For *my* 'Chas' with all my love.

# SHADOWS OF THE PAST

*A Selection of Recent Titles by Janet Tanner*

DAUGHTER OF RICHES
DECEPTION AND DESIRE
THE SHORES OF MIDNIGHT

ALL THAT GLISTERS *
HOSTAGE TO LOVE *
MORWENNAN HOUSE *

* *available from Severn House*

# Shadows of the Past

## Janet Tanner

This first world edition published in Great Britain 2003 by
SEVERN HOUSE PUBLISHERS LTD of
9–15 High Street, Sutton, Surrey SM1 1DF.
This first world edition published in the USA 2003 by
SEVERN HOUSE PUBLISHERS INC of
595 Madison Avenue, New York, N.Y. 10022.

British Library Cataloguing in Publication Data

Tanner,  Janet
    Shadows of the past
    1.    Frontier and pioneer life  -  New South Wales  -  Fiction
    2.    New South Wales  -  Social life and customs  -  19$^{th}$ century  -  Fiction
    3.    Love stories
    I.    Title
    823.9'14 [F]

    ISBN 0-7278-5926-9

Typeset by Palimpsest Book Production Ltd.,
Polmont, Stirlingshire, Scotland.
Printed and bound in Great Britain by
MPG Books Ltd., Bodmin, Cornwall.

**New South Wales, Australia, 1860**

The boy heard the raised voices from some way off as he approached the homestead. His heart sank. After long weeks on the trail his father was home – and the drink was in him.

The boy's footsteps slowed. Why did it have to be like this? Joel Page was a drover, away, sometimes, for months on end, and in his absence young Will longed for his return, remembering only the good times when Joel took him hunting, or swam with him in the creek. Will knew that Jenny, his little sister, longed for her father too, for he spoiled her dreadfully and she hero-worshipped him. As for Mammy – well, Mammy sang a great deal as she worked when Pa was away, and Will was not sure how glad she was to see him come riding up the track.

Will stopped, listening, and wondered if he'd give things a chance to quieten down a bit before going in. He wished he could stop Pa going for Mammy like that, and one of these days when he was a few years older he certainly would – with his fists, if need be. But for now there was nothing much he could do. Pa would only go for him as well. The last time he'd tried to intervene, Pa had given him the hiding of his life, and although he'd have willingly taken that and more if it had spared Mammy, he knew it had only made things worse, for Mammy had gone hot and holy for Pa, who had beaten her senseless. The trouble was that at fourteen he was still too small and thin to be any match for the great raging bull that was his father.

Well, at least Jenny wasn't there today to hear them rowing. She'd gone off this morning to play with the Chaytors children and wouldn't be back till dusk. Not that Pa would turn on

1

Jenny. She'd lie low and he'd forget she was there. Even if he remembered, he'd never lay a finger on her. Not on his Jenny.

There was a lean-to against the front wall of the house where firewood was stored. Will crept inside and sat with his arms hugging his knees, a reluctant eavesdropper to the quarrel, the sounds of which carried clearly through the open window just feet away.

'How can you do this, Joel?' His mother, shrill as a kookaburra in a stringy-bark. 'How can you spend half your wages in the grog shop before you even get home?'

'They'm my wages, ain't they?' His father, roaring with indignation. 'I earned 'em! I'll do what I like with 'em!'

'With no thought for me or the children? When we've barely enough to buy food and clothes? How can you be so selfish, Joel Page? What kind of a monster are you?'

'Mind your tongue, woman!' he snarled. 'Shut that ugly mouth of yours! Or I'll shut it for you.'

'Just try . . . ! Just try . . . !'

Will buried his head in his arms, then jerked it back again on his shoulders as he heard the sickening crack of his father's fist smashing into his mother's face. She screamed in shock and pain. Joel hit her again and again. Will knew he had because he heard her stumbling into the furniture, crying out to him to stop, to leave her alone. Dear lord, it was every bit as bad as he had feared. He had to do something. He couldn't just sit here and listen to the beating . . . This time he had to do something . . .

Will wriggled out from beneath the lean-to. The screaming and shouting had stopped by the time he reached the door. The only sound in the ominous silence was the heavy rasp of Joel's breath.

Will pushed open the door. And walked into a hell that would live with him for the rest of his days.

## New South Wales, eight months later

'Will . . . don't go! Please don't go!'
The little girl grabbed at his sleeve, looking up at him imploringly. A lump rose in his throat; he swallowed hard at it.

'I've got to, Jenny. You'll be all right with Mrs McCann. She'll take good care of you.'

'She won't lock me in my room like Mrs Mason did? Promise me she won't, Will!'

'I don't know, do I, Jenny? She might if you're bad and try to run away again.'

'But I want to be with you, Will! I don't want to be with stupid Mrs McCann! I don't . . . I don't . . . !'

Her lip quivered and again he felt the painful tug on his heartstrings. She was his little sister and she needed him. He was all she had left in the world now – and she was all he had too. But there was nothing he could do. He was too young to have the wherewithal to care for Jenny himself and too old to be fostered along with her by the worthy women of the settlement. A job had been found for him, helping out – and living in – on one of the big cattle stations, but Jenny could not, of course, go with him.

'Oh, why did Mother and Father have to die?' she asked now, tears filling her eyes and spilling into her voice. 'It's not fair! It's not!'

Will said nothing. What was there to say? Life wasn't fair. It was often harsh and cruel. And the poorer you were, the closer to the bottom of the heap, the harsher and crueller it was.

'But I don't understand what happened to them!' Jenny persisted.

3

His brow lowered. He looked away from her screwed-up face, the eyes that were full of tears.

'You know what happened to them, Jenny. The bushrangers got them. They came to steal stuff we didn't have, but they didn't know that. And when they couldn't find anything of any value they beat Mammy senseless and shot Pa.'

She frowned. 'But Mrs Mason said . . .'

'What does Mrs Mason know?' he asked roughly. 'Anyway, you're not going to be with her any more, are you? You're going to be with Mrs McCann.'

'Oh, Will . . . please . . .'

'You have to stay with her for now,' he said urgently. 'You know you do. But I promise you that I'll work and save and get enough money together to make a home for us, where we can be together, just as soon as I'm old enough to select a piece of land. Anyone is allowed to do that now, for just a quarter of the purchase price, since they brought in the Robertson Selection Acts. I'll build us a house and I'll farm the land and we'll be together.'

She looked at him wonderingly. She had never known anything but a little daub-and-wattle shack with just a small square of dusty garden around it; 'land' to her meant the endlessly rolling acres which belonged to the squattocracy, the wealthy upper crust of Australian society, quite beyond their means or aspirations. But all the same, Will was wonderful. Will could do anything, be anything he liked.

'Really, Will? We can live on a farm? Just you and me?'

He laughed. 'Well, not just you and me. I shall have to have help. Hired help.'

'Hired help!' It was all totally beyond her wildest imaginings.

'Yes. Just so long as you promise to be good and not try to run away again. You mustn't do it, Jenny, truly you mustn't. If you come looking for me you'll only get lost and no one would ever find you again. It's wild, lonely country. Do you promise me now?'

She nodded slowly.

'I promise.' Then: 'Just as long as you promise me too,' she added.

'What?'

'That you really will build a house for us and take me away from Mrs McCann's really soon.'

He bit his lip, doubts assailing him. All very well to say it. All very well to dream. But where was someone like him going to get the money to put down on a plot of land?

There was eagerness in her small, tear-stained face, an eagerness that tore at his heart, and the resolve hardened in him. Somehow he would do it. Whatever it cost him, if he had to lie and cheat and steal he would do it. Jenny had suffered enough, and none of this was her fault.

He took her hands in his, looking her straight in the eyes.

'I swear to you, Jenny, on the grave of our mother and father. I'll get a piece of land and I'll make a home for you before too long. Do you believe me?'

She nodded trustingly, the tears drying on her cheeks.

'I believe you, Will.'

# One

The gig stood in the stable yard, brand spanking new and sparkling in the winter sunlight; the pair of bays in the shafts pawed the ground restlessly, their breath making lacy white castles in the frosty air. A few yards away a young woman stood looking at them thoughtfully, one hand hidden in the folds of her blue woollen gown, the other playing with the fastenings of her cloak. Hazel eyes were narrowed behind the thick fringing of dark lashes, full lower lip caught and puckered between two rows of even white teeth.

Cerys Page very much wanted to climb into the gig, flick the reins and drive it out of the stable yard. She wanted to drive it all the way to Medlock, the little settlement twenty miles down the dirt road that was fast becoming a bustling town. Michael Costello, who ran the general store, had told her he was expecting a consignment of fabrics fresh from Sydney and she could not wait to go through them and pick out a few lengths before the best ones were snapped up. The trouble was, Cerys was not at all sure whether she was up to driving the buggy and not at all sure either what Will, her husband, would have to say if he knew she was contemplating it.

No – that wasn't true. She knew all too well – Will would be horrified. When she had married him and come to live on his isolated little holding, it had taken all her powers of persuasion to get him to teach her to drive at all.

'I can't ride, Will,' she had argued. 'I've lived all my life in Sydney and had no occasion to learn. I'll be so cut off out here if I can't drive a carriage either.'

'I can take you anywhere you want to go,' Will had said flatly. 'You just said it yourself, Cerys, you have no experience with horses and if you don't show them who's

6

master they have a mind of their own. I'd never stop worrying about you.'

'You don't worry about Jenny,' Cerys had objected. Jenny was Will's young sister, for whom he had been responsible since the death of their parents.

'Because Jenny has been in the saddle since before she could walk,' Will said shortly. 'It's quite different, as well you know.'

'Oh Will, please! *Please* teach me!' Cerys had put her arms around his neck, looking at him with those dark-fringed hazel eyes, the pucker of her mouth making deep dimples play in her cheeks, and he had weakened, just as she had known he would.

'Oh, very well, when I've got time I'll see what I can do.'

Good as his word, he had given her some lessons in the little sulky with solid, plodding, good-tempered Lady between the shafts, and Cerys had done reasonably well, although she would have been the first to admit she would never be half the horsewoman Jenny was if she lived to be a hundred and practised every day. Jenny seemed to have a natural affinity with horses Cerys knew she never would have.

Before long the children had come along, first Molly and then Ritchie. There had been little time then for carriage driving and Cerys's already doubtful skills had become rusty from disuse. She could, at a pinch, still manage Lady and the little sulky with reasonable competence. But Lady was lame, Will was away and would doubtless be unable to spare the time to take her into Medlock even if he were here, and the bolts of cloth would be growing thinner by the day as the ladies of the district fell on them like hungry vultures on a dead ewe. If Cerys did not want to miss out on the pick of them there was only one way to make it into town – and that was to take the new gig with the pair of bays – Will's pride and joy, bought only after many hours of totting up columns of figures and working out complicated calculations. But oh, it looked so big and cumbersome compared with the little sulky she was used to, and the matched bays were mettlesome and positively frightening compared with gentle, patient Lady. She *should* be able to handle them . . . but could she? Cerys was not feeling very confident.

Clearly Duggan Priest had his doubts about her competence too. Duggan looked after the horses for Will amongst his other duties and when Cerys had asked him to make the gig ready and harness the bays he had fixed her with a very straight look.

'Are you sure that's wise, missus?'

His obvious disapproval had made Cerys all the more determined. What right did he have to question her? She was the mistress here and he was just the stable boy – though 'boy' was something of a misnomer, since Duggan was sixty if he was a day, a wizened little man she rather thought had come to Australia in the days of transportation – and not of his own volition, either.

'I only want to go to Medlock, Duggan,' she said. 'It's a straight road and I'll be back long before it begins to get dark.'

Duggan chewed on a wad of tobacco, his startlingly blue eyes narrowed in the leathery face that had been tanned walnut-brown by years of exposure to the elements.

'Couldn't it wait till Mr Page gets back?'

'No, Duggan, it couldn't,' Cerys retorted. 'I need to buy material to make new clothes for the children. They're growing so fast they've nothing to fit them.'

That much at least was true. At three years old Molly was quite a little beanpole and now that Ritchie was walking she couldn't keep him in Molly's cast-offs any more. Nor did she want to. Ritchie was Cerys's pride and joy; nothing was too good for her son and she longed to see him in clothes that had been made especially for him. But what both she and Duggan knew, if truth be told, was that she was not being altogether selfless in wanting to get at the fabrics whilst the choice was still there. She really would like a new gown for herself too – hers were all growing dreadfully shabby and she had never quite lost the extra weight she had gained when she was carrying Ritchie either. The wool she was wearing today, for instance, was too tight for comfort under the arms . . .

'Well, I suppose you know best,' Duggan said, sounding as

if he did not actually think anything of the kind, and Cerys's patience, never her strongest attribute, snapped.

'Please make haste, Duggan, or it will be too late for me to go today.'

He had done as she asked, but now that the gig was ready, nervous doubts assailed her once more. It was only when she saw Duggan standing in the shadows, arms folded, watching her disapprovingly, that she made up her mind.

Oh, for heaven's sake, of course she could do it! She couldn't possibly lose face by backing down now. If she did, it wouldn't just be first choice of the fabrics she would forfeit, it would be Duggan's respect too. And that was not something she could afford to lose if she was to retain any sort of authority here. With a quick characteristic toss of her head, Cerys hitched up her skirts, climbed up into the gig and took up the reins. Then, with a brief nod in Duggan's direction, she walked the horses out of the stable yard and soon had them trotting along the dirt road in the direction of Medlock.

As she bowled along the open road Cerys found that she was beginning to enjoy herself. She couldn't imagine why she had been so apprehensive – heavens, there was nothing to it! The road was arrow-straight as far as the eye could see and the winter drought and weeks of hard frosts had made it hard and smooth almost as rock. No deep water-filled ruts to negotiate today, no mud flying from the wheels, no dust, even, to speak of. And it was such a beautiful morning! The sky was clear sharp blue above the rolling green pastureland, dotted with stands of trees and orchards, bare now for winter, and in places where the sun had not reached, frost still silvered the banks. As yet there had been no snow, but Cerys thought there might be if the temperature were to rise a little, and the thought made her smile.

Her mother and father worried about her, she knew, used as they were to Sydney's year-round balmy climate. They had questioned the wisdom of her going to live in the high tablelands of New England, just as they had questioned the wisdom of her marrying a man they felt she scarcely knew, and their objections had only made her the more stubbornly determined, just as Duggan's disapproval had done.

'They say the climate is very like England,' she had said. 'You grew up with that, Papa – well, in Wales, anyway. Why should it do me any harm?'

'I was used to it, Cerys. You're not. I'm not even sure that *I* would want to go back to it now – being cold is not very pleasant.'

'But you are always talking about how beautiful the mountains were!'

'That's true, yes, cariad. I suppose for the mountains I would put up with a lot . . .'

'There you are then,' Cerys said triumphantly. 'I expect it's the Welsh in me makes them call to *me*.'

'Correct me if I'm wrong,' her mother said tartly, 'but I thought it was Will Page's good looks that were doing the calling.'

Cerys had laughed then, blushing, because, of course, Mama was right. She thought that Will Page was the best looking young man she had ever set eyes on – and, living in Sydney with the military and the ship's officers and the thrusting young businessmen out to make a fortune, she had set eyes on quite a few. But the moment Will had walked into her father's store a few months earlier Cerys had been smitten and by the time he had left town to return to his farm she had completely lost her heart. She would have followed Will wherever he had taken her and they both knew it.

'I am lucky, Mama,' she had said. 'I'll have Will and the mountains too. I'm going to love them, I just know I am.'

And she did. Though the thermometer had been known to dip as low as ten degrees Fahrenheit on the Ben Lomond range, Cerys loved the fact that the sun almost always seemed to shine. She loved the orchards, bright with blossom in spring and heavy with fruit in autumn, and the fields where clover grew thickly and many wildflowers she had never seen before spangled the fresh green grass. Most of all she loved the cleanness of it all and thanked her lucky stars that Will had selected to purchase the land for his farm here, not in the dusty, fly-infested outback.

It was, she thought, the best place in the world for Molly and Ritchie to grow up. Only sometimes, like today, she wished it was not quite so far to reach civilization. But even that had its compensations. Why, if she had still lived in Sydney she would certainly never have learned to drive a gig, never experienced the pleasure of the reins running through her hands and the exhilaration, sharpened with fear, that came from knowing that she and she alone was handling these two mettlesome horses . . .

Carriage-driving when you weren't used to it was tiring though. By the time the first slab-and-bark buildings signified to Cerys that she was nearing Medlock, fatigue was beginning to numb her, and she gave her head a small determined shake. This certainly was not the time to lose concentration. Medlock was quite a busy little town. There would be other carriages, pedestrians crossing the street or even walking along the middle of it, horsemen, dogs . . . The main street was deeply rutted, too, from all the traffic that passed over it day after day. A little lump of nervousness rose in Cerys's throat. Well, she'd come this far, she'd just have to cope!

As luck would have it there was plenty of room at the hitching posts outside the Commercial Hotel. Cerys pulled up the horses with an inward sigh of relief, climbed down and led them to the water trough. They drank lustily, blowing and dribbling, and Cerys watched enviously. She was thirsty herself, but she didn't think she should go into the Commercial Hotel alone. True, it was owned and run by a woman – Kitty Jackson – but she was no lady. On the few occasions Cerys had glimpsed her standing in the hotel doorway, Cerys had been shocked by how low-cut Kitty's gown was, and how much paint she wore on her face. Kitty Jackson, with her flaming red hair and silk gowns to match, was a scarlet woman in more ways than one, Cerys rather thought, and Will would be even less likely to approve of his wife setting foot under her roof than he would be to approve of her driving his buggy.

Today, however, there was no sign of Kitty Jackson, for which Cerys was grateful. When the horses had drunk their fill she looped the reins around the hitching post and set off down the street to Costello's Store.

Without a doubt, Costello's occupied the finest business premises in Medlock. Whilst most of the other stores were stringy-bark and slab, Costello's was built of weatherboard and shingle, and the sign on the gabled roof was freshly painted, not faded by the blistering heat of the summer sun as so many of the signs were. M. COSTELLO. TAILOR, DRAPER AND GENERAL OUTFITTER, that sign read. Cerys smiled to herself and hurried eagerly inside.

'Why, Mrs Page!' Michael Costello emerged from the little back room beaming with pleasure as he recognized her. My, but she was a sight for sore eyes and no mistake, her cheeks whipped rosy by the chilly wind, eyes sparkling behind that thick fringing of dark lashes, and hair blown into disarray around the framework of her bonnet. 'How can I help you this lovely day? No – don't tell me. Word has spread about my new stock and you have come to see it.'

Dimples played in Cerys's cheeks as she smiled at him a little flirtatiously. A respectable married woman she might be, but she could never resist flirting for all that.

'I certainly have, Mr Costello! I wanted to get here before the vultures moved in too. Tell me you haven't sold out of anything yet!'

'I'm afraid a bolt of furnishing fabric has gone already,' he admitted. 'Beautiful blue velvet it was, too. Mrs Macleod from Birramindi wanted to redo all her curtains.'

'Oh, I don't want furnishing fabric!' Cerys said dismissively. 'My curtains will have to last for years yet. No, it's clothes I'm after.'

'And I've just the thing for you! The softest green wool you ever laid eyes on – or felt either. It'll bring out the colour of your eyes and kiss your skin like a whisper . . .'

His work was a passion with Michael, and that, together with the Irish in him, made him wax lyrical about fabrics the way a poet might about natural beauty.

Cerys's eyes went longingly to the back wall where the bolts of fabric were stacked, one on the other, a tantalizing rainbow. Then she pulled herself up sharply.

'I have to think of the children first, Mr Costello. Perhaps when I've sorted out something for them . . .'

'Oh yes, of course! The children! How are they?'

'Growing,' Cerys said. 'Growing very fast.'

Michael Costello nodded. 'Come with me then and we'll see what we can find.'

Cerys spent a most pleasurable half-hour choosing half a dozen dress lengths in the prettiest colours for Molly and plainer, more hard-wearing fabrics for Ritchie. But she could not resist a length of navy-blue silk to make a little sailor suit for him. He really would make it worthwhile, she thought, with his bubbling fair curls and cheeky grin, for he really was the most adorable baby the world had ever known.

Then and only then did she allow herself the luxury of choosing some fabrics for gowns for herself – the green wool Michael Costello had recommended, a soft heather pink, and a sensible grey. By the time she left the shop the sun was well past its zenith and Cerys had quite forgotten her anxieties about having to drive the gig home again.

The horses had grown restless. Cerys could see that as she walked back along the street with Michael Costello's assistant, Frank Newton, trotting beside her, laden down with her purchases. They were pawing the ground and tossing their heads as far as the tethered reins would allow them.

Another conveyance had been tied up outside the Commercial Hotel too – not a carriage but a wagon, large and flat-bedded, and on the road beside it a sizeable crate stood, waiting to be loaded. As Cerys supervised Frank stowing her packages, two men came out of the hotel and began attempting to manhandle the crate into the wagon. They were, Cerys thought, employees of the hotel and were perhaps more used to heaving barrels of ale, for they seemed to be making heavy weather of it.

She thanked Frank for his help and tipped him a gold coin – more than she had ever tipped anyone in her life, and more, in truth, than she could afford to tip now. But spending so much in the store had given her the illusion of wealth, and treating the boy with such generosity reinforced the illusion, making her feel good about herself and the world in general. Frank's eyes widened, he pocketed the coin and went off whistling down the street in the direction of the store.

Cerys loosened the reins from the hitching post, scarcely able to tear her eyes away from the two men attempting to load the cart. What on earth could that enormous crate be concealing? And were they ever going to get it on board? Certainly there was enough sweating and swearing going on! As she made her way round the gig she saw them heave it up and balance it precariously on the tailgate of the cart, but she could not imagine where they were going to go from there. Surely they needed the help of at least one more man to steady it whilst they shoved . . .

What happened next happened so fast it took Cerys completely by surprise. The bays, their reins now loose, decided they had been still – and looking at the rump end of the ugly cart and the heavy shires pulling it – for long enough. Before Cerys could do a single thing to stop them they took off, veering wildly around the cart with the gig lurching behind them. For a horrified moment Cerys was certain it was about to mow down the hotel worker on the road side of the cart. And the worker must have thought so too! With a startled yell of pure panic he dropped his end of the crate and jumped for his life. Unable to take the weight alone the other man too let out a shout, staggered for a moment as if he had consumed too much ale, eyes and mouth both wide open, then let go of his end, jumping aside as the crate crashed down on to the dirt road.

And what a crash it made! What an incredible cacophony of sound, as if the gates of hell were opening!

Cerys screamed, clapping her hands over her ears as the awful discord hung in the air. What on earth was happening? And her horses . . . oh, her horses . . .

Sparing no more than a horrified glance at the crate which had emitted that earsplitting row and the two red-faced men who had been unable to prevent it falling, Cerys began to run down the street in pursuit of the gig. Oh dear Lord, what if the bays decided to start racing? She'd never catch them – never! They could be badly hurt, and the gig jolted to finderjigs! Will was going to be furious! He'd never forgive her . . .

Then, to her enormous relief, she saw a figure step out into the road. Frank Newton, on his way back to Costello's store,

14

had heard the commotion, looked around to see what was going on, and realized the horses had got away from Cerys. As they passed, he grabbed the bridle of the one closest to him, ran a few paces with it, and brought it to a halt. Cerys slowed down, pressing her hand to her heaving chest and sending up a prayer of thanks.

By the time she reached them Frank was holding the horses steady with the expertise of a stable lad. He looked at her anxiously.

'You all right, Mrs Page?'

'No, Frank, I'm not!' Cerys was shaking all over and tears of shock were gathering now in her eyes. 'I've just had the fright of my life.'

'What was all that noise?' Frank asked curiously.

'Oh, those stupid men dropped whatever it was they were loading into the cart.'

'What – and frightened your horses?'

'I suppose so,' Cerys agreed guiltily, not wanting to admit that it was her own incompetence that had caused the accident in the first place. 'Oh, Frank, thank you so much – you deserve a reward . . .'

'Don't talk so silly, Missus,' Frank said, though his callow, pimply face flushed with pleasure. 'I didn't do nothing.'

'Only saved my life!' Cerys said. 'Will would have had me hung, drawn and quartered if any harm had come to his horses or his gig.'

'They'd have stopped in any case before they'd got very far,' Frank said humbly. 'And you already gave me more than I earn from old Costello in a week, and just for doing my job. Now, do you want me to help you get turned around?'

'Oh yes, please!' Cerys said gratefully.

Good as his word, Frank turned the gig and held the horses steady whilst Cerys climbed up and took the reins from him. She was still shaking inwardly and it was all she could do to hold the reins steady but she told herself all she had to do now was drive out of town and keep driving, just as she had on the way here. She moved off slowly back along the street once more in the direction of home.

There was quite a little group now gathered around the cart

15

– and the oversized crate. Amongst the men, Cerys saw the scarlet flash of Kitty Jackson's silk gown. A nerve jumped in Cerys's throat. Clearly the commotion had been heard inside the hotel and had brought Kitty and the others running out.

As she approached them, Cerys kept her eyes straight ahead, as if by ignoring them they would also ignore her. It was, of course, a vain hope. As she drew level with the shires, a man broke away from the group and strode furiously towards her. Still Cerys tried to pretend she had not seen him, but he made a grab at the horses' bridle, bringing them to a stop.

'Just a minute!' he said harshly. 'I want a word with you!'

Cerys swallowed hard and with difficulty. Her throat had gone very dry – and not just because this very angry man had accosted her, but because of who he was.

She'd recognized him at once – how could she not? Chas Wallace was one of the most important pastoralists in this part of New England. His holding, Wells Court, had been in his family since his father, Edward, had arrived and claimed squatter's rights in the 1820s; now it covered most of the vast open space between the town of Medlock and their own modest little farm. The cattle run carried almost two thousand head of stock, Will had told her, and Chas not only carried on the shorthorn stud his father had founded, but also bred thoroughbred horses and racehorses.

And it was not only his land and his wealth and his superior position in the New England squattocracy that made Chas Wallace a highly recognizable personage either. There was, Cerys thought, probably no more imposing figure for many miles around.

Tall, strongly built, with the long lean muscles of a man who spends his life in the saddle, Chas Wallace on one of his highly bred horses was an impressive sight and one that set female pulses beating fast the length and breadth of the district, for, unbelievably, at thirty-five years old, he was still a bachelor.

Cerys had no interest in him, of course – she had eyes for no one but her adored Will – but she had often thought it was not difficult to see why he set so many hearts a-flutter, with his thick fair hair bleached fairer yet by the sun, his skin tanned

16

to a rich mahogany, and his eyes blue as the mountain streams when the sun shone on them.

Now, however, those eyes blazed furiously, and the lines which exposure to all weathers had drawn between nose and mouth were deep, hard-set chasms. Cerys quailed inwardly even as she wondered what Chas Wallace was doing here in Medlock and what her piece of carelessness had to do with him.

However nervous she might be feeling, however, Cerys's usual form of defence lay in attack, and she assumed that line now. Pinching her lips together to keep them from trembling, she glared at him. 'Let my horses go at once!'

He ignored her order, glaring back at her with eyes narrowed so that the corners crinkled into creases almost as deep as those that ran between nose and mouth.

'It's Will Page's wife, isn't it?'

Cerys felt a stab of surprise that he should have recognized her. Neighbours they might be, but socially she and Will were far beneath Chas Wallace, and her path and his had rarely crossed.

'Will Page is my husband, yes,' she said tightly. 'And if he knows that you have been interfering with me, you will have to answer to him, I promise you.'

A muscle worked at the corner of Chas Wallace's mouth. 'Oh, he'll know all right. I shall make sure of that. What is he thinking of, letting you out with this gig, anyway? Clearly you haven't the first idea of how to manage it.'

'He doesn't know . . .' Cerys retorted before she could stop herself, then clamped her lips tight shut over the words, wishing she could take them back.

'Well, he is going to have to know, isn't he?' Chas Wallace's voice was very hard, very controlled. 'I shall be expecting him to compensate me for damage to my property.'

'Your property . . .' Cerys's courage was fast deserting her.

'My property, certainly. Do you realize that create contains a most valuable grand piano which I have had shipped from England at great expense?'

Cerys shook her head, her eyes wide with disbelief. A grand

17

piano . . . ? Well, that explained the terrible noise when it had hit the ground, anyway. But . . .

'What is it doing here?' she asked before she could stop herself.

'I had it delivered to the Commercial Hotel, if it is any business of yours,' Chas Wallace said abruptly. 'I preferred not to trust it to the bullocky who serves Wells Court. It seems I might just as well have done. I dread to think what damage has been done to it now – thanks to you.'

'It wasn't me who dropped it!' Cerys said with asperity and a great deal more confidence than she was feeling. 'It was too much for those two men to manage – any fool could see that.'

Chas Wallace's mouth tightened. 'I haven't the time to argue with you. All I know is that the accident would never have happened if you had had your horses under control. And I shall be expecting to hear from your husband in the near future so that as soon as I have had the damage assessed we can agree on how much he owes me by way of compensation. Good day to you, Mrs Page.'

He let go the harness, turned on his heel and marched back to the little group around the splintered container.

Sharp tears stung Cerys's eyes. Will was going to be furious with her! Bad enough that she should have caused an accident, but that it should have been Chas Wallace whose property had been damaged . . . ! And worse still, he almost certainly would insist on compensation, even though he could buy and sell her and Will several times over. Men like him didn't get – and stay – rich by chance. They made their money – and kept it – because they were hard and ruthless and didn't care for anyone.

Heaven alone knew what it would cost to repair a fine-tuned grand piano that had taken such a crashing fall. A great deal of money that they didn't have, in all likelihood. And that on top of all that she had just spent on fabrics . . .

Cerys glanced over her shoulder and through tear-blurred eyes saw Kitty Jackson place a hand on Chas Wallace's sleeve. So – that was the kind of man he was! One who consorted with scarlet women like Kitty Jackson! All the acres in New

England couldn't make a gentleman out of someone who would stoop to that – and certainly not a stupid grand piano!

Fired up with disgust and loathing, Cerys flicked the reins and the bays moved to do her bidding with a quick obedience that would, under any other circumstances, have pleased her.

As it was, she could think of nothing but how she was going to confess what she had done to Will, and how very angry he was going to be.

# Two

'Mama! Mama!'

As Cerys tethered the horses in the stable yard, a small round bundle of petticoats and boots came scampering out of the stringy-bark homestead and ran to greet her.

'Steady now, Molly!' Cerys said sharply. The last thing she wanted was for the horses to be startled again.

'What did you buy, Mama?'

'We'll see in a minute. Just give me a chance, will you?'

Some of the brightness went out of the little girl's eager face, but she crept forward anyway, lower lip caught between her teeth in a look of stubborn determination that was the very image of her mother's. With an enormous effort, she scrambled up on to the step of the gig, peering beneath the seat.

'Packages, Mama! I can see them!'

'Molly – get down from there at once! I told you I'd show you what I bought in a minute,' Cerys snapped, too tired and worried to have any patience with the child. 'Is your Papa home yet?'

Molly shook her head.

'No. And Aunt Jenny said you'd be back before he was if you knew what was good for you.'

*Out of the mouths of babes* . . . Cerys thought ruefully.

'Duggan!' she called. 'Duggan – where are you?'

'Just coming, missus.' The old stable boy emerged from one of the outbuildings on the other side of the yard looking decidedly bleary.

He had been taking a nap as like as not, Cerys thought crossly. And when there was so much to be done too!

'See to the horses, will you please, Duggan?' she ordered.

'You got back in one piece then,' Duggan said equably, and the comment touched a raw nerve.

'Well, of course I did!' she retorted – and only just stopped herself from adding: *You should have more confidence in me.* Today's drive had hardly been a triumph – as Duggan would doubtless learn soon enough.

She retrieved the packages from beneath the seat of the gig, much to Molly's delight.

'Which is mine? Can I carry it? Oh please, Mama!'

'I don't know which is yours until I open them all up,' Cerys said. 'It's only material, in any case. Nothing very exciting. But you can carry this one for me if you like.'

She laid a package across Molly's outstretched arms and made a pile of the others to carry herself.

As they crossed the yard, the door of the homestead opened again and Jenny appeared, Ritchie in her arms.

'Oh, it *is* you! Molly said it was. But you've taken your time coming in.'

'Duggan wasn't there to see to the horses for me,' Cerys said, her eyes on Ritchie, who was beaming and holding out his plump little arms to her.

Oh, how she loved that child! Just the sight of him could make her go warm and weak inside, lift her spirits, lighten her mood. She dumped the armful of packages on the table and took him from Jenny, loving the feel of his round, solid little body against her chest, rubbing her cheek against his soft curls and breathing in the smell of him, sweet, soapy, still the smell of baby – though not for much longer.

The thought was a sharp pain deep within her. Cerys held her little son more tightly and the tears, still dangerously close to the surface after this afternoon's disaster, threatened to fill her eyes again.

'Mama, can I . . . ?' Molly, balancing her package on one arm, was tugging at Cerys's skirts.

'Oh, if you want to,' Cerys said impatiently.

'Cerys, are you all right?' Jenny was looking at her narrowly.

She didn't miss much, Cerys thought. In fact, she missed nothing at all. Will's sister she might be, but while it was

21

easy to pull the wool over his eyes, the exact opposite was true when it came to Jenny.

But then, of course, that was probably because she was a woman. Whatever family traits she might or might not share with Will, first and foremost she was a woman. And everyone knew women were at least twice as canny as men.

Cerys glanced at her now over the top of Ritchie's golden head.

At seventeen, Jenny was quite a beauty. Her features were chiselled, with high cheekbones, a small straight nose and well-defined chin, her eyes tawny brown. Her hair was tawny brown too, thick and untamed, the sort of hair that constantly resisted being caught up with combs, and it was somehow a perfect reflection of its owner's nature, for Jenny, like her hair, was wild and untamed.

And that was scarcely surprising, Cerys thought, for Jenny had been orphaned at seven years old and pushed from pillar to post until Will had selected his land, built the farm and taken her to live with him there. On the whole she seemed remarkably unscathed by what had happened, but sometimes a mood of depression would descend over her like a cloud across the sun, a mood that nothing could shift. It had been like that these last few days, ever since her last visit to her young man, David Harris of Glenavon, and Cerys had wondered if there had been a falling out. But Jenny would say nothing. She had stalled all Cerys's questions and retreated into a world of her own. Now, however, after a day spent looking after the children, Jenny seemed more herself. Sharp as needles!

'Something's wrong, Cerys,' she said now. 'You can't fool me.'

'Oh – it's nothing.' Cerys tried to sound nonchalant, but she could feel the foolish tears welling. 'I had a bit of a mishap, that's all.'

'What sort of mishap? The horses aren't hurt, are they?'

It was typical that Jenny's first concern should be for the horses, Cerys thought.

'No, the horses are fine,' she said tautly. 'And so is Will's precious new gig. But they got a bit out of control and frightened some men who were loading a grand piano belonging to Chas Wallace and they dropped it and it's probably badly damaged and Chas Wallace is going to make Will pay compensation and Will is going to be absolutely furious with me and . . .'

'Stop! Stop!'

Annoyed, Cerys realized that Jenny was laughing. Actually laughing! The bad mood of the past days might never have been. Her hands were pressed to her mouth but her shoulders were shaking, and tears of mirth were escaping the corners of her eyes and trickling down her cheeks.

'It's not funny!' Cerys exploded.

'No. No – it's not.' With an effort, Jenny gained some control over herself. 'You're right. Will certainly is going to be furious. Of all people to cross – Chas Wallace! And a grand piano! Oh, Cerys, you certainly do things in style! A grand piano!' A giggle burbled in her throat again. For a few moments she struggled to contain it, small hiccuping sounds escaping from behind her hand. Then the unequal struggle was lost and Jenny exploded with totally uncontrollable mirth.

'Well, I'm glad I've cheered you up, at least!' Cerys said, annoyed and hurt.

'Mama, Mama . . .' Molly had torn the wrapping paper from her package and was staring in disappointment at a folded length of grey woollen cloth. 'Is this for me? I don't like it!'

Quite suddenly the tears that had been threatening for so long overwhelmed Cerys.

'I *told* you it was only material, Molly!' she cried. 'And that one's not for you in any case. It's for me. And I expect your father will make me take it all back when he hears what I've done, so it doesn't matter who it's for . . .'

Then, not wanting Molly to see her cry, she ran from the room, Ritchie still in her arms. As her tears moistened his head and he felt the shaking tension of her body, Ritchie began to cry too.

Will was still not home when it was time for Molly and Ritchie to go to bed.

23

Cerys had recovered her composure by now but she was still desperately worried as to what Will was going to have to say about her misadventure. He had quite a temper when he was roused.

Jenny helped her to bath the children in the big tub in front of the fire, and then she took them through to the bedroom they shared. Though the stringy-bark homestead was single-storeyed it was quite roomy. At least space was not at a premium here, and when Molly had been born Will had built an extension behind their own bedroom to make a nursery. Molly had slept there from the time she was big enough to go through the night without needing to be fed, but Ritchie had only recently been moved in with her, at Will's insistence.

'He's far too big to be in that crib beside our bed,' he had said, and Cerys had not been able to argue the point. Ritchie *was* too big for the crib, and too big to be sharing their room too, but her heart sank all the same at the inevitability of the right of passage – just one more step to independence and the day she would lose him.

Tonight he had fallen asleep almost the moment his head had touched the pillow, but Molly was a little restless and Cerys had sat down on the floor beside the bed they shared, wrapped a spare blanket around herself because it was bitterly cold away from the warmth of the living-room fire, and begun singing lullabies. Usually she fretted if the children were still awake after the first few minutes, all too aware of the hundred and one chores still awaiting her attention, but tonight she drew comfort from the little ritual, enjoying the feel of Molly's hand in hers, enjoying the soft regular snuggle of Ritchie's breathing, enjoying singing even, the selfsame melodies her own mother had sung to her. At last Molly's breathing too became deeper and more even. Cerys was just easing her hand free of the small curled fingers when she heard raised voices coming from the kitchen.

Will – yelling at the top of his voice. He was home at last then – and in all likelihood Jenny had already told him about the events of the day. He was furious, just as she had known he would be. Cerys quailed inwardly, half expecting him to come bursting in to chastise her. But, of course, however angry he was with her he wouldn't want to wake the children.

For a few minutes Cerys held back, sitting there on the floor with the blanket wrapped around her. If she waited a little while perhaps some of his anger would have spent itself. Jenny was well used to her brother and his rages; it would be water off a duck's back to her, particularly since what had happened had nothing to do with her. She might even be able to calm him down a bit . . .

After a while everything went quiet. Cerys stood up, folded the blanket neatly and dropped it on to the foot of the bed. Then she crept across the room, let herself out, and headed back towards the kitchen.

Will was at the table but he was not eating the meal she had laid out ready for him – not even sitting down, but leaning over the tin caddy which they used as a piggy bank and which was open on the table in front of him. He looked up as Cerys came in, his handsome face dark with fury.

'There's hardly anything left in this tin,' he grunted. 'Have you been going to it, Cerys?'

A fresh wave of guilt washed over Cerys as she thought of the money she had taken out to go into Medlock, and the gold coin she had so blithely given to Frank Newton as a thankyou for his help.

'Well, yes . . .' she began, but he was scarcely listening.

'I don't know where the money is going to come from to pay off Chas Wallace. Chas Wallace of all people! My hard-earned money going to that jumped-up swine!' He threw the handful of coins back into the tin in disgust, jammed on the lid and sent it spinning across the table.

'You've heard about what happened then,' Cerys said resignedly.

'Yes I have – and I can hardly believe it!' Will fumed. 'How the devil it came to happen at all, I don't know, and for it to be Chas Wallace . . .'

Cerys lifted her chin. 'It was his own fault, anyway. Expecting two men to hump that great big thing! They just weren't up to it.'

'Wallace won't see it that way,' Will said. 'He'll make sure

25

someone else pays. What I don't understand is how Jenny could be so stupid.'

Cerys stared at him. 'Jenny?' she repeated blankly.

'She's so good with the horses as a rule,' Will went on without noticing her interjection. 'I'd have trusted her anywhere. All I can think is that her mind was on some boy. David Harris over at Glenavon, I shouldn't wonder. She's been spending too much time over there these last few weeks. Well, she'll have no allowance for fine clothes to take his eye until this debt has been paid, that's for sure. Perhaps that will teach her to keep her mind on what she's doing and think a little less about her beau.'

'What are you talking about, Will?' Cerys demanded.

Will reached for the money caddy, returning it to its place on the shelf with a clatter. 'Jenny's brush with Chas Wallace, of course. What do you think I'm talking about?'

'But . . . she didn't . . . it wasn't . . . it wasn't *her*, Will. Why should you think it was?'

'Because she admitted it. Told me all about it.'

'Told you what?' Cerys pressed him.

'How she took the gig into Medlock and got careless. How she caused Kitty Jackson's men to drop Chas Wallace's grand piano. What's the matter with you, Cerys?'

Cerys had closed her eyes briefly as he spoke, and was chewing at her lip.

'Where is she now?' she asked.

'I don't know. Gone off in a huff because I told her what I thought of her.'

Cerys took a deep breath. This was exactly like Jenny. She knew how worried Cerys was about Will's reaction and in a fit of bravado and misplaced generosity had decided to take the blame herself. No doubt she thought she could handle her brother better than Cerys could and would have to endure fewer censures. But to pretend she had been unable to handle the horses when her ability in that direction was her greatest pride was a sacrifice indeed. And certainly not one Cerys could allow her to make.

'It wasn't Jenny who caused the accident,' she said. 'It was me.'

Will's jaw tightened. 'Don't try to cover up for her, Cerys.'

'I'm not . . .'

'She has to learn to bear the consequences of her actions. She's wild, and getting wilder . . .'

'It wasn't her, Will!' Cerys said again, more emphatically. 'I'm not covering up for her – in fact, it's quite the other way around. I was the one who took the gig into Medlock, and if she says it was her, then *she* is covering up for *me*.'

Will stared. 'But you can't drive the gig, Cerys.'

'No, I know that now. But I wanted to get some dress lengths to make new winter clothes for the children and I thought it would be all right . . .'

'I don't believe what I'm hearing!' Will stormed. 'You didn't take the gig into Medlock?'

She nodded dumbly, then managed: 'Yes, I did.'

'And Duggan let you? Damn it, I'll get rid of him! The man's as useless as he is idle . . .'

'It wasn't his fault,' Cerys said. 'He tried to stop me but I wouldn't listen.'

'And where does Jenny come in?'

'She doesn't,' Cerys said. 'I don't know why she told you it was her, but it must have been for my sake.'

'It was a lie!'

'It was a really nice thing to do . . .'

'It was a lie!' Will repeated furiously. 'I won't be lied to! And I won't be disobeyed either. Do you realize what you've cost me today, Cerys, with your pigheadedness? Do you realize what a knife-edge this farm is balanced on? You could ruin me with this!'

'Oh, don't exaggerate, Will!' Cerys retorted, frightened but defiant.

'And what do you know about it?' Will blazed. 'What have you ever known about it? You don't know what it cost me to get this place and you don't care what it costs me to keep it going. I work from morning to night for you and the children to live in luxury . . .'

'Luxury!' Cerys flared. 'You call this luxury?' She waved a hand dismissively, encompassing the shabby furniture, much of which had belonged to Will's mother and father. 'And you

27

don't just work for us, Will, you do it for yourself – and for Jenny . . .'

'Why, you ungrateful . . .' Will was beside himself, his hands balled to fists, his face dark and snarling. Cerys flinched, honestly believing for a moment that he was going to strike her, though he had never done such a thing. Then his hands tightened on the back of the chair, he lifted it and flung it with all his strength across the room. It struck the stone sink with a crash and a leg came off.

'Now look what you've done!' Cerys cried.

But Will was not listening, nor even looking at her. He was staring into space, eyes half closed, breath coming hard and fast. With a low groan, he turned towards the door and blundered out into the night.

The frosty air hit him like a sharp blow in the face, sobering him and cooling the hot tide of anger. He lifted his chin and tilted his head back on to his shoulders, breathing in slowly and deeply so that the knife-edge of cold ran into his lungs too, sharp and clean.

What in heaven's name had he been thinking of? Dear Lord, he had almost struck Cerys a moment ago. Shame coursed through his veins, and with it the old, dark fear.

He knew who he got his temper from. It was his father all over again.

Oh, it had partly been the grog with Joel, of course. After seeing throughout his childhood what it could do to his father, Will abstained from strong drink, though he told Cerys it was because they could not afford it. Yet still he experienced flashes of blind fury followed by the same black depressions that had plagued his father, and it was his greatest fear that history might repeat itself.

Will laid his forehead against the stringy-bark wall, rocking gently and trying to shut out the pictures that were rising unbidden from the dark recesses of his mind to torment him as they had done down the years. History would not repeat itself. He would make sure of that. He might have inherited his father's traits, but he was not his father. And goodness knows, what Cerys had done today was enough to make a saint mad!

28

All very well for her to dismiss it as nothing, but it could have been very serious indeed. Goodness knows, as it was it was bad enough. The margins on which the farm were run were so tight there was just no room to cover unexpected extra expense such as this, particularly as he did not even know yet exactly what the damage was. And if he should be unable to meet his debts now . . .

Will shuddered. He could not even contemplate losing the farm. Not only was it their home, it was also the embodiment of a vow he had made long ago. He had sworn to make a home for Jenny and in doing so had set himself the goal of becoming a respectable and hard-working landowner, not a footloose and feckless drover as his father had been. It had become his holy grail – and he had achieved it. But no one knew just what he had done to achieve that goal. No one knew what it had cost him . . .

A sudden movement in the shadows beneath the window of the homestead caught his eye and he swung round sharply.

'Jenny – is that you?'

In the crisp darkness nothing stirred.

'Jenny!' he called again, aware she was out here somewhere, working out her temper just as he was. But it wasn't like her to sulk and skulk, more likely she would be in the stable with the horses. Whatever he'd thought he'd seen moving in the shadows, it must have been his imagination.

Will drew a deep, steadying breath. Jenny would come back when she was good and ready. For himself . . .

The guilt for his burst of temper was weighing heavily on him now and he could feel the beginnings of the familiar depression that inevitably followed. Best he should go back in and make his peace with Cerys before the blackness closed in.

He pushed open the door. Cerys was holding the broken leg of the chair, trying vainly to jam it back into place. She looked up at him, pulling a wry face.

'We'll be a chair short.'

'Leave it,' he said. 'I'll fix it tomorrow.'

She came towards him, the chair leg still in her hand.

'I'm sorry, Will. It's all my fault. I shouldn't have taken the gig.'

29

'No, you shouldn't,' he agreed.

Of course, it was Cerys all over. Impetuous, stubborn – yes, and fiery too. But he wouldn't have had it any other way. Infuriating she might be but he worshipped the ground she walked on. Will did not think he could have endured the tedium of a little mouse for a wife.

'I'll take the materials back to Costello's to help pay for the damage to Chas Wallace's grand piano,' she said. 'Well – not the ones I got for the children – they need new clothes – but the ones I bought for myself . . .'

Unexpectedly Will felt his lip twitch. 'So it wasn't just for the children then?'

'No. But I will take them back, I promise.'

He sighed. 'No, you can't do that, Cerys. What would Michael Costello think? And what would he do with cut dress lengths? No, we'll manage somehow. Just promise me you'll never do such a stupid thing again.'

'I won't. And I'll go and see Chas Wallace . . . try to put things right.'

'Oh no you won't.' Will's jaw was set. 'You'll leave Chas Wallace to me.' He ran a hand through his hair. 'You could have been killed, Cerys, you realize that? If you'd lost control of the horses on the road . . .'

'Well, I didn't, and I wasn't,' Cerys said. 'Now, why don't you eat your supper and I'll go and look for Jenny. She shouldn't be wandering about outside in the cold and dark. I'll just get my shawl . . .'

She broke off suddenly as the homestead door was thrown open and Jenny came bursting in.

'Will – come quick! There's someone in the sheds, I'm sure there is . . . !'

'The devil! Then I was right!' Will moved as he spoke, all else forgotten. Why had he not followed up on the movement he had seen in the shadows? But at least now he could arm himself before he tackled the intruder and that was only wise. It could be some harmless vagrant, hoping to steal an egg or two from the nesting boxes or even to wring the neck of a chicken and make off with it. But harmless was not a word one usually associated with vagrants. Cold and hunger made men desperate; most of those who roamed the countryside were themselves armed – and dangerous. From the bushwhacker to the robber, from the former convicts to the settlers gone bad, these were not men to tangle with lightly.

Will threw open the door of a wall cabinet and grabbed his gun.

Cerys was standing frozen now, hands pressed to her mouth, eyes wide and anxious above them. But Jenny was at the gun cupboard too, taking down a second rifle.

'I'll come with you, Will.'

'No, you stay here,' Will instructed her. 'If he should come to the house I don't want Cerys and the children left without protection, and you're a good shot, Jenny.'

He strode out. Jenny followed him to the door, the rifle cocked and ready on her shoulder. Cerys, desperately worried for Will's safety and at the same time ashamed that she was dependent on his little sister for protection for her and the children, ran to the window, peering out anxiously into the farmyard.

In the bright moonlight the ground glittered with frost and the scattering of outbuildings threw sharp black shadows. But nothing stirred now, nothing but Will striding across the open space, gun at the ready, head jerking from side to side like a clockwork toy as he scanned his surroundings for any sign of the intruder.

Cerys's heart pounded unevenly against her ribs. She knew the dangers just as Will did and she could not help feeling it was downright foolhardy of him to go out there alone. He was a good shot, she knew, quick on the trigger and with as accurate an aim as any man. But shooting at a bottle stuck up for target practice or a pigeon on the wing was one thing – this was quite another. The intruder could be anywhere, even inside one of the outbuildings. He could take a shot at Will and Will would never even see him.

Will reached the other side of the yard and kicked open the door to the nearest outhouse. Cerys heard him shout something – an order to come out to anyone who might be hiding inside, no doubt – then, after a moment, he disappeared inside and she held her breath until he appeared in the doorway once more.

Evidently he had drawn a blank with this outbuilding at any rate. *Oh, dear God, let him draw a blank with the others too!* she prayed. *And don't let him be taken unawares . . .*

'Where has the blackguard got to?' Jenny grated from between gritted teeth.

'Are you sure you saw someone?' Cerys asked.

'Of course I'm sure!' Jenny snapped.

'I wish you'd kept quiet about it!' Cerys moaned. 'There might be more than one of them, and even if there isn't, he's got the advantage of Will. He could shoot him in the back as easy as winking. Oh, you should have kept quiet about him!'

'And let him steal the horses?' Jenny was indignant. 'What ever next? Oh . . . !'

Her voice tailed into a small scream as a sudden shot rang out, the crack explosive in the quiet of the night.

'Oh, sweet Jesus!' Cerys sobbed.

Will was out of her line of sight now and she had no way of knowing what had happened and whether the shot had come from his gun or the gun of the intruder. But concern for Will made her throw caution to the winds. She dived across the room and pushed past a startled Jenny.

'Will! I have to go to Will!'

She ran out into the night, looking around wildly. She thought the shot had come from the furthest cluster of out-buildings but she could see nothing. In spite of the brightness of the moon, the sheds were too closely clustered together to give up any secrets.

'Will!' she called. 'Will!' Then she screamed as she was grabbed from behind and dragged into the shadows. For a terrifying moment she was quite sure the intruder had caught her, then Will hissed roughly in her ear.

'What do you think you are doing?'

'Oh Will!' Her knees were weak – from shock and from relief. 'I heard a shot! I thought . . .'

'That was me. I thought I saw something. I'm jumping at shadows. But you shouldn't be out here. It's not safe. Go back to the house.'

'Not without you! Have you searched everywhere?'

'Not yet.'

'Then at least I can watch your back. He could jump you from behind, Will!'

Will shook his head. Argument was useless, he knew. And he didn't want Cerys going back across the open space of the yard again either until he was sure there was no one waiting to take a potshot at her. Besides . . . like it or not, she was right. He could do with another pair of eyes.

'Stay close then,' he ordered. 'Come on – we'll check out the next shed.'

Together they moved on, and though Cerys's heart was still beating a tattoo, the tension was far more bearable than waiting helplessly in the house.

One by one they checked the outhouses but as far as they could see, no one was there. No one rushed out to attack them at least, but there were so many places an intruder could hide if he did not want his presence to be detected . . .

'I'm beginning to think whoever it was must have hightailed it,' Will said, rasping a hand across his chin.

'If there ever was anyone,' Cerys suggested.

'Oh, there was someone here all right. I saw something myself when I was outside just now and if Jenny saw them too . . . But I reckon they must have made a run for it when they knew we were on to them. I don't think they're here now.'

Cerys drew a breath of relief.

'Shall we go back inside then?'

He nodded. 'We might as well, I think. We'll keep a sharp eye out from the window as long as the moon is bright enough to see by though.'

Taking her hand, he led her back across the dirt yard.

Jenny was still in the doorway, alert as ever.

'You found nothing?'

'Nothing.' Will shivered, chilled to the bone now that the adrenalin was no longer heating his blood. 'Come inside and close the door. We'd best call it a night if we're not all to catch our deaths of cold.'

Jenny did as he told her, but she was clearly reluctant to put down the gun.

'There was someone, Will. I know there was . . .'

'Will thinks he's gone now though,' Cerys said briskly.

'I don't like it, Will – someone creeping around out there. It makes me nervous, and I would have thought it would make you nervous too after what happened to Mother and Father . . .' Her eyes on him were sharp. Cerys thought that the strange expression in them showed just how deeply she had been affected by the tragedy for all her apparent resilience.

'Oh, for the love of . . .' Will broke off, sensing Cerys's disapproval. She hated to hear him swear, particularly oaths she regarded as blasphemous. 'What happened to Mother and Father was quite different. It's not going to happen here. Now, you can do what you like, but I'm going to get warmed through and have my supper.'

# Three

W hen they had all unthawed their frozen fingers and managed to stop shivering, Will ate his supper whilst the girls took turns at watching from the window for any signs that the intruder was still lurking. There were none. Either he had gone, Will concluded, or both he and Jenny had been mistaken and there had never been anyone there at all.

At around eleven the moon disappeared behind an errant bank of cloud, so there was no hope of seeing any movement around the outbuildings anyway, and Will decided the best thing would be to put what had happened out of their heads and go to bed. But he had a last look around anyway and by the time he went to their room Cerys was in her nightgown and sitting at the dressing table brushing her hair as she did every night.

She smiled as he entered the room, watching his reflection in the mirror as he wearily discarded his shirt and breeches, and revelling in the pleasure she still gained from the ripple of his muscles beneath bare, weather-tanned skin.

Such a revelation it had been to her, the sight and the smell and the touch of a man's body. She had no brothers and her father had never, to her knowledge, so much as stepped out of his bedroom any less properly attired than was considered fitting for a respectable Sydney businessman. Heavens, she could scarcely remember even seeing his feet bare and not encased in the highly polished boots he invariably wore, much less anything else! So the sight of Will's forearms, ridged with muscle and feathered with soft dark hair, had stirred a dark and unfamiliar excitement within her, and his chest, broad and similarly feathered, had made something sharp and sweet twist deep within her. As for his legs, his hips . . . oh! When she could bring herself to look, the pleasure was so intense it was almost painful.

Four years of marriage had done nothing to make that pleasure pall, though sometimes Cerys had the distinct feeling that there were other, deeper pleasures that she had somehow never experienced. Sometimes, just sometimes, she was aware of a sort of yearning sadness that her greatest pleasure came from just looking. She slept with Will, she had borne him two children, and yet she felt somehow that their union was never quite complete. There was a remoteness about him, a secret place that she could never quite reach. On the one hand it made him all the more deliciously desirable, on the other she felt cheated as a woman and a wife. The promise of the foreplay when he held her tenderly in his arms was never quite fulfilled; when he made love to her it seemed there was something approaching desperation in the hurried act and when he turned from her she wanted to weep. In a strange way she did not want him to make love to her, for the anticipation was much better, and these days, truth to tell, he often did not, for the strains of their life were telling on them and they were both often too tired to be bothered.

Tonight, however, tired or not, Cerys felt a crying need to be in Will's arms. All the traumas of the day had conspired together to make her feel desperately vulnerable.

Will was at the window, taking one last look out, though it was too black now to see anything. He crossed to the bed, turned down the counterpane, and fell heavily into the bed. Cerys gave her hair one last stroke and put down the brush. If she delayed any longer Will would be snoring before she could cuddle up and arouse his interest! She turned out the lamp and padded across the room; his head was turned away from her as she slid beneath the covers, though he muttered a weary goodnight.

'Will?' She curved her body round his.

Will made no response. Cerys laid her face against his shoulder, twisting her arm beneath his so that her fingers could stroke his chest, play with that soft feathering of hair that ran thickly down his breastbone.

He shifted slightly, shrugging her off. 'Cerys, I'm dog-tired.'

'Will . . .' She parted her lips, pressing a kiss on his shoulder. His skin tasted slightly salt and it made her want him the more. She ran her hands lower, over his hard, flat stomach, and again he shifted, pulling away from her.

'Not tonight, Cerys.'

'But . . . Oh Will, you could have been killed out there tonight. I could! We could *both* have been killed . . .'

'But we weren't. Go to sleep, Cerys, there's a good girl.'

Hurt flooded her. 'You're still angry with me.'

'No, I'm not. I'm just tired. It's been that sort of day.'

'For me too!'

'Then get some sleep while you can.'

He sighed, turning over, and Cerys realized that, no matter what, there was no way Will was going to make love to her tonight. She moved abruptly, turning away and humping the bedclothes with her so that Will had to pull them back again or sleep uncovered.

Within moments his breathing became deep and regular. In spite of the depression that had closed in, in spite of the demons he could never be free of, Will was asleep. He would wake, in all likelihood, in the small hours and lie tossing and turning, sweating and fretting, but Cerys had no way of knowing that. She only knew that whilst she was in such need of him, Will had simply fallen asleep.

She lay staring into the darkness whilst the hurt and frustration and the feelings of vulnerability which the day had laid bare washed over her in waves. It was a long time before Cerys, too, eventually fell asleep.

The feeling of rejection was still with her when she woke, and with it an unfocused apprehension. It hovered like a cloud around her and weighed in the pit of her stomach as she hurried to dress in the chill of the early morning.

Will was already up and gone – his day began even earlier than Cerys's – so there was no one to confide her strange unease to, though she doubted she would have mentioned it even if he had been there. Will had no time for what he called 'that kind of nonsense'. He was a practical, down-to-earth man who believed only the evidence of his own eyes and ears. But

Cerys had learned to trust her intuition. Whenever she felt this way, something bad happened.

She took a quick peek out of the window, wondering if perhaps the intruder had returned during the night, but Duggan was going about his work looking as slow and unruffled as ever. It wasn't that then. If the outbuildings had been broken into or – worse – the horses stolen, there would be some evidence of it.

The children then. Cerys hurried to their room, anxious all of a sudden for their well-being. But here too – to her immense relief – everything seemed quite normal. Molly was still fast asleep, her little face rosy on the pillow, one thumb stuck firmly in her mouth, and Ritchie was awake, standing on the bed and engrossed in trying to unfasten the window catch.

Cerys shook her head, smiling. Ritchie was clearly going to be the practical one. He was totally fascinated with finding out how things worked. He must take after Will in that – he certainly hadn't got it from her. But she must tell Will of Richie's interest in the window catch and ask him to do something to fix it more securely, for, if she knew Ritchie, he'd work out how to open it before long and then he could be out of the window and taking a nasty tumble.

She reached across the sleeping Molly to pick him up and he turned and saw her. A broad grin split his engaging little face and, his interest in the window latch forgotten, he held out his plump arms and tried to take an unsteady step towards her. Cerys grabbed him before he could topple on to Molly and wake her, and those plump little arms fastened themselves around her neck.

Instantly her mood lightened a little. Perhaps this time the bad feeling didn't mean anything. It was just a hangover from all the upsets of the day before, not a premonition at all. But she wasn't convinced.

With Ritchie in her arms she went through into the living room, then set him down to play with his wooden building blocks whilst she cleared out the grate, laid a fire, and got it going. Then, as it began to blaze up, taking some of the chill off the air, she dressed Ritchie in front of it and set about making breakfast – a pan of thick, sweet porridge, thickly sliced ham and a pot of strong coffee. By the time it was ready Molly had appeared in the doorway, thumb still in mouth, complaining she was cold, and Cerys dressed her too in front of the fire. But of Jenny there was no sign. It was not unusual. Jenny was not an early riser, though when she did deign to get up she often rode out with Will, helping him with the stock or checking fences.

Cerys fed the children and ladled out some porridge for herself. She didn't normally wait for Will. He and Duggan would come in when they were ready. Everything revolved around the farm as far as they were concerned.

The children were racing one another on all fours now, round and round the kitchen table. Though he could walk, Ritchie still enjoyed the speed and safety of crawling, and Molly loved to copy him. Cerys smiled to herself at the sight of the two plump bottoms, side by side in the air.

Yesterday and its traumas were behind her, the bad feelings of foreboding almost forgotten. Today was going to be just another day.

Cerys had been wrong in assuming Jenny was still in bed. She had a great deal on her mind which had been worrying her for days, and the events of the evening had brought much of it to a head. Unusually for her she had spent a sleepless night and when she had heard Will moving about she had got up too, pulling on her warmest clothes and joining him in the kitchen.

He looked round in surprise as she came through the door. 'Jenny?'

'Will – I really need to talk to you.'

He frowned. 'Now? Won't it wait?'

She shook her head decisively. 'No, it won't. I want you to tell me the truth, Will. About how Mammy and Pa came to die.'

He froze momentarily. She saw how much she had shocked him. Then his breath came out in a short, disbelieving grunt.

'What are you talking about?'

She folded her arms about her waist, looking at him levelly.

'Mammy and Pa,' she repeated. 'I need to hear the truth, Will. From you. And please don't give me the story about bushies killing them again. I'm not seven years old now.'

His eyes narrowed. 'Who have you been talking to?'

Her lip trembled. So – he wasn't going to try to deceive her this time. After all the years of lies she was at last close to hearing from Will's own lips what had happened that day when their family had been destroyed and their lives changed for ever. Oddly, now that the moment had come, she didn't want to hear it. But it was too late now. There could be no turning back.

'Who have you been talking to?' he repeated. 'No one round here knew us back then.'

'It doesn't matter who I've been talking to,' she said flatly. 'It isn't the first time I've heard a version of this story, anyway. All those years ago, that Mrs Mason who took me in said something of the sort. But you told me it wasn't true, and I believed you. Because you were my brother, I believed you.'

Will flushed a dull red.

'If I kept the truth from you, Jenny, it was for your sake. Bad enough you should have been orphaned at seven years old without . . .' He broke off, snatching up his coat from where it lay across the back of a chair and pulling it on. 'I haven't got time to talk about this now. I've work to do. It's hardly something that won't keep. It's kept for ten years. Another day won't make any difference.'

'Does Cerys know?' Jenny shot at him, and knew instantly from the guilty look that crossed his face, quickly followed by a flash of anger, that she did not.

'For God's sake, Jenny! You think it's something I'm proud of? That our father should have . . .' He broke off.

'Yes?' she screamed at him. 'Go on!'

'I told you, I haven't got time for this now!' he snarled, his face contorting as it did when he was in danger of losing that short temper of his.

'But she's your wife, Will. Don't you think she has a right to know the truth? Didn't you think I had a right to know?'

'Some things are best left alone, Jenny. And if you've any sense, you'll keep quiet, just as I have.'

'You still haven't told me yourself . . .'

'No, and I'm not about to. I'm going to work. Someone has to keep a roof over your head – as I have these last six years, let me remind you!'

He slammed out.

For a moment Jenny stood taking deep breaths. She was trembling from head to foot and the thoughts and emotions were churning again, around and around. She really needed to think – about what Will had more or less confirmed for her, and what she was going to do about it. But first she needed a good gallop. As always, when the world closed in about her, Jenny turned to her horses.

Mindful of the fright they had experienced last night over a possible intruder, Jenny took the smallest of the handguns and stuck it into her belt. Who knew if he might still be hanging about? But when she went outside she could see nothing untoward. In the cold grey light of early dawn everything shimmered pearly white with frost. The dirt yard crunched beneath Jenny's boots and her breath made puffy clouds in the still, cold air.

As she went into the stables the horses shifted in their stalls and wickered a welcome. A nose or two was thrust in her direction and she rubbed them idly as she passed.

Merlin, her gelding, was in the farthest box. He nuzzled her in greeting and she unfastened the gate and led him out. He must be surprised at such an early visit, she thought, but as always he was ready and raring to go. As soon as she had him tacked up, his ears pricked and when she climbed into the saddle and touched his flanks with her heels he moved off at once, powerful muscles rippling. She walked him across the dirt yard but the moment they reached turf she bent low, whispering in his ear. 'Come on, Merlin! Let's go!'

He was almost straight into a canter and then a full gallop, hooves thundering on the frozen ground, mane flying. Jenny's hair was flying too, coming loose from the pins she had hurriedly stuck into it, streaming out behind her and whipping around her face. For the moment all the anxieties and emotions that had kept her awake half the night were forgotten. It was always the same, the thrill of the ride, the exhilaration that came from the icy wind in her hair and the feeling of oneness with a horse, any horse, but especially her beloved Merlin. It was the greatest pleasure Jenny could imagine, and also the greatest relief.

It had been the same for as long as she could remember. Her earliest memories were of riding with her father, propped before him on the saddle with her little legs spread as wide as they would go across the broad back of Digger, Joel's trail horse. She had clutched at the pommel, eyes wide with a mixture of fright and delight as she bobbed like a cork in a swollen river with the trot, then cried out in excitement as the horse's stride lengthened and the ground passed faster but much more smoothly beneath the thundering hooves.

'All right, Jenny?' Joel had asked as the horse slowed once more, and she had nodded vigorously but wordlessly, for the canter had stolen all her breath.

And: 'Oh Father, can we do it again?' she had begged when he had lifted her down.

As a child, Jenny had lived for the times when Father came home and best of all were the times when he took her riding. Once he had come home rich – Jenny never had known where that unexpected windfall had come from, gambling, maybe – and he had bought her a pony. But scarcely had she had time to begin to learn to ride when they were suddenly dirt poor once more and the pony had had to go. It had broken Jenny's heart – but feed cost money, her father had explained, and Jenny had been forced to agree she would not like Barley, as she called him, to go hungry.

And then it had been back to riding in front of the father she adored, and who adored her. Often as he lost his temper with Will and with her mother, Joel never once lost it with Jenny. She was his 'little sunshine', and he was her hero, and when he was at home she scarcely left his side.

She had not been there, though, on that terrible day when he and her mother had died. She had been over at the Chaytors' place, playing with Ellie and Sam, whose father, like Joel, was a drover, and she had never quite been able to forgive herself for that. Even at seven years old Jenny had somehow felt that

42

if she had been at home she would somehow have been able to prevent what had happened.

Now she knew different. All these years she had believed what Will had told her – that her parents had been murdered by a gang of bushrangers. Since she had grown, she had tormented herself with wondering if they had raped her mother too. She did not know why she had thought it, unless it was because she somehow knew instinctively that Will was not telling her the whole truth. And of course, such terrible things *did* sometimes happen in this wild and lawless country.

Now she knew different, and wished she did not, for it had totally altered her perception of Will, her brother and her hero.

Since their parents had died he had been everything to her. She had trusted him – and she had worshipped him – with reason. When she had been taken into the care of one family after another in the nearby settlement, Will had sworn to make a home for her, and somehow – she had never been able to imagine how – he had achieved it. When she was twelve years old he had purchased the little plot of land that was Kanunga, built the homestead, and stocked the farm. Life was hard, they had little money and Will was forced to work all the hours that God sent, but at least they were together.

It had been Will who had acquired her first horse for her, too, since the short-lived ownership of Barley. Bramble had been retired by a family who had selected a neighbouring plot of land, and, patient and slow, he was exactly the right temperament for her to learn to ride on, since she had no one to teach her. She seldom rode Bramble now; he spent his days quietly grazing in the paddock with Muff, the donkey, for company, whilst Jenny had progressed to Merlin.

The pedestal on which she had placed Will had been so high; now the reality sucked her dry and filled her instead with a sense of betrayal and bitterness. If only he would talk to her, even now, discuss with her the circumstances that had made her an orphan, and explain his part in it all, then maybe she would feel differently. As it was . . .

At the borders of the farm Jenny slowed Merlin to a trot,

looking ahead with eyes narrowed against the sun, which was beginning to rise, low and bright.

Wallace land lay ahead. Usually she did not think twice about trespassing – good heavens, there was enough of it, acre upon rolling acre, and she did not think Chas Wallace would even know. Even if he did, what did it matter? She was doing no harm. He could only shout at her to get off and she could show him a clean pair of heels. But today . . . Well, perhaps, given Cerys's altercation with him yesterday, it would be wisest not to risk upsetting Chas Wallace today. At the moment, it was true, there was no one to be seen. The land stretched green and silver and inviting as far as the eye could see. But all the same . . .

Reluctantly Jenny pulled Merlin up at the boundary fence. Briefly she thought that it seemed unfair that Chas Wallace should have so much land when they had so little, especially since she doubted Chas Wallace had paid so much as a penny piece for it. His family had been squatters; they had simply taken the land for themselves in the days when that sort of thing was allowed to happen, and now it was his. But then, as Will was so fond of saying, life was not fair. And she had other things on her mind this morning.

The exhilaration of the ride went from her in a rush, leaving her high and stranded and traumatized once more. Her mouth set in a hard line. She couldn't let this go. She had to talk to Will and force the issue. Especially given what had happened last night. With a sudden decisive movement that made Merlin toss his head and rear a little in protest she turned for home.

Cerys, pounding dough to make the day's fresh bread, was puzzled. The men hadn't been in for their breakfast yet and she could not understand it. Moreover, when she had looked in to see if Jenny was awake, she had found her bed empty. Cerys hoped fervently that something untoward had not occurred during the night – though Will had surmised that the intruder had left the premises she was not so sure. Still, surely if the barns had been broken into and the horses or farm equipment stolen he would have come in and told her by now.

She crossed to the door, wiping her floury hands on her

apron, and peered out. Everything looked perfectly normal; Duggan was forking up a pile of soiled straw which he had cleared out of the stables but of Will there was no sign.

'Duggan!' she called.

No response. Duggan was getting dreadfully deaf.

'Duggan!' she called again, and this time he happened to glance up, saw her speaking to him, and made his way across the yard towards her.

'Did you say some'ut, missus?'

'You haven't been in for your breakfast yet,' she said.

'No, that's right. I'm waiting for Mr Page, like I allus do.'

'Well, where is he?'

'I don't rightly know,' Duggan admitted.

'Well, go and look for him, will you, and tell him his porridge is spoiling. And that you're hungry if he's not.'

Duggan laid down his fork with alacrity.

'Is Miss Jenny out riding?' Cerys asked as an afterthought.

'I think she must be. Merlin's not in his stall,' the old man replied.

'Oh, perhaps they're together somewhere,' Cerys suggested.

'Merlin's the only horse that's missing.'

'Well, find Will anyway and tell him to come in,' Cerys said again. Then she turned and went back into the house.


Ten minutes or so later and Cerys was beginning to grow anxious. The men were still not in.

'Where on earth can they be?' she muttered.

'Don't *worry*, Mama!' Molly, standing on a stool to knead a small ball of dough of her own, echoed the words that Will so often used to Cerys. Molly could be quite a little parrot. Imitating grown-up people made her feel grown-up too, Cerys guessed, and usually it amused her. But today she was too preoccupied to smile at her small daughter's funny little ways. She really did not know just why she was so anxious, only that she simply could not go on with her bread-making for a moment longer until she knew what was keeping Will.

'I'm going out to look for him myself,' she said.

'Me come too!' Molly climbed down from the stool, splattering flour across the kitchen floor in her haste.

45

'No, Molly. It's too cold for you outside without a cape. Stay here and keep an eye on Ritchie for me.' Cerys crossed to the door and went out, closing it behind her.

Though it was now broad daylight she had a sense of déjà vu. Just so had she come out looking for Will last night, only then she had known the reason for her anxiety and now she did not. Cerys shivered and knew it was not just the frosty air that caused it.

There was no sign of either Duggan or Will. Calling Will's name, she started towards the cluster of outbuildings. Where *were* they?

A small bent figure emerged from one of the sheds. Duggan. He was alone. But something about him arrested Cerys's attention and made the anxiety gather in a great lump in her throat.

Duggan looked somehow stunned. Never these days a speedy mover, he seemed to be staggering, as if wading through a swollen river. He looked, she thought, like a sleep-walker caught in a bad dream.

In that first moment when she caught sight of him and registered something amiss, Cerys checked, standing stock-still with her hands clutching the folds of her skirt. Then she began to run towards him.

'Duggan? What is it?'

Duggan seemed to come out of his trance, but stood firmly rooted to the spot, arms spread wide as if to stop her from passing him.

'Don't, missus. Don't go in there.'

She screwed up her face. 'What do you mean? What are you talking about, Duggan?'

Beneath that leathery tan Duggan had turned pale and he had aged somehow, his face gone slack, so that suddenly he looked like a very old man.

'Just don't, missus. It's best you don't . . .'

'Will!' she screamed. 'It's Will, isn't it? Oh, sweet Jesus . . . !'

Ignoring Duggan's warnings she pushed past him then, running to the shed. Her heart was pounding, her breath coming in painful shallow gasps. Duggan had left the door of the shed ajar; she wrenched it fully open and stepped inside.

46

At first she could see nothing. The morning sun had not penetrated here; the barn was dim and still.

*There's nothing here*, she thought, her heart lurching with relief. *There's nothing here . . .*

And then she saw him, a dark shape at her feet, so close she had almost trodden on him.

'Will!' She dropped to her knees beside him, feeling for his hand. 'Will, what's happened to you?'

There was no reply, but his hand was warm in hers.

'Will!' She lifted his head, laying it in her lap. 'What have you done? Don't worry, my love, you'll be all right. I'll send for the doctor – Jenny's bound to be home soon and she rides like the wind – she'll have him here in no time . . . It will be all right, you'll see . . .'

'Oh, missus.' Duggan's voice from the doorway, a harsh sound wrenched from him, which was almost a wail. 'Don't, missus, don't!'

He had the door open wide; a little extra light filtered in and in any case her eyes were becoming accustomed to the gloom.

She looked down and saw that Will's head was angled awkwardly on his neck. And something else. A dark pool was spreading across her skirts, dripping on to the ground beside her.

Her eyes widened. Shock coursed through her in waves, icy cold and debilitating. The use seemed to go out of her muscles, her insides turned to water.

She moved her hand against Will's thick curling hair and realized her fingers were warm and wet and sticky.

It was then that Cerys began to scream.

# Four

It was a nightmare, a nightmare from which she could not wake; a nightmare that seemed to go on for ever.

To begin with, in those first hours and days, there was a total sense of unreality. Cerys simply could not believe that Will was dead. She kept expecting him to walk in the door, thought she heard his voice and spun round, her heart lifting, before it fell away again into the bottomless pit. And yet, at the same time, a part of her knew with no doubt at all that it was true. Her cheeks and eyes burned as if with fever, her head throbbed, her chest and throat ached. And all the while she looked at the world through a thick, impenetrable fog that was punctuated only by moments of grief so sharp it was almost unbearable.

The police came – a constable and a trooper – and she told them all she could as to what had happened, her voice a monotone as if she were reciting a series of events that had happened to someone else. Mr Chalmers, the minister from Medlock, came, uttering platitudes that made her want to scream at him to leave her alone, Will had never been a churchgoer anyway and had been impatient with what he had termed 'mumbo jumbo'. And womenfolk from neighbouring homesteads came too. Cerys resented their intrusion; they had never come calling when Will was alive, she could only think their motive now was curiosity. But she couldn't bring herself to shut the door in their faces. It was Jenny who did that – a Jenny who remembered all too well the despised do-gooders who had made her life a misery after the death of her parents.

Cerys knew Jenny was suffering too, and, in her own way, just as much. Her pretty face was ravaged, dark circles beneath red-rimmed eyes, cheeks hollowed, skin grey and lifeless. She had scarcely eaten since she had returned from her ride to find Cerys hysterical and Will dead, and Cerys did not think she was sleeping either, for she could hear her pacing and weeping night after night. Yet Cerys could not find the necessary energy to break through the suffocating fog that surrounded her to share their grief. In some strange way she felt that sharing would mean taking on board some of Jenny's anguish without any relief of her own, and it was just too much for her. She simply could not do it.

Bad enough to have to cope with the children. They were both too young, of course, to really understand the enormity of what had happened, but they picked up on the moods of their mother and aunt, and Molly's tragic expression was a window on the fear and turmoil she was enduring. But at least caring for them gave a semblance of normality. Cerys could not simply retreat into that black world beyond the fog, there were meals to be prepared and clothes to be washed, and the necessity of it helped her to hold on to her sanity.

The nights were the worst, lying alone in the bed she had shared with Will with nothing to cushion her from her thoughts.

What had happened to him that morning? The police seemed to think that the intruder Will had chased the previous night had never left the property at all. He had simply gone to ground in the shed, they said, and spent the night there. Then, when Will had disturbed him the next morning, the intruder had shot him and made good his escape. Well, perhaps they were right. Certainly, even as they had searched that night, Cerys and Will had acknowledged the impossibility of being certain no one was there. In the dark there were so many places a determined man could hide.

But how long had Will lain there before he was discovered? Duggan could be of no help at all in that respect. He had not seen Will that morning, he said, and he had simply gone on with his work thinking Will must be somewhere out on the land. And he had heard nothing. Not the shot that had killed him and not the hoof beats of a horse galloping away. But that, of course, was not surprising, given how deaf the old man had become.

The very thought that Will had been lying dead whilst she had been going through all the motions of a normal day made Cerys feel sick.

She thought, too, of the altercation they had had on the day before, how upset Will had been about her taking the gig to town and damaging Chas Wallace's piano, and how they had quarrelled. Worst of all was thinking that Will had still been angry with her when they had gone to bed. Nothing would seem as bad, Cerys thought, if they had made love that night. At least everything they had shared, their lives together, would have been rounded into some meaningful order by the act of love and she would have had something good to remember and to cling to. As it was, Will had turned away from her and she had lain resentful and frustrated beside him instead of falling asleep in his arms.

Now he would never again make love to her and Cerys thought she could not bear it. Lying alone and sleepless in the bed they had shared she wept until she had no tears left and still the pain was there, wracking her body with its intensity.

And of course it was not just the emotional loss that kept her awake. There were the practicalities, too, creeping into her consciousness and making her feel almost guilty that she should think of them.

It had been Amy Hawker, one of the village women, who had first raised the question.

'How are you going to manage, Cerys?'

And Cerys, who at that juncture was still too stunned and grief-stricken to have even thought of the future, had looked at her with a puzzled frown.

'You'll have to let the land go, of course,' Amy Hawker had said.

*Let the land go.* The land Will had saved for, sweated over, died for. The very suggestion was an outrage.

'No,' Cerys said. 'I'll manage somehow.'

Amy Hawker exchanged a glance with the other women, a look of sympathy and resignation and scorn. Clearly Cerys Page was so upset she wasn't able to think straight.

And perhaps that was no more than the truth. All Cerys knew was that somehow she would keep the farm together.

For Jenny, devotion to whom had inspired Will to select it in the first place, for the children, whose heritage it was, and for herself. With Will gone she needed a dream to aim for, something that would require all her courage and determination.

Kanunga was their home. Cerys had no intention of letting it go without a fight.

Will was buried three days later in a corner of the land he had loved and as she followed his rough wood coffin across the pastureland, holding Molly by the hand and with Ritchie cradled against her shoulder, Cerys was more determined than ever. How could she leave Kanunga now, when Will lay there?

Mr Chalmers, the minister, had tried to persuade her to have him taken into Medlock, to the little graveyard there, but Cerys had proved herself as stubborn in this regard as in so many others. Will would have wanted to be buried on his own land, she insisted, and in the end Mr Chalmers had concurred, though there was great concern over the digging of a grave out here on the farm when the bitter weather had frozen the ground so hard. Maurie Trickett arrived with his pick and shovel and a Chinaman to help him, and eventually they had managed to excavate a shallow hole.

'Oh well, at least it ain't gonna fill up with water like the graveyard ones do when we get a downpour,' Maurie said, lugubrious as ever, but Cerys scarcely heard him. She couldn't bear thinking about graves that had to be bailed out before the coffin could be lowered – that was someone else's problem, and she had enough of her own.

A few neighbours had gathered around the grave, though for the life of her Cerys could not have said who was there, with the exception of the Harris family from Glenavon. They had come, she presumed, because of Jenny's friendship with David, and for Jenny's sake she was glad. The other mourners were lost in the fog that suffocated and isolated her, making her feel quite alone no matter how many others surrounded her, and she could not see their faces, nor did she try.

All her efforts were concentrated on getting through this

ordeal without 'letting herself down', as her mother would have put it. Having hysterics at the grave side would certainly be 'letting herself down' and would also frighten the children, even weeping was not, she thought, something she wanted to do. The tears were there, a knot in her throat that threatened to choke her, a mist in her eyes that threatened to blind her, and she thought that if she gave in to them, if she allowed so much as a single tear to fall, the others would come too, a deluge that she would be quite unable to control. Then the hysterics might very well follow. Better to keep herself on a tight rein. Better to swallow hard and blink furiously. Better to stare into space and bite her lip and hang on to the children as the little bit of Will that was still with her, still within reach, not lying cold and bloodied in that rough coffin . . .

'Ashes to ashes, dust to dust . . .'

Mr Chalmers' voice was reed-thin on the sharp cold air; the handful of dirt, hard with frost, sounded loud on the coffin lid.

*Oh Will, I can't bear it!* she thought, feeling the upsurge of emotion threatening to consume her. *I can't let them do this to you, I can't . . . !* And yet she stood motionless, her chin in Ritchie's hair, her eyes dry.

*They'll think I don't care*, she thought. But it didn't matter. Nothing mattered except getting through this and away from these strangers who had come to watch Will – her Will – laid to rest.

At last it was over. Mr Chalmers was saying something to her but she did not know what. His words sang in her ears like a swarm of bees. She saw David Harris step tentatively towards Jenny, saw Jenny lower her head and turn away from him, and knew that Jenny's breaking point would be reached if anyone so much as touched her. Ritchie was heavy in her arms, but he was a good burden; she moved Molly round to her other side so that she could change arms with Ritchie and still hold Molly's hand.

'Mrs Page . . .' She jerked her head around and saw Jem Routledge, the constable, standing beside her. He was in uniform; it looked as if he was on official business. Her heart lurched.

'You've got him? You've got the man who did this to my Will?'

He shook his head. 'No, Mrs Page. We're no further forward with our enquiries, I'm afraid. All the likely suspects seem to be accounted for. The Beavan gang are in the lock-up at Derry Cross, so it couldn't have been them, and Lightning was sticking up an inn on the Tamworth Road the night before your Will was shot.'

'Lightning?' The fog was still thick around her; none of this made any sense.

'Lightning. You know – that's the nickname for the bushranger who's most active around here. If the man who shot your Will was the same as the one young Jenny disturbed the night before, then it couldn't have been Lightning. And even if it wasn't the same man, I still don't think Lightning would have travelled so far so early in the morning. He got a good haul at the inn – there was a jeweller among the guests, with gold and diamonds hidden in his shoe. And in any case, he'd never have been panicked into running without taking some sort of haul with him.'

Cerys could feel the beginnings of the hysteria she was so desperate to avoid. Though they were out in the open air she felt as trapped as if the four walls of a prison cell had been closing in on her.

'Why are you telling me this?' she demanded. 'If you haven't found Will's attacker, then why are you here bothering me? Please . . .'

'Mrs Page.' Constable Routledge's tone was heavy with the exaggerated patience Cerys might have found annoyingly patronizing had she been up to noticing such a thing. 'I'm telling you because I think you should be warned. Now I know there are plenty of lawless characters on the loose, but we know for more or less certain that none of the obvious suspects killed your Will. Whoever it was didn't steal anything so far as you've been able to tell me, and they got clean away. Nobody's been able to give us any information at all. Nobody saw any strangers in the area, not young Jenny, who was out riding, and not any of the hands who were working out on the land. And there's another funny thing. Why didn't a bushie out

53

this way pick on Wells Court? He'd do far better out there than at your little place.'

'Wells Court is better protected than we are,' Cerys said. 'Any bushie would know he'd be likely to come off the worst if he tried anything at Wells Court.'

'That's as maybe,' Constable Routledge went on stoically. 'But what I'm thinking is, there might have been some reason he was interested in Kanunga, and that's why I'm having a word with you now, warning you, so to speak.'

'I don't know what you mean,' Cerys said helplessly.

'I mean, I'm thinking it was more personal, like,' the constable explained. 'Someone who had a grudge against your Will. Can you think of anyone like that, Mrs Page? Someone who might have wanted your Will dead . . . ?'

Cerys's face was hot, the world seemed to be going away from her. For a moment she was very afraid she might be going to faint. It made sense. It explained all the little things that had been niggling at her. She let go Molly's hand and clutched tightly with both arms to Ritchie. As she swayed, Jenny appeared from nowhere to support her.

'Cerys . . . let me have Ritchie!'

'No!' Cerys held him more tightly than ever, as if holding on to a lifeline. 'No, I'll be all right, Jenny. It's just—'

'I know what it is!' Jenny blazed, turning on Jem Routledge. 'It's this stupid oaf upsetting you. Can't you leave her alone, Constable? This is her husband's funeral, for heaven's sake!'

'I know that, but . . .' Jem Routledge had turned very red. Bad enough that Mrs Page was so upset by what he'd felt it his duty to say, but that Jenny should be chastising him for it . . . Like most of the young men of the district, Jem had a soft spot for the lovely, spirited girl. 'Look, I'm sorry, Miss Jenny, but I'm worried the murderer might not be just a bushie,' he said, awkward but determined. 'I'm worried he might come back to finish whatever it was he started. You and Mrs Page shouldn't be out at this farm alone.'

Jenny tossed her head. 'Oh, for heaven's sake! I can handle a gun as well as any man – and it didn't save Will in any case, did it? Don't worry about us. Cerys and I will be all right. So just stop frightening her with your stupid ideas.' She slipped a hand beneath Cerys's elbow. 'Come on, Cerys. Let's get you home.'

And with Molly clutching at her skirts she led the sad little party back across the fields to the homestead.

The days passed and still the black fog clammed in around Cerys, worse somehow now that the funeral was over. Much as she had dreaded it, it had at least been something to be worked towards and got through, something firm to aim for in this terrible fluid world where everything that had once seemed solid and dependable was now nothing but shifting sand.

But she couldn't go on like this, she knew. The farm had to be worked, the animals cared for, or they would be ruined. Thank heaven the sheep had already been shorn – Will had always made the necessary arrangements for the team of itinerant shearers to come and do the necessary, and she would not have known where to begin. But if the weather turned much harder, then feed would have to be distributed to the cattle. And when lambing came around, and the heifers began to calve, Cerys had not the first idea what she would do. Duggan, she knew, would be no help at all – or very little. He was first and foremost an odd-job man – and almost past that. It had been Will who had looked after everything that needed doing out on the farm.

'We shall have to take on some hired help,' she said to Jenny.

Jenny looked at her blankly. If anything, she was still in deeper shock than Cerys.

'Jenny, please, listen to me!' Cerys said sharply. 'Do you think the Harrises would help out until I find someone suitable?'

'The Harrises?' Jenny still looked bemused.

'Yes, the Harrises!' Cerys repeated emphatically. 'David is your friend – more, for all I know – you've been over there a good deal recently. Perhaps they'd lend us one of their hands – or perhaps David himself would come over. He'd jump at the opportunity, I shouldn't wonder.'

'No,' Jenny said shortly.

'What do you mean – no?'

55

'I mean – no! I don't want to ask the Harrises favours, and I certainly don't want David here.'

Cerys frowned, remembering the way Jenny had turned away from David at Will's burial. She had thought it was because Jenny was so grief-stricken; now she realized it was more than that.

Jenny and David had had some serious falling out, and it could scarcely have come at a worse time.

'I can do some of what Will used to do,' Jenny said, as if reading her mind. 'I used to go out with him, remember?'

'To help him, yes. But doing his job is something quite different!' Cerys objected. 'You're a girl, after all.'

Jenny shrugged. 'What's that got to do with it? I might not be as strong as a man, but I can ride and I can drive cattle – I learned that at my father's knee. Anyway, we may not have any choice. Can we afford to take anyone on? I thought money was tight.'

Cerys sighed. 'I'll have to go over the books, Jenny. I've been putting it off, but that's one thing, at least, that *I* can take over. I'd have done it before if Will had let me – book-keeping is something *I* learned at *my* father's knee – he was a shopkeeper, after all.' She broke off, biting her lip as she remembered the argument she and Will had had when she had offered to look after the accounts.

'I could easily do it for you,' she had said. 'You're always saying how much you have to do – well, it's something I could take off your hands.'

And: 'I do my own books,' Will had said stubbornly. 'I always have, and I'm not going to change now.'

'But Will, you'd have more time to spend with me and the children if I—'

'I can make the time,' Will had said, and his tone had told her that she was wasting her breath.

Well, now she was going to get to do the book-keeping not from choice but from necessity. And Cerys found herself wondering anxiously just what she would find when she did.

The books were kept in a large wooden-fronted wall cupboard

in the living room, the twin of the one where the guns were housed.

When the children were in bed Cerys got the books out and carried them to the kitchen table. For a moment she trailed her fingers on the leather tooling, her eyes blurring as she envisioned Will doing the selfsame thing night after night as, weary from a long day in the fields, he recorded the day's expenditure and, sometimes, the profit he had made from the sale of wool or some head of cattle. Then, as she opened the book, the tears pricked more sharply than ever.

Will had kept accounts with such pride! The first pages were as neat as the ledgers of any trained clerk, the writing forward-slanting and even, the figures meticulously executed. Cerys could just picture him, the tip of his tongue protruding between his lips as he wrote carefully.

The figures balanced too. In those early days the farm had, it appeared, been making a profit, and the balance of Will's capital looked reasonably healthy.

As she turned the pages, however, Cerys saw that the standard of neatness Will had set himself was declining. The writing was higgledy-piggledy now, sloping in all directions, and the columns were disfigured with the occasional blot. Because he was overtired, no doubt – and worried too, for the scrawled figures could not disguise the falling profit margins and the shrinking sum of capital.

Cerys swallowed hard. The decline had begun soon after the date of their marriage and dipped sharply after first Molly and then Ritchie had been born. You didn't need to be a financial genius to work it out – the little farm had supported Will and Jenny quite comfortably, but with three more mouths to feed, and three more bodies to clothe, it was a different story.

So that was the reason Will had been unwilling for her to take over the books! He did not want her to see just what a difference she and the children had made to the profitability of his enterprise. And, in all likelihood, he hadn't wanted her to be worried, either.

A feeling of enormous guilt washed over Cerys as she remembered all her little extravagances – and the extra burdens she had placed on Will's already overstretched margins the day before he died. No wonder he had been so angry with her! He certainly hadn't been exaggerating when he had told her furiously what a fine line lay between them and ruin.

By the time she closed the ledgers again Cerys was close to despair. If it had been this difficult to keep the farm going when Will was alive, how much more difficult would it be now, without him? He had known what he was doing and struggled; she and Jenny would be approaching it like a game of blind man's buff.

But they'd manage somehow. On that score Cerys was determined. She couldn't see the farm that was their home sold. She couldn't fail Will in this. Somehow she would find a way.

She laid her hands on the leather tooling of the ledger, palms down, fingers slightly splayed, as if it were not an account book at all, but a Bible.

'I'll do it, Will,' she whispered. 'I won't lose Kanunga. And I swear it will be here, better than ever, when it's time for your son to take over. I'll do it for all of us. For you, for Jenny, for Molly, and for Ritchie. Yes, most especially, I'll do it for Ritchie.'

It was, she knew, a vow that would take every ounce of her courage and resourcefulness to keep.

# Five

Jenny put her head around the kitchen door. She looked hot and untidy, face flushed, hair coming loose from its pins, though her fingers were blue and swollen from the cold.

'Cerys? Could you come out and give me a hand?'

Cerys, elbow-deep in suds at the sink, sighed bad-temperedly.

'*Now?* If I don't get this washing out it will never dry today.'

'And if I don't have some help, there won't be any logs for the fire,' Jenny snapped back.

'Oh – all right.' Cerys pushed the washing in to soak and reached for a dry towel. Her hands too were puffy, but red rather than blue, and long painful cracks ran from the quicks of her nails back down her fingers and thumbs. 'What is it you want me to do, anyway?'

'Just help me move the wood. There's a really heavy log on top. I can't shift it on my own and I don't know where Duggan has got to.'

'That man is worse than useless!' Cerys fumed. 'Will always said he was, and I stood up for him. Now I know what Will meant.'

'Oh, he's all right.' Jenny's nose was dripping from the cold; she wiped it on her sleeve like the farm hand she was becoming. 'We just don't notice what he does, that's all. If he wasn't there to do it we'd notice soon enough. And he doesn't seem to mind not being paid. As long as we feed him and keep a roof over his head he's happy enough.'

Cerys said nothing. Now that she had taken over the books and learned the true state of their finances she had become even more parsimonious than Will had been, and she even begrudged Duggan his share of the food when he seemed to

59

do so little in return for it. But it could be that Jenny was right and he did more than she thought. If so, then perhaps he wasn't such a bad bargain.

Molly and Ritchie were playing together quite well, building some sort of structure with the wooden blocks Will had made for them. How long that would last she didn't know. It would inevitably end in tears when Molly became the bossy big sister, refusing to let Ritchie help, and Ritchie got impatient and knocked the whole lot down. But for now, at least, they were quiet.

'Will you watch your brother for a few minutes, please, Molly?' Cerys said, pulling on Will's coat. It was warmer than any of her own, and tougher for standing up to the hard physical jobs around the farm, which she had never had to do before but which now seemed manifold. A bit of dirt on Will's coat would scarcely show; if she spoiled her own, heaven only knew when she would be able to replace it.

Molly, engrossed in balancing an archway over two square blocks, ignored her.

'Molly!' Cerys said more sharply. 'I'm talking to you! I want you to look after Ritchie while I go and help Aunt Jenny with something outside. Will you do that for me, please?'

Molly nodded, still more interested in what she was doing than in Cerys. Her tongue, peeping from between her lips, was reminiscent of Will deep in concentration.

'Mm.'

'And you won't let him go near the fire?' Cerys had it guarded but, little monkey that Ritchie was, she did not trust him not to play about with the guard and perhaps have it over if the fancy took him. 'You hear what I'm saying, Molly?'

'Mm.'

'I won't be long then.'

With one last look at the pair of them, Cerys followed Jenny outside.

As soon as they went into the woodshed she could see why Jenny had encountered a problem. The autumn storms had brought down several large trees and Will had stacked high the timber he'd carted home. The log Jenny had mentioned was lying across the others, thick and heavy. It would make the most wonderful logs, but not only would Jenny need help moving it into position, it was also likely Cerys would have to take the other end of the two-man saw to help her cut it into manageable lengths before she could set to work with the chopper. But at least they had plenty of firewood to see them through the winter and for that she should be grateful, she knew. If the worst came to the worst they might be hungry, but at least they wouldn't be cold.

'Right, tell me what you want me to do,' she said to Jenny now, acknowledging without doubt that when it came to jobs outside the house Jenny was unquestionably the gaffer.

The girls worked together for some minutes before Jenny said: 'It's all right. I can manage now.'

Cerys straightened up, relieved. The cuts in her fingers and thumbs were throbbing unbearably.

'Sure?'

'Yes, sure. You get back to the children.'

Cerys went back across the yard. The kitchen door was ajar. She groaned inwardly. She couldn't have closed it properly behind her; now the cold would have got in and chilled the kitchen.

She pushed the door fully open and went inside. Molly was still sitting on the floor with the building bricks – the edifice was now quite large and impressive. Of Ritchie, there was no sign.

'Molly!' Cerys said. 'Where's Ritchie?'

No response. This way Molly had of ignoring her when she was engrossed in something really was infuriating.

'Molly!' she said again. 'Will you answer me when I speak to you!'

Molly looked up, her eyes wide, innocent and pained.

'Where is Ritchie?' Cerys asked again.

Molly looked around and her expression changed to concern – and guilt.

'Where is he?' Cerys repeated.

Molly got up, knocking over the carefully constructed house in her haste. 'I'll find him.'

'Ritchie!' Cerys could feel the beginnings of panic. Stupid, really – he couldn't be far away, but the events of the last

61

weeks had left her raw and vulnerable. Terrible, unbelievable things didn't just happen to other people. Sometimes, however unlikely it might seem, they did actually happen to you.

'Ritchie – where are you?'

No reply – but then, there wouldn't be. Ritchie was, after all, only a year old. But clearly he was not in the kitchen.

Molly had disappeared in the direction of the bedrooms; Cerys followed, hurrying from room to room.

'Ritchie! Ritchie . . . Are you here?'

'No,' Molly said. 'He's not.'

She sounded really worried now, and aware that she had failed in her duty. Cerys felt no sympathy for her, only anger born of her escalating anxiety. She caught Molly by the shoulders and shook her hard.

'Why couldn't you keep an eye on him like I asked you? Honestly, Molly, you are impossible! I only wanted you to watch him for a few minutes. I don't know where he's got to!'

And then, quite suddenly, she remembered the open door and her heart seemed to stop beating. Perhaps Ritchie was not in the house at all! Perhaps he had toddled outside . . .

'Oh no!' Cerys groaned. She let go of Molly and ran back through the kitchen, the panic rising once more.

Ritchie wasn't dressed up for the cold – and there were so many dangers outside! And though she wouldn't have expected him to go far, she certainly hadn't seen him when she'd come back from the woodshed. He could be anywhere – anywhere!

She tore open the door and ran out, once again forgetting to shut it behind her. The yard was as deserted as it had been when she had come in. Cerys looked around wildly. She did not have the first idea as to where to begin looking and she was beset with the most dreadful feeling that she would never see Ritchie again.

She dashed to the woodshed and wrenched open the door. Jenny, the chopper in her hand, stopped in mid-swing, looking at Cerys in amazement.

'Ritchie's missing,' Cerys said urgently. 'Help me look for him, Jenny!'

'He can't be far . . .' Jenny soothed.

'He could be anywhere!'

She ran back outside, calling his name.

Duggan appeared like a genie from a bottle, looking, Cerys thought, a bit guilty. 'What's up, missus?'

'Ritchie's missing!' It was all she could do to keep from striking him. If he hadn't gone skulking off somewhere, Jenny wouldn't have needed to ask Cerys for help and none of this would have happened.

She was scuttling round now like a headless chicken, quite certain something terrible had happened to the little boy she worshipped and adored, and fast becoming hysterical.

'The stable! He loves the horses . . .' Visions of Ritchie crawling beneath the door of a stall rose in front of her eyes. He knew no fear; he could easily be kicked . . . in the head, in the stomach . . . She made a dash for the stables, Duggan following, shaking his head.

'He's not in there, missus. I'd have seen him . . .'

And, true enough, Ritchie was not in there.

'One of the other outhouses, then. Perhaps he's gone to the hen house . . .'

'Mama!' It was Molly, sounding frightened. 'Mama – I've found him! He's on the pond!'

'What?' Cerys's initial relief was short-lived. 'What do you mean – *He's on the pond*?'

'Come and see!'

She tugged at Cerys's hand, drawing her across the yard. Duggan followed. As they rounded the corner of the stable and the duck pond came into view, the relief and the fear came at her again in equal measures.

The freezing winter weather had skimmed the pond over with a thin covering of ice, so that the ducks strutted forlornly beside it. Not so Ritchie. He had toddled, or crawled, his way right into the middle of it.

'Oh dear God!' Cerys whispered.

'He shouldn't be there, should he?' Molly said censoriously.

'No, he certainly should not!'

'The ice won't hold him, will it?'

'Oh, be quiet, Molly!' Cerys screamed at her. She ran to the edge of the pond. She could see how inviting it could be for a little child – smooth and shiny beneath the pale sun. But a death trap – oh, a death trap. If the ice were to give way beneath him and he fell through, he could easily drown before she could find him. Molly knew not to venture on to the ice – she'd been told often enough to stay away from the pond, frozen or not. But Ritchie was too little to be aware of danger.

'Ritchie!' Cerys screamed.

'Don't frighten him, missus,' Duggan cautioned her.

She ignored him. 'Ritchie!' she called again, trying to sound calm but authoritative. 'Come here! Come here this minute!'

'You want me to go and get him?' Molly asked, anxious now to redeem herself.

'No! You stay here! You've done enough . . .'

'We could try a ladder,' Duggan suggested. 'I've seen it done – spread the weight, you know. But . . .'

'I don't think it would take it. I think we'll just make things worse . . .'

'Oh for goodness sake!' Jenny was at the pond side too now, as horrified and helpless as the others.

There was nothing for it, Cerys realized. The only solution was to persuade Ritchie to come off the ice under his own steam and pray that it held. But at the moment he was showing no inclination to do that. Whether this was because he was enjoying himself or because the slippery surface had frightened and unnerved him she was not sure, but she suspected the latter. Ritchie was sitting there with eyes that were very wide and a mouth that was pursed up, and he looked ready to cry.

'Ritchie!' she called again in a tone that was more encouraging than chastising. 'Come here now, there's a good boy.'

'Come on, Ritchie!' Jenny echoed, and Molly added her voice for good measure.

'Yes, come on, Ritchie!'

All Ritchie did in response was to hold out his arms, asking to be picked up – begging to be rescued! The sight of him tore at Cerys's heart and she wanted to weep, but that, of course, would do no good. Again she called his name, and this time he did indeed wriggle a little in their direction.

For long, seemingly endless minutes they coaxed him and as, little by little, he crawled closer across the ice, they prayed it would withstand his weight. Every so often there was an ominous cracking sound that sent a wave of terror around Cerys's heart, as cold as the water beneath that thin layer of ice.

And then: 'I think I might be able to reach him!' Jenny said.

She was taller than Cerys by several inches and her arms were correspondingly that much longer. She lay flat on her stomach on the hard ground, stretching her arms out towards the now-forlorn little figure. The cold of the ice on his little hands and bottom had finally taken all the fun out of the adventure for Ritchie, and though he did not understand the peril of his predicament, yet somehow he had picked up on the desperate anxiety of his family on the bank, and realized he was in danger.

'Come on, Ritchie, and we'll go and find you a biscuit!' Cerys urged.

His face screwed up, he tried to get to his feet, and then everything happened at once. As he slipped, landing heavily on his bottom, the ice cracked and gave way. Cerys screamed, her hands flying helplessly to her mouth, but, quick as a flash, Jenny made a grab for him, and by some miracle got a hold of his arm. With gritted teeth she hauled him towards her – cold, wet, screaming with fear – but safe!

Cerys grabbed him, clutching him to her as if she would never let him go.

'Ritchie! Oh, Ritchie . . . !'

She was weeping unashamedly now, and as she ran with him back to the homestead to get him out of his wet things and into some warm dry clothes, her knees felt as if they would give way beneath her.

Oh dear God, if she had lost him too she didn't know what she would have done!

Relief, irrational anger against Molly, gratitude to Jenny, irritation with Duggan, and, strangely, resentment against Will that he had left her to cope with all this alone, came together in one great wave of emotion, and it was only later that Cerys was able to think straight and realize the truth.

She'd been angry with Molly, blamed her for what had happened, but it wasn't Molly's fault. The child was only three years old – she couldn't be expected to be responsible for her little brother. That was Cerys's job, and she hadn't been there to do it.

No, the simple fact was they *couldn't* cope alone. However short money might be, somehow they had to make it stretch to pay for some sort of hired help. As things were, they were too tired, too overstretched, and if a remedy wasn't found, something would have to give. If a remedy wasn't found, something terrible would happen.

The only miracle was that it hadn't happened today.

Two days later, however, and they were still struggling along in the same old way, for there was, after all, no quick and easy solution. Jenny had gone out checking stock and taken Duggan with her, and Cerys was preparing a stew for the evening meal when there was a knock at the door.

Puzzled, she put down her vegetable knife. Visitors out here at Kanunga were few and far between, and there had been no do-gooders offering their sympathies since the day of the funeral.

Before she reached the door the knock came again, harder this time and more insistent.

'All right, I'm coming, I'm coming!' Cerys muttered.

She opened the door and almost took a step back in surprise. Standing there in the doorway, his tall frame almost blotting out the pale winter sun, was Chas Wallace. He was well wrapped-up today against the cold, with the collar of his greatcoat turned up and his hat pulled low, but the bit of his face that was visible in between was as daunting as ever. Chas Wallace was a hard man – and it showed.

For a moment grief and everything that had been worrying her went out of Cerys's head and she felt nothing but the same acute embarrassment she had experienced when she had realized she had been the cause of the accident which had damaged his piano and which could, but for fortune smiling on her, have been so much more serious. It might have happened across the great divide, in another lifetime, but the emotion she felt now was just the same, the shame of a wilful child who has caused some catastrophe through disobedience. Then the memory of how unpleasant he had been to her joined the others and she got a grip on herself.

'Mr Wallace,' she said shortly.

'Mrs Page.' Those very blue eyes were disconcerting in their directness. He was not angry now, yet still he conveyed the impression of power – and arrogance. As well he might, she thought, a little in awe, and annoyed that he should have this effect on her. Yes, perhaps he *was* a rich and powerful landowner whilst she was the struggling widow of a small farmer. Yes, perhaps he could buy and sell her and her family many times over. But that didn't give him the right to stand on her doorstep as if he owned the place and her with it. It didn't give him the right to make her feel so *small*.

Cerys took a deep breath and met his gaze squarely.

'This is quite a surprise, Mr Wallace.'

One eyebrow lifted; he looked at her with a quizzical expression.

'Really? Why?'

Cerys felt a slight flush colour her cheeks.

'I never thought . . .'

'That I would hold you to paying me compensation? I'm afraid if that was what you thought, then you have got the wrong man, Mrs Page.'

Her eyes widened. She could scarcely believe what she was hearing. Oh, she knew Chas Wallace was hard and ruthless, but surely not even he could be this callous? To come knocking on her door, demanding compensation for his stupid piano, with her husband scarcely cold in his grave . . .

'I had expected to hear from you before now,' he went on. 'I don't like letting things drag on, Mrs Page. I think it's best to tie up loose ends so that we can move on.'

Cerys shook her head, speechless. She had begun to tremble from head to foot. But Chas Wallace was standing there, regarding her squarely, waiting for an answer. From somewhere she found her voice.

'You'll get your money, Mr Wallace. I don't know where I'm going to find it, but rest assured, I will. I would appreciate it if you would send me a bill for the damage so that I can balance my books.'

A corner of his mouth quirked.

'Thank you. Yes, I'll do that.'

'And much good may it do you!' she flared before she could stop herself. 'I suppose that's how you've got – and stayed – rich. By trampling on people when they're down, and robbing the graves of the dead. Well, all I can say is I would rather be poor than have that sort of thing on my conscience.'

He was frowning now. 'I beg your pardon?'

'You heard me. Oh, I know I damaged your precious grand piano, and I'm sorry about that. But to come here, at a time like this, for something so . . . trivial . . . It's despicable. You were afraid, I suppose, that you wouldn't be paid any compensation now that Will is gone, but the accident was my fault, and I'll pay my debts.'

'What did you say?' Chas Wallace asked.

'I said I pay my debts. It may surprise you, but . . .'

'No – about your husband. He's gone . . . Gone where?'

She grasped the door ready to shut it in his face.

'Don't play games with me, Mr Wallace.'

She pushed the door, encountered an obstacle. It was his foot.

'Please take your foot out of my door,' she said coldly.

'Not until you tell me what you are talking about, Mrs Page.'

Her mouth twisted. She was so angry she could barely speak.

'Don't tell me you hadn't heard what happened, Mr Wallace. It's been the talk of the neighbourhood.'

'I haven't heard. I've been away in Sydney. I left the day of the accident and only got home yesterday. Are you saying something has happened to your husband?'

Something in his tone, something in his face, told her that he was speaking the truth.

'Will was murdered,' she said. 'Shot. The police think

he surprised an intruder. We'd thought there was someone prowling about the night before.'

'When was this?'

'The day after I damaged your precious piano. It seems everything happened that day, doesn't it? Was it a full moon? I don't remember . . .'

Her voice was rising hysterically. She could hear it, and do nothing about it.

'My dear Mrs Page, I really am so very sorry. I had no idea.' Chas Wallace did, indeed, look genuinely shocked. 'How are you managing?'

Her head jerked back. How dare he? How *dare* he?

'We're managing, thank you. And you *will* get your money as I promised, just as soon as—'

'Don't worry about that,' he interrupted her. 'I can see that you have other things on your mind just now. Is there anything I can do? Send over a couple of hands to help you out perhaps?'

So angry with him was she, that she could feel no gratitude for his offer and certainly not accept it. She knew now how Jenny had felt when she had suggested asking David Harris for assistance. She would work herself into the ground before she would place herself in the debt of a man like him.

'We are managing, thank you,' she repeated. 'There's no need for you to concern yourself.'

For a long moment those very blue eyes, narrowed in his handsome, weather-beaten face, seemed to bore into her. Disconcerted, Cerys wanted to look away, but would not allow herself to do so. She lifted her chin and determinedly held his gaze. After a moment, he nodded brusquely.

'Very well, Mrs Page. But if you change your mind, please remember the offer is there. In the meantime, my condolences to you and your family in your loss.'

He pulled his hat a little lower and turned away.

Cerys did not wait to see him go. She retreated into the house, slamming the door shut and leaning against it. She was trembling, and now that the encounter was over, the tears were very close.

'What's wrong, Mama?' Molly was tugging at her skirts, looking up at her anxiously. 'Who was that man?'

Cerys took a deep, steadying breath. 'No one.'

Molly continued to regard her with a serious expression.

'Go and play. It was no one,' she repeated.

With a quick, impatient movement, she returned to the pile of vegetables waiting to be prepared, but still her heart was beating hard and irregularly, and still the tears pricked behind her eyes.

Perhaps Chas Wallace *hadn't* known what had happened to Will. But his unexpected visit had upset her badly nevertheless. And not just because he'd been demanding money she didn't have, either. There was something about the man that was totally disconcerting, though for the life of her she couldn't have said exactly what it was.

As she went on peeling her vegetables, Cerys kept seeing him standing there in the doorway, kept seeing the hard, leathery lines of his face in the gap between hat and upturned collar, and her heart continued to pound in her chest.

Chas Wallace stood for a moment staring blankly at the firmly closed door. His eyes were narrowed with shock and he was cursing himself for the unforgivable blunder he had just committed.

Yet how in heaven's name was he supposed to have known Will Page had met an untimely end? As he had told the widow, he had been away in Sydney. But even if he had not been, there was always the possibility that the news would have passed him by. Chas Wallace was not one to do much conversing, or, as he would term it, gossiping. Though he supposed Jem Routledge or the troopers would likely have called out to Wells Court to ask if they had heard or seen anything . . .

Chas Wallace frowned. Perhaps they had been to Wells Court, and Billy Mottram, his overseer, and Mary Lightfoot, his half-caste housekeeper, had decided to say nothing to him about it. He would certainly have a word with them when he got back – allowing him to be placed in a position such as this was intolerable. Just because the Page family were poor selectors they should not be treated so dismissively and they certainly did not deserve the careless cruelty he had just inflicted. But Cerys had spirit, he'd give her that! And she was a pretty woman, too, though ravaged by grief. No, he wished with all his heart that he had not added to her misery.

But, for all that, Chas was not kindly disposed towards the likes of the Pages. He let his eye run over the dirt yard and the outhouses to the land beyond. It upset him very much that such people were now allowed to select and purchase tracts of government land for as little as one quarter of the asking price. Heaven only knew where it would end. Poor little farms like this one ruining the sweep of the countryside, pastoralists like himself squeezed off what they had always considered their own land, and the aboriginals losing even more of what land remained to them. Unusually for one of his class, Chas had a certain amount of sympathy for the aboriginals.

At the moment, though, his sympathy was all for Cerys Page, widowed so suddenly and shockingly. And there were children, too – a little girl at least, and he thought he had glimpsed a baby playing on the kitchen floor too. How would she manage? Well, the short answer was that in all likelihood she would not. Chas Wallace's eyes narrowed. It could very well be that her land would come up for sale before too long. If it did, then he would make sure he was on hand to snap it up. He didn't want some other dirt-poor farmer taking over where Will Page had left off. But for the moment . . .

Chas Wallace unhitched his great grey gelding, Lupus, from the post, and felt another stab of guilty conscience as he glanced back at the house. He would never have made this call if he had known. He would have waited a decent interval, and perhaps he would never have made it at all. As it was, he certainly would not press Cerys Page for payment. She had enough troubles.

The decision eased Chas Wallace's sense of guilt, though enough remained to make him feel a little irritable.

He swung into the saddle and rode back towards the track, over land that he could not help thinking might shortly be his. But in his mind's eye he could still see a spirited girl with dark-fringed hazel eyes and a determined set to her chin, a girl whose pride was still intact even if her heart was broken.

*　　*　　*

71

The idea came to her when she had calmed down a little and fallen to pondering how on earth she was going to pay Chas Wallace whatever compensation he was demanding. She would sell the ring Will had given her when they were betrothed. He had told her once that it was quite valuable, though at the time that had not mattered to her at all. It was the fact that he had chosen it for her which made it precious to her. Now, however, it occurred to her that it was one of her few possessions that could be turned into hard cash.

Cerys wiped her hands on her apron, went to the bedroom and opened the little jewellery case which lay on her dressing stand.

Besides the ring, the case contained only a few worthless trinkets. Though her mother and father had given her a silver locket for her sixteenth birthday, she had managed to lose it soon afterwards. Perhaps annoyed with her for what they saw as her carelessness, they had never given her any other jewellery of value – a little unfair, perhaps, since Cerys was fairly sure it had been the chain or the clasp which must have given way, but it had never really bothered her until now. Though she would have felt bad selling something that had been a gift from her parents, it would have been preferable to giving up the precious ring that had set the seal on her and Will's love.

She took it out of the box now and the light caught the little cluster of diamonds, making them wink and glint. Slowly she slid the ring on to her finger and stood looking down at it. Memories of happier times were there now, all around her, and a lump rose in her throat. Could she bear to part with the ring? It would break her heart, but what choice did she have? If she could sell it, at least she would have some money to pay off Chas Wallace, and maybe, if she was lucky, something over to help buy some of the necessities of life.

Cerys wrenched the ring off her finger and returned it to its box. Tomorrow she would take it into Medlock, to the jeweller's. For now, she would try not to think about what she was sacrificing.

# Six

'Did I see Chas Wallace riding down our drive?' Jenny asked when she came in, rubbing her hands together to bring some life back into her frozen fingers.

Cerys nodded. 'Yes.'

She told Jenny briefly what had passed between them, but not that Chas had offered to send a hand over to help out. Jenny might want to take him up on his offer!

'What are you going to do?' Jenny asked.

Cerys lifted the lid of the stewpot, stirring the contents so as not to have to look Jenny in the eye.

'I'm going to take my diamond ring into Medlock and try to sell it.'

'You mean the ring Will gave you when you were betrothed?' Jenny looked shocked. 'You can't sell that! It has always been so precious to you, and now, with Will gone . . .'

'I don't think I have any choice,' Cerys said shortly. 'And I don't want to talk about it, Jenny.'

Jenny pursed her lips. 'It's your decision, I suppose, but what would Will have to say if he knew?'

'I think he'd say it was the right thing to do,' Cerys said. 'Will always was the sensible one. It's me who's too ready to follow my heart.' She smiled briefly. 'In any case, he could hardly be crosser with me than he already was for taking the gig into Medlock and causing the accident.'

Jenny said nothing. A shadow crossed her face, deep and dark, and she turned quickly away.

'I've never had the chance to thank you, Jenny, for trying to cover up for me,' Cerys said. 'Why did you do it?'

Jenny shrugged, not looking round, and her tone was guarded. 'I suppose I was worried for you.'

'But . . .' Cerys was puzzled now. 'It was a really nice thing to do, Jenny, and I'm very touched. But I still don't understand why you should have been *worried* for me.'

Jenny spun round. Her mouth was a tight line but a nerve was jumping in her cheek.

'I just knew Will would be furious with you,' she said shortly. 'And I was right, wasn't I?'

Cerys nodded ruefully, remembering the way Will's control had snapped and how he had broken the kitchen chair.

'Yes, but he was just as furious with you, I'm sure – and without cause.'

'He wouldn't hurt *me*.'

'Jenny!' Cerys said, shocked. 'What on earth do you mean? He wouldn't hurt me either.'

Abruptly Jenny turned away again. 'No, of course he wouldn't.'

'Mama!' It was Molly, running into the kitchen. 'Mama – Ritchie's turned everything out of the cupboard in your room. It's all over the floor . . .'

'He is such a rascal!' Cerys groaned, hurrying to see what Ritchie was up to and what damage he had done. But, of course, she wouldn't be cross with him. Not really. Being cross with Ritchie just never happened.

Cerys went into Medlock next day, taking the sulky with big, gentle Lady in the harness. She seemed to have recovered from her lameness and for that Cerys was more than grateful. She would have been terrified of driving the gig again after what had happened last time, but she wanted to get her ring to the jeweller's without delay. For one thing she wanted the money to pay Chas Wallace as soon as his bill dropped through the door, for another she thought that if she delayed she would lose the willpower she had summoned up to bring herself to sell it at all. It meant so much to her and she was very afraid that when it came to the point she would be unable to bring herself to part with it.

Jenny had offered to go for her, but this was something Cerys felt she had to do for herself. Instead, she suggested Jenny should find some jobs around the homestead, and, leaving the children in her care, she clambered up into the sulky and set off.

The journey into Medlock was a painful one, reminding her as it did of that last, fateful trip. That day when she had left home everything had been perfectly normal, the only cause for apprehension her inexperience in managing the two mettlesome horses. The present had been pleasant enough, the future stretched ahead rosy and promising. Cerys's only dilemma had been how much she should spend on fabric for clothes for herself and the children.

Now her world had turned upside down. The present was a morass of grief, the future bleak and uncertain. But at least she was doing one positive thing. However little she wanted to, at least she was taking steps in the right direction.

When she reached the main street that was Medlock, Cerys found herself wishing there was somewhere else she could tie up the sulky rather than outside the Commercial Hotel. Suppose Kitty Jackson should be outside, or the men who had dropped the piano when they had been forced to jump for their lives . . . Cerys thought she would die of shame. But she did not know of another hitching post, and Lady certainly needed a drink from the trough there.

To Cerys's enormous relief there was no one in evidence at the Commercial. She watered Lady, tied her up, and walked down the street.

Johnson's, the jeweller's, was just a few doors beyond Costello's store. Michael Costello was in the doorway; when he saw Cerys he disappeared hastily inside, embarrassed, no doubt, at the prospect of coming face to face with her. Why was it, she wondered, that some people could not wait to turn up on the doorstep offering their condolences almost as if they were revelling in being a part of the tragedy, whilst others would go out of their way to avoid any contact with the bereaved?

Outside the jeweller's shop Cerys stopped and searched in her reticule for the ring. She deliberately hadn't worn it; she had felt that if she'd had to remove it from her finger it would have been even more upsetting. Now, however, she desperately needed to see it there one last time. As she slipped it on to her finger the diamonds glinted in the pale winter sun and again

75

she remembered, with a lump in her throat, how happy she had been when Will had given it to her.

'A talisman,' he had said. 'A token of how much I love you, now, and through all the years ahead.'

'I love you too, Will,' she had said. 'You'll never know just how much.'

The words came back to her now. Had he known how much she loved him? Oh, if only she could put her arms round him and show him, right this minute! And if he knew what she was doing now, would he understand? She had told Jenny she was sure he would, but it didn't alter the fact that she felt horribly guilty, as well as sad.

Cerys swallowed hard, slipped the ring off her finger again, and into the palm of her hand. She had been right about one thing, she would never be able to bring herself to take it off under Mr Johnson's gaze. Then, before she could change her mind, she pushed open the door and went into the shop.

Thomas Johnson was there, carefully polishing a silver mug. He was a little dark round man with a large hook nose. Cerys thought he was Jewish but since she did not know any other Jews she could not be sure. As she went into the shop, Thomas Johnson first looked startled, then hurried to position himself behind his counter. There was not a great deal of call for a jeweller's in Medlock; many of the townsfolk expressed surprise that Mr Johnson had not gone out of business before now.

'Yes? How can I help you?' Mr Johnson asked, rubbing his chubby little hands together.

'I don't want to buy, I want to sell,' Cerys said. She opened her palm and carefully laid the ring on the counter. 'I've always been given to understand it's worth quite a lot of money.'

Mr Johnson's smile of welcome faded to be replaced by a frown.

'I'm afraid I don't have a great deal of call for this kind of thing. It's an engagement ring, isn't it?'

'A diamond ring, yes,' Cerys said eagerly.

'As I said, an engagement ring. Young couples don't care to buy second-hand, I'm afraid. They prefer to go for new, even if it costs them that bit more. They feel somehow that if an engagement ring is for sale, then the betrothal must have been called off for some reason. It's an unhappy connotation, you see. They feel that somehow the ring is jinxed, and the last thing they want to inherit is someone else's ill luck. Foolish, perhaps, when they might well get themselves a bargain, but there it is. I'm sorry.'

'Oh!' Cerys stared at him in dismay. It simply had not occurred to her that Mr Johnson might refuse to buy the ring from her. 'Oh, but surely . . . Do you have to say it's not new? Couldn't you pretend? Really, I've scarcely worn it . . .'

A shocked expression crossed Thomas Johnson's florid features.

'I wouldn't dream of doing such a thing!' He looked at Cerys a little more closely. 'It's Mrs Page from Kanunga, isn't it?'

Colour tinged her cheeks.

'Yes. I'm sorry – I shouldn't have suggested . . .'

'You are having a hard time of it, I suppose. I was sorry to hear about your husband.'

'Thank you,' Cerys said automatically, but she thought she could do without his sympathy. A little practical help was what she needed.

As if he had read her mind, Thomas Johnson picked up the ring, turning it over in his hand. Then he proceeded to put a glass in one eye so as to examine it more closely and squinted thoughtfully for what seemed to Cerys to be long minutes.

At last he removed the eye glass and returned the ring to the counter.

'I'll tell you what I'll do, Mrs Page. I'll take your ring and try to sell it for you. I'll even make you a small advance now in anticipation of a sale to help tide you over what must be a difficult time.'

'How much?' Cerys asked.

'Five gold sovereigns,' Thomas Johnson replied. It was well below what Cerys had hoped for.

'Is that all?' she said before she could stop herself. 'Couldn't you make it ten?'

The little jeweller pursed up his lips. 'Mrs Page, I am already being far more generous than I normally would be, because of your circumstances. I may never find a buyer for your ring at all, which would mean that I should have to go the loser of the advance I have proposed.'

'Yes, I see that,' Cerys persisted. 'But if you do sell it . . . ?'

'If I sell it, then, of course, I'll send you the balance – after I've taken my commission, of course. That would be ten per cent. I don't hold out much hope, but you never know, I suppose. It's the best I can do, Mrs Page, I'm afraid. But if you think you can do better elsewhere . . .'

He pushed the ring an inch or so closer to her across the counter. Cerys made no attempt to pick it up. She knew when she was beaten. And, of course, Thomas Johnson knew too. He was very well aware that there was no other jeweller's shop within hundreds of miles and that she had no other option but to go along with him if she wanted to try to find a purchaser for her ring.

She nodded. 'Very well, Mr Johnson, I'll leave it with you.'

'If you are sure . . . ?'

'Yes,' she said firmly. 'I'm sure.'

He opened the till, counted out five sovereigns, and handed them to her. With as much grace – and dignity! – as she could muster, Cerys took them and put them in her reticule.

'Thank you. And you'll let me know . . . ?'

'If and when I sell your ring. Yes, of course. Please rest assured, Mrs Page, I am an honest businessman. I won't cheat you.'

She nodded. Now that the ring was gone there was a great lump in her throat. She really did not want to carry on this conversation a moment longer than was necessary. Choked, she left the shop and went out into the street.

There was another gig tied up outside the Commercial Hotel, and a sense of déjà vu enveloped Cerys as she recognized the matched pair in the shafts. That was Chas Wallace's gig if she was not much mistaken!

She hesitated, uncertain whether to hurry up and get as far away as possible, or slow down and hope that he was gone by the time she reached the hitching rail. The last thing she wanted was to run into Chas Wallace now – even if it was only metaphorically speaking on this occasion. But as she approached the Commercial Hotel she saw him standing on the steps with Kitty Jackson. At the same moment he turned and saw her.

Well, she decided, better to take the bull by the horns than to let him think he frightened her. Taking her courage in both hands she flounced up to the hotel verandah.

'Mrs Page.' Those very blue eyes were regarding her levelly. 'I didn't expect to see you again so soon.'

'Nor I you,' Cerys said shortly, very aware not only of Chas Wallace but also of Kitty Jackson's rather hostile stare. Why she should be hostile, Cerys could not imagine, but then perhaps she always looked at other women that way, as if they represented some kind of threat to her. A woman like her could no doubt be fiercely jealous of her position amongst her gentleman friends.

'I expect you'd like to know, Mr Wallace, that I have taken steps to get the money to cover your bill when you present it to me,' Cerys said, with as much hauteur as she could manage. 'I've just taken quite a valuable ring to the jeweller's and when he has been able to sell it for me I shall be in a position to settle my debts to you.'

'Mrs Page, I did tell you not to concern yourself for the present,' Chas Wallace said coolly.

Cerys lifted her chin a shade higher. 'I don't like owing money.'

'As you will.' He looked towards the hitching post. 'Is that your sulky? I hope you can handle it better than you handled the gig or you'll be landing yourself with more compensation claims. Coming into town will prove to be rather an expensive business.'

Her face flamed. Bad enough he should say such a thing at all, but that he should say it in front of Kitty Jackson . . .

The horrible woman was actually smirking now, Cerys thought, and burned with resentment at being made a figure of fun.

'I'm glad you think it's a laughing matter,' she flared.

Kitty Jackson's dark eyes remained levelly on her for a long moment, as if she were considering whether Cerys was worthy even of a reply. Then: 'I assure you, Mrs Page, what happened when last you drove into town was not in the least funny,' she said archly. 'My men could have been seriously injured or even killed. The damage to Mr Wallace's piano could well have been the least of your worries.'

'And I'm paying for it!' Cerys said passionately. 'I believe in paying my way with hard cash, not with favours. Even if it does cost me my most treasured possession – the ring Will gave me when we were betrothed.'

Then, unable to bear the unpleasantness of this unlooked-for confrontation a moment longer, she turned on her heel and marched back to the sulky, glad only that the one thing she could be fairly sure of was that Lady, at least, would not disgrace her.

As Cerys walked, straight-backed, towards her sulky, Kitty Jackson shook her head slowly.

'Pathetic.' Her tone was scornful.

Chas Wallace gave her a quick sideways glance. 'You can be very wicked at times, Kitty.'

'And you can be a fool. Just because Mrs Cerys Page has a pretty face . . .'

Chas's eyes narrowed. 'She has had more than her fair share of misfortune, Kitty. I would have thought you could have been more charitable towards her.'

Kitty smiled archly. 'I haven't got where I am by being charitable to anyone.'

'Admired her, then. She hasn't let any of this break her spirit. She's still out there, fighting the world, much as you were when I first met you.'

Kitty tossed her head. 'Don't compare me with her, please, Chas! I would never have looked to a man to set *me* up in life! I make my own way, and always have.'

Chas smiled slightly. It was true enough. Kitty had arrived in town alone, got herself taken on as a barmaid in the Commercial Hotel, and had somehow managed to end up owning it. Just where the money had come from to buy out old Clayton Jennings he did not know and had never asked.

There were some things that were best left alone. The fact remained that Kitty Jackson was quite a woman. He admired her for it and the two were firm friends. More than friends. Both lone, independent souls, they fulfilled a need in one another. Kitty made no demands on him; he made none on her. And he found her hard edge refreshing. Generally it amused him. Only today he found it a little irritating.

'You see, to get herself out of a hole, she is dependent now on a ring he gave her,' Kitty was saying archly. 'And coming over all sentimental about it into the bargain. She has just been to Johnson the jeweller with it, I dare say, and much good will it do her. He's as tight-fisted as any that I've ever known.' She glanced at Chas out of the corner of her eyes, her expression almost feline. 'Pathetic,' she repeated. 'There's no other word for it.'

Chas shook his head. 'When you get an idea in your head you won't let it go, will you, Kitty?'

'Hmm.' She pursed her scarlet lips, looking at him speculatively, then she laid her hand on his arm.

'Just don't make a fool of yourself over her, Chas.'

His mouth hardened. 'Don't worry. I won't do that.'

'Are you sure?' she pressed him.

'Quite sure. There's land at stake here, Kitty – or will be. And where land is at stake, I can be every bit as hard as you. Harder.' He patted the hand that lay on his arm, smiled at her. 'Come on. Let's go and have a drink before I have to head home.'

Allowing himself one last glance at the slim, upright figure unhitching her horse, he turned towards the hotel, Kitty Jackson on his arm.

As she gave Lady another drink from the trough, Cerys saw someone else she recognized walking down the main street – the compactly built figure of David Harris. Everyone seemed to have chosen today to come into Medlock, it seemed! But at least – unlike Chas Wallace – this was someone she was pleased to see. Though she did not know him well, what she did know she liked and he was of course a great friend of Jenny's. Glenavon, the Harris farm, bordered their own land on one side just as Chas Wallace's did on the other, and Cerys felt a far greater affinity with them since, like themselves, the Harris family had selected land under the Robertson Act and were struggling to pay for it.

'David!' Cerys called.

He turned and saw her and tipped his hat.

'Mrs Page.'

At any other time Cerys would have suggested he should drop the formality and call her by her given name. He was, after all, a neighbour, not much younger than she was, and, if he played his cards right where Jenny was concerned, he could yet end up as her brother-in-law. But today Cerys found a certain comfort in being addressed as Mrs Page. It was Will's name – one of the few aspects of him that were left to her.

'I'm glad I've seen you, David,' she said. 'I've been wanting to thank you and your mother for coming to Will's burial. It was very kind of you.'

David nodded awkwardly. He was a good-looking boy, Cerys thought, with a magnificent head of thickly curling brown hair and eyes to match, and his mobile mouth was always ready to break into a smile. He was not smiling today, however. In fact, Cerys thought he looked slightly ill-at-ease.

'It's the least we could do,' he said. 'We were very sorry about what happened to Mr Page. We'd have come over to help, only . . .' He broke off.

'You've got enough to do on your own farm,' Cerys finished for him. 'I understand, David.'

'No, it's not that . . .' He broke off again. 'Are they any closer to finding out who did it?'

Cerys shook her head. 'I'm afraid not. Or at least if they are they haven't been back to tell me. Jem Routledge said it couldn't have been the Beaver gang or Lightning, the bushie. They were all accounted for at the time of the shooting. And nobody saw anything suspicious it seems – no strangers, nothing.'

'We certainly didn't,' David agreed. 'And we told the bobbies so. But it worried my ma, that's for sure, thinking there's someone that dangerous on the loose in the vicinity.'

'Whoever it was, he's long gone now,' Cerys said. She

didn't care to think of the rest of what the constable had suggested – that he suspected Will's killer was not a bushie or a former convict, but someone who had known Will and had a grudge against him. That just made it all so much worse. Bad enough to imagine some armed and desperate stranger roaming their land. But if Will had been shot for a reason, by someone he knew, then the chances were that she, Cerys, knew them too. It could be anyone – a friend, a neighbour, anyone at all, and that meant there was no one she could trust.

'How is Jenny?' A faint colour had risen in David's cheeks and the awkwardness was back in his voice.

A little smile lifted a corner of Cerys's mouth. Oh, David was smitten, all right! Just so had she asked eagerly after Will when he had first come into her life. She could almost feel the tremble in David's hands, share in the aching longing she was sure he was feeling.

'She's bearing up,' she said. 'But she and Will were very close, as I'm sure you know. He was the only family she had.' She reached out and touched his arm. 'Why don't you come over and see her? She'd be pleased, I'm sure.'

'Oh, I don't know.' David's face had gone shut-in. 'I tried to speak to her at the burial but she really didn't seem to want to.'

'Because she was upset,' Cerys said. 'Heavens, I know how *I* felt when Jem Routledge tried to talk to me! Sometimes you push people away when you don't mean to, David. I'm sure that's what it was with Jenny. After all, you and she . . . Well, she spends a lot of time over at your place, doesn't she?'

'She used to.' David still looked reluctant to be having this conversation despite his obvious interest in Jenny.

'Used to!' Cerys exclaimed. 'Why, she was hardly ever at home before Will died. Now, of course, she's very busy trying to cope with the work he used to do – that's the reason she hasn't been over to Glenavon.'

David shook his head. 'It's more than that, I'm afraid, Mrs Page. She hasn't been over for a long while now. No, I don't think Jenny cares for me any more – if she ever did.'

'But . . .' Cerys frowned, puzzled. She had not been exaggerating when she had said Jenny had scarcely been at

83

home in the few weeks before Will's death, and certainly she had given them the impression she had been at Glenavon. If she hadn't, then where had she been? It was puzzling to say the least of it, and she only hoped Jenny had not been up to some mischief. Well, if so, Will's death had put an end to it.

'Don't give up too easily, David,' she said. 'Jenny has always been very fond of you, I know, and I expect she could be again.'

She saw the hope flare in his eyes and smiled briefly. She was certainly right to think he carried a candle for Jenny. But whether Jenny returned the feeling, she had no idea.

As she drove home Cerys soon forgot the puzzle of where Jenny had been all those times she and Will had thought Jenny was at Glenavon. There were too many other things on her mind to waste time worrying about something that was clearly over and done with. Since Will's death Jenny had not so much as left the property, and with so much to do there was little prospect of her doing so in the near – or even the distant – future.

The journey took longer than it had done in the gig, for Lady was a good deal slower than the mettlesome matched pair, but she was also a good deal easier to handle, so that Cerys found it much less tiring.

At the border of the Kanunga property she noticed a fence down and groaned. The stock were, she thought, off to the north, and hopefully none had been lost – yet – but the fence would have to be mended quickly if they weren't to stray. Cerys could not understand why she hadn't noticed it when she had passed on her way to Medlock – perhaps she had been concentrating too hard on handling Lady and the sulky – but at least she had seen it now and she could send Duggan out to attend to it. Mending a fence was something he should be able to cope with. If he couldn't, then he really was totally useless!

She turned the sulky into the drive, keeping a sharp eye out for any other potential problems. Strange, really, how she had never really appreciated just how much Will had done when he had been there to do it. There had even been times when she had felt vaguely resentful at the long hours he worked – as if it were from choice that he stayed out on the farm, neglecting her, the children, and the homestead. Now she could see all the day-to-day jobs piling up she realized just how much she had taken Will for granted.

As she drove into the dirt yard her eyes narrowed and a puzzled frown creased her forehead.

There was a strange horse tied up at the rail – a magnificent bay gelding. She gave it a good look as she passed, noticing the highly polished but well-worn saddle and the length of the stirrups. The rider was tall, then – almost certainly a man.

She drew up in front of the stables, looked around in vain for Duggan, and unhitched Lady herself. As she emerged from stabling the horse the house door opened and Jenny came out. She waved to Cerys, more animated than Cerys had seen her since Will's death, and beckoned eagerly.

Cerys's puzzled frown knitted more deeply as she saw the figure of a man at Jenny's shoulder. A tall man, wearing a greatcoat but no hat. The owner of the horse, no doubt. But who was he? Why was he here? And why was Jenny looking so pleased with herself?

As Cerys drew closer, Jenny came running to meet her, smiling so broadly that Cerys could not help smiling back.

'Jenny . . . ?'

'Cerys, I think I've found the answer to all our problems!'

'What do you mean?' Cerys asked.

Jenny linked her arm through that of her sister-in-law.

'Someone to manage the farm for us. Come and meet Hal Tucker.'

# Seven

He was, Cerys thought in that first startled moment, quite simply the most handsome man she had ever seen. Beside him all the other men she considered good-looking paled into the ordinary. His features were classically perfect yet totally masculine, his hair thick and dark, his eyes blue and almost opaque, like pieces of glass.

There was something about those eyes she did not care for, though she could not for the life of her have said why. Jenny, clearly, had no such reservations. She was all smiles, her cheeks flushed and her eyes alive for the first time in weeks.

The man was extending his hand to Cerys; she did not take it, instead looking at him coolly. What had Jenny said to him? She wondered. Surely she had not been so foolish as to offer him a job when they knew nothing whatever about him? Well, if she had, it could always be undone. The farm belonged to her now, as Will's widow, and hiring and firing was her responsibility, nothing to do with Jenny at all. This man, whoever he was, would have to accept that.

'So, you are Hal Tucker,' she said tautly.

He withdrew his hand, which was, she noticed, still leather-gloved – but returned her close stare.

'I'm Hal Tucker, yes. And you are Will's wife . . . widow. Cerys, is it not?'

Her eyes narrowed. 'I am Mrs Page. Did you know Will? It sounds as if you did.'

He threw back his head and laughed. 'Did I know Will? Oh, most assuredly! We were the best of friends at one time – when we were both young and foolish. We worked together on Barlinney – one of the biggest cattle stations in New England.'

'That's where Will went after our parents died,' Jenny said, her face shadowing for a moment. 'I was put into the care of a settler family and Will . . .'

'Will learned his trade on Barlinney,' Hal said. 'As I did. Only, Will put it to better use. He bought himself this place whilst I . . . I've gone on working for other folk and spending my hard-earned wages on enjoying myself, not putting down roots for the future.'

Cerys's lips tightened. 'At least you are alive, Mr Tucker. Will's thrift and ambition cost him his life.'

'Yes, and I was truly sorry to hear it,' Hal said sombrely. 'My condolences, Cerys.'

Again she bristled for some reason at the use of her Christian name. Why was she so touchy about it? Unlike the feeling she had experienced when she had been talking to David Harris, this was not about wanting to use Will's name, it was about the familiarity with which this man was addressing her. He might have known Will, worked alongside him, roistered with him, perhaps even shared a billet – but he did not know *her*.

'How did you come to hear of it?' she asked shortly.

'Bad news travels fast, I'm afraid,' he said. 'It's the way everywhere – but especially out here among the farming communities.'

At that moment there was a scream from inside the house, followed by Ritchie's lusty wail.

'What's going on?' Cerys, totally distracted, pushed past Hal.

'Oh – he was asleep.' Jenny followed her, trying to explain. 'Molly has woken him, I expect.'

Cerys pushed open the door. Sure enough Ritchie was sitting on the floor beside the sofa, where he had been taking his afternoon nap. His face was scarlet, his hair damply plastered to his forehead, and he was beating a furious tattoo with his little fists.

Cerys scooped him up. She couldn't let Ritchie cry, even if he had nothing to cry about.

'What did you do to him?' she demanded of Molly.

'Nothing! I . . .'

'You woke him up, didn't you?'

'He *wanted* to wake up!' Molly protested.

'No, he did not want to wake up. He wanted to finish out his sleep. It was you who wanted him to wake up,' Cerys said crossly. Ritchie was likely to be fractious now for the rest of the day.

Jenny and Hal Tucker had followed Cerys into the house. Jenny pulled a face at Molly, making the little girl giggle. Cerys felt a stab of annoyance. It was good to see Jenny more like her old self, but she wished she would not undermine her this way when she was disciplining Molly.

'You were saying how you came to hear of Will's death,' she said to Hal Tucker.

'That's right. I've been shearing for the past few years and I was working a shed over at Nelson.' To Cerys's extreme annoyance he leaned comfortably against the dresser as if he were totally at home. 'I was pretty shocked, I can tell you. Anyways, as soon as I'd finished the shed I came hightailing over here to see if there was anything I could do to help.'

'That was very kind of you, Mr Tucker,' Cerys said, swallowing her irritation.

'No worries. I figured it was the least I could do when Will and I used to be such good mates. I knew he'd bought the farm to make a home for Jenny here, and I had heard he'd married, so it didn't take much working out that there would be two women in a pretty pickle.' He nodded towards Molly and Ritchie. 'I didn't know there were children too, though knowing Will I should have guessed as much.'

Hot colour flooded Cerys's cheeks. The man was definitely overfamiliar. How dare he make reference to her and Will's private lives!

'We certainly are in a pickle!' Jenny said. 'The only man about the place now is old Duggan, and he's no use at all. There's just too much to do for us to be able to keep up with it all.'

'Yes – while I think of it, Jenny, there's a fence down bordering the Medlock road,' Cerys said.

'There you are then!' Hal Tucker said easily. 'A job for me already.'

Cerys turned to look at him directly.

'As I have already said, it's very kind of you, Mr Tucker. But I'm not at all sure that we can afford to pay help just at the moment.'

Hal Tucker crossed one leg over the other, leaning back against the dresser even more comfortably.

'Who said anything about paying? And please, won't you call me Hal?'

'But you can't afford to work without being paid!' Cerys exclaimed, ignoring his last plea.

Hal Tucker shrugged. 'Not for ever, it's true. But for an old friend . . . If you are going through a bad patch I reckon the least I can do is help you out for a while. As long as I've got my food and a bed to sleep in, there's nothing else I need. And the shearing paid well. Henry Dunning is a generous man – not like some of the tight-fisted sheep masters round here.' His mouth twisted and his face darkened momentarily. It crossed Cerys's mind to wonder if it was Chas Wallace he was referring to.

'Call it a loan of my services for the sake of an old friendship,' he went on. 'You can pay me up for whatever I've done when you're back on your feet again.'

Cerys bit her lip. It went against the grain to put herself in debt to this man who was a stranger to her, even if he had been a friend of Will's – truth to tell it would go against the grain to put herself in debt to anyone. But what choice did she have? They *couldn't* manage, she and Jenny alone. The farm would go down and down and eventually they would lose it. And in the meantime – what else might they lose? She thought of what had happened just the other day when Ritchie had been left alone. It was only by the grace of God that he hadn't fallen through the ice on the duck pond and drowned. Next time they might not be so lucky.

And at least when spring came and she could get some of the stock to market she could make paying Hal Tucker what she owed him the very first priority.

'It makes sense, Cerys,' Jenny said urgently.

Cerys nodded. 'I suppose you're right. Just as long as you understand, Mr Tucker, that I'll pay you a fair wage the moment I can.'

'Hal,' he reminded her.

89

'Yes – very well – Hal.'

'It's a bargain then.' He held out his hand to her again and this time she had no choice but to take it. The grip of the hand, still encased in the leather glove, was firm and the light blue eyes were steady on her face. But, for all that, Cerys's discomfort seemed to increase rather than lessen and she wished she could pull her hand away.

What was it that was unsettling her so? She wondered. Was it because she did not like taking on a hand in the full knowledge it would be some time before she could pay his wages? Was it the man himself, with his disconcerting familiarity? Was it that she felt that somehow she had been manipulated into a corner? Or was it purely and simply that she was replacing Will in one area of her life and she just was not ready to do so, on any level.

Cerys could not be sure. She only knew that she did not feel relieved and happy that, as Jenny had said, all of their problems had been solved. Instead she merely felt miserable and oddly apprehensive.

A week or so later and Cerys was forced to admit that things seemed to be turning out a great deal better than she had anticipated. To be able to hand over all the worries about the day-to-day working of the farm to a man who knew what he was doing was the most enormous relief – though Jenny had done her best, Cerys had never been quite sure how capable she was of handling things, quite apart from her lack of sheer physical strength. The problems were so many and so varied, a man could work a farm for half his life before he knew how to deal with all of them. A girl who had only dabbled when the fancy took her had no chance at all.

Hal Tucker was not the aggravation about the homestead that she had expected either. Determined not to have a man of whom she knew absolutely nothing sleeping under her roof, Cerys informed Duggan that space would have to be made in his quarters. Had Duggan protested too vigorously she had made up her mind he would have to be given his marching orders, but in the event the old man did not protest at all. Hands were used to sharing billets – in Duggan's case, Cerys felt fairly sure, that billet had at one time been a prison cell – and Duggan merely said he would be glad of the company. Cerys fixed an additional cot and Hal moved into it.

Like Duggan, he took his meals with the family; unlike Duggan, he lingered after supper yarning with them. He was, she soon learned, a born entertainer who could spin a story about almost anything.

Sometimes he talked about the days when he and Will had been lads together on Barlinney Station, and though the reminiscences made her sad, she found them rewarding too. The Will Hal talked of was a different Will to the man she had known – young, fun-loving, always up for a spot of mischief. Hal told of how they had once used lengths of twine to tie up each leg of a pair of working trousers belonging to an old hand who had been making their lives a misery. The hand – Joss, Hal called him – was in the habit of reaching for his trousers and stepping into them in one quick movement when the men were woken before dawn for a day's hard work. Will and Hal had not known whether their trick would work or not, but it did, spectacularly. In the pitch dark of the early morning, Joss had shoved a foot into each trouser leg and heaved himself up with his usual forward thrust, lost his balance when his feet did not emerge at the other end of the legs, and fallen flat on his face.

'He knew it was us that had done it,' Hal said. 'And he promised to thrash us to within an inch of our lives if he could prove it. But he never could – and even if he had, it would have been worth it. To see him thrashing about on the floor and swearing – oh, that was the funniest thing!'

He broke off, laughing at the memory, and Cerys laughed too, though her heart was aching.

'He was a bit of a scamp, then,' she said, and Hal nodded.

'He was that, all right. Every bit as bad as I was – and I tell you, I was bad! But he was always more serious than me, too. He never forgot the promise he'd made to Jenny to make a home for her, and he saved every penny he could get his hands on so he could get the deposit together to select some land.'

'Never mind the serious side,' Cerys said. 'I saw enough

91

of that for myself. Tell us about the mischief you used to get up to.'

And so he did, story after story.

'Did I tell you about the Tarsbrook Ghost?' he said one night.

'No! You saw a ghost?' Jenny exclaimed. She was, Cerys had noticed, continually animated in Hal's company though she was still lost in the depths of grief for Will when he was not there, and she rode out with him with noticeable eagerness too.

Hal laughed. 'You want to hear the tale?' The two girls nodded. 'Have you never heard of the Tarsbrook Ghost?'

'Tarsbrook?' Cerys said. 'You mean the Tarsbrook we pass through if we are going to Sydney? The place where the river crossing is?'

Hal nodded. 'That's the place. It's supposed to be haunted – a story every drover knows. A fugitive on the run from the law tried to make the crossing once when the river was running high. The troopers were right on his tail, and he got reckless. Without stopping to think of the dangers, he plunged right into the torrent. Well, maybe he had nothing to lose. They'd have hung him, like as not, if they'd caught him. Either way, he wasn't in luck that night. The current was too strong, his horse lost its footing and the poor soul was washed away and drowned. His ghost still haunts the place, it's said, and on nights when the moon is full he can be seen galloping at full tilt, still trying to make his escape from the troopers on his ghost horse.'

'Quite a story!' Jenny said. 'But where do you and Will come in? You still haven't answered my question. Did you see it?'

'No, but half a dozen of the strongest, bravest drovers in all of New England did – and it scared them out of their wits, I can tell you! They had made camp for the night on the bank of the river and were sitting round the fire, enjoying a drink, and a bit of a song when suddenly – there it was! The ghost! Milky white in the moonlight and galloping across the high ground above the crossing.' Hal chuckled at the memory. 'They hightailed it, every last one, left their cattle and ran for their lives. When they got up the nerve to come back, a few head of the finest cattle had gone missing. They reckoned the ghost must have been hungry that night.'

'But . . .' Jenny was looking puzzled. 'If you were there . . . and *they* saw it, then why didn't you?'

Hal chuckled again. 'That would be telling, wouldn't it? Let's just say me and Will were a bit better off that week than we would have been with just our wages, and a few prime head of beef found their way to a farm where they shouldn't have been, and went to market with a different band of drovers.'

'*You* took the cattle?' Jenny asked. 'While they were scattered, frightened, you and Will . . .'

'It was more than that, wasn't it?' Cerys said, fixing Hal with a stern eye as if he were still a young tearaway. 'You and Will were the ones who made the ghost appear, weren't you?'

Hal laughed outright. 'There's no fooling you, is there, Cerys? Yes, it was me and Will, up to another of our larks – and that one made us a tidy profit, too!'

'But how did you do it?' Jenny asked. 'How did you make a gang of grown men believe they were seeing the ghost of the fugitive?'

Hal tapped the side of his nose.

'That's for me to know and you to find out. And maybe you will one day, but it's a story for another time.' He laughed again. 'Oh, it was good, though! You should have seen those drovers run! Like frightened girls, they were! Oh, it was a sight for sore eyes!'

'And that, I think,' Cerys said sternly, 'is quite enough of that. It's time we turned in, Hal. I don't care to burn the candle at both ends, if you do.'

He said his goodnights and left, not in the least disconcerted at being turned out.

'He's really nice, isn't he?' Jenny said.

Cerys, laying the table ready for breakfast in the morning, frowned.

'He seems to be, yes.'

'Well of course he's nice!' Jenny said quickly. 'He would never work for us for nothing, just out of friendship for Will, would he, unless he was nice?'

93

Cerys set the knife across the bread board and looked up at her sharply.

'Be careful, Jenny.'

Colour flared in the younger woman's cheeks. 'What do you mean?'

'You know very well what I mean,' Cerys returned tartly. 'You've set your cap at him, haven't you? I just think you should tread a little warily until we know him better.'

'Oh, for goodness' sake!' Jenny flared. 'He was Will's friend, wasn't he? Isn't that good enough for you?'

Cerys nodded slowly. 'I suppose it has to be.'

But she still did not understand why Hal made her feel so uncomfortable, even when she was laughing with him, enjoying his outrageous stories, and appreciating the difference his being there was making to their lives. Caution, perhaps, the caution of a woman whose whole world had fallen apart about her. But, whatever, she couldn't quite put it aside. She couldn't quite forget that they only had Hal's word for any of this. And most of all, she did not want to see Jenny hurt. She was so vulnerable just now, the brittle euphoria when she was in Hal's presence covering what Cerys knew to be a deep well of grief. If Jenny was badly hurt by Hal it could very well prove to be the straw that breaks the camel's back. The thought was a very worrying one.

Next day the bullocky came by with a letter addressed to Cerys. Puzzled, she carried it to the kitchen table where Molly was playing with a piece of pastry dough that she had kneaded so much it had turned grey.

'What's that?' Molly asked.

'A letter, for me,' Cerys told her.

'Who is it from?'

'I don't know. I'm going to open it and find out.'

She sat down and tore open the envelope. Molly, still kneading the piece of dough between her plump little hands, came to her elbow to watch.

Cerys drew the paper out, her eyes widening as she saw it was headed with the address of Thomas Johnson, the jeweller in Medlock. Then, as she read on, she didn't know whether to laugh with relief or cry.

The ring she had entrusted to him to sell for her had found a buyer, Mr Johnson said. If she would like to come into his shop he would be pleased to hand over the proceeds to her.

Cerys pressed a hand to her mouth.

'What is it, Mama?' Molly asked. 'Is something the matter?'

'No, sweetheart, it's good news,' Cerys told her, but there was a hollow space where her stomach should have been.

So – her ring had gone, finally and for ever, and she would never see it again, never slip it on to her finger and admire the way the stone caught the light, never feel it biting comfortingly into the flesh that was puffed now from washing and scrubbing in hot water and chilled by the biting wind when she hung the laundry on the line to dry. The sadness was very sharp in her; another part of the old life was gone for ever.

But it was no use feeling like that. It *was* good news. At last she could pay off the horrible Chas Wallace – at least, she supposed she could, for he had not yet been back with the bill she had asked for, and so she could not be sure just how much she owed him.

But it would be enough, surely? The figure Thomas Johnson mentioned was far more than she had expected to get. Twenty sovereigns! Her ring must have been more valuable than she had realized.

Unexpectedly she thought of the story Hal had told them of how he and Hal had rustled cattle under cover of the Tarsbrook Ghost. Had something like that paid for her ring? No, she wouldn't think it. That occasion had been a prank only; Will wouldn't have done anything so bad a second time. He had scrimped and saved to buy the ring for her because he loved her, she just knew he had . . .

'Mama,' Molly said seriously. 'Why are you crying?'

Cerys swallowed hard and wiped her wet cheeks with her fingers. Until Molly had mentioned it she had not even realized she *was* crying.

'Because I miss your papa, Molly,' she said simply.

Molly's face crumpled. 'I miss him too.'

'I know you do, sweetheart.' Cerys put her arms round the little girl and Molly climbed on to her lap, twining her plump little arms around Cerys's neck, so that the piece of greasy pasty dough pressed into it. But Cerys scarcely noticed and would not have had the heart to say anything about it if she had. 'We just have to be very brave,' she said softly.

'Brave,' Molly echoed.

A cry from the other room interrupted them. Ritchie, who had been having a sleep, had woken up and was seeking attention.

'Molly, I have to go to Ritchie,' Cerys said, making to get up, but Molly clung on tightly.

'Mama, no, stay with me!'

'Ritchie is crying,' Cerys said.

'I'm crying too!' Molly whimpered, hanging on for dear life. 'You always go to Ritchie.'

Cerys experienced a great wave of guilt. It was true, she never really seemed to have time for Molly. But that was just the way it was.

'Ritchie is not as old as you,' she said, carefully untwining Molly's arms and setting her down. 'You are the big girl and he is just a baby.'

Molly crumpled on to the floor. 'Molly want to be a baby, too!'

'No you don't, sweetheart,' Cerys said tiredly, and thought that it wasn't just a question of age. Molly was a girl, she was going to be a woman. Women had to be strong to take everything that life threw at them – childbirth, a home to hold together, bereavement, working until they were bone-tired and still having to go on. 'There are times when I would like to be a baby, but I can't be, and neither can you.'

She crossed to the room where Ritchie had been sleeping. On the floor, Molly lay and kicked her legs miserably. The ball of dough, unnoticed, rolled beneath the covers of the chaise.

Cerys would have liked to go to Medlock immediately so that she could collect the money due to her from Thomas Johnson and settle her debt with Chas Wallace. Also she had the totally unreasonable fear that if she did not act at once Mr Johnson might change his mind and tell her she had no money to come after all. She knew that was stupid – if he'd sold the ring, he'd sold it, and she'd never heard that the jeweller was anything but scrupulously honest.

But what she wanted to do was neither here nor there. As usual these days Jenny had gone out with Hal, and there was no one to look after the children. No one but Duggan, that is, and Cerys certainly would not trust him with them. No, there was nothing for it but to wait until Jenny came home.

Cerys busied herself with all the hundred and one tasks of running a home. There were the vegetables to be prepared for dinner, and that took longer than it had since Will had died, for Hal was an extremely hearty eater, there was the interminable washing, and the kitchen floor seemed to need sweeping constantly since every time the door was opened the gusting wind blew flurries of dirt and dead leaves in. She couldn't leave it in a mess – Ritchie still crawled almost as much as he walked, and she hated the thought of him getting himself dirty, or, worse, stuffing something totally unsuitable into his mouth and swallowing it before she could stop him.

At last – at long last – Cerys heard hoof beats on the yard and looking out, caught sight of Jenny going into the stables with Merlin. Perhaps, she thought, there would still be time for her to make it into Medlock if she was quick.

'Be a good girl – I'm just going across the yard,' she said to Molly, and scooped Ritchie up. Since the near disaster when he had wandered off to the duck pond she had not let him out of her sight.

The wind was bitingly cold; Cerys tucked Ritchie inside her shawl, loving the way he snuggled against her. He might be big enough to toddle now, but he still liked nothing better than a good cuddle. It was, Cerys thought, the one bright spot in a dark world.

Jenny had not yet emerged from the stable; Cerys crossed the yard and pushed open the door.

Then she stopped abruptly, colour rushing to her cheeks as a great wave of confusion overcame her.

Jenny was still in the stable, as Cerys had guessed, but she was not alone. Hal was with her. He had her in his arms and he was kissing her most thoroughly.

# Eight

S wiftly Cerys backed out of the stable door, banging into the frame as she did so. But Jenny and Hal were far too wrapped up in one another to notice. She hurried back across the yard and into the house, only stopping in her foolish wild flight when the door was safely closed behind her.

'What's the matter, Mama?' Molly asked, round-eyed.

'Nothing. Nothing at all.'

And, of course, in reality there was not. What harm was there in a kiss in the stables between Hal and Jenny? A kiss she should have seen coming? Jenny was eighteen years old – plenty of girls were married at that age – and Cerys thought it quite likely Jenny had been kissed before now. As for Hal, he was young, handsome, and, as far as they knew, free. Perhaps it was not wise for a young lady to allow such liberties, but when had wisdom ever had anything to do with it? Cerys was still young enough herself to remember the kisses she and Will had shared before they became man and wife – kisses that were all the sweeter for being stolen behind the backs of her mother and father.

But it was embarrassing, all the same, to have come upon Hal and Jenny like that, even if they had been quite unaware that she was there. And not only that . . .

The strange disquiet was there again, gnawing at her. Why was it that Hal had this effect on her? What was it about him that unsettled her so?

Ritchie began to wriggle; Cerys put him down and stood, undecided. Then she returned to the door.

She couldn't leave Jenny with Hal for much longer like that, either for her peace of mind as to what the two of them were up to or for the fact that she really wanted to go into Medlock.

But neither was she going to risk surprising them again. That was far too embarrassing.

She went into the yard, made a great show of looking around, then called Jenny's name loudly. A few moments later and Jenny emerged from the stables – alone. She was a little flushed and some strands of hair were escaping from their pins, but otherwise there was nothing to indicate that she had just been sharing a passionate embrace with the new farm manager – if Cerys had not known differently.

'Ah – there you are!' Cerys said innocently. 'I thought I saw you come home.'

'Yes, I was just settling Merlin.' Jenny sounded ever so slightly flustered.

'Can you look after the children for me for a little while?' Cerys went on to explain about the letter from Mr Johnson.

'He didn't take long to find a buyer for your ring then?' Jenny said. 'It's good, I suppose, but . . .' She broke off, biting her lip. 'Yes, I can look after the children for you now. I'll harness up Lady for you if you like.'

'Oh, yes, thank you.' Cerys went hot realizing how close she had come to causing herself – and Jenny – more embarrassment. Hal must still be in the stable, skulking out of the way so she should not realize he and Jenny had been in there together. If she had gone barging in to get Lady and found him there, their secret would not only be out – they would know it was.

'I'll go and get a coat on while you're doing it,' Cerys said, turning away swiftly and escaping back into the house.

Mr Johnson seemed surprised, and a little put out, that Cerys should have come for her money so soon.

'Good gracious, I only gave the letter to the bullocky yesterday!' he complained. 'I certainly didn't expect you to be in my shop today!'

'Well, I am,' Cerys said briskly, 'and I hope you've got my money ready for me.'

'Naturally. Naturally!' Mr Johnson rubbed his hands together. 'You say it as if you didn't trust me, Mrs Page. I am an honest businessman and I would be very angry if anyone should think differently.'

'Of course I trust you!' Cerys said hastily. 'I would never have left my ring with you if I didn't. And you wouldn't have written to tell me you'd sold it, would you? You would simply have kept the proceeds for yourself. No, all I meant was that . . .' She broke off, not quite sure how to explain herself and what had caused her to make the comment. She did trust Mr Johnson, of course, not to keep the money due to her. She simply thought that he had wanted to hold on to it as long as possible because he liked money just as he liked gold and jewels.

'I'm surprised it sold so quickly, too,' she ran on. 'Who bought it?'

'Oh!' Mr Johnson pursed his lips togther so that they made a tightly stitched little seam in his plump face. 'I don't think I am at liberty to tell you that.'

'Why ever not?' Cerys asked, genuinely surprised.

Mr Johnson huffed a little.

'Client confidentiality, Mrs Page. Client confidentiality. And in any case, with an item such as that, of great sentimental value to you, I have to say that I do think it is best you don't know who is the new owner.'

'You think I might go and steal it back from them?' Cerys said. 'Now who is casting aspersions on whose honesty?'

'Of course I think no such thing, Mrs Page!' Thomas Johnson hastened to reassure her. 'I just believe it is for the best.'

'I know,' Cerys said simply. 'Though I have to say I'm not altogether sure I would trust myself. It's why I'd like to be prepared. If I were to see it on the finger of one of the local –' She hesitated, on the point of saying 'busy bodies' – 'One of the local . . . ladies . . . I think I might just tear it off her finger.'

Mr Johnson smiled smugly. 'I think, Mrs Page, that it is unlikely you will see it again. Now, shall we attend to the business aspect? You'll want to get home whilst the daylight is still good, I expect.' He crossed to a wall safe, set beneath a shelf where three or four clocks ticked, all displaying different times, opened it, and took out a velvet pouch. 'The purchase price is here, minus my commission, of course. Did you want to count it?'

'No,' Cerys said, anxious not to upset the testy little jeweller again. 'It's all right, I do trust you.'

'If you are quite sure . . .'

'I'm sure,' she said.

She took the pouch from him and slipped it into her reticule. As she did so she felt a sense of guilt bubbling up inside her. That was it, then, her love sold for thirty pieces of silver. But she must not think of that. If Will were here now he would tell her she had done the right thing. If Will were here, he would understand.

'Thank you, Mr Johnson,' she said, and her voice seemed to belong to someone else.

Then, before he could see the tears sparkling in her eyes, she turned and hurried out of the shop. It was, of course, too late to call on Chas Wallace that day. By the time she was back at Kanunga it was time to give the children their tea and see to the evening meal for herself, Jenny and the men.

Hal came in early, long before Duggan. Cerys saw the colour rise in Jenny's cheeks and the sparkle in her eyes, and looked at Hal to see if the signs were as obvious where he was concerned. But Hal seemed just as he always did – pleasant, charming even, but paying no special attention to Jenny. If he made a fuss of anyone it was Molly – and she, little minx, seemed to be enjoying every minute of it.

As she checked on the vegetables, Cerys watched surreptitiously, and was unable to suppress a quiet smile. Molly would give Jenny a run for her money if she were fifteen or twenty years older! The adoration she already felt for Hal was quite obvious – and hardly surprising really considering the way he treated her. The little girl missed her father so badly and Hal seemed to be making an effort to fill the gap. Just now Molly was sitting on his lap whilst he showed her pictures in a book, and Cerys had scarcely ever seen her more rapt.

Only when Cerys set the cutlery on the table beside her did she come out of her trance, grabbing Cerys's hand by the wrist almost bossily and spreading her mother's fingers.

'Did you sell it, Mama, your ring? Has it really gone for good?'

'Yes, Molly, it has.' She felt annoyed that the little girl had

101

raised such a personal matter in front of Hal, yet, oddly, bound to offer him some kind of explanation.

'I've had to sell my engagement ring to pay my debts,' she said. 'That's what we're reduced to, I'm afraid.'

Hal's eyes darkened, whether with sympathy or with acrimony she could not be sure.

'That is very sad, Cerys.'

'Yes, but necessary.' Her glance went to the dresser shelf. She had propped Mr Johnson's pouch up behind the china shepherdess her mother had let her bring with her to New England from Sydney, a little reminder of home. There had not been room to place it in the cash tin as it was and she had not wanted to put the sovereigns in loose. Having them all together in the pouch gave her an odd feeling of security. 'What I got for it will be a great help, anyway.'

Hal looked away, his attention returning to the story he was reading to Molly, but Cerys had the feeling he was still thinking about what she had done, judging her perhaps, and finding her wanting. It was not a pleasant feeling, and it added to all the other discomforts that Hal was able to arouse where Cerys was concerned.

The very next day she set out for Wells Court, leaving the children collecting fresh eggs in Jenny's care. Hal was out on the farm and Cerys had had to especially ask Jenny not to go with him though the girl was very well aware of Cerys's plans. Really, Jenny was totally besotted, Cerys thought, and for the first time felt a wave of irritation rather than concern for Jenny, who might very well be on the point of having her heart broken.

Though Chas Wallace was their nearest neighbour, Wells Court was still a good fifteen minutes' drive away. As she trotted up the drive Cerys wondered if she would find Chas at home or if this would be a fool's errand, but at least, she thought, he would know she had made the effort.

Wells Court was a large, impressive building, surrounded by lawns and flower beds that would, in spring and summer, be bright with flowers and flowering shrubs. To one side and the rear of the house the outbuildings clustered, some of them as big and as substantial as the Page house! Clearly no expense had been spared on its upkeep, but then Cerys would have expected no different. Chas Wallace was, after all, the closest thing New England had to aristocracy.

As she tied up Lady to a hitching rail, a lump of nervousness rose in Cerys's throat. Angry with herself, she swallowed at it. Why should she be nervous of Chas Wallace? She was every bit as good as he was, even if he could buy and sell her many times over. And if it was his wrath she was afraid of, then there was no real reason for that either. She had brought every penny of the money her ring had fetched with her – she couldn't believe Chas Wallace could legitimately tell her the repair of the piano would cost more than she could give him. But . . . an awful thought struck her . . . suppose it did! Suppose the piano had been beyond repair – what then? There would be no way she could ever hope to be able to replace it. The shame she would feel if such a thing were to happen washed over her in a cold wave as if it were already so, and she stood for a moment with her fingers pressed to her lips, eyes closed. Then, with an effort, she pulled herself up.

*Don't even think such a thing. Just get on with what you came here for . . .*

Head held high, reticule clasped firmly between both hands, she marched up to the front door and knocked. For what seemed a lifetime nothing seemed to stir within the house. So – perhaps Chas was out already, inspecting his stock, riding his boundaries, or whatever it was he did when he employed enough hands to live the life of a gentleman of leisure if he so chose. Cerys was just wondering whether perhaps she should go around to the rear of the house, where she would surely find either a servant or a stable lad so that she could at least ask them to tell Chas Wallace she had called, when she heard footsteps inside the house.

The door was thrown open and Cerys found herself face to face with a small, dark-skinned woman who was almost as wide as she was high. Black beady eyes fastened almost accusingly on Cerys, and the woman folded her arms across her ample bosom.

'Yes?'

Cerys could not help but be surprised to find an aboriginal employed at Wells Court. Aboriginals were not known for their keenness to work, nor for their reliability – quite the opposite. Freedom was the most important thing in the world to an aboriginal, and they were quite likely to 'go walkabout' whenever the mood took them.

Still, Cerys thought, if Chas Wallace chose to have one working for him it was none of her business.

'Is Mr Wallace at home?' she asked briskly.

The little woman's scrutiny of her became even more intense.

'Who wants him?'

'Mrs Will Page.' For some reason Cerys took comfort in using Will's name. 'Is he at home or not?'

The woman declined to answer.

'What do you want with him?'

Cerys, already nervous and now disconcerted too, began to be angry.

'I think that's my business. Mine and Mr Wallace's.'

Still the woman stood her ground, for all the world as if she were a sentry guarding the entrance to a royal palace.

'If you won't tell me, I can't tell him.'

'Look, I don't want you to tell him anything, except that I am here,' Cerys said furiously. Intransigence was something else aboriginals were known for; she could imagine this stand-off going on for some time. 'Please do so at once!'

The woman's eyes, dark and full of resentment, held hers. Then, with a movement that was unusually quick for one of her race, she shut the door in Cerys's face.

For a moment Cerys stared in utter disbelief, then her quick temper, already simmering, boiled over. How dare a servant treat her so! She hammered on the door so hard that all the cuts in her fingers began throbbing in protest, and the pain only served to make her more cross than ever.

'Come back!' she yelled furiously. 'Open the door this minute!'

To her surprise it began to open.

'I should think so too!' Cerys fumed. 'How dare you . . .'

She broke off. It was no longer the aboriginal woman on

104

the other side of the threshold. Shocked, Cerys found herself face to face with Chas Wallace.

'Oh!'

Quick colour rose in her cheeks, confusion swamped her. She had come here with the intention of handing over her dues in a dignified manner and correcting Chas Wallace's impression of her as a silly, irresponsible girl, and ended up being caught banging on his door and shouting like a fishwife. It was not at all the right foot to start on.

But it wasn't her fault! It wasn't! If the aboriginal hadn't shut the door in her face she would never have lost her temper like that!

'Mrs Page,' Chas Wallace said.

There was something that sounded suspiciously like amusement in his voice – and something that gave the impression of amusement, too, in the way he was looking at her, one eyebrow slightly cocked, one corner of his mouth lifting.

With a supreme effort, Cerys got herself together.

'Mr Wallace.'

For the moment it was all she could think of to say.

The eyebrow cocked a little more. 'You wanted to see me?'

'Yes – yes, I did. Why else would I have driven over here? But that woman . . .'

'Mary Lightfoot, my housekeeper,' he said. 'I must apologize for her. She is very protective of my privacy, for some reason, and sometimes, I am afraid, she exceeds her brief.'

His housekeeper! Not just a servant, but his housekeeper! Oh well, more fool him!

'You'd better come in,' Chas Wallace said, standing aside. 'It's cold outside. Is your horse . . . ?'

'I tethered her,' Cerys said sharply. 'Don't worry, she's quite secure.'

'Good.' A corner of his mouth quirked, but Cerys did not notice it. All she was aware of as she went past him, following the direction he was indicating, was a pair of jet-black eyes glowering at her from a doorway.

Inside, the house was spacious and light, and furnished with

105

the kind of artefacts Cerys had not laid eyes on since leaving Sydney. The room into which Chas took her would, no doubt, in more social circles have been called a drawing room, for it was furnished with ornate Regency chairs, a blue velvet chaise and a highly polished table. A fire blazed cheerfully in the wide grate; on the mantel above, Cerys saw a carved case clock, a mounted tiger's claw and a pair of Oriental china vases, tall enough to dwarf the clock. But it was what stood in the corner of the room that caught her eye and brought the colour rushing back to her cheeks again.

The grand piano, in all its glory. The top was propped up, the lid open, revealing keys of sparkling ebony and ivory. A sheet of music was propped on the stand, a brocaded stool set in just the position for a player to reach the pedals. It looked for all the world as if someone had recently been playing it.

Cerys turned her glance quickly, not wanting to be seen staring at it, but not before Chas Wallace had noticed.

'The famous piano,' he said with a slight smile. 'That is why you are here, I take it?'

'It doesn't look too badly damaged,' Cerys said hopefully.

'The leg was broken, but I know a good carpenter and he has mended that,' Chas Wallace said. 'Unfortunately it's not so easy to get someone to attend to the workings.'

'There's damage to the workings?' Cerys asked, her heart sinking.

'One or two of the hammers appear to be broken,' Chas replied matter-of-factly.

'But you've been playing it . . .'

'Me?' His mouth quirked again. 'Oh no, not me. I don't play.'

'Then who . . .'

'At the moment, no one. Fortunately for you, I acquired the piano because a friend of mine thought I should. In her opinion, every drawing room needs a grand piano to grace it. And who knows? One day I may have a wife who is musical, and children who could learn to play. For the moment the piano is strictly for decorative effect, which, as I say, is most fortunate, since I have no idea how long it will be before I can find someone to repair it.'

'So you still don't know how much you want from me by way of compensation,' Cerys said faintly.

Chas Wallace thrust his hands into his pockets, tilted his head to one side and regarded her directly.

'I think the best thing would be to forget all about it – for the time being, at any rate.'

'But . . .' Cerys's mind was working overtime. Though it would be nice not to have to part with any of her ready cash, she did not like the idea of the debt hanging over her. If she didn't know how much she was going to have to pay Chas Wallace, she didn't know how much of the ring money she would have left to pay for the day-to-day necessities of life, and she really had no idea at the moment where the next decent slice of income was going to come from, or when.

'I'd rather settle things now and know where I stand,' she said stubbornly.

'But I've just told you – I don't yet know – apart from the carpenter's fee, that is. And quite honestly that isn't worth bothering with.'

Not worth bothering with! Probably a whole day's work for the craftsman involved, not to mention whatever materials he had needed to use, and Chas Wallace thought it 'not worth bothering with'! Oh, to have his kind of money!

'Mr Wallace,' Cerys said stiffly. 'It has cost me a great deal emotionally to get the money to reimburse you. I really would like to settle the matter now I'm here.'

Chas Wallace sighed. 'Very well. Give me a couple of sovereigns to cover it if you insist.'

Cerys swallowed hard. The money Mr Johnson had given her for her ring seemed to be burning a hole in her reticule.

'And what about the damage the instrument specialist will have to put right?' she asked.

'I told you – I don't know how much until it's been examined.' He was beginning to sound impatient.

'The trouble is, Mr Wallace,' Cerys said, 'that I don't know whether I'll have the money to pay you then. At the moment I've got it. But two, three . . . six months hence . . . I just don't know.'

He shrugged. 'I'll have to take that chance.'

'Well I don't want to, Mr Wallace,' Cerys said proudly. 'I may be poor but I like to pay my debts. And whatever you may say now, you did come to my door telling me that was exactly what you expected. Perhaps you're feeling sorry for me at the moment, but I wouldn't expect that to last, and I don't want your pity in any case. I want to pay my dues. Surely you must have some idea what the repairer will charge?'

Chas Wallace was no longer smiling. His eyes had narrowed; there was a speculative look about them.

'Perhaps you're right, Mrs Page. Very well, I'll make a bargain with you.'

'Good.' Cerys opened her reticule. 'How much?'

'No.' Chas Wallace stretched out a hand – lean, brown, authoritative. 'No money at this stage. As I say, I really have no idea how much to demand and I want to be fair to both of us. Now, you say you might not have the money to pay me when the time comes . . .'

'I might not. No.'

'In that case I suggest a surety. The deeds to your land.'

Cerys gasped. She could scarcely believe she had heard aright.

'The deeds . . . ?'

'Why not? If you are unable to find a few paltry sovereigns to settle your debt, the chances are you will be unable to keep your farm going anyway. I'd like the land – I'm always looking to expand my own, and this government initiative for selection has proved very restrictive for me.'

'But my land has to be worth a lot more than the repairs to your piano, however expensive the repairer proves to be!' Cerys cried, outraged.

'And, at the time, I would make up the difference – give you cash in hand to pay for it,' Chas Wallace said calmly. 'That's a far better deal than you would be likely to get if you were forced into bankruptcy.'

Cerys lifted her chin. 'And what makes you think it will come to that?'

'Two women – trying to run a farm alone?' Chas Wallace's tone was dry. 'Realistically, Mrs Page, I cannot see that it can come to anything else.'

'Perhaps, but we are not alone, Mr Wallace.' Cerys was unable to avoid allowing something of her triumph to show through. 'We have a manager to help us. A friend of Will's, who knows all about farming.'

Chas Wallace's eyes narrowed and Cerys was even more pleased that she had seemingly surprised him.

'So you see, we may very well yet make a great success of our little farm,' she said smugly.

He nodded slowly. 'Very well, I grant you that. But I still think my offer is an unbeatable one. You have nothing to lose by accepting it, Mrs Page. Deferment of your debt to give you the chance to get back on your feet again, and the chance to gain a good price for your land should things go wrong. In such a case you'd get a pittance for it by selling it back to the government, you realize? And, because they would be looking to sell it on again, you'd have to vacate your home. I wouldn't make you do that.'

Cerys looked at him narrowly. 'You wouldn't?'

'Why should I? It's the land I want. As far as I'm concerned you could stay in the house as long as you wanted to. And . . .' He looked at her levelly. 'You have a son, don't you?'

She nodded.

'Well, there would always be a job for him on my holding,' Chas Wallace said evenly.

Cerys laughed slightly and did not know why. Nothing about this was even remotely funny.

'He's only just over a year old.'

'And in no time at all he'll be fourteen years old and big enough to be of good use around the place – though not up to a farm of his own.' Chas Wallace shrugged slightly. 'It's up to you, Mrs Page. You've nothing to lose by accepting my offer. Either you can pay, in which case you are doing well enough not to need my assistance, or you can't. But you will still have a roof over your head and a future for your boy. I can't say fairer than that.'

Cerys took a deep breath. Her head was spinning. Oh, if only Will were here to talk things over with! But then, if Will were here she wouldn't be in this mess . . .

'And if I refuse to accept your offer, Mr Wallace?' she said.

'Then of course I would be much harder on you, Mrs Page.' He moved abruptly. 'Very well. If you insist on settling your debt here and now I estimate it to be in the region of a hundred and fifty guineas.'

Cerys blanched. A hundred and fifty guineas! It was a fortune she had no hope whatever of finding. Whether she liked it or not, it seemed she had no choice but to go along with Chas Wallace's suggestion.

And perhaps it wasn't such a bad one. If she could make the farm pay then she would give him his money and settle the debt once and for all – though in all conscience the figure seemed unreasonably high when the piano was standing there within her line of vision looking remarkably unscathed. And if she couldn't . . .

All she could hope for was that Chas Wallace was a man of his word.

'Very well,' she said stiffly. 'I'll have the deeds sent over to you.'

His eyes held hers, teasing. '*Sent?*'

'I'll bring them myself,' she said, furious that he knew very well she was in no position to order anything.

He smiled. 'I must say you are very trusting, Mrs Page. You'd put the deeds of your property into my hands without so much as a receipt?'

Her face flamed. She simply hadn't thought . . .

'No, it's best we do this properly, for both our sakes,' he went on. 'I'll instruct my lawyer in Medlock to draw up a legal document setting out the terms of our agreement. Then I suggest we go into town together to sign it. I can pick you up in my gig and drive you in.' His mouth quirked. 'That might be safest for all concerned.'

So – he was still alluding to her loss of control of the gig! Cerys thought, annoyed.

'Can't we please forget about what happened?' she said stiffly. 'I'm afraid I'm finding the joke has worn a little thin.'

He straightened his face with difficulty. Something about the manoeuvre made the deep lines play about his mouth so that he looked impossibly attractive. The suddenness of the transformation took Cerys unawares, shocking her as much by the fact that she had noticed it as anything else.

'I'm sorry, Mrs Page. I really shouldn't tease you about something you obviously find very embarrassing,' he said.

'Not only embarrassing – expensive too!' Cerys flared, discomfited now also by the unexpected way she had felt a moment ago.

Once again a muscle moved in his jaw; once again she found herself noticing it.

'Perhaps,' he said evenly. 'I think we should look on it as fortuitous. An opportunity that might prove of benefit to us both.'

She moved impatiently. 'I must be getting back, Mr Wallace. Will you . . . ?'

He nodded. 'I'll let you know when the legal documents are ready for signature. Good day, Mrs Page.'

'Good day, Mr Wallace.'

As she went back through the spacious hall to the front door, Cerys was aware of a pair of beady black eyes following her from behind a door, and aware, too, that there was nothing friendly in the gaze.

Chas Wallace stood in the doorway watching Cerys leave. His eyes were narrowed thoughtfully, but a small smile was playing about the corners of his mouth.

Not a bad morning's work! The land was, he thought, almost as good as his. If he could get the document handing the deeds over to him signed and sealed he could relax safe in the knowledge that when the Page farm failed it would go, not on the open market, or even back to government control, but to him, as settlement of a debt. He'd have to pay off whatever was still owing on the land to the authorities, of course, but that wasn't important to him, and he felt sure a consideration slipped into the hand of whatever official he had to deal with would allow it to go through smoothly.

But it seemed he had not acted a moment too soon! If a friend of Will's had turned up on the scene he did not need to be clairvoyant to see the man's motives. He had his own eye on the farm, no doubt. Well, unless he were to go so far

111

as to marry Cerys there was no way he would get his hands on the Page land now.

Not, Chas thought, that Cerys would be looking to wed again for some long while. She was clearly a woman devastated by the loss of her husband, though she was bravely doing her best to rebuild her life.

Well, at least he had eased his conscience somewhat by promising that she could stay on in her home even if she lost the land. And it would be no hardship to him. None at all . . . No, all in all, not a bad morning's work.

He went back inside the house, closed the front door, and pushed open the door to the dining room. Mary Lightfoot was still lurking there.

'And what did you make of all you overheard, Mary?' he asked conversationally.

The aboriginal shrugged, not in the least worried at being caught listening.

'Land should be free and clear. Like in Dreamtime.'

Dreamtime, for the aboriginals, was the dawn of the world, their equivalent of the Garden of Eden.

'Dreamtime is over, Mary,' Chas said flatly. 'Now the land belongs to people like me.'

She snorted, flaring her flat nostrils, turned away, then turned back to him once more.

'Woman does not belong to you though.'

'No – I know you don't,' he said.

'Not me – her. She don't belong to you even if her land does.' She nodded sagely. 'And she never will.'

Chas Wallace moved impatiently, his good mood dissipated.

'Get on with your work, Mary,' he said dismissively.

As she drove back to Kanunga, Cerys's thoughts were spinning. She could scarcely believe she had actually agreed to hand over the deeds to Chas Wallace, and yet – was it such a bad decision? If things went wrong for them it could turn out to be a blessing in disguise.

What would Jenny have to say about it though? Fiery little Jenny, fiercely loyal to Will's memory, would likely be furious.

But in the last resort it wasn't up to her. Kanunga might be her home at the moment, but it wouldn't always be. Jenny would marry one day and have a husband to provide for her and a place of her own. It was Cerys who would have to soldier on, Cerys who had to do whatever was necessary to keep a roof over her children's heads, and Will would have expected no less. Will would have understood.

Perhaps it would be best if Jenny did not know about her arrangement with Chas Wallace, Cerys decided. She would simply tell her they had sorted things out amicably and if things went right, Jenny need never know. After all, no one would ever dream Chas Wallace would have asked so much for the repair of a piano, grand or not, and one he didn't even play! It was outrageous! And what was it he had said? A lady friend had suggested no drawing room should be without one. Well, it didn't take much to guess who that friend might be – though she was no lady! Kitty Jackson, as like as not.

Cerys felt an uprush of irritation. So, it was all down to Kitty Jackson that she was in this position. Well wouldn't it just be? And what Chas Wallace saw in someone like her, she simply could not imagine!

Cross again without really knowing why, Cerys flicked the reins and pushed a lazy Lady to a faster trot.

# Nine

Cerys was growing more and more concerned about Jenny. Once, in another lifetime, it seemed, she had been a happy-go-lucky girl, quick-tempered, yes, rebellious and a little wild, yes, but basically sunny-natured and remarkably unscathed by the experiences of her early years. Now, however, her mood swings were violent, and the depressions that descended on her as black as Will's had sometimes been.

She was still grieving, of course, Cerys realized, for the adored brother she had lost, and everyone grieved in their own way. But all the same there was something almost frightening about the intensity of Jenny's grief, an edge of aggression that could be turned on Cerys, on Hal, or even on Jenny herself. Her face would darken, her voice become a snarl, she would slam things about and make the most hurtful accusations. Then, inevitably, it would end with tears when she would sob almost hysterically for a long while before exhaustion overcame her. The first time it had happened, Cerys had gone to her, thinking that they could share their grief, but there was no reaching Jenny. She simply yelled at Cerys to get out and leave her alone, that Cerys did not, and never would, understand.

'What do you mean, I don't understand?' Cerys had said, hurt. 'He was my husband, Jenny. The father of my children. Of course I understand!'

But Jenny refused to reply. She glared at Cerys with such hatred in her eyes that Cerys withdrew a pace or two, wrapping her arms around herself protectively, and when Jenny stormed past her, heading for the stables, Cerys let her go. She was, after all, grieving desperately herself. If Jenny chose to react so then she would have to get on with it. Cerys had no reserves to deal with such unreasonable behaviour.

On that occasion Jenny had taken Merlin and rode out her mood, but at other times the outcome was more sinister. One morning after a night of wild and heartfelt sobbing, Cerys noticed long scratches on Jenny's arms when she rolled up her sleeves to wash the dishes.

'Jenny – what have you done to your arm?' Cerys caught her wrist, trying to examine the angry score marks which had clearly been deep enough to bleed, but Jenny jerked her arm away.

'It's nothing. I caught it on a nail in the stable, that's all.'

'You should put something on it,' Cerys said. 'If the nail was rusty you could get an infection.'

'It's all right! Stop fussing, Cerys!' Jenny snapped. She pulled her sleeve down to cover the scratches and as she did so alarm bells rang in Cerys's head. At this time of year Jenny never went to the stables without wearing her coat – it was far too cold to do otherwise. So how had she come to scratch her arm on a nail?

She was lying. She had to be. And Cerys thought with a sinking heart that she knew the reason. It was no rusty nail in the stable that had drawn blood. Jenny had caused this injury to herself, a measure of her terrible destructive grief.

The second time it happened Cerys was beside herself with anxiety. Will would never forgive her, she thought, if she allowed Jenny to harm herself, but what could she do? She couldn't be with Jenny all the time, and if she tried to impose herself when Jenny wanted to be alone, then Jenny would either storm off or turn her anger and despair at what had happened on to Cerys. All she could do was hope that the grief would begin to lessen a little before Jenny did anything too drastic.

And at other times, even now, she was almost crazily euphoric. The reason for this, Cerys felt, was almost certainly Hal, and this, too, worried her. There was absolutely no doubt whatever of the way Jenny felt about him, even if Cerys had not seen them kissing. It was there in her eagerness to be with him from morning to night, the way her eyes followed his every move, her quick brittle laughter at his quips. Jenny, who had flirted outrageously with every young man in the neighbourhood but never lost her heart, was utterly besotted with Hal Tucker.

Hal, on the other hand . . .

In spite of the kiss, or perhaps because of it, Cerys had the unmistakable feeling that Hal was stringing Jenny along, enjoying the power he undoubtedly had over the pretty, vivacious girl. But oh! She was so vulnerable just now! So much on the edge! Cerys was very much afraid of what would happen if Hal let Jenny down, but there was absolutely nothing she could do about that either, except hope with all her heart that if – when! – it happened, it would not be yet.

Just let Jenny get on more of an even keel so it doesn't affect her too badly, Cerys prayed.

And wondered whether there was a God who might listen to her, or whether he was just a comforting father figure for children like Molly and Ritchie.

It was not to be long before Cerys's worst suspicions concerning Hal's intentions towards Jenny were to be proved right – though in a way that had never entered her head in her wildest dreams.

It was late in the afternoon, the wintry sun was setting pink in the pale grey sky over the outbuildings, and Cerys was busy preparing the evening meal.

For once she was quite alone. Molly and Ritchie had both spent a very active day running around the yard and now both of them were asleep, curled up together on Molly's bed. It was unusual for Molly to nap in the day now, and if Cerys had noticed her growing sleepy she would have done her best to keep the little girl awake, for this snooze would surely be at the expense of an early night tonight. But Cerys had not known. Molly and Ritchie had been playing together and it was only when she had gone to see why they were so quiet that she had found them curled up together and dead to the world.

Jenny was out too. She had driven the gig into Medlock to pick up some provisions they needed – flour, potatoes, butter and pork. Cerys had, in fact, cast a concerned eye over her store cupboard and worried that they had not preserved enough vegetables to last them through the winter. She could

116

not understand how she could have underestimated so badly how much they would need. The shelf in the larder had looked to be as laden as ever when she had squeezed the last jar on to it in the autumn. Hal was here now, of course, but Will was not. The one should have cancelled the other out. But seemingly the beans and beetroot, the plums and pears and gooseberries were not going as far this year. Well, there was nothing she could do about it now. She'd just have to make sure she put up more next year.

If they were still here . . .

Cerys sighed, all the worries weighing down on her, opened the oven door and peeked at the piece of lamb she was roasting. Yes, it was doing, but not as evenly as she would have liked. She needed to turn it. Cerys dug in a fork at each end and lifted the joint carefully. Then a sound from behind her startled her and she spun round to see Hal standing there.

'Oh! You made me jump!' But she was no longer concentrating on the task in hand. The joint dropped from one fork and plopped heavily down into the hot fat, which splashed up on to Cerys's wrist. She squealed in pain, setting down the other end and grabbing a cloth to wipe the fat from her arm.

'Oh – look what you've made me do! I've burned myself now!'

Hal was across the room in a couple of quick strides.

'Wash it off quickly!'

He grabbed her good arm, led her to the stone sink where she had been washing the vegetables and dunked her wrist into the cold water.

'Leave it there a minute,' he advised.

Cerys, however, yanked it out again.

'I've got the meat out. If I don't put it back in it won't be cooked. And look at all those fat splashes on my skirt! I'll never get them out . . .'

'Don't worry so much,' Hal drawled.

'Don't worry! It's all right for you!' She finished turning the meat, managing to splash herself again in the process. 'Oh, what's the matter with me!'

Her voice rose angrily; quick tears gathered in her eyes. Normally she would have taken a little thing like this in her stride, now the burning pain of her wrist and the fat splashes on her skirt where it was not covered by her apron were just too much to bear.

'What are you doing in here anyway?' she asked bad-temperedly. 'You shouldn't be in here at this time of day.'

Hal leaned back easily on the back of a chair.

'Well, I came to see you, of course.'

'What for?' Then, as she saw the way he was looking at her, quizzical, teasing, she tossed her head impatiently. 'Oh, don't be so stupid!'

She turned back to the joint, lifting the tin carefully with the cloth and putting it back into the oven. Then, as she closed the door, she felt his hands on her waist.

'Stupid, is it?'

He was close behind her, his chin against her ear, those hands on her waist holding her fast, pulling her against him. She felt his breath on her cheek, and then the moist warm pressure of his mouth against her neck.

'Hal!' She tried to turn and push him away, but somehow succeeded only in facing him whilst being held as securely as ever.

'What do you think you are doing . . . ?' The words were cut off as his mouth covered hers. 'Oh!' she squealed, twisting her head to one side and thrusting at his chest with both hands. Then, with enough room to swing, she managed to land a slap on his face.

It was not a hard slap, but it was enough to make him release her, his hand going to his cheek.

'What d'you do that for?' For a moment he glared, a glare almost frightening in its intensity, and his blue eyes were as cold as ice chips. Then his features relaxed and he grinned at her. Actually grinned! Fury rose in her in a great tide.

'How dare you!' she yelled at him. 'How *dare* you?'

'Because I wanted to.' He was still looking at her with that rather rueful amusement. 'I've wanted to from the first time I set eyes on you. You fascinate me, Cerys. And you've wanted it too, don't deny it.'

'I most certainly have not!' she spat at him and raised the

fork threateningly. 'Get away from me now! Get out of my house!'

'All right, all right!' He raised his hands placatingly. 'I read things wrong. I'm sorry.'

'I should think you were!' Cerys was fuming.

'All right, I said! There's no need to keep on about it. I won't try to touch you again.'

'I should hope not!' Cerys said emphatically. 'I'm grateful to you for what you are doing for us, Hal, but I won't have you taking liberties, and you'd better understand that.'

'I understand now – though you can't blame me for trying. And I said I'm sorry. What more do you want?'

Cerys drew a couple of deep, steadying breaths. What she wanted was to tell him to pack his bags and leave. What she wanted was never to set eyes on him again. But she dared not be so hasty.

'If there's nothing else then . . .' She glanced pointedly towards the door.

Hal leaned back easily against a chair, still looking at her in a way she felt was overly familiar.

'The real reason I came in was to look for my hammer. I'm fairly sure I left it here . . .'

'I haven't seen it,' Cerys said, not knowing whether to believe him or not.

'It must be somewhere else, then.'

'Yes,' Cerys said. 'It must.'

Hal tipped his hat, grinned at her and crossed to the door. When he had gone, Cerys pressed her hands to her mouth. She was trembling violently and the tears were very close again.

What an unpleasant thing to happen! And she'd been right, too, to think that Hal was a womanizer. Oh, he had tried to flatter her into believing it was her he was interested in, but of course it wasn't. It was any woman. Perhaps he would have been less ready to try to fool her if he'd known she had seen him in the stables with Jenny – and then again, perhaps he would not. His sort was incorrigible. But for him to think that he could actually seduce her with Will scarcely cold in his grave . . .

Cerys shook her head in disbelief. She wished with all her

heart that she could have acted on her first instinct and told him
to pack his bags and go. She really did not want him here. But
neither could she afford to lose him. There was simply no way
she and Jenny could manage alone, and until they could afford
to pay for labour it would be folly to dismiss Hal Tucker just
because he had tried to take a liberty with her.

The familiar feeling of being trapped by a vicious fate closed
in on Cerys. Wretched, still shaken, but resigned, she went back
to preparing supper.

'Cerys! Cerys! Wake up! Wake up!'

Cerys came through the layers of sleep in a rush, the urgency
of Jenny's voice making every nerve tingle. As she opened her
eyes she was aware that her room was bathed in red light – a red
light that was dappling the walls. Dappling? No – flickering!

'What . . . ?' Cerys flung herself out of bed.

'It's the barn!' Jenny's voice was urgent, full of panic. 'It's
on fire!'

'Oh my God!'

Cerys's mind was racing now in time with her hammering pulses. Waking up too suddenly, and full of awesomely
nightmarish thoughts . . . The barn full of winter feed – on
fire! They could not lose it – they could not! And suppose
the fire spread – to the other outbuildings – to the stables –
to the house itself!

'The men!' she cried. 'We must wake the men!'

'They're already awake and fighting it,' Jenny said. She
sounded quite calm, but that was Jenny all over. Calm,
capable when danger threatened, all dark moods and edge-
of-the-nerves afterwards. 'Hal woke me. I'm going to help
them, Cerys.'

'I'll come too!' Cerys was pulling on her clothes. Then a
thought struck her. 'The children – I can't leave them!'

'The children are fast asleep,' Jenny said. 'They won't
wake.'

'Oh, maybe not . . .' Their room was on the back of the
house, it was true. No flickering red light should reach their
window. 'If I close the door securely . . .'

She took the time to look in on them all the same, but as

Jenny had said they seemed to be sleeping soundly. Then she grabbed Will's overcoat and ran outside.

At once she could see that the barn was well alight. But – thank God! – it was the one farthest from the other outbuildings and the stables, and at the moment there was no wind to carry sparks. The fire was roaring throatily, though, as it devoured their precious stock of hay and shot up through the flimsy roof.

Cerys saw the figures of the men silhouetted against the flames – Duggan bent and wiry, Hall tall and strong. He was working like a Trojan, she realized.

'What can we do?' Jenny called to him.

'Fetch more water,' he yelled back.

Grabbing buckets they raced to the trough in the yard. It was already half empty. When the water in it had gone they would have to hope there was still rain water in the butts, or run all the way to the duck pond. There was no time though to worry about that yet – no time for anything but helping Hal and Duggan to fight the fire. Cerys became a mindless automaton as she ran to and fro with the buckets, past allowing herself to even acknowledge what was happening, or might happen.

Several times the fire seemed to be dying down, then it would flare up again as a fresh area caught, and flames lit up the night sky. Cerys's eyes burned from the thick smoke, her throat rasped, and once or twice a bout of coughing almost overcame her, but somehow she soldiered on, finding reserves of strength and energy she had not known she possessed.

Silver dawn was streaking the sky by the time Hal finally pronounced the fire to be out.

Out! There was next to nothing of the barn left to burn! Cerys thought. As the first pale morning light illuminated the sorry scene it was clear that she was not far wrong. All that remained was a soggy, smouldering heap of what had once been best hay – good, now, for nothing – and one wall, smoke-blackened and tottering. Cerys rubbed her stinging eyes and wanted to cry, but crying would do no good, and at least, thank God, the fire had not spread beyond the barn. Hal – and the good fortune of a still night – had contained it. But oh – the waste! The terrible waste! And what would they do now for hay for the horses and extra feed, if it were needed, for the stock?

As she stood, hands covering her mouth, surveying the desolation, Jenny materialized at her elbow.

'This is just awful,' Cerys said through her fingers.

'It could have been a whole lot worse,' Jenny pointed out briskly. 'And you have Hal to thank that it is not.'

'Oh – yes . . .'

The irony of it struck her; just a few short hours ago she had been on the point of telling him to pack his bags and go. If he had . . .

'It was Hal who discovered the fire,' Jenny went on. 'His room overlooks the barn and he couldn't sleep. If it hadn't been for him starting to fight it right away, heaven only knows what would have happened.'

'I know. It doesn't bear thinking about.' Cerys knew she had to swallow her pride and thank Hal properly for what he had done. But, grateful though she was, it would not come easily.

She crossed to where he was forking hay out into the open space of the dirt yard and damping it down.

He looked up as she approached. His handsome face was smoke-blackened, his hair tousled from the sleep from which he had been so roughly awakened. He stood surveying her, hands on hips.

'Not a bad night's work, eh?'

It seemed a strange thing to say.

'I want to thank you, Hal,' she said awkwardly. 'If you hadn't seen the flames and started to fight the fire when you did . . . Well, things would have been a good deal the worse for us, I'm sure. I'm grateful, really I am.'

He passed a hand across his face and the dirt rubbed into streaks and furrows.

'Just doing my job.'

'A bit more than that, I think.'

He shrugged. 'Like I said before, it's what friends are for.' Then the effort of talking whilst his throat was parched and catchy proved too much and he began to cough.

Duggan was coughing too. Cerys could hear him kecking

and hawking across the yard. It worried her; Duggan was an old man.

'The two of you had better come over to the house,' she said. 'I'll make some soothing drinks.'

'You're sure now?' Hal managed between rasping bouts, but there was no mistaking the heavy sarcasm in his tone.

'Of course I'm sure. And thank you again,' Cerys said.

If Jenny had been besotted with Hal before, the fire certainly bolstered and cemented the way she felt about him. He was, in her eyes, a hero, who had saved them from almost certain ruin, and her adoration became even more clear for all to see than it had been up until now.

But there was also a subtle change in Hal's treatment of Jenny, Cerys noticed. He was, without doubt, paying her far more attention, the charm which had radiated indiscriminately now focused on her. Naturally Jenny was lapping it up, but Cerys found the development even more worrying. It was, she thought, as if Hal were putting on a performance for her benefit, trying to show her how little he cared for her rebuttal of him and how much she was missing, both at the same time.

She simply could not see that his sudden keen interest in Jenny could be genuine, and it disturbed her that he should be playing with Jenny's feelings at a time when she was so vulnerable. But in all honesty she couldn't see that there was anything she could do about it. The whole affair would blow itself out in time, of that she was fairly certain, and if Jenny's heart was broken, well, she wouldn't be the first or the last to suffer so. And there were so many other things to worry about – the loss of the barn and the hay principally amongst them.

One evening when the children were in bed, Cerys got down Will's ledger and started doing sums. As she had feared, the extra expense of having to buy in hay was a drain that would stretch the budget to its limits. Certainly there was no money at the moment for rebuilding the barn, and with everything so uncertain, the last thing she wanted to do was to borrow more from the bank, even if they would lend it, which was far from certain.

The only reserve which stood between them and the bread-line was the money she had got for her ring. She didn't feel justified really in dipping into it when she still owed Chas Wallace an unspecified amount, but until spring came and she could get some stock to market she couldn't see that she had any choice. Even then it was going to be tight. Almost every penny that could be expected had been taken into account in Will's forward planning. As far as Cerys could see there was just enough to tide them over on the necessities of life until next year's shearing, and no more. It was a hand-to-mouth existence and no mistake. And now this . . .

Cerys had not touched the pouch Mr Johnson had given her since she'd brought it home intact from her visit to Chas Wallace and propped it behind the Dresden shepherdess on the mantelshelf. Now she felt the need of the comfort of seeing hard cash. She got it out, loosened the tie and tipped the sovereigns out on to the table, counting them into neat piles. Then she stopped, frowning, and counted them again. She was mistaken, surely! But no, there were ten less than there should have been. Cerys sat motionless, chewing her lip and staring at the sovereigns as if just by looking hard enough she could make them materialize. Then she got up and crossed to the door.

Jenny was on the porch with Hal, and flirting as usual if the sounds of the laughter which floated into the kitchen were anything to go by. Cerys called to her and she looked round, not best pleased at being interrupted.

'Can you come in here a minute?'

Jenny said something to Hal, too softly for Cerys to hear, and Hal whispered something back. Cerys felt her hackles rising. It was as if they were deliberately trying to shut her out. Oh well, let them play their silly childish games. She had more important things on her mind, and she raised them the moment Jenny deigned to come in, her face flushed and rosy above the collar of her jacket.

'Jenny – have you taken any money out of Mr Johnson's pouch?'

'No.' Jenny looked genuinely surprised. 'Why would I do that?'

'It's ten sovereigns short,' Cerys told her.

Jenny pulled a face, looking at the neat piles of coins.

'Well, isn't that what you gave Chas Wallace?'

'No, it's not!' Cerys said. 'He hasn't had anything yet.' She hesitated, not wanting to tell Jenny about their arrangement. 'I'm not paying Chas Wallace until he gets an estimate for the repair. I told you that, I'm sure. And if you think I didn't, then you just weren't listening.'

Jenny shrugged. 'All right, I wasn't listening. But I haven't taken your ten sovereigns. What would I want them for, anyway?'

It was true enough. Since Will's death, Jenny had been nowhere where she could spend any money at all, let alone ten sovereigns. And she'd barely changed out of the cut-down pair of men's breeches and the shirt and coat she wore to work out on the farm either.

'Well, ten sovereigns have gone,' Cerys said flatly. 'Do you think it might be Hal?'

'That is an awful thing to say!' Jenny flared. 'He wouldn't steal from you! Why, he's refused to take a wage . . .'

'I know. But perhaps . . . Well, we know nothing about him, Jenny. Nothing at all.'

'He was Will's friend,' Jenny said heatedly. 'That's good enough for me. I don't know how you can even think such a thing of him, Cerys, when you think of all he's doing for us. And what about the fire? The way he fought it was as if it were his own barn that was burning down, not ours.'

'Yes, you're right.' Cerys sighed. 'Well, I can only think the full amount was never there in the first place. I didn't check it when Mr Johnson gave it to me, and when I got home I don't think I did it as thoroughly as I should have . . .'

'You didn't check it?' Jenny interrupted, astounded. 'Cerys! Why ever didn't you check it?'

'Oh, I don't know. Mr Johnson asked me to, but the way he said it was implying I didn't trust him. He seemed a bit testy about it . . .'

'You should have checked it!' Jenny scolded.

'I know I should.' Cerys sighed again. She could scarcely believe she had been so stupid. To allow Mr Johnson to cheat her out of ten sovereigns by shaming her into trusting him . . . Oh, she had a great deal to learn, and no mistake.

But she had trusted him. She really had. And she couldn't understand how he had survived so long in business if he was crooked. In a small town like Medlock reputations could be destroyed so quickly and easily.

But there it was. The money was gone. Either Jenny or Hal had taken it, or it had never been there in the first place. Either way, she was ten sovereigns worse off than she had believed.

'I'm sorry, Jenny. It's just that I'm so worried,' Cerys said. 'I really, truly don't know how we're going to manage.'

Jenny frowned. 'Things are that bad?'

'Worse. This is about all the ready cash we have until we can get some stock to market. Will borrowed, I think, when times were hard, but I don't want to do that, even if I could. To be honest, I don't think the bank would be as happy to make a loan to me now I'm on my own. In fact, I wouldn't be surprised if they didn't start chasing me for what we already owe them. And then there's the rest of the money outstanding on the land – the next payment on that will be due shortly.' She rubbed her eyes tiredly with her fingers. 'We are going to have to make some big economies, that's all. The first thing that will have to go is the gig and the matched pair.'

'Cerys – no!' Jenny cried, horrified. 'You can't get rid of the gig and the matched pair! Don't you remember how proud Will was when he brought them home? He was so pleased with them!'

'He would do the same if he was here,' Cerys said firmly. 'We don't really need the gig any more. I'm not proficient at driving it – I can handle the sulky much better. And you don't ever use it. You always ride Merlin, and if you needed to drive, you could use the sulky too. There will be two less horses to feed if we get rid of the matched pair, and they and the gig should fetch quite a reasonable sum. Actually—' she broke off, biting her lip – 'I'm afraid Lance is going to have to go too.'

Lance had been Will's horse.

Jenny looked horrified. 'Not Lance!'

'I can't afford to feed him,' Cerys said flatly. 'We have to be sensible about this. I'm going to ask Hal to take them all to Medlock next market day and see if he can find a buyer for them.'

Even in the depths of winter, a monthly market was held in Medlock. It might not produce the highest prices, but it was the best chance of a quick sale that Cerys could think of.

Jenny sighed. 'I suppose you're right.'

She looked utterly downcast, right on the edge of falling into one of her depressions once more and for once Cerys was almost glad that Hal was here and making such a fuss of her. Whatever the long-term outcome, at least tonight, hopefully, he would lift Jenny's mood – or take the brunt of it at any rate. Cerys felt that with everything she had on her mind, her sister-in-law's woes were just one burden too far.

'Go on – go and chat with Hal and leave me to sort things out here,' she said. 'And open a bottle of apple brandy, why don't you? There's one left on the shelf in the pantry. I was saving it for Will's birthday . . .' Sudden tears pricked her eyes; angrily she blinked them away.

Heavens, she didn't even have time for grieving!

'We might as well drink it,' she went on briskly. 'Goodness knows, we deserve a treat, and it's going to be a long while before there's anything to celebrate again.'

'Oh Cerys!' Quite suddenly Jenny ran to her and threw her arms around her sister-in-law. She hugged her tight, her head buried in Cerys's shoulder, and Cerys felt her body shaking with sobs.

'Jenny, don't!' she begged. 'Don't cry, please.'

'Oh Cerys, I am so sorry! So sorry . . .' Jenny, who, for all her depressive moods, rarely cried, was almost beside herself. Cerys felt a twinge of alarm, her thoughts flying to Hal and his persuasive ways, and how besotted Jenny was with him. Oh no! she thought. Oh Jenny, no!

'What are you sorry for, Jenny?' she asked gently.

'Oh – everything . . .' Jenny hiccuped.

'You haven't . . . done anything foolish, have you?' she pressed the sobbing girl.

'Foolish?' Jenny looked up at her, bewildered.

'You and Hal . . .'

For a moment Jenny's face creased so that Cerys thought she was going to burst into gales of hysterical laughter.

'No, of course not!' she exclaimed.

'That's all right then,' Cerys said, relieved.

'No – it's not all right.' A tear rolled down Jenny's cheek and she let it go. 'All that's happened, Cerys. It's my fault. All my fault.'

'Oh Jenny,' Cerys groaned. The depression really had bitten now; Jenny was at the stage of blaming herself for everything. 'How do you work that out?'

'If it hadn't been for me Will would never . . .' She broke off, weeping hard.

'Never have come out here? Well, I guess that's true, Jenny. But then again, he might. He wanted to be a farmer, didn't he? He didn't want to be a drover all his life, any more than Hal does.'

The truth of what she had just said struck her. Was that the reason Hal had come here and stayed to work for no wage – that he had seen an opportunity to take over Will's life? Was it the reason he had made a play first for her, and now for Jenny? Was it the reason she, Cerys, was so uneasy about him? She'd think about it later . . .

'You can't take any of this on yourself, Jenny,' she said. 'So let's hear no more about it. Come on, I could do with some of that apple brandy, never mind you! Dry your eyes and we'll go and get it.'

For a moment longer Jenny remained motionless but for the heaving of her chest, staring down at the floor. Then she wiped her wet cheeks and blew her nose.

'I'm so sorry, Cerys . . .'

'Oh, don't start that again!' Cerys begged. She collected the sovereigns, dropped them into the pouch and went to return it to the mantelshelf. Then, thinking better of it, she took it to one of the wall cupboards, reached down a two-pint jug from the top shelf and dropped it inside. Perhaps Jenny had been right to be outraged that Cerys should suggest Hal might have been helping himself, but she still thought she would feel safer if the cache was in a different hiding place, one Hal did not know about. Even Jenny hadn't seen where she'd put the sovereigns, she felt sure, for the girl was still drying her eyes, her back towards Cerys. Then Cerys replaced the ledgers on their shelf and put an arm about Jenny.

'Come on, let's have that apple brandy.'

When she opened the door, Hal was leaning against the wall. Cerys, whilst chiding herself for being overly suspicious, nevertheless could not avoid thinking it was very cold for hanging about outside, and neither could she avoid the strong impression that he had been listening to everything she and Jenny had been saying.

# Ten

'Mama! Mama! There's a man outside our house!'

Cerys's heart leaped into her throat as Molly came rushing into the bedroom, where she was making her bed. A man? Oh dear God, not the intruder returned, surely? Hal, Jenny and Duggan were all out working on the farm and she was left alone at the homestead with the children.

She hurried through to the kitchen and ran to the window. There was indeed a man outside the door, a big man, with his hat pulled low and the collar of his greatcoat turned up against the biting wind and the splattering of icy cold rain that it had blown in this morning. His back was towards her but she knew at once who it was.

Chas Wallace.

For some reason Cerys felt her heartbeat quicken. He'd said, of course, that he would let her know when he had set something up with his lawyer to formalize their agreement, but still it was somehow a shock to see him standing on her doorstep.

At least he had come, though, when Jenny and Hal were both out, and for that Cerys was grateful. She would not have known how to explain his visit to Jenny, and although she was certainly not obliged to offer any explanation at all to Hal, he would certainly have been curious as to why Chas Wallace was here. He missed nothing, Cerys thought, with the same quick flash of almost unreasonable resentment that always accompanied any thought, however fleeting, of Hal Tucker.

'Who is it, Mama?' Molly was asking.

'Someone to see me.' Cerys thought it unwise to name names; Molly might very well remember and blurt it out over supper.

She hurried to the door and opened it. Chas Wallace turned, rain dripping off the brim of his hat and pooling in the crease below his collar.

'Good morning, Mrs Page.'

'Good morning. Do come in.' She didn't know why she'd said it like that, as if this were a social visit. She only knew she couldn't leave him standing on the doorstep in the rain, and that she felt strangely awkward.

'I'm very wet,' he said ruefully. 'I shall drip all over your kitchen floor.'

'It's all right. I can always wipe it up.' She laughed nervously.

'If you're sure . . .' He came in.

'Would you like something to drink? A cup of coffee, perhaps?' She didn't know why she'd said that either when she really was anxious for him to tell her whatever he had come to tell her and go again before Jenny or Hal returned and found him here.

'A cup of coffee would go down very well.' Completely at home, he crossed to the sink, took off his hat, and tipped the water out of the brim.

Cerys reached for the coffee pot, which was sitting on the hob, glad that she had made a fresh brew not quarter of an hour ago.

'Mama!' Molly squealed. 'Mama – the man is on fire!'

Cerys wheeled round, and both she and Chas burst out laughing. In the heat of the kitchen his sodden greatcoat was steaming copiously.

'No, Molly, he's just wet,' she explained.

'But . . . that's how the barn looked the day after the fire!' Molly argued.

It was true enough, just so had the heaps of soggy blackened hay steamed after Hal had damped them down.

Chas Wallace was looking at her curiously, one eyebrow raised.

'You had a barn fire?'

She nodded. 'I'm afraid so. The other night. I've lost almost all my stock of hay, and the barn is completely destroyed.'

'Oh dear. Disaster seems to be seeking you out at present.'

'Yes,' she said tersely. 'It does.'

'How did the barn come to catch fire?' he asked.

She shook her head, pouring coffee. 'I don't know. The hay can't have been properly dried when Will harvested it, I suppose.'

'Hmm.' He was frowning, thoughtful. She thought he was on the point of saying something, then he smiled at Molly, who was staring at him curiously. 'Did you see the fire?'

'No – no. It was all out when I woke up. But I saw the hay steaming like you did . . .' Molly's words came tumbling out one on top of the other.

Chas Wallace laughed. It was a nice laugh, Cerys noticed to her surprise, deep and hearty.

'So what's your name?'

'I'm Molly. And that's my brother Ritchie,' she said proudly, pointing. Ritchie had just rounded the kitchen door, toddling for once instead of crawling.

'Well I'm Chas,' he said. Again Cerys was taken by surprise. 'Chas', not 'Mr Wallace'.

'Do you want to take your coat off?' she asked, heading for him with the coffee.

'Better not. I'll drink this and be on my way.' He took the cup from her. 'I really only called by to tell you my lawyer has the papers we discussed ready for signature.'

'Ah.' Cerys glanced at Molly. The little girl was all ears.

'I thought perhaps we could make an arrangement to go into town together,' Chas Wallace went on. 'I could drive you. Not today, obviously, unless you want a soaking, but . . .'

'Yes, of course. I'll have to take the children with me, though –' she hesitated, lowered her voice – 'I really would prefer it if my sister-in-law didn't know anything of this. Perhaps I could say we are going to see the piano tuner?'

He laughed aloud again. 'And bribe the children with bonbons not to let on that the piano tuner is a very starchy old man with an even older, even starchier, clerk? I see you are a very devious woman, Mrs Page.'

'Sometimes I have to be,' she said shortly, fairly confident this conversation was beyond Molly's comprehension.

132

'So when shall we make the trip? Would the first fine day suit you?'

Cerys hesitated. She really did not like this at all. Signing her deeds into a surety for Chas Wallace was something she really did not want to do. But what choice did she have? And there was another consideration, too. Tomorrow was market day – Hal would be going to Medlock to try to sell the horses and the gig and the last thing she wanted was for him to see her going into the lawyer's office with Chas Wallace.

'Very well,' she agreed after a moment. 'As long as it's not tomorrow.'

He did not question her as to her reason.

'About this time of day?'

She nodded again. 'We'll be ready.'

'Good,' he said. He drained his coffee cup and set it down. 'I'll be on my way then, before I completely flood your kitchen.'

He returned his hat to his head, pulled it low so that once again only his eyes, nose and leathery cheeks were visible. Then he pinched Molly's cheek, ruffled Ritchie's hair, and headed for the door.

'Thanks for the coffee, Mrs Page.'

'You're welcome.' Cerys was surprised to find she meant it.

'Who was that man?' Molly asked when the door had closed after him.

Cerys considered. There was no way she could lie.

'Our neighbour,' she said. 'His name, as he told you, is Chas, and he is going to take us to Medlock the very next day when the weather is fine. We have to see a gentleman there. But I don't want you to say a word about it to Aunt Jenny, Molly. Do you understand?'

Molly nodded solemnly, but her eyes were very round.

'Can I trust you?' Cerys reiterated. 'Not a word? This is to be our secret, Molly.'

Molly considered. 'Can I tell Ritchie? He is my best friend.'

Cerys smiled. 'Yes, you can tell Ritchie. But no one else. Right?'

'Right,' Molly echoed.

'Now,' Cerys said, 'I have to finish making the beds. But after that we'll bake some cookies. Would you like that?'

'Oh yes!' Molly cried.

Already, Cerys thought, she had forgotten about their visitor. But, of course, Molly had not forgotten. She was totally fascinated and curious about the visitor.

When he left the house, Chas Wallace crossed the yard for a closer look at the burned-out barn. There certainly was very little left of it! Cerys seemed to have accepted the explanation that the fire had started because Will had not dried out the hay properly before baling it and stacking it away. Chas himself would not have been so easily satisfied. It was a long while now since harvest; fires that were caused by spontaneous combustion usually occurred much sooner in the season than this. But, of course, Cerys was no farmer. She wouldn't know these things.

His eyes narrowed thoughtfully as he inspected the remains of the damped-down hay and the charred stump of the wall. No one, it seemed, had been hurt. More hay could be made next year and a shed could be rebuilt. But it was unlikely Mrs Cerys Page could afford to do it. The destruction had brought his ownership of the land a step closer, not a doubt of it.

He glanced back at the house. No sign now of Cerys. She really was quite naive, he thought, for all her fighting spirit. Naive enough to be totally oblivious to the fact that somebody might be out to ruin her.

Ah well. Life out here, like nature in the raw, could be wild and cruel. The survival of the fittest. Though Chas Wallace knew without doubt that he was a survivor, he could not help feeling a twinge of regret over the fact that he was very much afraid that, for all her courage, Cerys Page was not.

Next day – market day – it was still raining. Cerys frowned when she saw it. Would the weather affect the number of people who made the trip to Medlock and lessen the chance of getting a good price for the horses and the gig? But the hardy regulars would still come – farmers needed the opportunity to buy and sell, and inclement conditions could not be allowed to alter that. In any case, Cerys had decided she had no choice.

She could no longer afford to feed the horses and they had to go. Whatever they fetched, it should be enough to buy more hay for those they could not manage without – Lady and Merlin, and Hal's horse too. And Jenny's dear old horse, Bramble, and Muff the donkey – no one would be likely to want to buy them, and Cerys couldn't bear the thought of them going to the knacker's yard.

She and Jenny said a sad goodbye to the matched pair and to Lance, and had watched Hal drive the gig out of the yard with Lance and Thor, Hal's own horse, tied up behind.

'Why are they going, Mama?' Molly asked.

'Because we can't afford to keep them, Molly.' Cerys felt she must tell Molly the truth.

'But why not?'

'We just can't,' Cerys snapped. 'Now come inside, Molly. We are all getting wet.'

'Like the man yesterday.'

Cerys threw her a quick warning glance and Molly, remembering that it was supposed to be a secret, clapped her hands over her mouth.

Cerys looked anxiously at Jenny, expecting a quick question as to what Molly had meant, and already wondering how she was going to explain without telling Jenny about Chas Wallace's visit and the reason behind it. But Jenny seemed to have wandered off into a world of her own. From the vacant expression on her face it didn't look as if she had even heard what Molly had said, let alone taken notice of it.

'Jenny?' she said anxiously.

Jenny came out of her reverie, tossed her head impatiently, and swallowed hard. Cerys could see the tears shining on her lashes.

'What?'

'Are you all right?' Cerys asked.

'Of course I'm all right,' Jenny snapped. 'Just let me come in for an extra waterproof and I'm off for the day. I've got work to do.'

Cerys nodded. She didn't know what Jenny planned to do, and was not at all sure that Jenny knew either, but she suspected the younger woman needed to be on her own for a while. Would that she could be allowed the same luxury!

The children were an enormous comfort, and she would not have been without them, but just sometimes she felt she had no time for herself, to do her grieving. It was all struggling on, from minute to minute, and day to day. With a deep sigh, Cerys shrugged her coat the better to cover Ritchie, who was clamped, limpet-like on her hip, took Molly by the hand, and went back into the house.

Late in the afternoon Hal returned, riding Thor. There was no sign of the other horses, or the gig.

He came into the kitchen, making dirty footmarks on the clean floor, though at least the rain had eased so he did not drip water to add to the mess.

'You found a buyer, then?' Cerys said.

Hal nodded curtly. 'In the end. It's been a long, hard winter. Nobody seemed that interested.'

'How much did you get?' It was, after all, the most important consideration.

Hal opened his coat, took out the proceeds of the sale, and laid them on the table. Cerys's heart sank.

'Is that all?'

Hal shrugged. 'Best I could do. Like I said, nobody was that interested.'

'So who did take them?' Cerys asked.

'A trader from Mitchellstown bought the gig and the pair. Has a general store, it seems, and is doing well enough to want to be able to take his wife out for a drive on a Sunday afternoon.'

'And Lance?' She was almost afraid to ask. The thought of someone else other than Will riding Lance was enough to bring a lump to her throat. She only hoped whoever now owned the horse would be kind to him.

'Oh, some farmer took him,' Hal said carelessly. 'Youngish fellow – didn't look like a horseman, but he handled him well enough.'

'Didn't you get the name?' Cerys pressed him.

'Harvey, was it?' He contorted his face in an effort to remember. 'Hargreaves? No – Harris, I think.'

'Harris!' Cerys exclaimed. 'Not *David* Harris?'

'Couldn't say,' Hal retorted shortly. 'Why, do you know someone called Harris?'

'I should think I do!' A little smile lifted the corners of Cerys's mouth. 'David Harris and Jenny are great friends. Or at least, they used to be. She was always over at the Harris place, Glenavon, and we quite thought she and David . . .' She broke off, biting her lip. 'Oh, it would be so nice to think David had Lance! The Harris family would take good care of him, I know. What did he look like, the man you did business with? Did he have curly brown hair? Lots of it?'

Hal shrugged impatiently. 'I don't know.'

'Oh, you couldn't miss it if it was David! He has a real mop . . .'

'It was raining,' Hal said. 'He was wearing a hat. He paid, didn't he? That's all that matters.'

'Yes, I suppose so, Cerys said. It wasn't all that mattered to her, of course. Who the new owner of Lance might be was equally important. And if it was David she didn't mind at all that he had got a real bargain. Perhaps it had been fortunate after all that it had been a wet day and there was not much competition for the horse. In all likelihood David would not have been able to pay a high price. But of one thing she felt fair sure, if David had bought Lance it had been because he had recognized him and wanted to give him a good home – and perhaps help her and Jenny out into the bargain.

Hal did not seem to want to talk about it, though. He was heading for the door and looking less than pleased. Hardly surprising, really, considering she had just as good as told him that David Harris had been Jenny's sweetheart.

Once again Cerys felt an edge of unease, quickly followed by a dash of guilt. Why couldn't she like Hal Tucker, when he did so much for them? Getting the horses and gig to market would have been a total nightmare if he hadn't been here, and willing to do it.

'Hal . . .' Cerys said.

He paused in the doorway, turned. His face wore that curious expression she sometimes surprised on it – a shut-in expression that seemed to conceal something – unspoken thoughts, or a

137

whole side of his personality that she had only occasionally glimpsed.

'Thank you, Hal,' she said quietly. 'I am really grateful to you.'

He nodded abruptly and momentarily something passed between them. Then the door was thrown open, and Molly came rushing in, face rosy above her warm coat.

'Hal! Hal!'

He rumpled her hair, grinning. 'How did you know I was here?'

'We saw your horse.'

Jenny was in the doorway, holding Ritchie by the hand.

'Hal.'

'Jenny.'

And there it was again, Cerys thought. Jenny's eager admiration, as badly concealed as three-year-old Molly's, and Hal's smug reaction.

Oh, someone was going to be badly hurt before this was over. And Cerys could not see that it was going to be Hal Tucker.

Next day the rain had stopped and the cloud lifted enough to show patches of washed-out blue.

When Jenny, Hal and Duggan had been in for breakfast and left again, Cerys changed out of her working dress into her best woollen gown, cleaned up the children, and dressed them, too, in their Sunday best. Then she wrote a carefully worded note to Jenny and propped it up on the table where Jenny could scarcely miss it. Cerys had not mentioned to her that Chas Wallace might be taking her and the children into town today and she hoped that if they got there and back whilst Jenny was out working on the farm she might not need to. But a note was needed just in case. Cerys did not want Jenny to come in, find them missing, and be worried as to what had happened to them.

'Where are we going, Mama?' Molly asked.

'To town, like I told you,' Cerys said. 'It was our secret, remember?'

'Oh yes. Like the man who was on fire.'

138

'Yes. And we are going to town with him. If he comes.'
Cerys was looking out of the window, watching the drive.
Perhaps Chas Wallace *wouldn't* come. Perhaps something had
happened to detain him at home . . .

Ritchie began to cry and Cerys detected the unmistakable
sign that his nappy needed changing. She groaned.

'Oh, Ritchie! Why now, just when I've got you ready to
go out?'

She hurried to change him, but as always she found it
impossible to remain annoyed with him for long. She let him
lie half-naked on the rug, kicking his legs happily, and smiled
at the rolls of chubby flesh.

'Mama! Mama – the man is here!'

Molly, who had been standing on a chair to take over her
mother's vigil at the window, jumped down and ran towards
the door, almost treading on Ritchie in her haste.

'Molly – calm down, for goodness' sake!'

But Molly, on tiptoe, was lifting the latch and, with a
struggle, managing to open the door.

Cerys, on hands and knees trying to secure Ritchie's nappy,
looked up to see Chas Wallace looking down at her.

Once again – as seemed to happen every time she met him
– Cerys felt at a total disadvantage.


The offices of Walter Spencer, the lawyer, occupied one of
the most substantial buildings in Medlock, and the interior
closely resembled any legal chambers in any town the length
and breadth of England.

Walter Spencer had been articled to an old-established firm
of lawyers in Bristol, and had even practised there for a year
or two before he had met his downfall. Large sums of money
were found to be missing from clients' accounts, and the finger
of suspicion had not so much pointed at Walter as reached out
and jabbed him in the chest. An investigation had discovered
he had been spending money way in excess of his legitimate
means, the false figures in the ledgers were in his hand, and
a hidden bank account containing a goodly sum had been
evidence enough for a jury to convict him and a judge to
sentence him to transportation. Walter Spencer had arrived in

Sydney early in 1840, one of the last convicts to be shipped in before transportation was abolished in New South Wales later that year.

Walter had been just twenty-nine years old, but he was too wily – and too well educated – to remain a prisoner of the penal system for long. He secured his release, moved to New England, and set up in practice in Medlock.

If any of the townsfolk were aware of his history, they did not let it concern them much. Walter Spencer was a good lawyer and he had learned his lesson. For almost thirty years he had served the community well, and in all that time there had been not so much as a hint of impropriety.

Cerys, of course, knew nothing of any of this, but she was suitably impressed when Chas Wallace brought his gig to a halt and led her into the office, filled with dark, heavy furniture which had clearly been shipped out from England.

She was impressed, too, to be greeted by a grizzled little clerk in his tight starched collar and formal waistcoat and startled by what she recognized as an English accent. There were those, she knew, who had come to the new country on free or assisted passages – wasn't that exactly what her own parents had done? – but few of them found their way to New England.

Josiah Cload had, however, been Walter Spencer's clerk in Bristol, and when Walter had set up here in Medlock he had managed to induce Josiah – out of work because of Spencer's own downfall – to cross the world to join him.

'Mr Wallace – good day to you, sir,' he greeted Chas, practically bowing and scraping.

He looked a little askance, however, at Cerys, who had Ritchie in her arms and Molly hanging on to her skirts. A woman in the lawyer's office was rare enough – unless of course it was Miss Kitty Jackson – and as for children, well, that was totally unheard of!

However, the door to Walter Spencer's inner sanctum was already open, and the lawyer was coming out himself to greet Chas Wallace, so the clerk had little option but to allow the family to pass.

Walter Spencer himself showed no such discrimination. He

had, of course, prepared the necessary documents, so Cerys's presence was not in the least surprising to him, and he knew better than to allow his distaste at having children in the office to show. One did not readily upset a client of Chas Wallace's stature!

'Find some paper and pencils to amuse the little ones whilst we are attending to our business, please, Mr Cload,' he instructed with a sickly smile at Molly, and the shocked-looking clerk had no option but to do as he was bid.

With Molly and Ritchie settled down, Walter Spencer laid the documents on the desk and ran through their contents with Cerys. For the most part it was just as Chas had suggested to her in the first place – the deeds of Kanunga were to be placed in the safekeeping of the lawyer as surety for the money owed to Mr Wallace by Mrs Page. But there was one glaring omission.

'Mr Wallace said that the agreement would allow me to stay in my house as long as I need to, even if the land has passed into his ownership,' Cerys said when she had read through the agreement. 'I don't see any mention of that here.'

Walter Spencer steepled his fingers and regarded her severely.

'As Mr Wallace's lawyer, I am very much opposed to such a thing being written into the agreement,' he said in the dry-as-dust lawyer's tones which no one would ever have believed could belong to a former convict. 'Such an eventuality would have to be at Mr Wallace's discretion and only decided upon at the time, when all the circumstances were clear, and I have therefore made no mention of it.'

Cerys turned to Chas. 'I'm sorry, but I can't sign anything unless my rights are clearly set out. I must know I would be able to remain in my house. It's the basis of the whole agreement.'

'You're quite right, Mrs Page, it is.' Chas Wallace looked – and sounded – faintly amused – as if this whole thing were a game to him, Cerys thought crossly. 'Please add that clause, Mr Spencer.'

'But Mr Wallace, I do urge you . . . I must counsel against any such undertaking.' The lawyer did not look best pleased. But then now neither did Chas Wallace.

'I am the client here, Mr Spencer, and I shall be grateful if you'll do as I ask,' he said coldly. 'And without delay, too. Both Mrs Page and I are anxious to get back to our duties at home.'

'If you insist on including such a clause, the document will have to be rewritten,' the lawyer said stiffly. 'The inner page, at least. To make alterations might well render it meaningless in a court of law.'

'Then get it rewritten,' Chas instructed. 'How long will it take?'

Walter Spencer pulled the double sheets of vellum towards him, looking at them critically. His mouth was a tight line.

'Fortunately the centre sheet is only half a page long. I can have that one rewritten to include the proviso you require in, say, an hour.'

An hour! Cerys's heart sank as she saw her chances of getting home again whilst Jenny was out receding. And Ritchie was becoming restless too, though Molly was still drawing on the paper she had been given with immense concentration.

She glanced imploringly at Chas.

'You have half an hour,' he said shortly. 'We'll leave you in peace so that you can get on with it. If it's not ready then, I shall have to look further afield for a lawyer who is able, and willing, to fulfil my requirements.'

He rose, and Cerys followed suit. Walter Spencer was fussing like a lap dog suddenly, falling over himself in his efforts to assure Chas his wishes would be adhered to. It occurred to Cerys how nice it was to be able to get one's way with such a minimum of fuss. A look, a tone of voice, and Walter Spencer couldn't do his bidding quickly enough. Cerys would have had to shout, scream and cry to obtain the same effect, and then it would not be so satisfactory.

As it was, she rather enjoyed scooping up Ritchie, taking Molly by the hand, and sweeping out of the office in the wake of Chas Wallace.

# Eleven

O nce outside, however, Cerys was in for a shock. She had not had time to wonder where they would go or what they would do in the half-hour Chas had given Walter Spencer to rewrite the last page of the contract, but Chas, clearly, was in no doubt whatsoever. As he strode purposefully along the street, Cerys experienced the first twinge of doubt.

'Where are we going?'

And her worst fears were realized when he replied: 'To the Commercial Hotel, of course.'

'I can't take the children there!' Cerys cried, horrified.

Chas glanced at her, mildly surprised. 'Why ever not?'

'But it's a . . .' Words failed her. 'They have strong drink there!'

'In the bar, yes,' Chas said. To Cerys's added annoyance he sounded mildly amused. 'We don't have to take the children into the bar, though I don't suppose it would do them any harm. It is a hotel too, remember. We can use the residents' lounge and get a cup of coffee to warm us up whilst we are waiting for Walter Spencer to do the necessary.'

Cerys was unconvinced. 'Oh, I don't think . . .'

He cocked an eyebrow. 'Surely you wouldn't rather keep the children out here in the cold and damp?'

'Oh, I suppose not,' Cerys said crossly. She did not like the idea of so much as crossing the threshold of the Commercial Hotel with the children, she did not like the idea of them coming face to face with that scarlet woman, Kitty Jackson, and she did not like feeling that she had been coerced into doing something against her will. But Chas was right, it was very cold and damp, the sort of cold that ate into the bones, and chilled them to the marrow, and Ritchie had a bit of a cough. Walking the streets with him for half an hour would do him no good at all. And it wasn't a prospect she cared for herself, truth to tell.

In all her life Cerys had never set foot inside an establishment that sold hard liquor. Her father and mother still adhered to the Wesleyan Methodist principles of their youth and were strictly teetotal; Cerys had been brought up to look on alehouses and sly grog shops as places of sin and wickedness.

Now, she half expected some thundercrack from heaven to reverberate around her head as she stepped through the doorway of the Commercial Hotel, Ritchie on her hip, Molly clutching her free hand. When it did not she looked around with some interest and was pleasantly surprised by the decorum of the place.

There was a reception desk in the entrance hall, as well as a small chintz-covered sofa, and the residents' lounge beyond was furnished comfortably and, Cerys was forced to admit, with some taste.

The owner was, of course, the woman who had urged Chas to get a grand piano to grace his drawing room, Cerys reminded herself. And it was as if she had brought that gracious style into her hotel. Most of the furniture, Cerys felt sure, must have been shipped out from England, and the drapes were finest velvet, not a one watermarked as so much of the fabric that arrived in the colony was. The lounge might well have been a drawing room in a grand English country house – or at least, as Cerys imagined the drawing room of a grand English country house might be, for she had certainly never seen one.

'Why, Chas!' The voice from the doorway behind them was drawling and low-pitched; Cerys recognized it at once, even before she turned and saw Kitty Jackson standing there.

As always, she wore red. Cerys saw Molly's eyes go round with astonishment and awe, and had to smile. In all her short life Molly had never seen anyone wearing such a bright shade or such shiny fabric, and her face clearly expressed her undoubted admiration. There was no doubt, Cerys thought, that it brightened up a dull day, but to be seen wearing it was a matter for shame!

144

'I've brought some clients for you, Kitty,' Chas said easily. 'You have already met Mrs Page, haven't you? And these are her children, Molly and Ritchie.'

Kitty swept a cursory glance over them.

'I hardly thought family outings were your kind of thing, Chas.'

He laughed, seemingly missing the acidity of the remark.

'There are things about me you still don't know, Kitty! No, Mrs Page and I have business in town with Walter Spencer but unfortunately he has let me down and it will be another half-hour before he has things ready for me. So we have come to take some of your excellent coffee whilst we are waiting. And the children . . . ? What would the children like, Cerys?'

'Oh, they don't need anything,' Cerys said hastily. She still had her doubts about the propriety of bringing them into such a place – and they might, in any case, spill drinks down their Sunday best clothes. Ritchie might even manage to vomit. He often did; where Molly had always seemed to have the constitution of an ox, the slightest little cough or keck could bring a hasty return of whatever Ritchie had just eaten or drunk.

To her annoyance, however, Chas overrode her decision.

'I'm sure they'd like something though, wouldn't you, children?'

'Yes! Warm milk!' Molly said promptly. 'And Ritchie would like some too.'

'I'm not sure I can manage *warm* milk,' Kitty said coolly. 'I'm very short-staffed. Will cold do?'

'Oh – I want warm! And so does Ritchie!' Molly groaned.

Kitty glared at her. 'I'm afraid we can't always have what we want in life, Polly.'

'It's Molly,' Cerys said sharply. 'And though cold milk will be perfectly fine for her, I wouldn't like to give it to Ritchie. It will probably make him sick,' she added with some satisfaction.

'Warm the milk, Kitty,' Chas urged. Cerys had the distinct impression he was rather enjoying all this. 'It will only take a minute. Why are you short-staffed, anyway?'

She tossed her head.

'My barmaid and my pot boy have run off together to the bright lights of Sydney. They'll be back soon no doubt, either together or separately, their tails between their legs. Sydney is not all it's cracked up to be.'

'Sydney is a very nice town,' Cerys said, bristling.

Kitty Jackson turned a frankly disbelieving look on her.

'You know it?'

'I was born and brought up there,' Cerys said.

'Well, well. A town mouse!'

'Not a mouse of any kind,' Chas said firmly. 'If you think that, you misjudge her. Why, it is entirely Mrs Page's doing that Walter Spencer's clerk is, at this very moment, hard at work redrafting something that was not to her liking, and wasting some of his precious heavy vellum in the process. Now, can we have the coffee and warm milk or no? You've still got your Chinese cook, no doubt?'

A half-smile lifted a corner of Kitty's mouth, but it was unmistakably aimed at Chas alone. For Cerys and the children there was only icy hostility.

'Oh yes, Chang is still with me. He, at least, has the sense to know when he's well off.' She inclined her head. 'I'll ask him to see to it right away.'

She swept out.

'Don't let Kitty's manner put you off,' Chas said with a smile. 'Her heart is pure gold.'

'Hmm.' Cerys could not help feeling that Kitty was very selective about who was allowed into that well-kept secret.

A few moments later Kitty was back with a pot of coffee and the milk for the children.

'You see what I am reduced to?' she demanded. 'Waiting at my own tables!'

'Not for long, I dare say,' Chas returned. 'Everyone knows you pay your bar staff most generously. You'll have would-be employees queuing up at the door once the word gets around.'

Kitty was pouring coffee into three cups. Clearly she intended to join Chas and Cerys.

'Well, it hasn't happened so far. It's five days now since

146

the lovebirds took flight. I'm beginning to think there isn't a single soul in Medlock looking for work.' She pushed a cup across the polished table towards Chas, leaving Cerys to reach for her own. Cerys was not concerned, however. She was much too occupied with making sure the children did not spill their milk on the very expensive Chinese carpet.

Fortunately they did not – and neither did Ritchie vomit. But Cerys could not help but be relieved all the same when Chas checked his fob watch and announced that it was time to return to the lawyer's office. The beautiful formal room and the hostility of their hostess, not to mention the fact that Cerys knew that just across the entrance hall, in the bar, strong drink was being consumed by men who did not even have the decency to wait until the sun was over the yardarm for their first tipple of the day, were all making her very uneasy.

'How much do I owe you, Kitty?' Chas asked.

She shook her head. 'It's on the house.'

'Kitty – you are in business,' Chas chided her. 'You'll never make a profit at this rate.'

'I make a very good profit, as well you know!' she retorted. 'And I do not charge my friends for coffee – or for warm milk.' She laid her hand on his arm, looking up at him from beneath lashes so black that Cerys felt sure she must touch them up with boot polish. 'I do not charge my friends for *anything.*'

'Come along, Molly,' Cerys said hastily.

The little girl was far too full of admiration for the 'scarlet woman' for Cerys's liking. She did not want her in Kitty Jackson's presence a moment longer than was absolutely necessary – especially when she was flirting so openly with Chas Wallace and making such suggestive remarks.

Cerys felt her hackles rising and could not be sure why. Of course, she had known right from the outset that he was heavily involved with the ghastly woman, so why should it bother her now? And, of course, it didn't. It was only Molly's moral welfare she was concerned with . . . wasn't it?

With Ritchie held tight against her shoulder, Cerys marched out of the Commercial Hotel dragging a reluctant Molly behind her. Thank goodness she was only three years old, and not thirteen, was all Cerys could say. She certainly

147

did not want her daughter corrupted by the likes of Kitty Jackson!

Back at the lawyer's offices Walter Spencer was waiting, rubbing his hands together virtuously and looking very pleased with himself.

'Everything is ready for you, Mr Wallace. I trust you will find it all to your satisfaction now.'

'I trust so too,' Chas said.

It was indeed all in order. But for all that, Cerys felt a twinge of anxiety as she put her signature beneath Chas Wallace's at the foot of the document. Was she doing the right thing? Really, she had no choice, and yet . . . and yet . . .

Something else of Will's had passed away from her. Oh, the farm was still hers as yet, but the onus was on her more than ever to make a success of it. If she failed, it would pass to Chas Wallace and the fact that she could stay in her own house, though a comfort and an enormous consideration, was not the same thing at all as owning the land as Will had worked and slaved to do.

Tears pricked her eyes. Walter Spencer and Josiah Cload were signing their names too as witnesses to the signatures and they seemed to swim beneath the fierce concentration of Cerys's gaze.

She glanced up. Chas Wallace was looking at her with an intensity that surprised her. She looked away, looked back again, and his eyes were still on her, thoughtful, speculative . . . and something else. It was only when she noticed the slight smile deepening the furrows between his nose and mouth that she realized what it was.

It was a look of triumph.

By some miracle they were indeed back at Kanunga before Jenny returned from the land. When Chas Wallace had dropped them off and driven away Cerys hastily changed both the children and herself out of their Sunday best things and into everyday clothes, swore Molly to secrecy once more, and rushed to prepare some food so it would not be immediately obvious that she had been out for a good part of the day.

It went against the grain to deceive Jenny so, but Cerys

honestly felt it would be best for her not to know about the agreement with Chas Wallace. It would only upset her again, and she had, thank goodness, been on a much more even keel the last few days. The prospect of her going into another depression was more than Cerys could stand.

'I like that man,' Molly said seriously as Cerys straightened her pinafore over her old – and rather short – dress.

'Chas.'

'Yes – Chas. I like him.'

Cerys's mouth twitched in a small, rueful smile. She was going to have problems with Molly in ten or fifteen years' time all right!

'Better than Hal?' she asked teasingly. 'I thought that Hal was your very favourite.'

Molly pulled a face. 'I don't think I like Hal any more.'

'Oh – and why is that?' Cerys asked.

'I saw him kick Elizabeth.' Elizabeth was the farm cat, a scrawny tabby who loved to stretch out in the sunshine after a long night's mousing.

Cerys frowned. 'Why would he kick Elizabeth?'

Molly shook her head, very deliberate, very self-important. She was not used to her mother listening with such seriousness to what she had to say.

'I don't know. Elizabeth wasn't doing anything. He put his boot underneath her and lifted her right off the ground!'

'Did he indeed!' Cerys said.

'Yes, he did. So I don't think I like him any more. I'd rather have Chas. He wouldn't kick Elizabeth, would he?'

'I really don't know, Molly,' Cerys said. 'Sometimes it's very hard to tell what people are really like until you have known them a long time. You just can't see what's going on inside them and whether they are really nice, or just pretending to be.'

'So Hal just pretends to be nice?'

'Kicking Elizabeth for no reason was certainly a very nasty thing to do. But perhaps he was just in a bad mood and took it out on her. That happens sometimes. Life can be very complicated, Molly.'

'So he might be nice after all, just cross?'

'He might be. I don't know.'

But she did know. Deep inside. Kicking a cat when he thought no one was looking was just the sort of thing Hal would do. And if he would do that, who knew what else he was capable of?

Once again Cerys shuddered at the thought of this man having the run of her farm and – even worse – enticing Jenny under his spell. And once again she thought, with a heavy heart, that for the moment there was not a single thing she could do on either count.

Had she but known it, Cerys had good cause to be concerned. Every one of her fears that Jenny would totally lose her head as well as her heart where Hal was concerned was perfectly justified. And at that very moment the two of them were together in the stable.

They had ridden out together to the very outskirts of Kanunga land, checking fences and the state of the feed available for the cattle, though, to be honest, Jenny's mind had been more on Hal than on any of the farming matters.

Oh, he was so handsome! she thought, glancing at him surreptitiously as they rode side by side. Just a glimpse of that chiselled profile between hat and collar could make her heart miss a beat, and when she took in the rest of him, broad shoulders, straight back, strong, muscled legs almost straight too because he rode with long stirrups, something sweet and sharp twisted inside her with such intensity that it was very close to pain, and yet still, unbelievably, intense pleasure.

Never before had she experienced anything quite like it. For a time she had thought she was in love with David Harris – he had made her heart beat faster too, but not like this – oh, not like this! Perhaps, she thought, it was because she had known David for so long, ever since Will had brought her here to Kanunga when she was really still just a little girl. David was kind and sweet and yes, he was handsome too, but compared with Hal he was so safe – and safe, in Jenny's book, these days at any rate, equalled uninteresting.

Hal, on the other hand, was dangerous. She knew it just as Cerys did – and it excited her.

It excited her too that she never felt sure of him, not even when she was in his arms. Even with his lips close to hers, whispering the things she so longed to hear, she still could not be quite sure she believed him. David had adored her and she had known it. This uncertainty was an aphrodisiac. She couldn't get Hal out of her head and that was in itself a blessing for it helped her to shut out other things, things she could not bear to think about, things that brought the all-consuming depressions and the moods that utterly defeated her shining fighting spirit. Hal was like a fever with her, heating her blood and prickling on her skin. With just a look he could reduce her to a jelly of desire.

It puzzled her sometimes that he and Will should have been friends. Will had been so serious, so determined, so driven, whilst Hal was so . . . free! And yet there was an edge to him that was driven too – by quite different motives and to quite a different end, she felt sure, though she had no idea what that might be.

And how could she? Will had been her brother, they had been so close and shared so much, and yet there had been a whole side to him she had not known, had not even suspected until such a short time ago.

Her mind closed like a steel trap before she could think the unthinkable. *Don't! Not even for a moment. Concentrate on the present, the here and now. Concentrate on Hal . . . and spare just a little thought for what you are supposed to be doing – checking fences and stock and feed . . .*

Jenny frowned. They were at the very farthest outpost of Kanunga. The cattle had congregated out here after eating their way across the pastureland that lay closer to the house and though the winter had almost run its course there were still great swathes where the grass was lush and green. But surely – there should be more cattle than she could see . . . By any reckoning, the herd was severely depleted.

Jenny reined in. 'Hal – how many head of cattle would you say there are?'

He narrowed his eyes, silently counting and estimating.

'Thirty? Thirty-five?'

'That's what I make it. There should be fifty. Where are the others?'

He pushed his hat back on his head. 'Strayed?'

'Help me check the fences.' Momentarily all her lustful thoughts were forgotten and Jenny became very much the farmer.

The fences out here were, on the whole, well maintained for the very reason that they were so far from the homestead and therefore the most vulnerable. At first Jenny could see no gaps where they were broken down. Then she found it. A gap where the posts had been pulled out of the ground and flattened – and the fencing with it.

'They've strayed all right,' Hal said.

Jenny shook her head. 'I don't think so.' She jumped down from the saddle, looking more closely at both the broken-down fence and the ground beside it. 'This fence hasn't been banged down by the animals or blown down by the wind – it's been deliberately cut, and the posts removed. And that looks like horse's hoof prints in the mud.'

'How can you tell, when the cattle have churned it all up?' Hal challenged.

Jenny pointed. 'There – it's as clear as day. And don't tell me they belong to our horses, either. We haven't been that far over. No, I think we've had rustlers out here, Hal. And they've got away with twenty or so head of our cattle.'

'Well, if that is so, there's not much you can do about it,' Hal said.

'Don't I know it!' Jenny swore, calling the rustlers by the very worst name she could think of, and Hal laughed. Jenny turned on him. 'It's not funny! We can't afford to lose twenty head of cattle, Hal! Get down off that horse of yours and help me mend this fence so we don't lost another twenty just wandering.'

He did so, though he was still, in Jenny's book, taking the whole thing very lightly. She could feel a black mood nudging her. How could they ever hope to survive when everything seemed ranged against them? Since Will's death it seemed everything that could go wrong was doing so. The fire had destroyed the hay and the barn, and now twenty prime beasts had gone missing – twenty prime beasts who should have brought in a tidy sum at market.

'Oh – let's get back,' Jenny said recklessly when the fence had been repaired. She touched Merlin's flanks and at once the gelding responded. For the time being Jenny forgot everything else as the horse flew over the heavy ground. She could hear the thunder of Thor's hooves close behind, and the thrill of the chase drove her on. She had a head start, of course, but all the same, to keep Merlin ahead would take every bit of her skill, for Thor was the bigger horse and, she thought, faster than Merlin, all things being equal.

'Go, Merlin, go!' she whispered, half-lying along his neck, her mouth close to his pricked ears.

Thor was drawing alongside; they were racing, neck and neck. Jenny gloried in the soaring exhilaration. Side by side they flew, and though Jenny felt sure Hal could overtake her if he chose, instead he settled into the same rhythm. Side by side. Neck and neck. The homestead was in sight now, the horses and riders thundered towards them. And they were still neck and neck as the yard came leaping up at them and Jenny pulled Merlin to a halt. She let out a wild, triumphant yell, reminiscent of a Wild-West rodeo and sat there for a moment, breathless, flushed and windswept.

'I gave you a run for your money, didn't I?'

'You certainly did. You're quite a girl, Jenny.' He was laughing too, exhilarated by the ride and by the girl. He could have beaten her if he had chosen, of course, but some races were won by holding back a little. And certainly she was a brilliant horsewoman. He had wanted to test her ability; he was more than satisfied with what he had seen.

He watched her now as she slid from the saddle, slim and graceful as a boy, and smiled to himself.

'Get the blankets, Jenny,' he called, dismounting himself.

She disappeared into the stable and he followed her. As she reached for the horses' blankets he grabbed her from behind. She squealed and he pressed his mouth close against her ear.

'Shh! D'you want everyone from here to Medlock to hear you?'

His hands were cupping her breasts, firm, full and definitely not like a boy. She wriggled for a moment but it was a wriggle of pure bliss and she tilted her head back towards him, covering his hands with her own.

'Oh Jenny, I have plans for us,' he whispered against her throat.

'Tell me about them.'

'Later.'

He slid his hands down to her waist, finding the fastening of the men's breeches she wore for riding, undoing it and slipping his hand inside. She gasped as his fingers moved slowly, purposefully across her flat stomach and down to the secret places between her legs. Already she was wet and eager, caught between his searching hands at the front of her body and his rock hard body behind.

He buried his mouth in the hollow between her shoulder and throat, kissing, sucking, biting at the soft flesh that was slightly salt from the perspiration the ride had drawn out like a bloom on her skin, making the moment last as long as he could bear it, whilst she moaned softly and writhed against him.

Then, when the desire for both of them was at its height, he turned her, lifting her bodily and laying her down on a heap of warm, scratchy straw.

The men's breeches, already unfastened, slid down with no effort at all and he was on her and in her, moving in the rhythm as old as time whilst she moved with him. He held back, prolonging the lovemaking until she cried out again and again as if she were in pain, her thighs tensing around him, her back arched, her neck corded. Then and only then did he give way to his own crying need with a few quick and violent strokes. As he rolled from her into the straw he let one arm lie affectionately around her still, and she nestled contentedly into his shoulder, too happy, too replete to care about what they had just done or anything in the world but the delight of the act and the closeness they had shared – and were still sharing.

Hal Tucker was not always such a tender and considerate lover. But he knew enough about women to know how to win them over. Yes, he had taken his pleasure with Jenny, but he had made sure she was pleasured and satisfied too. That way she was his, for the moment at least – though he felt fairly sure she was his in any case. That way she was much more likely to agree to his plan when he put it to her.

And strangely enough it was she who raised the subject when the aftershocks of passion had died away and she lay in his arms, more relaxed than she had been in weeks.

'What are your plans for us, then?'

'Ah!' Still he kept her waiting.

'Go on – tell me! You can't keep anything from me now.'

'Very well.' His fingers found a strand of her hair, twisted it into a corkscrew curl. 'I want to be with you, Jenny. You know that, don't you?'

She laughed softly, but with a little of the old uncertainty.

'I hope so!'

'I do, and you know it. But we've got nothing, either of us, to set up a home. This place belongs to Cerys; it will never be yours, and I have no money to buy it off her – if she'd sell – or to put down a deposit on a selection of my own. I need something behind me, Jenny, so I can ask you to marry me.'

Her heart leaped in her throat. Oh, this was more than she had dared dream of!

'Just ask me, Hal,' she whispered. 'Money doesn't matter. Just ask me!'

'I can't do that, Jenny. I have to have something to offer you. God knows, you deserve the best.'

'Oh, Hal . . .' Jenny felt she would burst with joy – and with frustration. For what hope did either of them have for getting together the sort of money of which he was speaking – especially whilst they were tied, morally, to helping Cerys to survive.

And then, as if in answer to her unspoken question, he propped himself up on one elbow, looking down at her in the half-light that filtered in through the stable door.

'There is a way, though. If you'd help me . . . It might even be fun!'

She looked up at him eagerly.

'What is it? Tell me, Hal!'

And he told her.

# Twelve

Cerys could not understand the change in Jenny. There was a luminous glow about her, and a euphoria, and Cerys felt fairly sure that Hal Tucker had something to do with that. But there were also days when she looked very tired – as if she had had no sleep at all, Cerys thought. Then there were dark circles under her eyes and she seemed to have dreadful difficulty in keeping awake.

On those same days Cerys thought that Hal looked tired too, though he hid it better. Could it be that they were having assignations in the small hours? But if so, where? Though there were definite signs that spring was coming, the nights were still bitterly cold – far too cold, Cerys would have thought, for them to be meeting outside. But Hal shared his quarters with Duggan, and Cerys didn't think there was anything untoward going on in Jenny's room. It was right next to her own, and the walls were thin enough for every sound to carry clearly – something which had always concerned her when Will was alive and it had been them who had wanted their privacy.

No, she simply could not work out what it was that was going on. But something was – she knew it in her bones.

Perhaps, she thought, she should raise the subject with Jenny. But she could well imagine the response she would elicit, and conflict with Jenny was something she could well do without.

And she had so much else on her mind, too, such as how on earth was she going to balance the books. Day-to-day living expenses for themselves and hay for the animals had already used up the meagre sum Hal had been able to get for the gig, the matched pair, and Lance, and was beginning to make inroads into her ring money. And she didn't even know yet how much

156

she was going to have to pay Chas – a vitally important debt to settle when the time came if he was not to gain possession of her land.

Sometimes, truth to tell, she felt like just giving in and letting him have it. At least that would mean she did not have to worry any more. She and Jenny and the children could just go on living in the house, they could have a vegetable plot and a few hens, and perhaps Chas would allow them to keep the cow for milk. It would be a hand-to-mouth existence, but they would manage.

And then she would think that giving in like that unless there was absolutely no option would not be fair to any of them, and not what Will would have wanted either. If only she had an income of some kind aside from the farm, perhaps it wouldn't be so bad. If she had a job . . .

When the idea first came to her she dismissed it out of hand. But for all that, it kept coming back to nag at her, insisting that at least she should give it due consideration.

She knew where there was a job going all right – and one that would presumably be mostly evening work, when Jenny would be in from her day on the land and able to look after the children. Kitty Jackson had been bemoaning the fact that she couldn't get a replacement for her barmaid who had run away with the pot boy. But could Cerys bring herself to do it? The very thought was anathema to her. To be on the premises where men came to buy and consume strong drink – worse, to have to serve them with it and presumably be convivial towards them – Cerys cringed and shied away from it with all the strictness of her upbringing.

Good heavens, her poor mother and father would die of shame if they knew she was even considering it for a moment! But could she afford to be so proud? When the deeds of her land were legally made over to Chas Wallace, wouldn't she wish that she had swallowed that pride and brought some regular money into the household?

Around and around the arguments went in Cerys's head, around and around. And the carousel was made the more giddy by the knowledge that if she didn't come to a decision soon the chance might be lost. Against all her expectations,

Kitty Jackson might find someone else to fill the post. But still Cerys was unable to bring herself to drive into Medlock and willingly offer her services to that dreadful woman.

I can't do it, Cerys thought. I just can't.

And little realized that something was about to happen which would not only solve the mystery of Jenny's bleary eyes but also push her into making a decision about approaching Kitty Jackson.

It was a fine and blustery spring morning and Cerys decided to take advantage of the sun and the wind to get as much washing as possible out of the way and outside to dry.

She did the children's things first, and the bedlinen, and then progressed to some of her own clothes. Jenny was out on the farm as usual but Cerys knew that she, too, had some garments in need of a wash, and with a tub of hot soapy water waiting she went to Jenny's room to collect them.

Usually it was a simple matter to know what to take – Jenny was not the tidiest of souls, and dirty clothes were all too often strewn around the room. But Cerys knew that the shirt that Jenny had been wearing yesterday should be somewhere. With an armful of small items, she yanked open the door to the wall cupboard that Jenny used as a wardrobe, then stopped, staring in amazement.

The cupboard was almost completely taken up with what looked, unbelievably, like a whole sheepskin. Or even two, bundled together. As the door opened, the thing fell out on to Cerys's feet, coarse, curly, and a dirty off-white colour.

Cerys took a step backwards. 'What in the . . . ?'

She dropped the laundry she was holding into a heap on the floor and pulled her find fully out of the cupboard. She simply could not imagine what something like this could be doing here in Jenny's room.

Then, in the corner of the cupboard, she noticed something else – what looked like a bundled-up shirt and a pair of the men's breeches Jenny wore for riding. She picked them up, annoyed at Jenny for leaving them here dirty where she might never have found them, and dropped them on top of the pile of laundry. Then she froze again, staring at the shirt. It was covered in splatters of dark, dried blood.

Cerys recoiled in horror. There was something going on here that she did not understand – and liked even less. Something Jenny was trying to keep from her. Well, whatever it was, Cerys intended to find out. If she had been free to do so, Cerys would have gone out on to the land there and then to find Jenny and demand an explanation. But she couldn't do that. Jenny could be miles away, and she had the children in her care. She would just have to wait until Jenny came in. But when she did, Cerys was going to waste no time in getting to the bottom of this. On that point she was absolutely decided.

It was early afternoon before Jenny returned and Cerys had worked herself up into a fine old state. When she saw the girl crossing the yard, she settled the children with a plate of biscuits she had baked, and the moment Jenny came through the door she confronted her.

'Jenny – I want to talk to you.'

Jenny pulled a face. 'Can't it wait until I've washed and changed?'

'No, it can't. Let's go to your room.'

'For goodness' sake, Cerys . . .' Jenny was half-laughing as she followed her sister-in-law, but the smile died on her face when Cerys threw open the door to her bedroom and she saw the sheepskins spread out on the bed. 'Ah.'

'I found these in the bottom of your cupboard when I was looking for anything you might need washing,' Cerys said bluntly. 'What in the world are they doing there?'

'Ah,' Jenny said again, clearly playing for time.

'And that's not all.' Cerys moved the sheepskins to reveal the bloodstained shirt and trousers. 'These were there too. Hidden. What are you up to, Jenny?'

Jenny blanched and her lip trembled. 'Oh Cerys . . .'

'Just tell me the truth!' Cerys demanded. 'You've been going out at night, haven't you? That's why you look so worn out half the time. It's no use denying it – I know you have – and it has something to do with this, doesn't it?'

Jenny's head was bowed. For a long moment she remained

silent, then she brought up her chin with a jerk, facing Cerys defiantly.

'All right – I'll tell you. If you really want to know – and be a party to breaking the law.'

'I knew it!' Cerys said sharply. 'I knew there was something going on here that shouldn't be! Yes, Jenny, I do want to know, since you are living under my roof.'

'I'm trying to help, that's all.' Jenny rubbed her face with a grimy hand, leaving a black smear across her nose. 'Trying to make a bit of money, since we don't have any.'

'But how?' Cerys demanded. 'Where do these sheepskins come in?'

Jenny half-smiled again. 'Do you remember the Tarsbrook Ghost? The story Hal told us?'

'The Tarsbrook Ghost?' For a moment Cerys stared blankly, unable to comprehend what Jenny could be talking about.

'Yes. You remember, Hal told us how he and Will pretended to be the ghost and frightened off the drovers.'

If Jenny had not been looking so perfectly serious Cerys would have thought she was pulling her leg.

'I remember. But what . . . ?'

'Well . . . we've been doing it again, Hal and I. I ride across the cut, very fast, with the sheepskins draped over my horse to make it look white and ghostly and sort of . . . well, woolly. And the drovers get scared and make a run for it and whilst they are out of the way Hal manages . . . Well, when they come back, a few prime head are missing, that's all.'

'You're rustling!' Cerys said incredulously. 'Jenny – I don't believe it! What are you doing with the cattle?'

'Oh.' Jenny shrugged. 'Hal knows farmers who will buy them. And we only rustle from the very big pasturalists who can afford it. Never from small farmers.'

'But it's still illegal!'

'I know that. But . . .'

'And what about the bloodstained clothes?' Cerys demanded. 'How did that happen? And whose blood is it?'

Jenny dropped her lashes and her lip trembled. Then she raised her gaze again to Cerys.

'A steer got frightened the other night. It hurt itself and we had to shoot it.' There was a wobble in her voice, but Cerys hardened her heart.

'Well, I'm sorry, Jenny, but it's got to stop. It's terribly wrong. And you'll be caught without doubt if you go on with it. Not everyone is stupid enough to believe in ghost horses and riders. Do you really want to go to jail?'

'No, of course I don't! But I don't want to be poor, either,' Jenny said defiantly. 'We've got nothing, Cerys, nothing at all. And I've helped out already. Someone had rustled ten head of our prime stock. I didn't tell you because I didn't want to worry you. Well, at least they've been replaced. I made sure of that before we sold on any of the ones we managed to take.'

Cerys stared. 'We had cattle rustled?'

'Yes. Out on the boundary. Hal and I found them missing.'

'And you kept it from me?'

'I didn't want to worry you – I said. And then Hal came up with this idea and . . .'

'I might have known he was behind it!' Cerys said furiously. 'He's trouble, that one! I wish he'd never come here.'

Jenny's eyes blazed. 'He's saved us from certain ruin!' she flared. 'I don't know what you've got against him, Cerys. Why, if I didn't know better, I'd think you were jealous that he and I . . .' She broke off.

'I am certainly not jealous of anything that's between you and Hal!' Cerys retorted. 'Quite the opposite. In fact, one of the reasons I don't like him is that he once tried something with me, if you really want to know.'

The moment the words were out she regretted them. Oh, perhaps Jenny should know of Hal's advances towards her, but all the same she would rather it had not come out like this, in anger. The last thing she wanted was to hurt Jenny when she was so vulnerable. But Jenny, instead of looking crushed, merely grew more angry.

'I don't believe you! He wouldn't! You're just saying that!'

'I'm not,' Cerys said. 'I'm sorry, Jenny, but it's the truth.'

'You must have misunderstood him. He wouldn't do that!' Jenny repeated.

Cerys sighed. There was no point arguing with Jenny when

161

she was in this mood. Maybe later, when she had cooled down, she'd think about what Cerys had said. At least now she had been warned.

'To get back to this rustling thing,' Cerys said. 'Are you telling me that we now have ten head of someone else's cattle on our land?'

'Yes. But they're not branded or anything. No one will ever know.'

'I'm not so sure about that,' Cerys said. 'In any case, it's not the point. I can't condone this, Jenny. It's illegal – and immoral.'

Jenny shrugged. 'So what are you going to do about it? Call the constable and ask him to take them into custody until they can be returned to their rightful owner?'

Cerys groaned with frustration. 'You know very well I can't do that – though believe me, I would if I could.'

'Even though we lost ten head to somebody else?'

'Two wrongs don't make a right,' Cerys said.

'So?'

'No, we shall just have to keep quiet about it and hope you don't get arrested when you take them to market. But I don't like it, Jenny.' Cerys drew herself up, facing her sister-in-law sternly. 'And this Tarsbrook Ghost thing has got to stop. If it doesn't, I *will* go to Jem Routledge, and that, I promise you, is no idle threat.'

'But—'

'No buts, Jenny. This disgusting thing –' she poked the sheepskin accusingly – 'will have to be disposed of and so will the clothes you messed up. There's no way I should ever be able to get the blood out of them, and I don't intend to try. Please deal with that without delay. And if I ever suspect you are doing anything of the sort again . . .'

'Oh, all right,' Jenny said sullenly.

'I mean it, Jenny. And I will know, I promise you. The lack of sleep stands out a mile where you are concerned. Your heavy eyes give you away at once.'

'I said all right, didn't I?' Jenny muttered.

'Mama!' Molly was in the doorway, Ritchie beside her. 'We've eaten all the biscuits and Ritchie feels sick.'

162

Cerys swung round, her mind still buzzing with all Jenny had revealed, to try to confront the reality of two small children.

'You've eaten *all* of them?'

'You didn't say we couldn't!' Molly said defensively.

'You should have known better! And letting Ritchie . . . No wonder he feels sick! You know what he's like. Ritchie . . .'

'Mama,' Ritchie said plaintively.

And promptly *was* sick.

The confrontation with Jenny was the deciding factor, Cerys thought. However wrong what Jenny had been doing was, at least she had been actively trying to improve their situation. Whilst she, Cerys, was pussyfooting around the niceties of whether or not she could bring herself to work in a bar – which was, at least, perfectly legal.

Well, she couldn't risk Jenny doing something like that again out of desperation. And she might. Heaven alone knew what madcap schemes she and Hal would dream up unless the situation improved.

There was nothing for it – Cerys would have to bite the bullet, swallow her sensibilities, and go into town to see if Kitty Jackson would give her the job.

Jenny, when Cerys told her what she planned, was noticeably shocked.

'Cerys – you can't work as a barmaid!'

'At least it's not illegal,' Cerys returned tartly.

'No, but . . . you'll hate it! Look, why don't I . . . ?'

'Don't be foolish,' Cerys said. 'You are needed here to work on the farm. And you can't work all day and at night too. That has already been amply demonstrated.'

'But that was in the middle of the night,' Jenny said, looking sheepish. 'This would be just evenings, I assume. And you're working all day too, looking after the home and the children.'

'It's not as demanding as being in the saddle all day, or heaving great bales of animal feed about,' Cerys said – though it had to be admitted, she was often bone-tired herself by the time the children were in bed. 'It may be you'll have to do a bit more for yourself, of course. Your own washing, for

163

instance. Not that that would be a bad thing,' she added, for her discovery in Jenny's cupboard still rankled. 'Anyway, there's no point wasting breath discussing it. My mind is made up, Jenny. I'm going to see Kitty Jackson as soon as I can – before she finds someone else to fill the vacancy. It's our best chance of getting a regular income – for the time being anyway.'

Jenny sighed. This, she thought, was a sure route to disaster. But trying to talk Cerys out of something when she was so determined really would be a waste of breath.

'You want me to mind the children whilst you go?'

'Well, yes, of course,' Cerys said with acerbity. 'I don't want them to have to endure such a corrupt environment. And I don't think Kitty Jackson would want them either. I don't think she likes children very much.'

Jenny gave her a sharp and curious look, and Cerys could have bitten off her tongue.

'Well – I'm assuming she doesn't,' she said hastily. 'A woman like that . . .'

Jenny seemed satisfied and Cerys heaved a silent sigh of relief. Oh, she had nearly let the cat out of the bag then and no mistake!

'Go this afternoon, if you like,' Jenny said carelessly. 'I've nothing more pressing to do today.'

'Thank you.' Cerys inclined her head. She only wished she could feel more enthusiastic about her prospective employment.

'Mrs Page, this is a surprise indeed!' Kitty Jackson was receiving Cerys in the same residents' lounge where she and Chas had taken coffee. In the reception area Cerys had spoken to a man passing through – a man who looked suspiciously like one of those who had dropped Chas's piano – and he had informed Kitty that Cerys was there to see her.

Cerys held herself very erect, uncomfortable not only with her surroundings, but also with Kitty's cool appraisal of her. The hostility she had felt when she had been with Chas was less apparent this afternoon, if anything there was an amused look playing about Kitty's painted mouth which Cerys found even more disconcerting.

There was, she thought, no point in wasting time on pleasantries. Best to come straight to the point.

'When I was here the other day I understood you to say you had lost your barmaid,' she began. 'If you have not yet replaced her, I wondered if you might consider me for the position.'

If she was taken by surprise, Kitty did not allow it to show in her face. Kitty liked to be in control and a person surprised was one with less than the greatest advantage. But the look of amusement intensified.

'You want to work for me – as my barmaid?' she asked levelly.

Cerys swallowed hard. 'Yes. I know I'm not the most likely candidate, but I'm honest and hardworking and . . . well, clean and presentable, I hope.'

'Indeed. Respectable, one might say. A great many young women who apply for this kind of work would not be able to say that,' Kitty observed shrewdly.

Cerys felt the colour rising in her cheeks. 'I hope you don't think . . .'

'Oh – not for one moment!' Kitty waved a hand airily. 'May I ask the reason why?'

'Why . . . ?'

'Why you are here, seeking employment.'

'Because I need the money,' Cerys said bluntly. It seemed to her at that moment that honesty was by far the best policy. 'I lost my husband a few months ago and I am finding it very difficult to make ends meet.'

'As I thought.' Kitty regarded her narrowly.

'And I have young children. So you see, I thought that if I could find paid employment in the evenings whilst there is someone at home to look after them . . .' Cerys broke off, biting her lip. 'You haven't filled the position, have you?'

'No, indeed.'

'Then will you consider me?'

The silence seemed to go on for ever. Then Kitty said bluntly: 'No.'

Cerys felt her heart plummet earthwards.

'Oh! But . . . Why not?' She had not meant to ask. It was very shaming. But somehow she could not stop herself.

165

Kitty looked at her from beneath those sooty lashes which Cerys had, on that other occasion, when she had been up to considering such things, been quite sure were darkened with boot black.

'I don't need to give you a reason, or explain myself in any way, Mrs Page, but I will do so anyway. In my opinion you are not in the least suited to the position. You are clearly uncomfortable here. I think you are probably more than a little critical of my clients and the activities they like to partake in, and would be unable to hide your feelings. You would be stiff, unfriendly, possibly openly hostile, and certainly not at all congenial company. A man likes to be served with a smile and a twinkle. He likes to be able to give a girl's bottom a pat without feeling she might turn and slap his face. He wants a whore, not a virgin. In short, Mrs Page, I think you would make a terrible barmaid – more likely to turn my customers away than attract them. Does that answer your question?'

The blood had rushed to Cerys's face; the tirade made her tremble, with outrage as well as shock. After she had summoned up the courage to come here – to be spoken to like that!

'You are probably right in every regard, Miss Jackson,' she said spiritedly. 'I don't approve of you, or your establishment, and I would almost certainly dislike the sort of man who frequents it. Without doubt I would slap the face of anyone who took liberties with me. So although I would have worked hard and willingly for you, and although I would never have been anything but pleasant to anyone who treated me as any decent woman should have the right to be treated, I would not dream of lowering my standards to become the sort of harlot you seem to want. Yes, I wanted the job, because I need the money. I admitted as much. But now I can see you have done me a favour in refusing to employ me, because I would certainly not wish to sink to the sort of level you appear to occupy.'

She stopped, breathless and furious, and suddenly, from the doorway behind her, came the startlingly incongruous sound of someone clapping.

'Bravo!'

It was a man's voice, and one she recognized. She swung round to see Chas Wallace standing there. The colour drained from her face, then returned in a scarlet flood.

'Bravo, Mrs Page!' he said again, and then, to Kitty: 'My, Kitty! I dare say no one has dared to speak to you so in a very long time – if ever they did. What price your town mouse now?'

The last remark was lost on Cerys. So horrified was she that Chas Wallace had heard her outburst, and so ashamed that he should know she had been seeking employment here at the Commercial Hotel, that all she could hear was the blood pounding in her ears.

'Will you excuse me please?' she said with all the dignity she could muster, and turned on her heel, sweeping past him through the doorway and out through the little reception area.

The cold fresh air hit her burning cheeks as she emerged through the front entrance and for a dreadful moment she thought her shaking legs were going to give way. But somehow she managed to walk on, head held high, towards her sulky, tied up at the hitching rail.

'Mrs Page!' Chas Wallace's voice behind her.

She scarcely dared turn around; tears were now stinging her eyes.

With long strides he was beside her. 'Don't run away!'

'I'm not running away!' she said indignantly. 'I am going home to my children, who need me.'

'They can wait a few more minutes, surely?'

Cerys reached for the reins to unhitch them, Chas put out a hand to restrain her.

As his fingers covered hers, Cerys felt a sharp sensation that seemed to spread from where they touched, prickling over her skin. Startled she looked up, and as her eyes met his, her stomach seemed to tip too. Dear Lord, what was happening to her?

Her eyes left his, went to his hand, staying hers on the reins, and as if she had rebuked him, he removed it. To her utter amazement Cerys found herself regretting the gesture.

'You were actually hoping to find paid employment here?' Chas said.

'That is the reason I came, yes,' Cerys replied. Her tone was brisk to cover the fact she was sure her voice would shake as much as her knees. 'I can see now I made a terrible mistake.'

'Would a job as housekeeper suit you better?' he asked.

She stared at him, uncomprehending, and he went on: 'Mary Lightfoot, my housekeeper – you remember her? She has, I am afraid, gone walkabout. Aborigines have a habit of doing that, as I'm sure you know. It has left me in a far worse position than Kitty finds herself in. With no woman to keep things in order, Wells Court is in quite a state. And I am wondering if you might feel able to help me out.'

'Oh!' Cerys could not think of a single thing to say.

'It may only be temporary, of course – until Mary decides to come back – and she most likely will, eventually. And it would be daytime work, not evenings,' Chas went on. 'But I would have no objection to your bringing your children along with you. Provided they were kept under control, of course – but I'm sure they would be. They seem extraordinarily well behaved.'

'Oh . . .' Still she hesitated.

'I am a generous employer,' Chas said. 'I think you would find yourself considerably better off. If you think it would not be too much for you, that is.'

At last Cerys found her voice – but little inspiration.

'Mr Wallace – I don't know what to say . . .'

'Well, think it over.' He smiled, turned away.

In a flash Cerys made up her mind. She would be a fool to turn down such an opportunity.

'Wait, Mr Wallace,' she said hastily. 'I don't need to think. I should like to accept your offer.'

He turned back, smiled again.

'Good. Shall we say you'll begin tomorrow then?'

She nodded, speechless once more. Then: 'Thank you,' she said. 'Thank you very much.'

And turned to unhitch the reins whilst Chas Wallace went back to the Commercial Hotel.


'Chas – what in the world are you thinking of?' Kitty asked with some hauteur.

'I don't know,' he replied thoughtfully, and it was no more than the truth.

He didn't know what had got into him to offer Cerys Page the job as his housekeeper. All he had said was true – Mary had certainly upped and 'gone walkabout' and as a result Wells Court was not functioning as well or as efficiently as it usually did. But to offer the job to Cerys Page of all people, to help her get her financial affairs on a more even keel, when what he really wanted was for her to go under so that he could get his hands on her land . . . It made no sense at all.

'It will only be until Mary chooses to come wandering back,' he said.

'I wouldn't have thought you'd want a woman like that in your house at all!' Kitty said with asperity. 'What a temper she has!'

Chas smiled slowly. 'Yes, hasn't she?' He did not add that it was at the moment he had heard her tirade that he had decided to offer her the position. 'She certainly put you in your place, Kitty!'

'Hmm!' Kitty turned away, tossing her head.

It never even occurred to Chas, simple man that he was, that what Kitty was feeling at that moment was a very severe attack of jealousy.

# Thirteen

C erys was feeling incredibly flustered. She had, in fact, been flustered for most of the time since she had accepted Chas Wallace's offer.

'I don't even know how I'm going to get there,' she said to Jenny. 'Do you think the children will be safe in the sulky?'

'It's a pity we sold the gig,' Jenny commented.

'Well yes, I know that now,' Cerys responded sharply. 'But I wasn't safe driving it, anyway. I think I can manage with the sulky if I squash Molly in and she has Ritchie on her lap. Well – I shall have to manage. I don't have any choice.'

'I expect you will – unless Chas Wallace sends his carriage for you. That wouldn't surprise me.'

'What are you talking about?' Cerys demanded.

'Well, he seems to be falling over himself on your behalf. I thought if you asked he might send the carriage,' Jenny said with irony.

'That is the silliest thing I ever heard!' Cerys snapped. 'A housekeeper being collected in a carriage!'

Jenny pulled a wry face. 'Oh, I don't know. No sillier than employing a housekeeper who can't live in and has to take two children to work with her.'

'I don't see why!' Cerys was getting annoyed now. 'I shall do a very good job for him. Looking after a house is something I'm very good at. And in any case, it's only temporary, until the aboriginal woman comes back.'

'We shall see,' Jenny said sagely.

Cerys wanted to hit her.

In the event she did manage to squeeze Molly and Ritchie into

170

the sulky beside her, and with instructions to Molly to hold on to him very tightly, they set off.

The door at Wells Court was opened by Chas Wallace himself. Cerys had wondered whether she was doing the right thing by going to the front door as she had before or whether, now that she was a servant, she should go to the back. But Chas did not seem in the least put out at her choice.

'Mrs Page – good morning!' He was in shirtsleeves and Cerys could clearly see muscles rippling beneath fine lawn. She averted her eyes. Looking at men's muscles had come to an end when Will had died.

'Good morning,' she said briskly.

'And the children, too.'

'Say good morning, Molly,' Cerys instructed.

'Good morning,' Molly said obligingly, and with the sort of pertness that made Cerys realize once more that Molly was likely to grow into a minx where men were concerned.

Ritchie, however, merely stared, his eyes very round. He was clearly taking everything in before deciding whether or not he would deign to communicate in his own fashion.

'Come through to the kitchen, Mrs Page,' Chas said. He led the way, but as he pushed open the kitchen door, Cerys was surprised to see a young girl there, washing dishes. Rather greasy-looking hair had been scraped beneath a mob cap and the girl was wearing what appeared to be a uniform of sorts – grey skirt, white shirt and grey striped apron.

'This is Florence,' Chas said by way of introduction. 'Florence – this is Mrs Page, who will be taking over Mary Lightfoot's duties as housekeeper until she returns.'

The girl threw Cerys a rather resentful glance from beneath stubby lowered lashes.

'Pour some coffee for Mrs Page,' Chas instructed. 'I'm sure she would like a cup before she begins work. And you can pour one for me too, and bring them to us in the parlour, if you please.'

It was, Cerys thought, as if she were not an employee at all, but a guest.

'Very good, Mr Wallace sir.' But the girl avoided looking at

171

Cerys. She was going to have trouble with that one, she rather thought.

'I didn't know you had other staff,' she said when they were ensconced in the parlour and safely out of earshot.

Chas Wallace looked surprised.

'In a place this size? Goodness yes! Surely you did not think you had to do all the menial work as well as the housekeeping?'

Cerys felt a flush warming her cheeks. She had shown herself to be very unsophisticated, she thought, and though she knew, of course, that Chas knew she had to do all her own washing and cleaning, she felt somehow ashamed that she should have thought for even a moment that he had no servants either.

'Time was when we had a whole band of convict women working for us,' Chas went on. 'In my father's day there were always at least four, though sometimes I think they were more trouble than they were worth. Nowadays there is just Florence and her sister Edith. You'll have to be strict with them, I'm afraid. They can be quite slovenly, and Mary Lightfoot is not the best disciplinarian.'

'How do they feel about me replacing her?' Cerys asked, remembering the resentful look on Florence's rather mean features.

Chas smiled slightly. 'None too pleased, I imagine. They doubtless expected to be able to do as they liked whilst Mary was not here. It's possible they even thought one of them might be promoted into her shoes, though neither of them is the least bit suited to responsibility, and both tend to be rather . . . slow on the uptake, shall we say.'

Cerys sipped her coffee, one restraining arm about Ritchie in case he should begin wrecking Chas's parlour. But the little boy seemed quite in awe of his surroundings and inclined to do nothing but cling to his mother's skirts, and even Molly was, for her, quite subdued.

'Shall we run over your duties?' Chas suggested. 'Then, when you've finished your coffee you can set about carrying them out in whatever way you think best.'

'Yes, yes of course.'

172

'You'll find your own way about the house, I trust?'

'Yes – yes, I'm sure . . .'

'I think,' Chas Wallace said, 'that this is an arrangement that is going to work out very well.'

His eyes met hers, holding them, and he smiled.

The most curious sensation prickled through Cerys. A sensation not dissimilar to the one she had experienced when his fingers had touched hers, except that that had rippled over her skin, whilst this seemed to begin in the pit of her stomach.

'I certainly hope so,' she said, the words coming to her lips automatically though her thoughts were racing like a flock of scattered sheep and she could not get hold of any of them.

Ritchie, growing suddenly bold, twisted out of her slack grasp and made a dash for it across Chas Wallace's expensive-looking Oriental rug. Grateful for the distraction, Cerys dived after him.

'If you're happy then, Mrs Page, perhaps you will excuse me,' Chas Wallace said, not giving the slightest hint either that he knew he had discomfited her, or that he had even been aware of whatever it was that had passed between them. 'I have a great deal of farm work that is awaiting my attention.'

With another slow smile he left the room and Cerys was left floundering.


Cerys settled in at Wells Court a great deal more easily than she would have believed possible. Each morning she drove over in the sulky with the children, each afternoon she drove home again in good time to prepare an evening meal for Jenny and the men.

Though housekeeping for Chas Wallace was something extra in her already fully occupied life, and Cerys had expected that taking up employment would leave her totally exhausted, she discovered to her surprise that she seemed to end the day less tired than before and each morning she was awake with the dawn, refreshed and ready to begin again.

Perhaps, she thought, it was the change of scene that had done it; to get away from the four confining walls of the undeniably dark farmhouse at Kanunga which, although they were her home, had hemmed her in with her grief and anxiety

173

throughout the long winter. Perhaps it was because that winter was at long last over, and the buds were beginning to burst on the trees and the grass to spring fresh and green beneath her feet.

Or perhaps it was simply that the work was less onerous at Wells Court. The manual work and the basic chores were done, as Chas had explained, by the Fenner sisters, Florence and Edith. Although they were slatternly in their appearance and, to begin with, resentful in manner, they seemed to do more or less what Cerys told them to. Her own duties consisted mainly of planning and preparing meals and catering for the needs of the household, supervising the laundry, and checking the store cupboard. She enjoyed the responsibility of ordering and organizing, though sometimes she felt guilty, for it seemed to her, steeped as she was in a Protestant work ethic, that she really did very little to earn the generous wage that Chas Wallace paid her each week.

As for the children, they were as good as gold. With all the extra space at Wells Court they were in their element, exploring room after endless room, or lurking in the kitchen with Florence, who had taken to the children. When there was a bowl to be washed up after making a cake, Florence would allow the children to scrape it out before she plunged it into the hot, soapy water, and more than once Cerys caught her giving them snacks of beef dripping spread on thick crusty bread and sprinkled with salt and pepper. Cerys was not at all sure this was good for either of them, especially little Ritchie with his sickly stomach, but she hesitated to upset Florence when so far at least it had not actually seemed to have done any harm to either of them.

With the improving weather they were able to get out of the house too, and play in perfect safety on the lawns and in the stable yard under the watchful eye of Chas's grooms and handymen, most of whom had taken to them just as Florence had.

'They are pleased to have children about the place,' Chas said when Cerys one day raised with him her concerns that Molly and Ritchie were getting in the way of the men and hampering their day's work. 'It's a very long while since there have been children at Wells Court, and I dare say it's just what the place needs.'

It occurred to Cerys then to wonder why Chas had never married and had children of his own, but she knew better than to ask.

Most of all Molly and Ritchie loved the farm dogs, who trotted out behind the horses, stretched out to sleep in the warm spring sunshine, and sprang to life barking madly and leaping about when someone they did not know came riding up the drive. Mostly they were tolerant enough of Molly and Ritchie's interest in that way that animals are tolerant of small children, but after she saw the pair of them hanging on to Rufus, a shaggy-haired cross-breed as big as a small donkey, one around his neck, the other on his hind quarters, Cerys had a sharp word with them about the dangers of becoming overfamiliar with them.

'Rufus wouldn't hurt us!' Molly said, round-eyed with indignation. 'He's a nice doggy!'

'I'm sure he is,' Cerys said. 'But you must treat him with more respect all the same. And the others too. They may not all be as good-tempered as Rufus, and you don't know them that well, and they don't know you.'

'Can we have our own dog then?' Molly asked reasonably. 'One who does know us.'

'Yes, one day you shall,' Cerys promised, and wondered briefly why Will had never had dogs at Kanunga. As a town girl, the daughter of a storekeeper, she had not been used to animals and had not really noticed the omission before. Now she thought it a little strange. Dogs and farms seemed to go together, and indeed most of them had at least two or three for work and for company.

'Ned says that Poll is going to have puppies,' Molly said. Ned was one of the stable lads. 'When she does, we could have one of them for our very own, couldn't we?'

Cerys shook her head, smiling. 'I don't think we can have a dog at the moment, Molly, with things as they are.'

'Oh please, Mama! Please!'

'Please,' Ritchie echoed.

'We'll have to see,' Cerys said, but she knew the children

would have to be disappointed. She couldn't leave a puppy at Kanunga whilst they were here all day – and anyway that would defeat the object of having one at all. But neither could she bring it here with her and take it home again. Fitting both Molly and Ritchie in the sulky was difficult enough without having a puppy to transport too!

But worrying about how to tell the children they simply must not set their hearts on a puppy of their own was such a little thing compared with all the problems she had faced in the last months! It made her feel quite light-hearted – and light-headed! – that life could have ever returned to such a mundane level.

One thing that was still concerning Cerys, in spite of her improved financial position, was her debt to Chas. For her, the grand piano seemed to dominate the parlour and one day when she was alone she could not resist taking a closer look at it. Sneakily, like a thief, she made certain that no one was about, and lifted the lid. The keys, ebony and ivory and quite pristine, looked back at her. It really didn't appear damaged, but Chas had mentioned unseen problems. Tentatively she touched one of the keys – a soft tinkling note pealed out. She depressed another key and another, moving nervously up the scale. Each note, it seemed to her, sounded perfectly in tune.

And very, very pretty.

Fascinated, Cerys touched some more notes and, gaining confidence, some more. No one could have described her tinkling as tuneful, but the sound pleased her. Once, when she was a child, old blind Mr Peake, the organist at their chapel in Sydney, had allowed her to sit on the music stool and play a few notes and the thrill of it had made her quite forget her nervousness of the old man with his strange, half-hooded, sightless eyes.

It was the same now. Totally entranced, Cerys forgot that she had no business playing Chas Wallace's piano, and that she would die of shame if anyone should catch her doing it. So engrossed was she that she did not realize Chas Wallace had returned home, let alone that he was standing in the doorway watching her.

She became aware of him quite suddenly; a creeping sensation prickling up her spine made her realize she was not alone. She spun round, hot colour flooding her cheeks, to see him lounging against the doorpost.

'Oh!' she gasped.

'You seem very drawn to my piano, Mrs Page,' he said. His tone was amused rather than annoyed.

'I . . . I wondered just how much was wrong with it,' she said lamely.

'Nothing now.' A corner of his mouth quirked. 'A travelling tuner came by one evening a week or so ago and carried out the necessary repairs for me.'

'Oh – then . . .' Her heart was sinking; this, then, was the moment of reckoning. 'You must tell me how much I owe you, Mr Wallace, so that I can repay you.'

He hesitated. Then: 'I haven't had the bill myself yet.'

'But you must have, surely?' she burst out. 'If the man was a travelling craftsman you would have paid him there and then, wouldn't you?'

'No, he is going to send the bill on to me,' Chas Wallace said smoothly. 'In any case, I have already told you not to worry your head about it at present.'

'But I am worried!' Cerys said sharply. 'When you are holding the deeds to my property as surety for the debt, of course I am!'

A dark shadow flashed across Chas Wallace's face. For a moment he looked brooding – almost dangerous.

'It's my opinion the deeds are safest where they are at the moment,' he said.

She frowned. 'What do you mean?'

He shrugged. 'Aren't you happy with the arrangement? I thought it was working very well indeed, and you must believe me now when I say I have no intention of turning you out of your home.'

'Yes, but . . .'

'Then let's leave things as they are for a little longer, shall we? Wait until you are back on your feet before you start worrying your head about it. The land is still yours – I'm not pressing for my debt to be repaid. And your deeds are safe in Mr Spencer's strong room. It's fair enough, isn't it?'

'Yes, I suppose . . .' But Cerys had the distinct feeling she had been manipulated somehow.

'It sounds to me like you are rather musical,' Chas said, changing the subject.

Her colour heightened once more. 'Oh – I don't know about that . . .'

'Would you like to learn to play?' Chas asked.

'Oh, I'd love to!' Cerys admitted.

'Then why don't you? I don't know of a tutor, I'm afraid, so you would have to teach yourself, but from what I just heard, I should think you'd manage it – to a degree at any rate. Why don't you do so?'

'Oh, I couldn't! I might damage it again . . .'

He laughed aloud. 'That's a risk I'm prepared to take, if you are. As I told you once before, as far as I'm concerned, the piano is for ornamentation only. But that seems a terrible waste when it's such a fine instrument. And especially since I have had it repaired,' he added mischievously.

'Well . . .' Cerys was sorely tempted. 'If you're sure . . .'

'Quite sure. There's just one thing. Fond as I am of them, I would rather the children didn't play on it.'

'Of course not!' Cerys agreed, horrified at the very idea.

'That's settled then.' His eyes met and held hers, and Cerys felt that strange, prickling sensation in the pit of her stomach.

She tore her eyes away from his and felt the hot colour still burning in her cheeks.

What *was* going on? For the life of her, Cerys could not understand it. But there was something extremely disturbing about Mr Chas Wallace.

Jenny had gone into Medlock to buy supplies from the general store – flour and sugar and cooking oil. Chas had given Cerys an afternoon off, so she was at home catching up with some of the chores and Jenny was able to take the sulky – much easier than trying to fit the bulky supplies into a pannier slung across her horse.

As she emerged from the little general store with her arms full of purchases she heard someone calling her name, and spun round to see David Harris trotting along the street on Lance, Will's old horse.

Jenny's heart sank and a faint colour rose in her cheeks. She knew she had treated David rather badly and felt guilty about it, and the guilt made her less pleased to see him than she might otherwise have been. It was a shock, too, to see him riding Lance, though she knew it was him that Hal had sold the horse to, and she did not like that one little bit either. It should be Will on that broad handsome back!

'David,' she greeted him, managing to hide everything she was feeling. 'How are you?'

'Oh, well enough, I suppose. And you? It's been such a long time since I saw you, Jenny.'

'Yes, well, we are very busy these days,' she said vaguely.

He nodded. 'I expect you are. I still wish you could find the time to come over to Glenavon sometimes, though, Jenny. I do miss you.'

'Oh, maybe I will sometime,' Jenny said, fobbing him off.

David, however, was looking at her narrowly. 'Is that farm manager still with you?'

'Hal?' Jenny was a little surprised at the description. 'He's not a manager, exactly. He's just a friend of Will's who's helping us out. And yes, he is still with us. Of course, you must have met him when you bought Lance.'

'Yes.' David appeared to be on the point of saying something more, and Jenny made a rapid effort to change the subject.

'Cerys was very glad Lance went to you,' she said. 'And to be honest, I'm glad too. We know you'll look after him as Will always did. How are you getting on with him?'

David patted Lance's neck. 'Very well. He's a very nice horse.'

'And quite a bargain, too,' Jenny said.

'A bargain?' David's eyes had taken on a puzzled look. 'I thought I paid a very fair price for him, Jenny.'

Jenny smiled faintly. 'I know Cerys was hoping for more. Though we would still rather know he went to a good home than make a lot of money out of him.'

179

'Jenny . . .' David was looking a little worried now. 'How much do you think I paid for Lance?'

Jenny told him, and his worried look deepened.

'I paid a great deal more than that, and if that so-called manager says I didn't, then he's not been telling you the truth.'

'Oh!' Jenny was both startled and alarmed. She did not like this one little bit. She did not want to believe that Hal had cheated Cerys out of some of what David had paid for Lance, but she could not think of a single occasion on which David had not been strictly truthful. It was one of the things that made him a little boring, really, in her opinion – he was always as open and honest as the day and totally transparent. Somehow, distasteful as it was to her, she could all too easily imagine Hal pocketing some of the proceeds and being rather pleased with himself for doing it too. And if he had been less than honest about what Lance had fetched, there was a pretty good chance that the gig and matched pair had gone for more than he had admitted too.

'Jenny – are you sure it's a good idea, having someone out at Kanunga you scarcely know?' David was saying anxiously. 'Some men might take advantage of two women alone and . . .'

'Oh don't fuss, David!' Jenny said impatiently, the anxiety she was feeling giving her voice a sharp edge. 'I expect I must have misunderstood what Cerys told me. And, of course, I should have known you would never have got a bargain at Cerys's expense. But now, I really am going to have to go. Cerys is going to wonder what on earth has become of me!'

He nodded, but he still looked concerned.

'Don't forget, Jenny, we are always there at Glenavon if you need us.'

'That's kind, David.' Jenny loaded her purchases into the sulky. 'I'll tell Cerys I saw you, and that you were asking after her.' Then, ignoring David's forlorn look, she unhitched the reins and climbed up herself. 'Take care, won't you?'

'And you, Jenny.'

As she drove off along the street she could feel his eyes following her. It only added to her discomfort.

180

# Fourteen

Hal Tucker was sprawled at the kitchen table, feet up on another chair, mug of tea between his hands, looking for all the world as if he owned the place.

Jenny came up behind him, wound her arms around his neck and put her head down close to his. He shrugged a little impatiently and her face clouded.

'Hal! What's wrong?'

'Nothing.' But his tone was impatient too.

'Don't you want me any more?' she asked, pouting.

'Yes, of course I do. But not all the time.'

She was insatiable, he thought irritably. Why did women constantly want reassurance? He had thought Jenny might be different, with an untamed nature to match his own. Certainly she was not the kind of woman to whimper and swoon, and she could ride and shoot and rope a steer as well as any man. But in this respect she was no different to the rest.

Sensing the gulf that had opened up between them, Jenny felt an edge of desperation.

'But I thought that you . . . that we . . . You said you had plans for us!'

His irritation grew. Kiss a woman and she wanted to be told you loved her. Bed her, and she wanted a ring on her finger. Well, the woman who caught *him* like that would have to get up very early in the morning!

'I made you no promises, Jenny. It's not my style. Now, can I drink my cup of tea in peace?'

She withdrew, hurt.

'Oh, I see!' she snapped. 'When you want to make love to me, that's one thing. It's all sweet words and "Jenny, I want to be with you". But when I want to make love to you, it's another matter entirely.'

'You've got it,' he said unpleasantly.

'Well, we'll see how you like it when I turn my back on you!' Jenny snapped.

But they both knew, even as she said it, that was not something that was going to happen.

She flounced to the dresser, banging cups. Hal pointedly ignored her and she felt her misery beginning to turn to anger. How could he treat her like this after all that had happened between them? It wasn't very nice. But then, she was no longer sure that Hal was a very nice person.

'There are things,' she said softly, 'that I know about you, Hal Tucker. Things you would rather nobody else knew, I'm sure.'

She glanced over her shoulder and saw him stiffen. Every line of his body was suddenly alert, like a deer who senses the hunter. She felt a small prickle of triumph.

'What are you talking about?' he snarled.

'Oh Hal, you know as well as I do,' she said, enjoying her moment of power.

He was on his feet in a moment, across the kitchen, grasping her roughly by the arms.

'What?' His handsome face was almost ugly suddenly, lips curled back to bare his very white teeth, eyes narrowed and dangerous. Towering over her, that handsome face very close to hers, he shook her so that her head jerked on her neck. 'What do you know about me, Jenny? What?'

She felt a frisson of fear. This was a new Hal, one she had not seen before. But besides the fear she also felt something that might have been excitement.

'I know you cheated Cerys over the sale of the horses for one thing,' she said, her eyes glittering.

'And what else?'

'Isn't that enough? I know you got a great deal more for Lance than you handed over to her. I saw David Harris in town the other day and he told me so. I expect you got more than you said for the gig and the matched pair too – and you kept most of it for yourself.'

182

His eyes bored into hers, his fingers bit painfully into her shoulders. Then, with a short hard laugh, he released her, turning away, then back to face her.

'Have you told Cerys this?'

Her chin was up, the colour high in her cheeks. 'Not yet.'

'And are you going to?'

'I don't know,' Jenny said. 'I should. It's only right that she should know. But . . .'

'Yes?' he grated.

'What good would it do? I don't suppose you would give her what you owe her. She'd tell you to leave because she wouldn't trust you any more, and we'd be back to struggling to run this place on our own. And I . . .'

A corner of his mouth twisted up in a smirk. 'You'd miss me.'

'You know I would,' Jenny said.

'In that case . . .' He reached for her again, but this time, though his grip on her was still like iron, the intention behind it was quite different. He pulled her towards him and as his mouth covered hers she melted inwardly, though for a moment she held herself stiffly, resisting. He kissed her hard and long, his teeth raking her lips, and she moaned with the helpless desire he could arouse in her; he tore open the neck of her shirt and as his hands grasped her breasts she made no move to resist.

'You won't give me away, will you, Jenny?' he whispered harshly, his mouth close by her ear.

For reply she only pressed closer, luxuriating in the feel of his hard body against hers, her treacherous heart beating so fast she thought she would die from the response he could evoke in her.

No, she would not give him away. How could she, whilst she still wanted him so? She might no longer quite trust him, but what she knew gave her at least a little power over him. She might not like what she knew, he might not be the man she would wish him to be. But that did not change her obsession with him.

Jenny knew nothing beyond that she could not bear it if he went away, could not bear never to be in his arms again.

Without the hope that she would one day be his, she would not want to live.

He was in her power; she was in his. For the moment it was enough.

Cerys knew, the moment she came home from Wells Court that afternoon, what had been going on. There was a smell of passion satisfied in the kitchen and Jenny's bright eyes and flushed face confirmed it.

Cerys's heart sank. She had actually been singing as she drove home, the silly little ditties and nursery rhymes the children liked to join in with. Molly had joined in, a bit tunelessly, but with great enthusiasm, and Ritchie had clapped his hands and added the odd word here and there, even more tunelessly than Molly, and usually a note or two too late because he was simply echoing them. For the first time since Will's death, it had felt almost as if they were a normal happy family, not one decimated by grief and worry.

Now that happy mood disappeared as if it had never been, and Cerys was plunged once more back into the abyss. Will was gone for ever, this man she did not like was there in her house, and something she liked even less was going on between him and Will's sister, whom she not only loved, but also felt responsible for. The weight of anxiety dropped back heavily on to Cerys's shoulders and she knew that she had to bear it alone.

Cerys turned it over and over in her mind as she prepared the evening meal. She had really thought, these last few weeks, that things were cooling down between Jenny and Hal. Oh, she could see that Jenny still worshipped the ground he walked on, but she had also observed that Hal was paying her less attention, and that the attraction, on his part at least, was beginning to pale. Jenny would be hurt and upset, she knew, but at least she would no longer be in danger of . . .

Cerys stamped quickly on the thought which she could not bear to form. That Jenny would forget herself, and allow Hal the kind of liberties that could mean the downfall of any young woman.

But tonight, for the first time, Cerys was in no doubt that

Jenny had been misbehaving with Hal. It was written all over them, in the looks that passed between them and the muffled giggles and whispers coming from the corner of the room where they were sitting together. And Hal was definitely paying Jenny more attention again. Not a doubt of it.

Something would have to be done. But what? Cerys wished with all her heart she could tell him to pack his bags and go. Jenny's honour was more important than keeping the farm going – or at least that was how it seemed to her at the moment. They would manage somehow. Why, Chas Wallace had once offered to lend Cerys one of his hands, and if he did so again she did not think she would turn him down this time. He had, after all, become a friend. And if the worst came to the worst, then she would surrender the deeds to him, let him farm the land, and continue to live in the homestead with Molly, Ritchie and Jenny as he had promised she could.

But suppose she was too late to save Jenny? Suppose the damage was already done? Cerys went cold as she thought about it. If Jenny should happen to have put herself in the position of being with child and she, Cerys, had sent Hal Tucker away, then the poor baby would be fatherless and Jenny would have to bear the shame – and the burden – of raising it alone. At least if Hal were still here he would presumably shoulder his responsibilities and make an honest woman of Jenny.

Or would he? Would he turn his back on her and his baby anyway? Cerys was horribly afraid he might. A man who could kick a cat, a man who could rustle cattle and persuade a young girl to help him, might very well also be a man with no conscience, who could walk away from the consequences of his shameless seduction without a backward glance. And was he, in any case, a suitable husband for Jenny? Cerys did not in all honesty think he was, and she did not believe Will, if he were here, would think so either.

Around and around her mind ran, leading her first to one decision and then another until she thought she would go quite mad. On one thing, however, she was decided.

However difficult it might be, however much trouble it

caused, she must say something to Jenny in the hope that she could make her see sense.

But for all that, Cerys did not feel overly optimistic that her efforts would meet with much success.

Her opportunity came later that evening when the children were in bed and Hal had left for his own quarters in the bunkhouse.

'Jenny – we need to talk,' she began firmly.

'Oh Cerys – can't it wait? I've had a hard day and I'm very tired,' Jenny demurred.

'Not too tired that you couldn't flirt with Hal all evening,' Cerys returned tartly. 'And not such a busy day that you couldn't canoodle with him this afternoon either.'

It was not at all the way she had intended to approach this delicate subject, but then, that was her all over, Cerys thought, cross with herself as she saw Jenny's hackles begin to rise. She just couldn't seem to stop herself coming out with things she didn't mean to.

'Oh, if you're going to start going on about Hal again I *am* going to bed,' Jenny retorted, getting up from her chair. 'I really don't want to hear it, Cerys.'

'Maybe you don't, but you're going to anyway,' Cerys said bluntly. 'I wouldn't be doing my duty by Will if I didn't say something.'

'Don't bring Will into this!' Jenny flared.

Cerys ignored her. 'What do you think he would say if he knew what was going on? He would be horrified, Jenny. As I am.'

'I don't know what you mean.' Jenny tossed her head, but guilty colour tinged her cheeks.

'You do know what I mean,' Cerys insisted. 'You've quite lost your head over Hal Tucker and I am very worried as to where it's going to end.'

Jenny stared her out. 'And is that any business of yours, Cerys?'

'Well of course it's my business!' Cerys returned angrily. 'You are my sister-in-law, Jenny – no, more. You're a true sister to me, and I can't help worrying about you.'

'There's no need,' Jenny said stiffly.

'There is every need!' Cerys's hands were clenched now; she beat them against her skirts in time with the words. 'Hal is a very attractive man, I know . . .'

'So you admit it?' Jenny interrupted triumphantly.

'I've never denied it. I can see he's a man who can easily turn a girl's head. That's what concerns me so. Please, Jenny, please think about what you are doing – for all our sakes. But most of all for your own. Think where this could end.'

Jenny's colour rose a little higher, but she glared at Cerys defiantly.

'I don't know what you're talking about.'

'Oh, I think you do,' Cerys returned. 'You're a country girl, born and bred, Jenny. You work with animals. You're not some overprotected little miss who has barely stepped outside her parlour, and whose mama has a fit of the vapours talking of such things. You know what happens when cattle and sheep breed – and you know what happens between men and women . . .'

She broke off, appalled at the crudity of what she had just said. They were not delicate little ladies, either of them, it was true. But all the same there were bounds of decency which should not be overstepped.

'You would be totally ruined, Jenny, and no decent man would want anything to do with you, she said, trying another tack. 'Your life would be as good as over and you'd never live it down. People talk so! Why, it's bad enough you're out on the farm with him every day unchaperoned! It can't be helped, I know, but it's enough to ruin your reputation, and—'

'Well!' Jenny exploded, interrupting her. 'You're a fine one to talk, Cerys, and no mistake! You are alone all day with a man too if I am not much mistaken. What about your reputation?'

'Oh don't be so silly!' Cerys snapped. 'That is quite different, and in any case I am not alone with him. There are servants in the house, and I have the children.'

'Servants can be banished to the kitchens, and the children can be found something to occupy them to leave you free,' Jenny said. 'Perhaps I am the one who should be talking to you, Cerys – warning you of the dangers of working for a

187

very attractive older man who has somehow managed to avoid saddling himself with a wife and is used to getting his own way. Perhaps I should be warning you of what people will be saying.' She raised the pitch of her tone to a shrill gossipy whine: '"Do you really suppose that Chas Wallace hired Cerys Page for her housekeeping skills? Oh no – it's her skills in the bedroom he pays her for!"'

The horrible mimicry was cut short as Cerys slapped Jenny full on the face. Jenny gasped, her hand flying to her stinging cheek, then took a step backward, her eyes wide with shock above her fingers.

'Oh Jenny – I'm sorry – I'm sorry!'

Cerys was equally shocked at what she had done. She could scarcely believe she had actually struck Jenny, however outrageous the things she had said.

'Well!' Jenny caught her breath. She was no longer angry either; the slap had burst the ever-expanding bubble for both of them. 'You don't like it, you see, do you, Cerys, when the tables are turned. It's all right for you to tell me how to live my life, but a different story if I bring yours into it.'

'Because what you just accused me of is utter nonsense, Jenny,' Cerys said. 'Surely you can't think . . .'

'I don't know what I think,' Jenny admitted. 'Oh, I don't think you are behaving improperly, not really. I was just stung into saying that. But I do think Chas Wallace must have some ulterior motive, Cerys. A man like him . . . he wants something, I'm sure. Our land, I wouldn't be surprised. You can't trust the squattocracy, you know. They didn't get where they are by honourable means.'

Cerys winced inwardly as Jenny's words hit her like a kick in the stomach from a mule, and suddenly the realization that the deeds for her land were sitting in the strong room of Chas Wallace's lawyer loomed large in her mind.

Unaware of her turmoil, Jenny was continuing: 'And I've seen the change in you, too, these last weeks, Cerys. You're happy, aren't you? And whatever his motives, you have Chas Wallace to thank for that.'

'Oh Jenny . . .' Cerys was overcome with confusion now.

'Surely you don't think . . . I could never be unfaithful to Will's memory! Never!'

A small sad smile twisted Jenny's mouth. 'But you will be, Cerys, you will be. However much you disbelieve that now, you are still a young woman with all your life before you. Will is dead –' her voice cracked; somehow she regained control of herself – 'but you are alive, and life is for the living. I don't begrudge you your happiness, Cerys. Please don't begrudge me mine.'

Cerys looked at Jenny mutely, at the pretty face bearing the angry red marks left by her fingers and the eyes brimming now with tears.

There was nothing more she could say. She opened her arms, and Jenny went into them. For the moment all their differences were forgotten in an uprush of sisterly love.

Cerys could not sleep, though when she had first gone to bed she had drifted off the moment her head touched the pillow.

When she and Jenny had come out of their long, loving hug Cerys had fetched the apple brandy and poured them a glass each, for they were both shaky and badly upset by the quarrel, and the apple brandy, to which she was not in the least accustomed, combined with tiredness, had sent her into a deep slumber.

But a few hours later she was wide awake again. Her mouth felt parched and dry; she got up and poured herself a glass of water, then went back to bed expecting to drift off once more. But it had not happened. Everything she and Jenny had said to one another was going around and around in her head in an endless carousel, and underlying it was the pervasive sense of unease that remained of her anxiety for what was going on between Jenny and Hal.

But strangely what kept coming back to haunt her most of all was what Jenny had said about her and Chas Wallace.

Was that really what people thought – that she was more than just a housekeeper to him? Her cheeks burned in the darkness as she imagined the town gossips with their tongues wagging and their heads nodding sagely. But how much more they would have had to talk about if Kitty Jackson had not turned her down so arbitrarily for the barmaid's position at the Commercial Hotel!

No, the thing that really kept coming back to haunt her was what Jenny had said about replacing Will in her life – and in her heart.

It was an awful thought, one that she shrank from with every fibre of her being. Will was her husband. He might be dead, but she still thought of herself as his wife, still yearned to touch him and hear his voice, still sometimes even expected him to come walking in through the door telling her this had all been nothing but a terrible dream. The very idea that she might one day wake to see a face other than his on the pillow beside her was anathema to her, the suggestion that she could be with someone else as she had been with him utterly repellent. She had given Will her heart, and dead or not, with him it would always remain. She simply could not imagine ever feeling about anyone the way she had felt about him.

And yet . . . and yet . . . guilt stirred within her. Jenny was right – she was already almost happy again at times. Only this afternoon, driving home with the children, she had been singing, and not just because children want, and need, to sing, but because she had wanted to sing too. Life had begun to return to something like normal . . . and with Will not there to share it.

She didn't want to be unhappy, of course, but perversely neither did she want to be happy without him. It seemed to her very like a betrayal. And even worse . . .

Cerys remembered the strange feelings she had experienced with regard to Chas Wallace, the touches that had prickled over her skin, the melting inside when his eyes met hers, and the trickle of guilt turned into a flood. Dear God, she could not be feeling anything for him! She must not! It was ridiculous, in any case, to imagine he might share those feelings, whatever Jenny might suggest. He was a bachelor, one who enjoyed his freedom and liked the company of women like Kitty Jackson. But supposing by going to work for him she had given him quite the wrong idea? Suppose, like Hal Tucker, he should try something with her? What would she do?

Oh, you are being ridiculous! Cerys told herself, humping

the bedclothes over her perspiring body. Chas Wallace had been kind, that was all, and if he had any designs at all they were not on her but on her land.

But the anxiety and the guilt and some other emotion she could not identify – or did not try to – refused to go away. It was a very long time before Cerys once more fell asleep.

'Mama! Mama! The puppies have been born!'

Molly came racing into the laundry room at Wells Court, where Cerys was sorting a pile of clean sheets, Ritchie tottering behind her on his fat little legs.

Cerys looked up. Her head was aching – a result, no doubt, of her sleepless night if not the apple brandy – and there were dark circles beneath her eyes.

'You've seen them, have you?' she asked.

'Yes! Yes! They're beautiful! And what do you think? Mr Wallace says we can choose one for our very own!'

'Molly,' Cerys said wearily. 'I have already told you, we cannot possibly have a puppy.'

Molly's face fell. 'Oh Mama! Please! They're only very little!'

'But they grow,' Cerys said. 'And anyway, a puppy takes a great deal of looking after. I'm sorry, Molly, but it is out of the question.'

'Come and see them!' Molly tugged at her hand. 'You must come and see them!'

Cerys sighed. 'Very well. I'll come and see them when I have put these sheets away. But don't think that means I am going to change my mind. We are not having a puppy, and that is that.'

Molly and Ritchie trailed after her whilst she took the pile of clean bedding to the linen cupboard, Molly still chattering excitedly and plainly impatient. Then Cerys took Ritchie by the hand and followed the little girl outside.

Chas Wallace was in the yard, examining the hooves of Lupus, his grey gelding – to see if he needed to be shod, Cerys imagined. He looked up and smiled at the little procession; Cerys, her inner turmoil of the previous night still very clear in her mind, felt her face grow hot. She nodded, managed a quick stiff smile of response, and hurried past him.

The puppies, together with their mother, Poll, were in one of the outbuildings. There were five of them, small round bundles, suckling on Poll, wobbling around her on stubby, uncertain legs, and falling one on the other.

Ned, the stable lad, stood in the doorway watching them, an inane grin of pleasure splitting his open, but rather ugly, face.

'Steady on, Miss Molly!' he cautioned her. 'Don't you go a-scaring them now! They ain't a day old yet!'

'Look, Mama, look!' Molly tugged at Cerys's sleeve. Her face was alight.

In spite of her reservations – and her mood – Cerys could not help smiling. The puppies certainly were adorable; it was not difficult to see why Molly was entranced.

'So – which one do you like the best?'

At the sound of Chas's voice, Cerys swung round. He was standing at her shoulder, very tall, very strong. With her new-found awareness, Cerys felt the colour deepening in her cheeks, and moved away a little.

'Molly says you offered to let us have one of them,' she said, and her voice came out sounding brisk. 'I'm afraid though that such a thing is out of the question.'

'Oh Mama, please!' Molly begged.

'Molly!' Cerys said sharply. 'I have already explained to you that we could not possibly cope with a puppy.'

'Oh, I wasn't going to suggest you took it home with you!' Chas said quickly. 'I can quite see the problems that would cause. My idea was that if the children were to decide which one they would like, I could keep it here for them. They are here every day, after all, and would be able to play with it and watch it grow.'

'Oh!' Cerys scarcely knew what to say. In truth there was nothing she could say. The decision seemed to have been taken out of her hands. 'It's very kind of you,' she said weakly. 'I'm sure it would give them a great deal of pleasure.'

Molly was jumping up and down with excitement now.

'So which one is it to be?' Chas asked, smiling at her. 'Or

do you want to wait a day or two before you decide? It will be six or seven weeks yet before they are ready to leave their mother in any case.'

Molly, however, was not about to let the chance pass her by. She was too afraid Cerys might come up with some objection and even yet foil her ardent desire for a puppy of her very own.

'That one!' she cried, pointing to a white pup with one black eye and three brown socks. 'That one, please!'

'A good choice,' Chas approved. 'Now you will have to think of a name for it, won't you?'

'Is it a boy or a girl?' Cerys asked.

'That one is a girl, isn't it, Ned?'

Ned nodded. 'Aye, that she be.'

'So what girls' names do you like?' Chas asked Molly.

Molly hesitated for only a moment. Then: 'Cinderella!' she cried.

Cerys could not keep from laughing. 'It's her favourite fairy story. But it's a bit of a mouthful for a dog's name, Molly!'

'You can always call her Cinders for short,' Chas suggested.

'No! She's Cinderella!' Molly insisted, but Cerys could not help thinking it would not be too long before the puppy did become Cinders.

'Very well, Cinderella it is,' Chas agreed gravely. 'Ned will look after her for you, won't you, Ned? And you can come and see her just as often as you like.'

'Oh, I shall stay with her all the time,' Molly insisted. And Ritchie, not to be outdone, echoed her.

'Stay! Me stay!'

His meaning was very clear, though it was the first time Cerys had ever heard him string two words together.

He must be going soft in his old age, Chas thought – offering to keep a dog here just for the benefit of two children who weren't even his. Wells Court already had its full complement of dogs; it had been his full intention to find homes for all this litter and drown the ones he couldn't. But Molly had been so eager, so excited – and little Ritchie, too, though he wasn't yet old enough to express it fully. They had got under his skin, these two little ones – he, who had never cared much for children – thought them nothing but a nuisance, in fact.

Perhaps, he thought, it had something to do with their mother. For she seemed to have got under his skin too. Where she and her family were concerned it seemed he behaved totally out of character.

He glanced at her, at her pretty face, marred this morning by dark shadows beneath her eyes – and just a little flushed, standing there with Ritchie in her arms. Her full lower lip was caught and puckered between her teeth – a habit he had noticed before when she was thinking hard about something. Quite suddenly Chas was filled with a desire to kiss it.

Abruptly he turned away. Good lord, never mind going soft – he was going mad!

It did nothing to detract, though, from the pleasure he was feeling in the children's excitement, and the good feeling that came from knowing he had done something to brighten their lives.

And that, for a moment, however briefly, he had shared their excitement.

# Fifteen

Cerys entered the last figure in the appropriate column of the accounts book, blotted the page, and laid down her pen. Then she nodded her head, slowly and with satisfaction. Things were definitely improving. The finances were much healthier. Her wage from Wells Court, which she still felt was generous to say the least of it, had made an enormous difference, and expenditure was down too, since both she and the children ate there in the middle of the day. Soon now they could get some of the stock to market, and that would be another boost. She would speak to Jenny about it when she came in.

With the lighter evenings Jenny and Hal had taken to walking out after dinner, and though Cerys was not happy about it, she had come to the conclusion it was best not to interfere. The last thing she wanted was another row with Jenny, and in any case she really could not afford to lose Hal just now. Already he had the new season's breeding programme under way, and without his know-how she did not think that would have happened. She was still of the opinion that Hal was leading Jenny on, and she still did not like him one little bit. But since the angry words she and Jenny had exchanged concerning him she had come to realize that trying to make Jenny see that would only do more harm than good.

Jenny would just have to find out the hard way if Hal really was leading her a merry dance. And perhaps he wasn't. Perhaps she was wrong, Cerys conceded, and he really had fallen for her. Certainly he seemed a good deal less careless of her feelings these days, and they were almost constantly in one another's company.

Cerys was just replacing the ledger on the shelf when there

was a tap at the door. A very soft tap, so soft that had the house not been so quiet she might not have heard it at all.

Puzzled, she crossed to the door and opened it. Old Duggan stood there, his wizened face looking anxious.

'Duggan!' Cerys frowned. 'Is something wrong?'

'Can I have a word with you, missus?' he said by way of reply.

'Of course, Duggan. Come in.' But she was even more puzzled when he glanced furtively over his shoulder as if he was afraid someone might see him entering the house.

'What is it?' she asked when she had pushed the door to behind him.

Duggan stood for a moment, staring at the ground. He had removed his cap, and was twisting it nervously between his hands.

'Come on, Duggan, out with it!' she urged him.

'It's about Hal Tucker,' he began, and stopped again.

'What about him?'

Duggan took a deep breath and let it out on a long sigh.

'I don't trust him, missus. I don't think he's to be trusted. There – now I've said it.'

Cerys looked at him narrowly. 'What makes you say that?'

Again Duggan hesitated. 'I don't rightly know. It's everything and nothing, as you might say. It's what he does, and what he doesn't do. It's what he says, and what he doesn't say. But I tell you this, missus, there's some'ut about him, and I've thought so for a long time now. That Hal Tucker is a wrong 'un. I can feel it in my bones.'

It was the longest speech Cerys had ever heard Duggan make in all the time she had known him, and it surprised her. But the gist of what he was saying did not. It was a confirmation of her own misgivings. Her heart sank at his words and the cloud of anxiety was back, settling in around her.

'Oh Duggan.' A strand of hair had escaped from its pins; she tucked it behind her ear distractedly. 'I don't know that I totally trust him myself, but—'

'I think I've missed one or two bits and pieces,' Duggan went on doggedly. 'Not that I've got much to miss, mind you, and I know I'm getting old and forgetful, but all the same . . .'

196

Cerys's mind flew to the ten sovereigns that had been missing from her ring money. Jenny had said it must have been Mr Johnson cheating her and she had gone along with that though she had never before heard Mr Johnson's honesty questioned. Now, however, the suspicion came back to her that it might very well have been Hal, helping himself.

'You think he's stolen from you?' she asked anxiously.

'I wouldn't like to say so, not to be sure. I've got no proof. And like I say, it's more than that. I haven't always been a good boy meself – I reckon you know that. I got meself in trouble when I was nobbut a lad, and I ended up . . . Well, let's say I didn't come over from England of me own free will. There was transportation in them days.' He paused and his faded old eyes had a faraway look in them as if he were seeing another time, another place, and reliving the harsh punishment of being shipped off in chains from one side of the world to the other. Then, abruptly, he came out of his reverie and went on: 'Mr Will knew, anyway, that I'd done me time, and he still took me on. I shall always be grateful to him for that, giving me a good home to see out my last years. And I don't want to see his missus taken advantage of by the likes of Hal Tucker.'

'That's very nice of you, Duggan,' Cerys said, touched.

'You see what I'm trying to say?' Duggan persisted. 'I can't put the finger on him, but I've been around his sort enough in my life to know 'em when I see 'em.'

He broke off as the kitchen door opened, and Jenny and Hal came in, a nervous, shifty look contorting his little weasel face. Both Jenny and Hal looked surprised to see him there, though Jenny greeted him warmly enough. But Hal's expression darkened, his brow lowering, his mouth becoming a hard line.

Worried, Cerys wondered if he had guessed the reason for the old man's call. He came to the homestead for his meals, of course, but never in the middle of the evening. And Hal was nothing if not sharp.

'Thank you, Duggan. I'm much obliged to you,' she said ambiguously.

He nodded jerkily, his eyes on Hal, and left.

'What did he want?' Jenny asked when the door had closed after him.

197

'Oh, nothing of any consequence,' Cerys replied, as casually as she could manage.

Jenny was too wrapped up in Hal to pursue the matter and by the time Hal too had left for his quarters Cerys thought she had probably forgotten all about it, and was glad. She did not want another confrontation with Jenny, and she knew that if she told her the reason for Duggan's visit it would only open up old wounds all over again.

But she could not forget. It was just another straw to add to the load that was building on the proverbial camel's back. And she did not like it one little bit.

'What was your gripe to the lady of the house, old timer?' Hal demanded unpleasantly of Duggan.

The easy smile with which he favoured Jenny – and Cerys – was gone now, replaced by a mean, narrow look that was somehow all the more unpleasant because of the handsomeness of his features.

The old man, stripped now to his underwear ready for bed, looked up sharply.

'That's no business of yours.'

'It is if it was me you were complaining about,' Hal said. His voice was low and dangerous.

'And why would I be complaining about you?' Duggan returned, but his guilty look was unmistakable – the same look that had given him away more than thirty years earlier when his then employers in faraway England had accused him of stealing from them, the same look that had convinced the magistrate of his culpability and brought him the sentence of transportation to the penal colony.

'Well, I think you were.' Hal approached him threateningly. 'I think you were bearing tales.'

'Got something on your conscience, have you?' The old man was suddenly defiant. 'Aye, I think you have, Hal Tucker.'

Hal's hand shot out, fastening around Duggan's throat, pushing him back against the wall of the bunkhouse and pinning him there like a butterfly caught on a pin.

'Have a care, old timer.' He brought his face down level

with Duggan's and just a few threatening inches away from it. 'Keep your nose out of my affairs.'

Duggan's eyes were wide and alarmed in his lined old face, but the spirit that had kept him going through his long convict days flickered still on occasions, and it flickered now.

'I can see right through you, Hal Tucker,' he managed.

Hal's lip curled. 'Is that so? Well, you'll keep what you see to yourself if you know what's good for you.'

He increased the pressure of his hand around Duggan's throat as if to choke him, then banged the old man's head back against the wall a couple of times, released him, and turned away.

Duggan gasped for breath, his own hands going to his throat where Hal's grip had compressed his Adam's apple, and reeled dizzily towards his bunk.

Hal towered above him.

'Let that be a warning to you, old timer. Next time I won't be so gentle. No one messes with Hal Tucker and gets away with it. Certainly not an old lag like you.'

With a vicious movement he kicked Duggan's feet out from beneath him. The old man went crashing down, catching his shoulder on the edge of the bunk and crying out in pain and shock.

Hal looked down at him for a moment, his eyes full of furious hatred. Then, with a satisfied smirk, he turned away.

There was something about Wells Court, Cerys thought, that was pure tranquillity. The moment she turned the sulky into the drive each morning her spirits began to lift and her troubles to drop away.

Strange, really, that such a busy working farm should have such an air of ordered calm – and yet, perhaps, not so strange, for it was indeed *ordered*. The men worked hard, but they seemed to take a pride and a pleasure in their labours, and each and every one of them brought with them years of experience and acquired skill. The fruits of their efforts were there all around her as she drove through the neatly edged paddocks and orchards and into the pristine stable yard where Ned sat in the warm spring sunshine polishing tack with loving care.

199

But it was the house itself that was balm to her weary spirits. The rooms were so large, light and airy compared with the dark, cramped rooms at Kanunga, and she loved the furnishings on which no expense had been spared and the artefacts from around the world that decorated the place and breathed out an air of luxury such as she had never known. Yet for all its grandeur there was nothing in the least overwhelming about Wells Court. Instead, there was a feeling of careless comfort that made one feel instantly at home, a feeling of open welcome and safe haven from a cruel, hard world.

Only Chas Wallace's presence could disturb her calm here, and oddly it was not an unpleasant sensation, merely unsettling in a way she could not truly understand. But today he did not appear to be in. There was nothing to ruffle her feathers, and the peaceful atmosphere and the sun shining in through the big windows was balm to her frayed nerves.

It was mid-morning when she glanced out of the window to see a sulky pulled by a solid-looking pony heading up the drive towards the house. Surprised, for visitors were few and far between out here in the country, Cerys tidied her hair, took off her apron, and went to the door.

Amy Hawker, one of the mainstays of the Medlock community, was standing there wearing what looked like the Sunday-best gown and bonnet she would normally deck herself in to attend services at chapel.

'Why, Mrs Page!' she said, affecting surprise, though Cerys had the distinct impression she was not surprised at all. If anything her expression was one of smug satisfaction. 'I never expected to find you here!'

'Hadn't you heard I had taken employment with Mr Wallace?' Cerys returned. 'I would have thought it was common knowledge in Medlock. Information of that sort usually spreads like wildfire.'

Amy Hawker drew herself up.

'Well, I'm not one to listen to gossip,' she proclaimed self-righteously, and Cerys was hard put to it not to smile. Amy Hawker was well known for the avid interest she took in the affairs of her neighbours.

'How can I help you, anyway?' she asked.

Amy Hawker arranged her reticule fussily on her wrist and folded her hands across her ample middle.

'It's Mr Wallace I came to see. Is he at home?'

'I'm afraid not,' Cerys said. 'And I don't know when he'll be back. Can I perhaps give him a message so that your journey won't have been entirely wasted?'

Amy Hawker considered. 'Well, yes, I dare say you could, she said, a little reluctantly. 'If you're quite sure there's no point in my waiting.'

'Come in and wait by all means, Mrs Hawker, if that's what you'd prefer to do,' Cerys said. 'But Mr Wallace could be out until late afternoon for all I know. If he's out on the stud farm, as I suspect he is, he is usually gone for a very long time.'

Amy Hawker sniffed. 'Stud', with all its connotations, was not a word she cared for, and not one, in her opinion, that should be in a lady's vocabulary.

'Very well. The reason I am here is to ask Mr Wallace if he might be so good as to donate a prize for the Spring Fayre we are holding at our church in Medlock,' she said rather pompously.

'I see.' Cerys could not help thinking that was only part of the truth. If she had wanted to be certain of catching Chas in she surely would not have chosen mid-morning, when it was quite likely he would be working, to make her call. In Cerys's opinion, it was probably an excuse – though a legitimate one, no doubt. In all likelihood she had heard a rumour that Cerys was working as Chas Wallace's housekeeper and she had come here with the intention of checking out the validity of the story so that she could be the one in the little town who was in the know, the fount of first-hand knowledge.

'Mr Wallace has always been very generous to us in the past,' Amy went on, 'and it is especially important we do well with the Spring Fayre this year. The church roof is badly in need of repair.'

*As you would know if you took the trouble to attend services.* The unspoken criticism hung in the air.

'Certainly I will pass your message on,' Cerys said. 'And if I know Mr Wallace, I'm sure he will be pleased to do anything he can to help you out.'

'I'm much obliged to you.' Amy Hawker hesitated, apparently reluctant to go. Then: 'How are you getting along yourself, Mrs Page?'

'We're managing, thank you,' Cerys said.

'Yes, of course, you have that young man to help you, haven't you?'

'Hal Tucker. Yes. He has been very good.'

'I'm sure.' Amy Hawker's beady little eyes were sharp. 'Jenny certainly seems very taken with him.'

Cerys was startled by the extent of the woman's knowledge. Word certainly travelled fast, considering how isolated the farms were from the township and from each other. But how could Amy Hawker possibly know about Jenny's attachment to Hal Tucker?

'Working together as they do it's almost inevitable they should become close,' she said evasively.

'Not just that, surely!' Amy Hawker's tone might almost have been crowing. 'When I saw them in Medlock . . . well, there was no mistaking it – they were certainly very taken with each other.'

Her words startled Cerys still more. She did not know Jenny and Hal had been to Medlock together.

'When was that?' she asked before she could stop herself – and immediately regretted it. When, oh when, would she learn to think before she spoke?

'Oh, some while ago now,' Amy replied smugly. 'Well, before poor Will died, anyway. I remember wondering what he would think about his little sister being alone in the company of a young man if he knew about it.'

'I think you must be mistaken, Mrs Hawker,' Cerys said, a trifle stiffly. 'Jenny only met Hal when he came to the farm after Will's death.'

Amy Hawker bridled. 'Oh well, if you say so.' But her tone indicated she still thought she was right and Cerys wrong. Women like her liked to think they knew everything, Cerys thought, irritated.

'I'll pass your message on to Mr Wallace,' she said briskly. 'When is the Spring Fayre?'

'In two weeks' time. Perhaps we shall see you and Mr

Wallace there. And Jenny and the young man too,' Amy added archly.

'Perhaps.' Cerys was anxious to bring this visit to a speedy conclusion and tacit agreement seemed the best way to achieve this, though she thought it highly unlikely that either she, Jenny or Hal would have either the time or the inclination to patronize the Spring Fayre. Chas, of course, was a different matter. His time was his own. But in all honesty, she could not imagine him wanting to dally at stalls and sideshows either.

When Amy Hawker had gone, disappearing at a slow and stately trot down the drive, Cerys went back to her work. But the woman's prying rankled, and her words kept coming back to Cerys.

She didn't like to think that Jenny and Hal were causing talk in the neighbourhood, though she supposed it was inevitable. A girl spending so much time unchaperoned in the company of a young man was bound to be seen by some as improper, and the fact that it was out of necessity would be overlooked in the avid enthusiasm to have something to gossip about.

It was disturbing her too that they had been into Medlock together, and she knew nothing about it. Amy Hawker was wrong when she said it had been prior to Will's death, of course. She had to be. But Cerys couldn't understand why they should have gone into Medlock together at all.

Something must have cropped up, she supposed, something they needed urgently, perhaps, to secure fence posts or . . . oh, any one of a hundred things. Since she was now away from the farm for the best part of the day she had lost touch with what was going on. But all the same . . .

The uncomfortable feeling that something she did not know about was going on still lingered. For Cerys, some of the brightness had gone out of the day and the tranquillity that was Wells Court was, for the moment, marred.

The middle of the day came and went with no sign of Chas. It was mid-afternoon and Cerys was thinking about leaving herself when he came in. She could see at once that something was wrong. He looked drawn, the long lines on his face deeper than ever, and his whole demeanour was dispirited

203

if not actually defeated. His appearance was dishevelled too, sleeves rolled back to the elbows, dirt splattering his breeches and shirt.

'Hell's teeth, what a day!' He flung his hat down on the table and ran his fingers through his hair.

'What's happened?' Cerys asked.

'I've lost my best stallion,' he replied bluntly. 'They called me early this morning to say something was wrong, and we have been fighting all day to save him. But in the end there was nothing we could do.'

'Oh I am so sorry!' Cerys knew how much the animals at the stud meant to Chas. Not only did he care for them, but also they represented years of careful breeding. 'What was wrong with him?'

'Twisted gut, I think,' Chas replied shortly. 'Is the water hot? I need a bath.'

'I can have it ready for you in no time,' Cerys said. 'But first I think you should have a cup of tea.'

He smiled briefly, the hard lines between mouth and nose softening.

'The woman's touch.'

'It will do you good,' Cerys said. 'You've had nothing all day, and there's nothing like a cup of tea when you're feeling down.'

'A good stiff brandy would be better.' He smiled again at her look of disapproval. 'A cup of tea will do fine for now. I'll have the brandy later.'

'When I've gone home, you mean.'

'When you've gone home, certainly. You think strong drink is the devil's brew, don't you, Mrs Page? And you don't care who knows it.'

'I've seen the trouble it can cause,' Cerys said primly. 'I once lived in Sydney, remember, and the men spilling out of the sly grog shops and bars were no better than animals, fighting and using bad language and—'

'You don't mean your parents allowed you near sly grog shops?' One eyebrow lifted.

'Since there was one on the corner of the street where my father had his store, I could scarcely avoid it!' she returned tartly. 'It was not a pretty sight, Mr Wallace, I assure you, to see men behaving so.'

'Indeed I am sure it was not. A small noggin, however, for medicinal purposes . . . surely you would not begrudge me that?'

'You are laughing at me!' she said, indignant.

'I wouldn't laugh at you, Mrs Page. Truth to tell –' his expression lowered again, the harsh lines reappearing – 'I do not at this moment feel like laughing at all.'

Remorse filled her. 'I am sure you do not. Oh, have your brandy if that's what you want, Mr Wallace. I don't suppose it will do you any harm, and it might do you good.'

'Well thank you, Mrs Page,' he said ironically. 'That is very kind of you.'

'Well go on then!' He made no move to get it, and she gave a small, impatient shake of her head, crossed to the cabinet where the brandy was kept, and poured him a glass. As she turned back towards him she saw that he was watching her, his eyes narrowed and intent.

Flustered by the depth of that look, she hesitated for a moment like a startled gazelle, then crossed the room and thrust the glass at him. As he took it, his fingers brushed hers, lingering for a moment, and the same thrill she had felt when he had restrained her hand on the reins shivered over her skin and set her whole body alight.

'Do you know, Mrs Page, I am not sure I need this now,' he said, his fingers still trapping hers on the glass, but lightly, so lightly that it might have been accidental. 'You've cheered me up and I feel better already.'

His eyes on her were still intent and unwavering, but also slightly amused. She pulled her hand free. Her heart was hammering, her cheeks hot. She turned quickly away.

'I must go and get the children. They're out in the stable with those puppies again, as you might guess, and Ned is keeping an eye on them.' She was chattering inanely, she knew, but it was anything – anything – to cover the confusion she was feeling, anything to overcome the awkwardness of the moment and return to something like normality.

She fled out the door. Halfway along the passage and she

suddenly remembered Amy Hawker's visit. Reluctantly she went back.

Whether Chas had still needed the brandy or not, he was drinking it anyway, leaning against the dresser, the glass cupped between his strong, weather-beaten hands.

'Back so soon, Mrs Page?'

His amused look and the tone of his voice disconcerted her all over again.

'I forgot to tell you Mrs Hawker came by.'

'Mrs Hawker?'

'Yes, you know – Amy Hawker, from Medlock. She's one of the stalwarts of the church there.'

'Oh, that Mrs Hawker. The famous busybody. What did she want? To save my soul?'

'She wanted you to give a prize, or something to sell at their Spring Fayre in two weeks' time,' Cerys said. 'I told her I was sure you would.'

'Really? Well, I suppose I shall have to then. Anything to keep the good people of Medlock happy.' He lifted his glass, glancing approvingly at the amber liquid. 'I think,' he added wickedly, 'that I shall donate a bottle of good brandy.'

Cerys's mouth opened wide, then she clamped it shut, gripping her lip with her teeth to hold back the giggle that was bubbling up inside her. If she disapproved of strong drink herself, how much more would Amy Hawker and the ladies of the church! The very thought of how such a gift would be received was amusing in the extreme.

'You are very naughty, Mr Wallace,' she said. 'And I am going home now.'

'You're sure you won't join me in a brandy?'

'And run my sulky off the road because I am incapable? No thank you, Mr Wallace.'

'Ah!' he said. 'You'd been on the brandy the day you let your gig go out of control in Medlock and damaged my piano, had you?'

Instantly her defences were up.

'You know very well I most certainly had not!' she returned indignantly. 'Good day to you, Mr Wallace.'

'Good day, Mrs Page.'

The suppressed laughter in his voice and the gaze of those narrowed eyes followed her out of the room.

As Cerys drove into the yard at Kanunga, Jenny came running out of the stable to greet her.

'Oh, thank goodness you're here, Cerys!'

'Why, what on earth is wrong?' Cerys asked, alarmed.

'It's Duggan.' Jenny was beside herself. 'He's had an accident. I think he's been kicked by one of the horses. He's unconscious, and there's a lot of blood. I didn't know what to do . . .'

Cerys stamped on a feeling of panic that twisted in her own stomach.

'Where's Hal? Isn't he here?'

'No – he's still out on the land somewhere. I'm all on my own . . .' The usually capable Jenny seemed to have gone to pieces.

'Go into the house, children,' Cerys ordered, trying to sound calm and authoritative. 'Molly – look after Ritchie until I come in.'

The children, looking solemn and frightened, did as they were bid, Molly taking Ritchie by the hand and urging him along, and Cerys went with Jenny into the stable.

Duggan was lying half in and half out of the stall with Fango, his old black horse, standing over him, more protective than threatening. He was not moving, and as Jenny had said, there was indeed a lot of blood oozing from his head and staining the straw on which he lay.

'He looks bad, doesn't he?' Jenny said worriedly. 'I can't understand it! Fango is usually as gentle as a baby!'

'Never mind that now.' It was Cerys's opinion that no horse could ever be totally trusted, but this was not the moment for a discussion on the subject. 'He needs a doctor, that much is plain. You had better ride into Medlock and fetch one. There's no way we could get Duggan into the sulky, and in any case, I'm not sure he should be moved.'

Jenny hovered for a moment as if mesmerized by the inert and bleeding body she had discovered when she had come to stable Merlin.

'Go on – and be as quick as you can,' Cerys instructed. 'I'll stay with Duggan, at least until Hal comes in.'

With one last look, Jenny left, and Cerys dropped to her knees in the straw, taking Duggan's worn old hand in hers and speaking to him softly as if he could hear her.

'You're going to be all right, Duggan. The doctor will be here soon and he'll make you better.'

But she did not really believe her own words. The day that had begun with such promise was going to end, Cerys feared, in tragedy.

# Sixteen

'I simply don't understand,' Cerys said. 'I simply don't understand how it happened.'

It was late evening now. Jenny had ridden like the wind into Medlock and summoned Dr Stewart. He had examined Duggan, shaken his head, and stated his doubts as to Duggan's chances of recovery. Duggan was an old man and he had taken a severe blow; Dr Stewart was not hopeful. Duggan might or might not recover consciousness; even if he did, it would be a long haul back and he might never be fit for much again. Whatever, he needed expert nursing care and medical attention and his best chance would be if Dr Stewart were to take him back to the little hospital he had set up in Medlock.

Between them they had managed to get Duggan into Dr Stewart's carriage and he had driven away.

Cerys was distraught. She was very fond of Duggan, and for such a fate to befall him seemed horribly cruel. Jenny, too, was very shaken, and the two women talked and were silent in bursts.

Only Hal seemed unaffected by what had occurred.

'He can't complain. He's had his life,' he said carelessly, and it was all Cerys could do not to strike him.

'How could it have happened?' she asked again now, pausing with her hands in the water as she washed the dishes. 'Fango is as gentle as a lamb.'

'You can't trust any horse,' Hal offered. 'If he's startled or provoked . . .'

'But what could have startled him? And Duggan would certainly never provoke him! Do you suppose he collapsed? He must have been on the floor to be kicked in the head like that,' Cerys said distractedly.

209

'Asleep, I shouldn't wonder.' Hal was lounging in one chair, his feet up on another, and suddenly his uncaring attitude was too much for Cerys.

'Isn't it time you were going to your own quarters?' she said sharply. 'There will be more for you to do tomorrow with Duggan in the hospital.'

'I can only do what I can do. And let's not pretend the old chap was much help anyway.' Hal got up in his own time and stretched lazily. 'At least I won't have to put up with his snoring tonight. I shall have the place to myself.'

Cerys bit her lip hard to keep from saying something that would really set the cat among the pigeons. When she turned back she saw that Hal had his arm round Jenny's waist and was whispering something in her ear. Cerys did not need to hear his words to be able to guess what he was saying. Jenny's blush and giggle said it all. He was suggesting that she would be able to keep him company in privacy now, no doubt.

Oh, how she wished she could tell the beastly man to pack his bags and go! But whilst they were so dependent on him, and whilst Jenny was so besotted with him, there was nothing she could do.

'I'm going to bed,' Cerys said when the clearing away was eventually done – in the state she and Jenny were in it had taken much longer than usual.

But she knew she wouldn't sleep, and she was right. She lay with the events of the day running around and around inside her head, every nerve and muscle taut and restless.

It was an hour or more later when she heard soft creeping footsteps going past her room, followed, a minute or so later, by the creak of the bolt and the sound of the kitchen door being closed softly.

Cerys closed her eyes and breathed out a deep sigh. She'd known it! Jenny was going to Hal. Oh, the silly, silly girl!

Suddenly everything became too much for Cerys. Tears gathered in her eyes and ran down her cheeks and she began to sob. When at last she was exhausted she drifted into a restless sleep. She had not heard Jenny return.

Next morning, tired and fraught, Cerys got the children dressed and set out for Wells Court. Life had to go on, and if she didn't appear, Chas would wonder what had happened to her. But it was all a greater effort than usual and the children, sensing that something was very wrong, played up more than usual.

At one point she had to stop the sulky and give them a talking-to because she truly thought they were going to fall out. With her nerves so frayed, another disaster seemed just a heartbeat away.

Chas was in the kitchen when she arrived. After yesterday's unsettling encounter she could have wished he would be out and she would not have to face him, but now, surprisingly, she was glad to see him there.

'How are you this morning?' he greeted her, but from the narrow way he was looking at her she thought that he could tell by her face that something was wrong.

'Oh, the most awful thing happened yesterday!' she burst out, and went on to tell him all about it.

'I'm sorry to hear that,' Chas said sympathetically when she had finished. 'You must be very worried.'

'I am! Poor Duggan . . . oh, Mr Wallace, he looked so ill! So frail! Just lying there, with this awful wound to his head . . .' Her voice trembled and tailed away.

'It's strange, I know,' she went on after a moment. 'He's just an employee and I've never really had a great deal to do with him apart from providing his meals. But now this has happened, and it feels like he's one of the family.'

'That's only natural,' Chas said soothingly.

'He's such a funny old soul,' Cerys went on reflectively. 'He was a convict, you know. But his heart's in the right place. Only the other day he came to me to tell me he was worried that Hal Tucker might be taking advantage of us.'

Chas's gaze sharpened. 'He thought that?'

'Yes. Well, so do I, really. I haven't trusted him for a long while. But what can I do?' She broke off again, her anxieties and distress clearly evident in her face.

'Would you like to go into Medlock and see how Duggan is this morning?' Chas asked suddenly.

Cerys raised her head quickly, surprised. 'Oh, I would! But . . .'

'I'll drive you in. I'm sure Florence or Edith will look after the children whilst we're gone.'

Molly, who was totally unsettled though not quite understanding what was going on, was holding on to Cerys's skirts, looking up at the pair of them, her eyes huge.

'Would you be a good girl for Florence for a little while if I were to go out?' Cerys asked her.

Molly nodded.

'And make sure Ritchie is a good boy for me too?'

Another nod.

'That's settled, then,' Chas said decisively. 'I'll go and have the gig made ready.'

He strode away and Cerys, overcome with gratitude, was left thinking what an astonishing man he could be.

Medlock was all a-bustle in the warm spring sunshine. Under normal circumstances, Cerys might have reflected how much it had grown in just the few years she had known it, as selectors took up parcels of land in the surrounding countryside and the town and its traders expanded to meet their needs. This morning, however, she could think of nothing but Duggan, her stomach tying itself in knots at the prospect of seeing him lying, perhaps unconscious still, in his sickbed.

Dr Stewart's house and the little hospital he had built beside it lay on the far outskirts of the town, a neat single-storey slab building with a shingle-roofed verandah, all edged in by a picket fence.

Cerys's throat closed with nervousness as the gig drew up outside, and she grasped her reticule with hands she could not keep from trembling.

'I was intending to go and seek out the good Mrs Hawker whilst you were visiting Duggan, but on second thoughts I'll wait here for you,' Chas said, and again she was struck by his perception and kindness.

She climbed down from the gig and pushed open the gate in the picket fence, wondering whether she should go directly to the hospital building or first knock on the door of the doctor's house. The matter was resolved for her when the door to the hospital opened and Dr Stewart's wife, Martha, who acted as his nurse, came bustling out, wrapped in an enormous apron and carrying a bowl.

Cerys recognized her at once – the doctor and his wife were well-known figures in the town, with good reason – but Martha Stewart had not the slightest idea who Cerys was. Though her husband had delivered Molly and tended to Cerys after the birth of Ritchie, the two women had never met.

'Can I help you?' she asked briskly in the broad Scots accent that had not been diluted one iota in all the years since she and Dr Stewart had left the Highlands to start a new life on the other side of the world.

'I've come to see Duggan Priest,' Cerys said. 'Dr Stewart brought him in from our farm yesterday afternoon. I'm Cerys Page.'

'Ah.' Martha Stewart's tight-featured face gave nothing away. It was an expression she had cultivated through years of nursing. Not for her to give a patient hope or drag them down into the depths of despair. That was left to her husband in his omnipotent position of qualified physician. 'You had better speak to Dr Stewart. I'll fetch him.'

She disappeared, not into the hospital, but the house, still carrying her bowl, which slopped a little water on to the doorstep as she pushed open the door. Cerys stood uncertainly, waiting. Was anyone with Duggan? Surely they wouldn't leave him alone and unattended?

It seemed to Cerys an age before the door opened again and Dr Stewart himself emerged.

'You had better come inside, Mrs Page.' His tone was gentler than his wife's, though overlaid with the same soft burr. Cerys hesitated, and he motioned to her with a quick, impatient gesture. 'Come on, lass. We'll not do you any harm.'

If this was an attempt to put Cerys at her ease, it had no effect. Cerys stepped nervously into the hallway, then followed the doctor into the small room off it which served as his surgery.

'Sit down, lassie.' He indicated an upright chair facing his own captain's chair, and though Cerys did as she was bid, her apprehension was growing by the minute.

'How is he?' she blurted out.

The doctor seated himself before replying.

'It's not good news, I'm afraid.' His tone was grave.

'You mean . . . he's no better?'

Dr Stewart settled his broad, capable hands on his plump thighs.

'I am afraid not.' He paused. 'Duggan Priest passed away in the night.'

'Oh!' Cerys's hand flew to her mouth. In a way she had been expecting this from the moment the doctor had invited her into the house, yet it was still a shock. It ran through her in an icy wave and she felt a sob rising in her throat. 'Oh no!'

'I'm sorry, lass, but it's most likely for the best. Mr Priest's injury was very severe. I doubt he'd ever have been good for anything again even if we could have saved him. I'm afraid there was nothing I could do,' Dr Stewart told her.

'I see,' Cerys said numbly. And then: 'Thank you, Doctor.'

The room was swimming round her. Through a haze she heard the doctor say: 'He was your employee, was he not? Doubtless you will be taking care of the funeral arrangements.'

'Oh – yes.' It wasn't something she had even thought about, but if she didn't take on the arrangements, who would?

'I'd be obliged, then, if you'd deal with it as a matter of urgency. I cannot keep Mr Priest here for long, you understand.'

'No – of course not.'

'And there will be the little matter of my bill. For coming out to Kanunga yesterday, and a night's nursing here at my hospital.'

'Yes, yes of course . . .' She had not thought of that either. A doctor's bill, on top of everything else . . .

'I'll send it out to you when it has been prepared,' he said with what Cerys thought was frightening matter-of-factness. But then, of course, Dr Stewart was used to coping with death. It was something he frequently encountered in his calling.

'Can I . . . Can I see him?' she asked in a small voice.

'Aye, that you can, if you wish. My wife has him laid out and decent.'

That was what Martha Stewart had been doing when she

214

had arrived, Cerys realized. The bowl of water she had been carrying was the one she had used to wash Duggan.

'Come with me, then.' The doctor rose and Cerys followed suit. Her legs felt shaky.

He led her back outside and opened the door to the hospital. Cerys felt a moment's fear. With the exception of Will, she had never seen a dead body. But she felt she wanted to pay her last respects to Duggan. Taking a deep breath and holding on to herself very tight she followed Dr Stewart into the hospital.

Duggan lay in one of the three beds, covered, for decency, with a clean white sheet. Cerys felt another bolt of panic as Dr Stewart made to draw it back and again she held on tight to her emotions.

'There you are, you see,' Dr Stewart was saying. 'He looks very peaceful, does he not?'

Cerys could not reply. Duggan did look peaceful, she supposed, and younger perhaps than he had looked in life, with all the frown lines wiped away. But he also looked even more shrunken and tiny and very, very vulnerable.

'Oh Duggan!' she whispered, her eyes filling with tears. She reached out to touch his hands, to cross one over the other on his chest, but somehow could not bring herself to do so. Her fingers hovered for a moment, then she withdrew them quickly, almost as if she was afraid of being burned.

'Don't be afraid, lassie.' Dr Stewart took her hand and gently eased it down towards Duggan's. As she felt the touch of cold flesh she shuddered, then relaxed. Dr Stewart was right; there was nothing to be afraid of.

'Goodbye, Duggan,' she whispered. 'I'll see you get a decent burial, don't worry. And . . . and thank you . . . for everything.'

Then she turned and walked, very upright, out of the hospital.

As he had promised, Chas was waiting for her outside and he could see at once that something was very wrong. Cerys was moving like a woman in a dream, her legs moving automatically, her reticule clutched tightly between both hands. He jumped down from the gig and went to meet her.

'Cerys?' It was the first time he had used her given name. 'Cerys . . . are you . . . ?'

She looked up at him, her eyes filling with tears.

'He's dead. Duggan is dead.'

'Oh, I am so sorry . . .' He was cursing himself now for not going in with her. She had suffered enough misfortune already without having to face this on her own.

'He's dead,' she said again, as if trying to convince herself of the truth of it. 'Oh Mr Wallace, it's so unfair! He has had such a hard life, and to die here like that, all alone, with no one who cares for him . . .' The tears spilled over and ran unchecked down her cheeks.

'He was unconscious, wasn't he? He didn't know anything about it.'

'How do you know that?' she demanded fiercely. 'How do you know he didn't wake up and wonder where he was? And how long did he lie in the stable before Jenny discovered him? Was he unconscious all the time, or did he know about that too?'

The tears were flowing freely now. She scrabbled in her reticule for a handkerchief and pulled out a tiny lacy square so clearly unequal to the task that it somehow emphasized her vulnerability. Chas Wallace was suddenly overcome with tenderness towards her. It was not an emotion he was familiar with.

'Here . . .' He offered her his own kerchief.

She hesitated. 'Oh, I couldn't . . .'

'Why not? You'll be the one supervising the laundering of it,' he said with dry humour.

She managed a weak smile and took the kerchief, blowing her nose hard.

'I'm sorry . . . I didn't mean to . . . I don't usually do this . . .'

'I know you don't,' he said. 'And you have nothing to apologize for. You have had a bad shock.'

'Yes. And now I have to organize a funeral for poor Duggan. If I don't do it soon they'll give him a pauper's burial, but I don't know . . .'

She broke off. She had been about to say 'I don't know

how I'm going to pay for it', but she could not bring herself to. It seemed so mercenary with poor Duggan lying dead.

Chas read her mind.

'Don't worry about a thing. Leave it all to me. We'll go and make the arrangements now. And I'll ask for the bills to be sent to me.'

Her eyes opened very wide and she began to protest, but he interrupted her.

'Look on it as a bonus on your wages. It's to my own benefit, anyway. A housekeeper worried out of her mind is no good to me.'

'Oh, Mr Wallace, I don't know what to say . . .'

'Don't say anything.'

He turned away abruptly. He was as surprised as she was by the offer he had just heard himself make. He was, it seemed, constantly surprising himself with his reactions where Mrs Page was concerned. The town would have a field day with it too – Chas Wallace, the ruthless landholder, paying for the burial of a former convict who did not even work for him . . . oh yes, he was going soft and no mistake.

But doubtless they would have been even more shocked if they could have looked into his heart. For what Chas had really wanted to do was take Cerys Page in his arms and comfort her. And he would have done it, too, if he had not been in the main street of the town. And if he had not thought that such a gesture would drive her away . . .

For the first time Chas Wallace admitted the truth to himself. He wanted Cerys, wanted her more than he had ever wanted any woman in his life.

The realization of it was even more of a shock than any of the others that had gone before.

They buried Duggan on a blustery spring day when skies as grey and lowering as any they had endured throughout the long winter months hung over the little cemetery, but the trees that surrounded it were already bursting with new leaf and the promise of the fine, warm summer that lay ahead.

In contrast with Will's funeral on their own land when so many other farmers and townsfolk had come to pay their last respects, the only mourners around the graveside were Cerys, Jenny and Chas Wallace. Jenny had done her best to persuade Hal to attend, but Hal had replied shortly that work around the farm did not stop for funerals, someone still had to do it, and Cerys was not surprised. There had, after all, been no love lost between the two men.

She was also relieved. She did not want to be around Hal Tucker more than was absolutely necessary.

Afterwards, Chas drove Jenny back to Kanunga, and Cerys to Wells Court, where the children were being looked after by Florence and Edith.

Cerys was silent, withdrawn inside herself, and very pale.

'Are you sure you feel like driving yourself and the children home?' Chas asked as he made the sulky ready for her.

'Of course.' She smiled faintly. 'What else would I do?'

'I could drive you and collect you again tomorrow if it would help,' he offered.

'Oh no – you've done quite enough already,' she said. But she felt a rush of gratitude and warmth and a reluctance to leave. She was beginning to associate the feeling of safe haven that Wells Court afforded her with Chas Wallace himself, and that was a dangerous thing to do. Her perception of him had already changed so much; he was no longer the ogre she had once thought him. But she must not allow herself to be carried away. He was her employer; she must not allow herself to think of him as her protector too. That way led to complications that could bring everything tumbling down around her ears.

'I'll be quite all right, thank you,' she said.

And managed to keep her head high and her hands steady on the reins as she drove away.

As she turned into the stable yard at Kanunga, Cerys had the oddest feeling that Duggan would come waddling out to meet her, and had to remind herself that he would not, and never would again.

She lifted the children down and told them to hurry inside whilst she unharnessed Lady; the fine rain was falling harder now, and she didn't want them getting wet through.

As she hurried across the yard herself the door opened and

Molly appeared. She had been subdued before; now her big solemn eyes seemed to dominate her face.

'Auntie Jenny is crying!'

Cerys's heart sank. Jenny in one of her black moods was something she could well have done without just now. But her first thought was that something had happened between Jenny and Hal. She didn't think Jenny cared deeply enough about Duggan to be sitting in the house alone and crying over his death, but certainly she had been upset by Hal's refusal to accompany her to the funeral. Perhaps she had remonstrated with him again over it, there had been harsh words, and he had told Jenny some things she did not want to hear. It was only the final outcome to the affair that Cerys had been expecting, and in many ways it would be a relief. But the timing, given her own fragile state, could scarcely have been worse.

Jenny was sitting at the table, head bowed, hair come loose and tumbling about her tear-ravaged face.

'Go and play in your room, children,' she told them.

Molly started for the door, but Ritchie ran to her holding out his plump little arms to be picked up.

'Not now, Ritchie,' she said firmly, and to Molly: 'Take your brother and amuse him, there's a good girl.'

When the door had closed after them, she turned to Jenny.

'What's happened? Is it Hal?'

Jenny shook her head wordlessly.

'What then? Oh, I know it's been a horrible day, but please try to pull yourself together. You're upsetting the children.'

Jenny covered her face with her hands, her whole body racked with distress.

'It's my fault. All my fault!' she sobbed through her tear-wet fingers.

'All your fault? What are you talking about, Jenny?'

'It's a curse,' Jenny wept. 'I'm cursed, Cerys.'

'Oh, don't talk such nonsense!' Cerys said briskly.

'It's true! I am! Everyone around me meets a violent end . . . My mother and father . . . Will . . . and now Duggan.'

'Duggan died because he was kicked by his horse,' Cerys said.

Jenny looked up at her with red, swollen eyes.

219

'Do you really believe that? Fango is so gentle!'

'Jenny, it's as Hal said – you can never totally trust any animal. I have to believe it. What else could it have been?'

Jenny's face contorted. 'Violence. That's what happens to people around me. Violent death, Cerys.' Her voice rose hysterically. 'I should get rid of me if I were you, before you and the children meet the same end!'

Cerys rubbed her aching head with her fingertips.

'Jenny, you are being quite unreasonable. This can be violent country, I grant you, and I know you have suffered more than most from the evil deeds of bushrangers and the like. I know both Will and his parents died at their hands, but . . .'

'They didn't, though,' Jenny blurted.

Cerys, brought up short, started at Jenny uncomprehendingly. 'What did you say?'

'Our parents weren't killed by bushrangers.' Jenny suddenly burst into hysterical laughter. 'Oh Cerys, you should see your face!'

'Have you taken leave of your senses, Jenny?' Cerys demanded. She had begun to shake, though she was not quite sure why. 'Will told me . . .'

'Yes, he told me too.' Jenny scrubbed her eyes with her hand; they were now very bright. 'Only it wasn't true. I found out what really happened. And when I told Will I had found out, he admitted it.'

'Admitted what?' Cerys asked through clenched teeth.

Jenny sat back in her chair and the words came spilling out like a raging river cascading through a breached dam.

'My father used to drink, and when he was drunk he became violent. He used to beat my mother. My father – who I loved so much – used to beat my mother senseless. Oh, I knew that really – I'm sure I knew – but I closed my mind to it. I couldn't bear it, you see. Anyway, Will couldn't bear it either. And one day he came home and heard them fighting and he hid . . . and then everything went quiet and he went in and he found –' she paused, gasping a little, with gasps that were halfway to being sobs – 'he found my father standing over my mother's body. He'd killed her, Cerys. Killed her! I don't suppose he meant to. He didn't know what he was doing. He never meant to . . .

but he did. And then he turned on Will and Will picked up the shotgun that was lying there on the table and . . . he shot my father . . . his father. My father killed my mother, and Will . . . Oh Cerys, say something! Please say something!'

Cerys tried, but no words came out. Her jaw seemed to be frozen rigid.

'I've shocked you, haven't I?' Jenny said with a hysterical giggle. 'I've really shocked you! And there's more . . .'

Finally Cerys found her voice.

'Well, I don't want to hear it, Jenny, whatever it is. I'm not even sure I believe you! Will might have lied to you to protect you, but he would never have kept something like that from me! Never!'

'Oh Cerys,' Jenny said. 'There is so much you don't know about us. Me and Will both. We are trouble, we Pages. It's like I say . . . a curse. The curse of the Pages!' She began to laugh again, the hysteria rising and rising.

Cerys took hold of her shoulders and shook her hard.

'Stop this, Jenny! Stop it now!'

The laughter ceased abruptly and the sobs began again, gentle at first, then racking her body.

'Oh Jenny, Jenny!' Cerys cried, her own tears starting to flow.

And once again the two girls clung together for comfort.

Her world had rocked again, slipped sideways on its axis. All very well to tell Jenny she did not believe her, but somehow Cerys could not deny the story had a ring of truth to it.

It seemed to her now that somehow she had always known there was something in Will's past that he had never spoken of. She had never consciously addressed this before, yet now that Jenny had opened the door it felt oddly familiar. It was not really a question of a hundred and one little things slipping into place; there had never been anything she had questioned and worried about. Unless it was his moods, those same black moods that so affected Jenny. Perhaps they were a manifestation of the scars inflicted on young children by seeing their father use violence on their mother again and again.

But Will . . . a murderer? Never! Except that even if he had done what Jenny said, it would have been with the intention of protecting himself and his mother, nothing else.

'If anyone ever hurt you I would kill them, Cerys,' he had once said. At the time it had made her feel safe and very much loved. Now the words – and the look in his eyes when he had said them – came back to haunt her.

Oh Will, she wept silently, why didn't you tell me? At least we could have talked about it! You could have explained it to me and perhaps I could have helped you to come to terms with it!

But he had not told her. Now he could never explain and she could never talk with him about it. And the bleakness that followed the complete and utter shock of it was for the fact that there had been something so important in his life that she had never shared with him, that the man she had thought she knew so well, she had never really known at all.

What else had he hidden from her? What other secrets had he taken to his grave? The questions tormented Cerys, and she thought they always would.

# Seventeen

A s spring turned to early summer the resilience with which
Cerys had been blessed began to reassert itself. There
were some things in life which one could do nothing about,
best to try to set them to one side and get on with the business
of surviving.

For all her problems, worries and heartaches, Cerys told
herself, things could have been a great deal worse. She had
two lovely children, and by some miracle they all still had a
home. She had employment that kept her busy and provided a
much needed income, and the farm was just about paying its
way. She had sent thirty head of cattle to market, and the price
they had fetched was far in excess of what she had hoped to
achieve – thanks, she felt sure, to Chas Wallace.

She had mentioned to him that she was not happy about
entrusting the transaction to Hal Tucker, and he had offered
to take them with his own. Hal had been disgruntled, but she
couldn't help that, and she felt quite sure that Chas's good
name as a breeder had helped secure a far better deal than
Hal could ever have achieved, even if he was scrupulously
honest about what he got for them.

Sometimes she wondered about the low price Hal had
obtained for the gig and the horses, but it was something
else she put to the back of her mind. That was water under
the bridge; there was nothing she could do about it now. But in
the light of her own feelings about him, as well as the warning
poor old Duggan had given her, she had resolved to be more
careful in the future.

And oddly enough Jenny had not taken umbrage when
Cerys had told her that Chas, not Hal, would be dealing
with the sale. Cerys had expected Jenny to rise angrily in

his defence, but she did not, merely nodding and saying it was a sensible plan.

Could it be, Cerys wondered, that Jenny was not quite as gullible as she seemed to be where Hal was concerned?

She was certainly as besotted with him as ever, though, and more than once Cerys heard her creep out to be with him when she thought Cerys was asleep.

It worried her greatly, but she did not see what she could do. She had made her feelings plain enough, and warned Jenny of the possible consequences of such a liaison, and it had only led to quarrels and Jenny carrying on exactly as before. She was the girl's sister-in-law, not her keeper, and all she could hope for was that the affair would run its course without too much damage done. Unless, of course, Hal really did care for Jenny, as she clearly cared for him. But Cerys could not believe that. At the moment, she thought, it suited Hal to play Jenny along. When it no longer suited him, he would break her heart without a second thought.

But the question remained – why was he playing her along? Why was he here at all? All very well for him to have said he was doing it for Will; Cerys didn't believe that any more than she believed Jenny was the love of his life. Hal Tucker, she thought, cared only for himself, and whatever his reasons, they would be ones that benefited him in some way. For the life of her she could not think what those reasons were – unless, of course, he thought that he might end up owning Kanunga himself.

Well, if he thought that, he was in for a disappointment. In the first place Kanunga belonged to her, not to Jenny, and in the second the deeds were lodged with Chas's lawyer and if things went wrong the land would go to him. Not for the first time Cerys was glad she had made the deal. With her growing friendship with Chas, the knowledge felt like a safety net beneath the feet of a tightrope walker.

Only sometimes Cerys wondered if she was wrong to place so much trust in Chas. Her land would, after all, be of tremendous benefit to him. But then, he could have called in the debt a long while ago if he had wanted to. He had

224

shown her nothing but kindness and generosity and she could not really understand that either.

Oh, it was all such a puzzle it made her head ache thinking about it. So she tried to push it to one side along with everything else and get on with the day-to-day business of living.

One fine morning in early summer Cerys drove as she usually did to Wells Court. The children were more excitable than usual – Christmas was coming, and Molly was telling Ritchie about it.

'We get presents, and we have a chicken. We even went to church last year, didn't we, Mama? It's exciting!'

Cerys's heart sank. She didn't think there would be any presents this year, and she didn't feel much like going to church either. The thought of townsfolk like Amy Hawker staring at them was not an inviting one. But it upset her to think how disappointed Molly was going to be, and she wished with all her heart she could do something to make the day special for them.

Ritchie, of course, was too young to really understand what Molly was so excited about, but he had caught her mood and was bobbing up and down so much that Cerys was afraid he might fall out of the sulky.

'Keep still, you two!' she said sharply, and wondered how much longer she could manage to fit them both in. They were growing so fast it was becoming a very tight squeeze indeed.

Today, however, they made it safely to the stable yard. She lifted the two children down and watched with a smile as they went running to where Cinders, the puppy Chas had said they might keep for their own, was romping in the sun, chasing flies and the occasional stray bumblebee. Ned was there, too, cleaning tack, and Cerys called to him.

'Good morning, Ned. Will they be all right with you for a little while?'

'I'll keep an eye on them, yes,' the lad replied.

He was looking at her a little strangely, but Cerys thought nothing of it. She crossed the yard, opened the door, and went into the kitchen.

Then she stopped short, taken totally by surprise. A rotund, dark-skinned woman with the blunt features of an aboriginal was in the kitchen, supervising Florence as she peeled potatoes, a woman who drew herself up and quivered with indignation as Cerys walked in, glaring at her just as she had glared the very first time Cerys had gone to Wells Court and knocked at the front door.

Mary Lightfoot was back.

Almost unconsciously, after all that had happened, Cerys had fallen into the habit of wondering where the next blow would fall. But somehow, the one thing that had never occurred to her was that Mary Lightfoot would walk, unannounced, back to Wells Court. Now, seeing her there, as much in charge as she had ever been, Cerys realized with a sinking heart how tenuous her position had always been. Chas had defined her role as 'temporary' when he had taken her on, and said that Mary might well be back, but as Cerys settled in, she had forgotten it. Now, the realization hit her like a bucket of cold water.

Mary Lightfoot was back. She, Cerys, would no longer be needed.

She stood helplessly, feeling suddenly like an intruder in the kitchen she had come to look on as her domain, totally at a loss as to what to do or say.

Mary Lightfoot folded her arms across her ample bosom.

'Mr Wallace is in the parlour,' she said with spiteful satisfaction. 'He would like to speak to you.'

Cerys nodded. She could not trust herself to reply. With as much dignity as she could muster, she marched across the kitchen. Florence was avoiding meeting her eye; her head was bent over the bowl of potatoes, but Cerys could feel the girl's eyes boring into her back.

The parlour door was closed; she tapped and opened it. At first she thought Mary Lightfoot had been mistaken in saying Chas was there. The room appeared empty. Her glance lit on the grand piano and a lump rose in her throat. Chas had suggested she should teach herself to play, but there had never been the time. Now she would never have the chance. And oh, how she would miss Wells Court! How she would miss . . . Tears welled suddenly in her eyes.

'Mrs Page.' Chas suddenly materialized from the depths of the big wing chair, whose back was towards her and had totally hidden him.

Cerys blinked furiously. The last thing she wanted was for him to see her cry again. Heavens, he would think she was one of those women who were forever weeping when things went awry!

'Mr Wallace,' she said, trying to keep her voice steady.

'Why don't you sit down?' he suggested.

'Thank you, I'll stand.' She did not know why she had said that, but somehow standing preserved her dignity. And she could make a speedier exit if the tears threatened again.

He took a few paces to the window, turned and faced her, hands on hips.

'You have seen, I expect, that Mary Lightfoot is back.'

She nodded. 'Yes. So I presume you have sent for me to tell me my services will no longer be required.'

'Ah.' An eyebrow quirked. 'Why do you presume that?'

'Well.' She laughed shortly, but it came out sounding more like a sob. 'You hardly need two housekeepers. And you did make it clear when you offered me the position that it was just until she turned up again.'

'That is true,' he said. 'Things have changed somewhat since then though, I think you will agree. I don't want to lose you, Mrs Page.'

Her lip wobbled. She bit fiercely on it.

'You mean you want me to stay on?'

'Yes, that's exactly what I mean. Will you?'

Startled, she tried to collect her thoughts. Little as she wanted to leave the house that had become her haven, she couldn't see what reason there could possibly be for her remaining. Mary Lightfoot had resumed control; nothing could be the same again. She would arrange everything, take over all the tasks Cerys had so enjoyed. She would become just another servant, like Florence and Edith. And Mary Lightfoot disliked her, she felt sure. The woman had never troubled to conceal her animosity from the first moment they had met. How much more virulent that would be now that Cerys had taken her place for the last months! Mary Lightfoot would do everything in her power to make Cerys's life a misery, of that Cerys had no doubt. No, she did not think she could bear to continue working here with her position so altered. Her fierce pride simply would not stand it.

'Thank you, Mr Wallace,' she said stiffly, 'but I really don't think . . .'

He regarded her seriously. 'You don't think what?'

'That I could work under Mary Lightfoot. I'm grateful for the offer. You have been more than kind to me and while I felt I was being of use to you, and earning my wage, that was one thing. But I don't want charity. So – thank you again, but I think it would be best if I refused your offer, took the children, and went home.' Her voice wobbled again on the last sentence.

A corner of his mouth quirked. 'That was quite a speech, Mrs Page. But who said anything about you working under Mary Lightfoot?'

She frowned. 'Well, I assumed . . .'

'Wrongly, but understandably.' He smiled crookedly. 'I'm not making myself very clear, am I? For that, I apologize, and can only excuse myself by saying I am not at all used to this sort of thing. No.' His eyes met hers. 'In my own rather clumsy way I am asking you to become my wife.'

If she had been startled before it was nothing to the utter astonishment she felt now. Her mouth dropped open; she stared at him, simply unable to believe she had heard aright.

'But . . .'

'I've shocked you.' There was something in his tone and in the way he moved away from the window, running a hand through his hair, that might almost have made her think he had become self-conscious and unsure of himself, had she been capable of registering such a thought, and if she could have believed such a thing possible of the powerful, confident Chas Wallace.

'For that I apologize. But it seems to me to be a reasonable solution to all our problems,' he went on.

'But why?' she said faintly. 'Why would you want to marry me?'

228

He laughed suddenly, as if her question had dispelled his momentary awkwardness and returned him to his usual status – back in control, both of himself and the situation.

'Mrs Page – that is not the question a lady usually asks when she is proposed to, surely? Not that I have personal experience in the matter, you understand. I am not in the habit of making proposals of marriage, but all the same . . . You underestimate yourself. You have a great deal to offer. Wells Court would not be the same without you. All these years it has been lacking a woman's touch. I think it's high time that was rectified.'

'But . . .' She was still totally at a loss for words.

'And it wouldn't be such a bad bargain from your point of view would it?' he went on smoothly. 'You and the children would live in comfort and you'd have no more worries about how to make ends meet. Your future and theirs would be secure. I am not, I realize, the easiest person in the world to get along with. I've been on my own too long, and I'm rather set in my ways. But I would do my best to make you happy.'

Somehow Cerys found her voice.

'I must admit, Mr Wallace, you have taken me completely by surprise. I'm deeply honoured, of course, but—'

'You find the idea distasteful?' His eyes on her were sharp.

'Oh . . . it's not that . . .' Colour flooded Cerys's cheeks; she put her hands up quickly to cover them. 'I just . . . don't know what to say.'

'Don't say anything for the moment then. Give yourself time to think it over.'

'There's Jenny,' she said, grasping at the practical to avoid the implications of his previous suggestion and the hammering of her heart. 'I have to think of Jenny.'

'Your concern is admirable. But Jenny is a grown woman now,' he reminded her. 'She could well be married herself before very long – perhaps to your farm hand, Hal Tucker. You told me yourself they are very close.'

'But I don't want her to marry him!' Cerys retorted. 'I've also told you he's a bad lot and I don't trust him.'

Chas's eyes narrowed thoughtfully. 'Kitty told me she

thought she recognized him from somewhere,' he diversified. 'I intended to mention it to you before. He stayed with her for a few nights when he first came to Medlock, and she thought his face was familiar.'

Cerys frowned. So – Hal Tucker had stayed at the Commercial Hotel when he first came to Medlock. But concerned as she was over the man who had come into their lives so mysteriously and entranced Jenny so completely, at this moment she had too much else on her mind to worry about it.

'If Jenny should decide to marry him there would be nothing you could do about it,' Chas pointed out. 'As I say, she is a grown woman. And I would be quite prepared for them to continue to live at Kanunga. I'd even take Hal Tucker on to my payroll if necessary – just as long as he doesn't try cheating or stealing from *me*.'

Cerys experienced another jolt as she took on board the fact that under the terms of what Chas was suggesting Kanunga would become his property. In effect it already was, of course, with the deeds lodged with his lawyers as surety against a debt she would be unlikely ever to be able to pay off. But the absolute fact of handing over Will's land, utterly and finally, was still something she shrank from.

'And of course, should you and she prefer it, Jenny would be welcome to live here at Wells Court,' Chas went on. 'There's plenty of room and perhaps you would feel less isolated having her here.'

'That is very kind of you,' Cerys said faintly.

'Just her, you understand.' The wicked twinkle was back in Chas's eye. 'Not Mr Hal Tucker. I'm willing to take a chance on giving him a job, but certainly not a home too.'

'Of course not!' Cerys said indignantly. 'Why, I would never have had him at Kanunga if I hadn't been desperate.'

'So . . .' He picked up her phrase and flung it back at her. 'Are you desperate enough now to consider my offer?'

He was teasing her, she knew. How could he tease about something so serious? Oh, it was his way, of course, his way of dealing with awkward situations. She should be used to it by now, but all the same . . .

'It's not a joking matter!' she said crossly.

'You are right, Mrs Page, it is not. And for all my flippancy, I assure you I was never more serious in my life. I've given this a great deal of thought, and I feel sure it would work to the advantage of us both. I hope, when you have had the chance to think it over too, you will agree with me.'

She nodded. 'I will think it over, Mr Wallace. But at present I just don't know what my answer will be.'

She turned for the door, desperately needing to be alone with her whirling thoughts and chaotic emotions. His voice stopped her.

'Just one more thing, Mrs Page.'

She turned back to see him crossing to the bureau. 'There's something I'd like you to have as a token of my good intentions.'

She watched, puzzled, as he pulled out his key ring, selected a tiny key, opened one of the small drawers and took something out.

'I have been wondering for some while when it would be appropriate to return this to you,' he said. 'I think perhaps this is as good a time as any.'

'What . . . ?'

She looked at him, bemused. He held out his hand towards her. To her utter and complete amazement, lying in his palm was the ring she had sold to pay her debt to him.

For a moment she was speechless. Then: 'My ring!' she whispered.

'Good.' He smiled slightly. 'I got the right one, then. Mr Johnson assured me it was yours and I took his word for it.'

'But . . . how did you come by it?' she asked.

'I bought it, of course. When I heard you were trying to sell it to pay my debt, I felt I could do nothing less. I realize just how much it must mean to you, and I didn't feel I should be the one responsible for depriving you of it permanently.'

She stared, totally transfixed, at her precious ring, which she had thought never to see again, lying there in his palm.

'Don't you want it?' he asked.

'Oh yes . . . yes, of course!' The tears were filling her eyes,

231

running down her cheeks. She reached out tentatively and took the ring, slipping it on to her wedding-ring finger and seeing the diamond winking at her through a blur of tears. Then she looked up at Chas once more. He was watching her with a half smile, but there was a bleakness she could not understand in his eyes.

'You're pleased?' he asked.

'Mr Wallace . . . how can I ever thank you?'

'Don't try. And please don't think that this is a bribe to persuade you to agree to my proposal – though clearly I hope you will. It's just something I wanted to do.'

'Would you very much mind,' she said softly, 'if I was to be on my own for a little while?'

'Of course not. I quite understand. I'll make certain you are not disturbed.' He crossed the room, opened the door. Then he turned and looked back at her.

'I very much hope, Mrs Page, that your answer to my proposal will be yes.'

Outside the door Chas stood for a moment, throwing his head back and staring up at the ceiling. Well, there, it was said now. For the first time in his life he had committed himself into a woman's hands. It was a strange feeling, and one he did not care for. Even now he was not sure it was a wise move for a committed bachelor such as himself. He enjoyed his freedom. He did not like being answerable to anyone but himself. And yet . . . and yet . . .

Somehow Cerys Page had breached his defences and got under his skin, and when Mary Lightfoot had walked back in the door last night and he had realized there was a very real danger that he was about to lose Cerys, the prospect had been unbearable. Not to hear her singing as she worked, not to see the smile that came more readily these days, not to smell the faint flowery perfume of her soap after she left a room . . . Chas had realized with a jolt just how much she had come to mean to him.

He should have realized, of course. From the moment he had met her, his actions had been totally out of character. He had done things for her he would never have dreamed of doing for

232

anyone else, and fooled himself into believing he did them for his own benefit.

Except, of course, buying her ring from Mr Johnson. But even that he had excused as common human decency. He was now unutterably glad that he had done it, at once, before it was lost for ever to a stranger. And she had clearly been so happy to see it again. But the moment had been marred for him when she had slipped it so joyfully back on to her finger. The gesture had reminded him too sharply not only that she had been another man's wife, but that her heart still belonged to that man. Jealousy was not an emotion with which Chas was familiar, but he had experienced it then, and he experienced it now, a surge of something close to anger in his veins, but bitter taste of gall in his mouth.

Dear God, he wanted Cerys as he had never wanted anyone before. He wanted her spirit, her courage, her warmth. He wanted to lift the burdens from her shoulders. He wanted to take her in his arms and love her. He wanted her, body and soul. And the only way he had any hope of achieving that was by making her his wife.

Chas Wallace could only pray she would agree to his proposal.

When the door closed after him Cerys covered her face with her hands and let the tears flow. For a few minutes she wept without a single coherent thought, simply giving free rein to all her pent-up emotion.

Then, as the tears ceased, her mind was whirling again. Even now, she could scarcely believe she was being called upon to make such a decision. Never, in her wildest dreams, had she imagined Chas Wallace would ask her to be his wife, and she still could not think why he should do so. They were, after all, poles apart – he a wealthy and powerful landowner, she the widow of a poor selector with two small children. He had his reasons, she supposed, but she could not imagine what they were. He didn't love her, clearly – a small shiver of regret ran through her at the thought – he'd never given her any cause to think that he might, in spite of his kindness to her, and he had certainly made no mention of love in his proposal.

233

But then, she didn't want love, did she? That momentary frisson of regret was nothing but vanity. Love was what she and Will had shared. It came only once in a lifetime; to experience it with someone else would be sacrilegious to Will's memory, a betrayal of a man who was no longer here to share the future with her.

No, what she wanted was security – for herself and for her children. If she married Chas Wallace she would never again have to pore over ledgers to try and make them balance against all the odds, never have to worry whether Hal Tucker was cheating her and stealing from her, never again have to sell her most precious possessions or humiliate herself by trying to gain employment as a common barmaid. It was a tempting prospect.

Chas Wallace had been kind to her. She scarcely knew him – but then she had been so sure she knew Will, and she had been wrong. Whatever secrets might be hidden in Chas's past, they could hardly be worse than the things she had learned about Will since his death. Chas would be good to her, she felt sure, and good too to the children. They, most of all, deserved the things that life at Wells Court would bring them. And Jenny . . . Chas had promised that as far as was possible he would make sure she had a home too.

How Jenny would react, Cerys had no idea. Jenny had once told Cerys that life should go on and one day she would meet someone else. But that was all very well when there was no real prospect of such a thing. If it actually came to pass she might feel very differently. She might not be able to help being resentful that someone other than her brother should be sharing Cerys's bed – her whole life – and so soon too.

Would I just be prostituting myself? Cerys asked herself, and thought uncomfortably that that was exactly what she would be doing. And yet . . . and yet . . .

Oh Will, what am I to do? Cerys whispered. If you were here, what would you tell me to do?

She stared down at her precious ring, so newly returned to her, twisting it on her finger, trying to still the questions churning around and around in her mind and listen instead to her heart.

\*      \*      \*

It was a great deal later when she went in search of Chas.

She found him in the stable yard, saddling Lupus. For just a moment she hesitated, then, drawing a deep breath, she started towards him.

He looked round and saw her; his whole body became still as a statue, as if he were carved in stone, one hand on the bridle, the other on the saddle. Only a muscle in his cheek tensed; his eyes never left her.

She reached him, folded her hands demurely in her skirts, and raised her eyes to his.

'I've come to tell you my decision.'

'What is it?' he asked, still without moving.

She swallowed at a lump of nervousness in her throat, but when she spoke, her voice was clear and unwavering.

'Yes. I'll be your wife, Chas, if you still want me.'

# Eighteen

Cerys knew that she should tell Jenny of Chas's proposal at once, but for all that, she found herself postponing the moment. She felt she needed time to become accustomed to the idea herself before she could begin sharing it with anyone else, even Jenny. Especially Jenny, she admitted to herself, for she was still uncertain as to how Jenny would receive the news. And there was no cause for urgency. Chas had accepted her suggestion that they should keep their agreement to themselves until she felt ready to tell the world, and that the marriage should not take place until at least a year had elapsed since Will's death.

'It wouldn't be right for it to be any sooner,' she had said. 'In polite society I should still be in mourning and hiding myself away. Circumstances being what they were made that impossible, but it would be most disrespectful to Will's memory if I married again so soon.'

Chas had nodded agreement. Personally he had no time for conventions that were observed more for the sake of respectability than anything else, but he knew that it would hurt Cerys deeply to be talked about in Medlock and knew too the anguish she had already experienced over what she saw as her betrayal of Will. She had accepted his proposal of marriage; that was enough for him. He could wait for her as long as was necessary.

'Perhaps, in any case, I should pay court to you in the proper manner,' he said, very gravely, though there was a twinkle in his eye.

'Oh, I don't see any need for that, Mr Wallace!' she replied quickly, the ready flush rising in her cheeks.

'I disagree,' he said. 'If you want to keep the wagging

tongues silent it might be the best course. And there's another thing. I'd like it if you were to call me Chas rather than Mr Wallace. And if I may call you Cerys?'

'Oh!' She caught her lip between her teeth. I don't mind you calling me Cerys, of course, but calling you "Chas" might take some getting used to.'

'You'll try though.'

'I'll try. Well – anyway – just in private . . .'

He laughed. She was a delight.

'And how are you going to explain the fact that you are no longer working for me?'

'Well, tell the truth, of course!'

'Of course!'

'Mr Wallace!' she said indignantly. 'You are laughing at me.'

'Chas.'

'Oh . . . Chas! I mean, of course, that it will soon be common knowledge that Mary Lightfoot has returned and my services are no longer required.'

'Very well,' he said. 'Then I think the best course of action will be that I shall come calling and bring you and the children here so that you may enjoy being a guest rather than a housekeeper.'

'Oh, I don't know . . . Mary Lightfoot . . .'

'I shall instruct Mary Lightfoot that she is to do as you tell her. And you will be able to do all the things I know you have wanted to do and never had time for – such as playing with the children and the puppies and teaching yourself to play the piano.'

She smiled. 'It does sound rather inviting.'

'And that, Cerys, is just the beginning. It's high time you were spoiled a little, and I intend to make sure you are. Just a little, mind you! I don't want you turning into one of those young ladies who expect the world to turn at their behest.'

'Oh!' she said indignantly. 'I wouldn't!'

'I know that, Cerys. I was only teasing you. Do you really think I would have asked you to be my wife if I thought you were capable of turning out like that?'

He reached for her hands, and suddenly she had begun

trembling, not visibly, but deep inside. He drew her towards him. Afterwards, she would try to tell herself that it was because in accepting his proposal she had given him the right; in fact it was no such thing. She was mesmerized by the touch of his hands on hers, his eyes, still teasing, the very strong masculine presence of him. Then his lips were on her forehead, kissing her very gently, and something sharp and sweet twisted within her. She felt nothing but regret when he held her away.

'So – how would you like to spend your first day as the future Mrs Wallace?'

That brought her back to earth with a thump. Mrs Wallace. Not Mrs Page. It was not only Will's memory she was betraying; she was abandoning his name too.

'I don't know.'

If he had noticed her withdrawal, he did not show it.

'I think we should take the children and go for a good long drive. It's just the weather for it.'

'What about your work?' she asked.

'My work can wait. It's not every day I acquire a fiancée. Would you enjoy a drive, do you think?'

'I don't know,' she said honestly. Her emotions were churning so madly she did not even know how she felt at this minute.

'Shall we find out then?' he suggested.

She had enjoyed it. The children were ecstatic at riding in the roomy gig – no danger now of them crowding one another out and tumbling on to the track – and as the matched pair bowled along in the sunshine a sort of euphoric madness had taken hold of her. Could this really be her – Cerys Page – sitting beside the rich and powerful Chas Wallace in the finest gig in all of New England with her children bobbing up and down happily behind her? One of the hands was working at the roadside, mending a fence; he touched his forelock as they drove by. Cerys swelled with pride.

'Don't expect that sort of deference all the time,' Chas warned her wryly. 'Fogerty is from Ireland, where they still do that kind of thing. Native-born Australians are less respectful.'

238

Cerys giggled like a girl. Such respect just once in a while was more than enough for her. But the mention of Ireland reminded her of her parents; though they had hailed from Wales, that, too, was one of the old countries.

'Do you think . . .' She broke off, biting her lip.

He glanced sideways at her. 'Yes?'

'My parents live in Sydney. Do you think perhaps we could go to see them and tell them about all this in person?' She was choosing her words with care so that the children would not begin asking awkward questions. 'You could speak to my father about it.'

A smile lifted one corner of Chas's mouth. 'You mean I should ask his permission? Well, I don't see why not!'

Cerys lifted her face to the sun. A bird soared overhead. On either side of the track the land spread out as far as the eye could see, green, succulent grass, stands of trees all now in full leaf. It was a moment out of time, and Cerys's heart sang with the joy of it.

It was only afterwards, as she struggled home to Kanunga, the children squeezed beside her in the little sulky, that reality returned with a rush. It was done. She had agreed to marry Chas Wallace. But was it the right decision? Whilst solving some problems, had she created others? And still the guilt plagued her.

'Oh Will, Will!' she whispered. 'You do understand, don't you?'

But there was no reply in the wind on her face, no absolution in the warmth of the setting sun. Cerys knew she had a long road to travel before she could truly begin to live again.

Keeping her secret from Jenny was not nearly as difficult as Cerys had imagined it would be, for Jenny did not seem at all her usual self.

She did, it was true, notice that Cerys was wearing her ring – which she could scarcely bear to take from her finger since it had been so unexpectedly returned to her.

'Cerys – what's that?' Jenny asked, pointing to it as Cerys served cold pork on to her dinner plate. 'I thought . . .'

'That I sold it. Yes, I did.' Cerys tried to keep her tone light. 'Chas bought it back for me.'

'You see?' Jenny said. 'Didn't I tell you? He'd do anything for you.' But she did not press the point. She seemed, in fact, almost uninterested, as if her mind was elsewhere.

That was how she was these days, slightly distracted. But Cerys had too much on her own mind to wonder about it too deeply. She was only grateful that Jenny, usually so perceptive, seemed to notice nothing at all.

In order to keep up the charade it was necessary, of course, for her to leave every morning as usual for Wells Court, but her days there could scarcely have been more different. She was now a lady of leisure, and the change in her routine both pleased and niggled her. It was wonderful to be able to spend more time with the children, an enjoyable luxury to sit at the grand piano and tinkle on the keys trying to produce a tune, enormously – and rather wickedly – satisfying to experience a sense of superiority over the dour and dismissive Mary Lightfoot.

But it also made her a little uncomfortable to have time on her hands. A strict work ethic had been drilled into Cerys from the time she was a little girl, expected to help out around her father's store and with household tasks. And since she had married Will there had never been enough hours in the day, so that even when she had snatched a few moments rest she was unable to relax, so conscious was she of all the things that needed to be done.

Now, her enjoyment of her new-found leisure was marred by a pervasive sense of guilt. It couldn't be right, just letting the days drift by! And there was still so much that needed doing at Kanunga! But if she returned home to do it, questions would certainly be asked, questions she did not yet feel ready to answer.

And so her days were slow and leisurely, her evenings as filled with endless chores as they had ever been. She laboured too over the accounts books long into the night, checking and rechecking the entries and columns of figures so they would be in perfect order when she came to hand them over to Chas, as she would soon have to do.

At least she did not think that Hal had cheated her again, though, of course, she had tried to ensure he had had no opportunity to do so. Her precious money pot seemed untouched too since she had found a new hiding place for it, unknown even to Jenny, since Jenny seemed so ready to trust Hal implicitly, and there was little of value in the house that would be worth Hal's while to steal, she thought with a wry smile.

How different it was at Wells Court! Anyone with a mind to try to rob Chas Wallace would find an Aladdin's cave of treasures, and Cerys, who had never had much in the way of possessions, and had never thought them necessary to her happiness, was continually shocked by the pleasure she gained from running her fingers over a smooth, perfectly turned piece of wood, or handling a delicate piece of porcelain or glass. But she thought it would be a foolish man who tried to rob Chas.

What would her parents make of him, she wondered – and of the fact that she was going to marry again? They had been worried about her, she knew, since Will's death, for they expressed their concern for her in every letter they wrote to her, and more than once had suggested that she and the children should return home to Sydney. But marriage again, so soon? They were so straight-laced she was not at all sure they would approve of that.

She wrote her letter to them in the parlour at Wells Court on Chas's heavy embossed parchment, and she chose her words with care, making no mention of Chas's proposal, simply that she would like to come to visit with the children and she would be bringing her friend and employer Chas Wallace with her. She read and reread it several times before sealing the envelope with a dollop of hot wax melted in the flame of a candle, and put it ready for collection by the bullocky when next he called. Then she tried to put it out of her mind. But still she was haunted by the image of the old-fashioned look that would almost certainly come over her mother's face as she read that Cerys had a 'friend' who was also a gentleman!

One morning when the children were playing happily outside in the warm sunshine under the watchful eye of Ned, Cerys was tinkling on the piano. She was beginning to be able to pick out simple tunes now, her ear becoming attuned and her fingers

241

remembering note sequences. Would she ever be able to put two hands together, she wondered, as proper trained pianists did? She tried, and winced at the discord she produced, then tried again. Better – but no, perhaps for the time being she should concentrate on keeping the tune going.

So lost in concentration was she that Cerys was quite unaware of Chas standing in the doorway behind her until she broke off and he began to applaud.

'Bravo!'

She turned quickly, a little embarrassed.

'Oh, I didn't know anyone was there!'

'Don't stop,' he said. 'I was quite enjoying it.'

'Oh, how can you say that? Why, Molly could do better! I'm not a very quick learner, I'm afraid.'

'Nonsense! You have got more tune out of that piano than anyone else has since the day it arrived,' he said. 'Always excepting, of course, the wonderful concerto you produced on the very first day without even trying!'

'Don't remind me!' she groaned.

'Oh, it wasn't such a catastrophe was it?' he asked. 'After all, if it hadn't happened you would not be here now.'

That, she realized, was no less than the truth. If her horses had not got out of control that day she would never have met Chas Wallace in the first place.

'I think,' he went on, 'that I should make enquiries to discover if there is anyone in the district who could teach you properly. You've an aptitude, without doubt, and I must say I rather like the prospect of you entertaining me in the evenings when we are married. When we don't have better things to do, that is.'

Her face flamed. 'Mr Wallace!'

'Come on, now,' he chided. 'You promised to call me Chas – in private, at least – and for the most part you have succeeded. Don't spoil it now.'

She could not think of a single thing to say. Strange how he could still discomfit her.

'Talking of our marriage,' he went on, still totally at ease himself, 'I have been thinking. The room we shall share is badly in need of redecoration, as I'm sure you know. The hangings and covers have not been changed in years – not since my father's day. I'd like it to be nice for you, and I wondered if you would like to choose new ones yourself. When we go to Sydney to meet your parents would seem an ideal opportunity for ordering them. You would have a far better selection of fabrics there, and we could be sure of finding a really competent seamstress to make them up, too.'

'Oh – I could make them myself!' Cerys said eagerly. 'I like sewing and I'm quite good at it. I make all my own clothes, and the children's too. And it would give me something to do.'

'Well, if you are sure . . .' he said doubtfully. 'You know I want to spoil you, Cerys.'

'No, I'd like to, truly I would!' Her face was alight now with excitement at the prospect of being able to furnish a room without a thought as to how much it would cost. 'Could I take a look around now, do you think, so that I can begin thinking about what would look nice?'

'Why not?'

He stood aside to let her pass through the doorway, and she ran ahead of him up the stairs. She had been in his room before, of course, in her capacity as housekeeper, and she knew how it looked – a very masculine room with heavy, functional furniture and drapes and covers of thick brown fabric. But she had never looked at it with a view to changing anything – with the exception of the bedlinen.

Now she stood for a moment in the doorway, considering, then crossed to the window. The room looked out over the verdant pastureland, a pleasant, open aspect, and she judged it would get the morning sun. Perhaps yellow would make the most of it. But the pastureland looked so inviting, cool, and not yet seared brown by the heat of the high summer sun, and suddenly she knew she wanted to bring it inside the house.

'Green,' she said, glancing at him over her shoulder. 'Would you be happy with green?'

'I shall be happy with whatever you choose, Cerys,' he said, smiling at her happy face.

'Green, then, if I can find the right shade. The drapes right down to the floor. It will take a lot of fabric though . . .' She stretched her arms wide, mentally judging the window. 'I'll have to measure properly, of course.'

He came up behind her and put his arms round her waist and she leaned back against him. Her hair brushed his chin and he could smell the sweet elusive perfume of her soap. Desire for her suffused him; he had been careful, so careful, not to do anything to frighten her off – the lightest touch, the purest kiss – but now he felt his self-control stretched to breaking point.

Afterwards, Cerys was never quite sure how she came to be in his arms, nor when her happy anticipation metamorphosed into desire. One moment, it seemed, she was leaning against him comfortably, her mind full of her plans for the room, the next he was kissing her – tenderly at first, so that she felt as if her soul was being drawn out of her body, and then more deeply – and yearnings she had all but forgotten were stirring within her, aching with a sharp and poignant insistence that was part pleasure, part pain. He was holding her close, so close she could feel every line of his hard, muscular body, and yet it was not close enough. She wound her arms around his neck, twisting her fingers in the hair that grew thickly down to his collar, drowning in the scent and the feel of him, male, all male.

'Cerys,' he said softly, his breath tickling her ear. 'Oh, Cerys.'

She did not reply. She was breathless, and in any case she did not want to use her mouth for talking. All she wanted was for him to kiss her again, to taste his tongue and feel the pressure of his lips. Nothing else in the world mattered. Nothing at all.

She felt his hand slide down to her hips, moulding her body ever closer to his. Her legs parted slightly and she thrust her hips up towards him.

He lifted her bodily then, one arm beneath her knees, the other about her shoulders, and carried her to the bed. The thick brown coverlet felt rough against her sensitized skin; she sobbed as the bed dipped beneath his weight too. There was a madness in her veins, invading every part of her, bringing every nerve ending alive with a singing passion such as she had never before known.

His face was buried in her bosom; her breasts tingled at the touch of his mouth. Then he was scrabbling up her skirts so that her legs were bare, and shamelessly she did nothing to stop him. It was only when he moved to divest himself of his own clothing and she felt the hard pressure of him probing between her bare legs that reality came rushing in like a flood tide.

Dear God, what was she doing? What was she doing?

'No!' she gasped, pushing at him frantically. 'No – please!'

The utter panic in her voice was like a bucket of cold water thrown over Chas too. He paused, looking down at her, shocked and puzzled.

'What . . . ?'

'No, please!' She tried to wriggle away from him. 'I can't! Will . . .'

She saw, but did not for the moment register, the hurt on his face. It was as if she had struck him. He released her abruptly, rolled away, stood up, rearranging his clothing.

'I'm sorry.' She was almost weeping now, trying to pull her skirts down to cover her legs. 'I just can't. I'm sorry.'

'I thought you wanted it,' he said.

'I did! God help me, I did! But I've never been with another man but Will. I just can't do it . . .'

'Well,' he said harshly. 'If you're going to marry me you are going to have to try.'

The moment the words were out he regretted them. They had been born of frustration and hurt, and were not at all how he had meant to woo her.

'Then I don't think I can marry you,' she said. 'I can't bring myself to betray him like that.'

Chas spun round. 'He's dead, Cerys,' he grated at her.

Her face crumpled; she covered it with her hands.

'Not to me he's not,' she whispered. 'It was like – oh, I don't know, just as if he was suddenly there watching me! I couldn't do it, Chas. I don't know if I ever can . . . I loved him so much, you see. There was never anyone else, and he's still there . . .'

'I see.' Chas's eyes were hard. 'Well, perhaps you had better do some serious thinking, Cerys, and decide what it is you want.'

He turned on his heel and left the room; the door closed with a bang after him.

Cerys curled herself into a ball, her face covered with her arms. She was shaking from head to toe, bewildered by the torrent of emotion that was assailing her. One moment she had been happy, planning for the future like an excited child, the next she had been consumed with a desire stronger than she had ever before experienced. And the next . . .

The next she had been frozen by an overwhelming guilt, a sense that she was betraying Will in the most terrible way. Perhaps if she had married Chas and come to his bed because she had known she must, she could have done it as part of her wifely duty. But to give herself to another man in passion greater than she had ever felt for Will . . . It was that for which she could never forgive herself. And it would always be the same, she realized. There was a spark between them that could ignite a raging inferno of desire; just a touch or a look could make her weak. She wanted Chas with every fibre of her being, and in so doing, Will could be shut out as if he had never been. She couldn't allow that. It was more than the physical. It was a betrayal in the worst possible way of the man who had been her husband.

And yet . . . and yet . . . In a single moment she had thrown away everything that could have been hers – and her children's. Security, a good home, a good man.

Oh, what am I to do? Cerys asked, tormenting herself. I want him so much! But I must not! I must not!

She pressed her hands to her eyes until flashes of fire arced through the blackness.

And suddenly she saw Will's face, smiling at her. And above the ringing of her ears she seemed to hear his voice speaking in her head.

'Be happy, Cerys.'

She uncovered her eyes, looking around wildly. The room was quite empty, only the dust motes dancing in a ray of sunlight stirred. Yet somehow she was more aware of Will's presence than at any time since she had lost him. And she could still hear the echo of his voice inside her head.

'Be happy, Cerys.'

And, quite suddenly, she was. Not ecstatic, not excited, but warmly peaceful. Will, she felt, had given her his blessing.

'Thank you,' she whispered. 'Oh, Will, I'll never forget.'

But the past was the past; it was time to move on.

A clatter of hooves sounded through the open window. Suddenly Cerys was shot through with a bolt of urgency. She leaped up and ran to the window.

Chas, on Lupus.

Cerys flung the window wide.

'Chas!' she called. 'Chas!'

He did not hear her. As she watched helplessly he kicked Lupus to a gallop and was gone down the broad drive.

Panic filled her. She ran from the room and downstairs just as if, on foot, she could catch him.

At the foot of the stairs she met Mary Lightfoot coming up with a pile of clean laundry in her thick brown arms.

'Where has Mr Wallace gone?' Cerys asked.

Mary Lightfoot glared with open scorn at her dishevelled hair and clothing.

'Mr Wallace has gone to Medlock,' she said, and the satisfaction in her tone left Cerys in no doubt as to his intended destination.

Chas had gone to Kitty Jackson.

It was in that moment that Cerys knew for certain that, in spite of everything, she could not bear to lose Chas Wallace.

# Nineteen

C has had not returned by the time Cerys left Wells Court for Kanunga.

She had spent a wretched day hovering near the window in the hope of seeing him come riding back down the drive, but he did not, and she was tormented by images of him with Kitty Jackson, with whom she had no doubt he was soothing his hurt feelings and relieving his frustration. The very idea of it was agony. In all her life, Cerys had never felt such jealousy, but she felt it now, sharp and all-consuming.

How could she have failed to realize until now just how strong were her feelings for Chas Wallace? She could not understand it. The signs had been there, but she had ignored them, stifled them with her certainty that there could never be anyone else for her but Will.

Only now, when she was terribly afraid she had lost him, had she acknowledged the feelings that had grown in the darkness like a spring bulb planted too deeply. They had at last forced their way through to the light of day, but perhaps it was too late.

She would apologize, of course, and try to explain, but would he be able to overlook the way she had behaved this morning? She had led him on almost to the point of no return and then not only screamed and fought him as if he were a rapist and she a victim, but told him in no uncertain terms that she loved someone else. Would he give her another chance? Oh, with all her heart she hoped he would, but she could scarcely blame him if he did not. It was not, after all, as if he loved her, and what had once seemed a satisfactory arrangement to him might look very different now in the light of her behaviour.

She had refused to allow him to make love to her and had told him in no uncertain terms that she could never allow it. Anything she said now he might simply see as expeditious on her part due to what she would lose materially. Even if she showed him by her actions that they were not merely empty words, he might very well remain unconvinced that once she had his ring on her finger she would not revert to the attitude that had caused this morning's fiasco.

No, there was a very real danger he would be unwilling to take such a risk. He would send her away, call in his debts and assume ownership of Kanunga and she would be left to pick up the pieces and try to eke out a living for herself and the children.

Cerys trembled with despair – and with helplessness. She had lost the man she now knew she loved and placed her own future and that of the children in jeopardy, and there was not a single thing she could do about it.

Next morning, after a sleepless night, she was still trembling, with a sense of urgency now. She simply could not wait to get to Wells Court, see Chas, and try to put things right, though she was also in a state of trepidation at the prospect of the interview and what its outcome might be.

She snapped at the children as she got them dressed, snapped at Jenny, who looked pale and unwell herself, and let fly with a tirade at Hal when he propped his feet on a chair as he drank his morning tea.

'If you are going to have your meals in my house, at least show a little respect for my furniture!'

Molly and Ritchie at least were behaving themselves, subdued, no doubt, by the realization that they were in danger of receiving a sharp smack on the legs if they became boisterous or silly.

Cerys's heart was in her mouth as she lifted them out of the sulky and hurried towards the house.

Mary Lightfoot was in the kitchen with Florence. She glared at Cerys as she came in, as if she knew Cerys no longer had any right to be at Wells Court.

'Mr Wallace isn't here,' she said shortly. 'He hasn't returned from Medlock.'

Cerys's heart sank. 'You mean . . . he didn't come home last night?'

Mary Lightfoot smirked unpleasantly. 'Mr Wallace has very good friends in Medlock,' she said unpleasantly. 'Lady friends. Perhaps you didn't know that he often stays over at the Commercial Hotel. He keeps a room and a change of clothes there.'

Cerys refused to rise to the bait, though she felt very sick suddenly.

'Do you intend to stay in his absence?' Mary Lightfoot enquired.

Cerys hesitated, thinking as fast as she could. What could she do here? She didn't even know that Chas would be back today.

'No,' she said. 'No, I won't stay, Mary, thank you.' She turned to the children, who were clinging to her skirts. 'Come along, you two. We're going home.'

'But Mama!' Molly risked a protest. 'We wanted to play with Cinders!'

'Not today,' Cerys said.

It crossed her mind to wonder if the children would ever play with Cinders again.

She drove into Medlock. It was all she could think of to do. She had to see Chas, and if he was at the Commercial Hotel, well, unappealing as the prospect was, she would have to speak to him there.

There was no sign of his horse tied up outside, but then, she reminded herself, there wouldn't be. If he had been there all night he would have installed Lupus in proper stabling. She tied up Lady and lifted down the children. She did not care for the thought of taking them into such an establishment, but she did not see that she had any choice.

She picked up Ritchie, and, with Molly trailing behind her, went up to the door and into the small lobby.

One of Kitty Jackson's employees was there. Cerys lifted her chin, summoning all her courage.

'I've come to see Mr Chas Wallace. Is he here, do you know?'

The man looked at her in surprise, and she realized how odd he must think it that an unknown woman with two small children should be looking for the wealthy landowner and confirmed bachelor.

'Mrs Page.'

Cerys spun round at the sound of Kitty Jackson's voice. The hotel owner stood in the doorway that led to the lounge. As usual she wore a scarlet gown, and the shiny fabric made a splash of bright colour in the dim lobby.

'This lady is looking for Chas Wallace,' the man said, and Kitty Jackson nodded.

'Yes, I heard. I'm sorry, Mrs Page, but Chas is not here.'

Cerys's heart sank. 'Oh, I thought . . .'

'He *was* here,' Kitty Jackson told her, 'but he left early this morning. He had business to attend to in Manilla. I think it's likely he'll be gone for several days.'

'Oh,' Cerys said again, bereft. Several days! It seemed like a lifetime.

'Why don't you come into the lounge and have a cup of coffee?' Kitty suggested. 'You look as if you could do with one. And the children too – now, what was it they chose last time they were here? Warm milk, wasn't it?'

Cerys was astonished – both at Kitty's turn of hospitality, and at the fact she had even remembered that Molly had asked for warm milk when Chas had brought them all here on the day she had signed the deeds over to him.

'Come through,' Kitty said, and Cerys, too numbed by all that had happened to argue, followed her into the residents' lounge.

'Excuse me a moment whilst I order it,' Kitty went on. 'At least this time I have help in the kitchen and won't have to make it myself.'

Cerys was not best pleased to be reminded of how she herself had asked Kitty Jackson for a job and been turned down, but compared with everything else on her mind it had shrunk in importance so as to scarcely matter any more.

A few moments later, Kitty was back with a box full of small ornaments which she set down on a low table.

'I had put these out ready to give away to Amy Hawker for

one of her interminable bazaars,' she said. 'Will they amuse the children for a little while, do you think?'

'I'm sure they will,' Cerys said, taken by surprise yet again.

Molly and Ritchie were already beside the box, eager to turn it out and play with the contents.

'Please do sit down,' Kitty invited.

Cerys did so, and Kitty drew up a chair close to the one Cerys had chosen.

'I think I can guess why you are here, Mrs Page.'

Quick colour rushed to Cerys's cheeks at the suggestion that Chas should have discussed their private affairs with Kitty Jackson. Bad enough that he should have come rushing to her for physical relief. But to think he might have talked about what had happened between them too . . .

'I scarcely think—' Cerys began stiffly.

Kitty smiled faintly, seeming to read her mind.

'Chas and I are very old friends. We know each other very well. Chas is not the type to discuss his most private affairs with me, don't worry. But I do know there has been something between the two of you, and I know too that something has gone very wrong. As I said, I know him well enough to be able to say that with confidence – and there was no need for him to tell me what it was for me to realize it. His manner when he arrived here yesterday was enough, and your coming here today looking for him has confirmed it. I'm right, am I not?'

'Yes,' Cerys agreed faintly.

'He wants to marry you, is that it? And you are not sure that he is the right type of man to make you a good husband? Oh . . .' She waved her hand dismissively. 'You don't have to tell me about it. I am sure discussing your private affairs with a virtual stranger isn't in your nature either. But for Chas's sake, I would like to set your mind at rest if I can. From everything I know of him, he is a good man. A hard one, yes. And sometimes he can be brusque and appear unfeeling. But that's just his way. Underneath it all, he can be very kind and caring.'

'I know that,' Cerys said. 'He has been very kind to me.'

'So – what do you have to lose? The Chas I know will take

252

good care of you, I'm sure.' She laughed, self-deprecatingly. 'I don't know why I'm telling you this, Mrs Page. I am doing myself no favours, am I? If Chas marries you, I shall lose the man I have been closer to than any other – and believe me, though I meet a great many men every day of my life, I can't think that any of them will ever fill the gap that Chas will leave.'

'Miss Jackson . . .' Cerys was at a loss to know what to say.

'No – I *do* know why I am speaking to you like this,' Kitty went on. 'It's because I know what you mean to Chas. In all the years I have known him, I have never before seen him so affected by a woman.' She chuckled again. 'I have never before seen him affected by a woman at all, if it comes to that. I was convinced he was the confirmed bachelor, wedded to his land and his stud farm and all the other things he does so well. But he has changed since he met you, Mrs Page – changed beyond all recognition. You have made him happy, as no one else ever has, and all he wants is to please you. No – it's not all he wants, of course. He wants *you*, I know. And whatever it is that has gone wrong between you, I hope you can find it in your heart to put it right. Men like Chas do not love easily, Mrs Page, but when they do, they love very deeply. That makes them the more vulnerable.'

Cerys was staring at Kitty wonderingly. 'Did you say . . . he *loves* me?'

Kitty raised an eyebrow. 'Hasn't he told you so? Goodness, I can see he has not. How very typical of him!' She leaned forward and laid a hand on Cerys's arm. 'Chas does indeed love you, my dear – though I might wish he did not. Chas loves you very much – which is why I am pleading with you to be kind to him.'

A tap on the door – a buxom young girl with the full breasts and hips of the typical barmaid came in carrying a tray of coffee and the milk for the children. Cerys stared at her almost unseeing. Her mind was in a whirl, but her heart was singing.

Kitty Jackson had said that Chas loved her – and somehow, incredibly, Cerys could almost believe her. Why would a woman like her say such a thing if she did not believe it herself? By her own admission she had nothing to gain by it, and a great deal to lose.

Perhaps there was a chance that things could work out after all! Perhaps Chas would find it in his heart to forgive her! Perhaps they could begin all over again, and this time . . .

'You look very surprised, Mrs Page,' Kitty said as she poured the coffee. Her usual arch smile was back.

'I am,' Cerys said simply. 'I never, for one moment, thought—'

'And that, I suspect, is the reason Chas loves you,' Kitty said. She carried the mugs of milk over to where the children were engrossed in playing with her cast-off ornaments, and returned to sit opposite Cerys. 'This changes things, perhaps.'

Cerys nodded. 'When he returns, will you please tell him I was here, and I want to see him?'

'Of course.'

'And you will tell him too, please, that I am so sorry . . .'

Kitty raised a finely arched eyebrow. 'I assume he will know what I mean by that?'

'He'll know.' Cerys sipped her coffee.

'Well,' Kitty Jackson said. 'I think I had better see the seamstress and order myself a new gown for the wedding.' She sipped her own coffee. Then, to Cerys's surprise, she set down her cup and leaned forward again, her face very serious.

'There's something else I think I should mention to you, since we are talking. It's about that man you have working for you at your farm.'

Cerys frowned. 'Hal Tucker?'

'Is that what he calls himself? Hmm.'

'What about him?' Cerys asked, beginning to be alarmed.

Kitty Jackson's eyes fastened on hers. 'You do know, I suppose, that he is an escaped prisoner?'

The cup rattled in Cerys's hand, coffee slopped on to her skirt, scalding her legs, but she scarcely noticed.

'He's what?'

'An escaped prisoner. Oh dear – I see you didn't know. I thought as much.'

'But what makes you think such a thing?' Cerys whispered.

'It's strange, really,' Kitty said pensively. 'It only came to me this morning – and after Chas had left too, or I would have mentioned it to him. I did tell him I thought the man's face was vaguely familiar when he stayed here for a week or so when he first came, but I couldn't think why, or where I'd seen it before. As I say, it came to me this morning, when I was thinking about you and Chas. I saw his picture on a wanted poster when I was down country a while back. Don't ask me why I should suddenly have realized now – but I'm sure I'm right. It's not a face one can forget entirely – he is so very handsome.'

'I knew it!' Cerys said. 'I knew right from the start he was a bad lot, and poor old Duggan warned me too. But we couldn't manage without him, and Jenny has fallen for him, and he claimed to be an old friend of Will's come to help us out for old time's sake.'

'Looking for a place to hide out from the law, no doubt,' Kitty said drily. 'Well, he may well be telling the truth about knowing Will – he certainly asked the way to Kanunga, if I remember correctly. But he is also a bank robber – and a murderer.'

Cerys's hand flew to her throat. She had turned deathly pale.

'A murderer, did you say?'

'That is certainly what it said on the poster. Look – I don't mean to alarm you. This is a lawless country. Shootings happen – well, you know that – and sometimes almost by accident. I'm sure he means you no harm. An isolated place to hide out is what he wants, I should think, and at Kanunga he's found it.'

'But Duggan suspected him – and Hal found out that he did,' Cerys said. 'Oh dear Lord, you don't think . . . ? I knew it was peculiar, old Fango kicking him! Perhaps he didn't! Perhaps it was Hal all the time who did something to him to try to keep him from warning me or telling anyone else of his suspicions!'

'Cerys – stop!' Kitty laid a hand on her arm. 'I'm sure your

255

imagination is running away with you. Hal Tucker is clearly a most undesirable character, but surely the last thing he would want would be to draw attention to himself here by doing away with your old hand.'

'I don't know,' Cerys said distractedly. 'I just don't know.'

'What we really should do,' Kitty said, 'is go to the law and tell them he is hiding out at your place. Jem Routledge would very likely send the troopers in to capture him and that would be an end of it. Would you like me to come with you to speak to him?'

'Yes . . .' Cerys hesitated, her mind working overtime. 'No! I must warn Jenny first. She is terribly fond of Hal – obsessed even. This is going to come as the most terrible shock to her. And if the troopers just turned up and took him away, I don't know what she would do. There might even be shooting. Hal is not likely to go willingly. If that happened, Jenny might be hurt . . .' She pressed her hands to her mouth as a dozen dreadful scenarios played themselves out before her fevered eyes. 'No, I have to warn her, get her out of the way first. I'll go home straight away and see if I can get her on her own.'

She stood up. The troubling urgency had returned – for quite a different reason now.

'Would you like to leave the children here with me?' Kitty offered.

Again, Cerys considered. But she didn't want the children out of her sight, and Ritchie, particularly, was likely to be upset if he was left with a woman he had scarcely ever seen before, much less knew. And besides . . . If she went home without the children suspicion was bound to be aroused as to the reason why.

'I think we'll be safe enough just as long as Hal doesn't realize I know the truth about him,' she said. 'You're right when you say he wouldn't want to do anything to draw attention to himself, and he certainly has never posed any direct threat to us. Once I've warned Jenny, I'll bring her back with me to Medlock out of harm's way, and then go to the law.'

'It's your decision.' But Kitty still looked worried. 'I wish Chas was here. If only I'd realized where I'd seen this Hal

Tucker's face before Chas left! He would have known what to do – and somehow I don't think he would have allowed you to go back to Kanunga alone.'

With all her heart, Cerys wished too that Chas were here, but he was not, and over the last dreadful months she had become more self-sufficient than she had realized.

'Perhaps he wouldn't, but it's something I have to do,' she said decisively. 'Come along, children, we have to go home.'

Reluctantly they abandoned the wonderful array of ornaments, Cerys picked up Ritchie, said goodbye to Kitty Jackson, and set out for Kanunga.

Throughout the drive home her heart was racing and her thoughts were keeping pace with it.

She had known there was something very wrong about Hal Tucker, but this was worse than her wildest imaginings. That a convicted bank robber and killer should have been sharing her home for the last months was so dreadful as to be almost unthinkable. Dear God, he could have murdered them all in their beds!

Had he ever known Will? she wondered, or had he simply heard that Will was dead and taken advantage of it – and her? That must be it. She could not believe that Hal had ever been a friend of Will's – and not only because of what he had done. Will would never have formed a friendship with someone like him, surely? Will had been upright and good and kind and . . .

And yet . . . With a jolt Cerys found herself remembering Jenny's revelations about Will's past, and how they had forced her to realize she had not really known him at all. Was there something else she did not know? Something involving Hal Tucker? What was it Jenny had said? 'There's so much you don't know about us – me and Will both.' It was as though there was something more than what she had told Cerys – something she had kept to herself. Could that something concern Hal Tucker? And if so, how did Jenny know about it when she did not? She had 'found out' the terrible truth of what had happened to her – and Will's – parents, she had said. She had gone to Will and he had admitted it. But how had she found out? If Will had not told her, who had? Could it possibly have been Hal Tucker? Suddenly Cerys was remembering Amy Hawker's assertion that she had seen Jenny and Hal together in Medlock *before* Will's death. She had dismissed it, assuming the woman had been mistaken. Now she found herself wondering if she herself was the one who had been wrong. Jenny had been absent from the farm a good deal in the days leading up to Will's death, and they had assumed she was with David Harris. But he had told Cerys himself that that was not the case. Could it be that in fact she had met Hal Tucker, and been with him in Medlock? Could it be . . . ?

Oh dear God! Suddenly the hairs were standing up on the back of Cerys's neck and all the blood seemed to drain from her body, leaving her icy-cold and trembling.

Will had been shot by an intruder – perhaps the same intruder they had sought on the evening before his death.

Hal Tucker, who claimed to have known Will, was a convicted killer – a desperate man on the run, looking for a place to hide out from the law.

Was it possible he had come to Kanunga to ask Will for assistance? Could it be that it was Hal Tucker who had shot Will when he refused him sanctuary, then calmly insinuated himself into the household?

Suddenly it seemed to Cerys that such a thing was all too possible. There were many questions that remained unanswered, but she could believe all too easily that she might have stumbled upon the solution to the biggest question of them all.

For the first time in her life Cerys used her riding whip on Lady's plump and lazy flanks. It was imperative she reached Kanunga without delay.

# Twenty

Jenny was in the kitchen, which surprised Cerys, since Jenny usually spent her days out on the farm with Hal, and Cerys had been wondering how she was going to cope with the hours until she could get Jenny alone.

'Where's Hal?' she asked, laying down her reticule on the table.

'Working, of course,' Jenny replied. 'I didn't feel like it today. I don't feel well.'

She was indeed very pale. Cerys, however, had a great deal too much on her mind to ask what was wrong.

'Go and play in your room, children,' she told Molly and Ritchie.

'Can't we go outside?' Molly asked.

'No, you can't. We have to go out again soon, and I want to know where to find you.'

They went off, Molly leading Ritchie by the hand, and Cerys turned to Jenny.

'I have to talk to you, Jenny. I have just learned something very disturbing about Hal Tucker.'

Jenny raised her eyebrows. 'Oh – not again! Why can't you leave him alone?'

'Jenny, please!' Cerys said urgently. 'This isn't something I can overlook. You have to prepare yourself for a shock. I have been talking to Kitty Jackson from the Commercial Hotel, where he stayed when he first came to Medlock, and she has recognized him as a wanted criminal. He robbed a bank, Jenny, someone was shot dead, and he is now on the run from jail.'

For just a moment Jenny looked shocked. Then she tossed her head.

'Oh, what utter rubbish!'

'No, Jenny, Kitty Jackson is quite certain.'

'And you believe a woman like her?' Jenny exclaimed. 'Why, she's little better than a prostitute! And in any case, if she recognized Hal, why hasn't she said anything before now?'

'Because she has only just remembered where she had seen his face before,' Cerys said. 'It was on a wanted poster, Jenny.'

'Well I haven't seen any wanted poster!' Jenny retorted. 'She's trying to make trouble, that's all. She's just jealous because of what's going on between you and Chas Wallace. Everyone in Medlock knows that she has been in love with him for years.'

Cerys shook her head. 'No, she wasn't just trying to make trouble, Jenny. She is seriously concerned that we are harbouring a man like that. And so am I. We have to turn him in. I almost went to the law whilst I was in Medlock, but I was afraid of what might happen if the troopers came out here with all guns blazing. I wanted to make certain you didn't get in their way. I'm going back now to speak to Jem Routledge and I want you to come with me.'

'No!' Jenny exploded. 'You can't do that, Cerys!'

'I have to,' Cerys said, trying to keep her voice level. 'I don't have any choice. I certainly can't let him stay here now.'

'Why not?' Jenny asked harshly. 'Even if he did what you say – which I don't for one moment believe he did – he must have had a reason for it. And he's turned over a new leaf. You've seen how hard he's worked! He's making a new life for himself. Surely he deserves to be given another chance?'

'Do you really think I could take a risk like that with the children here? With you, out alone with him all day long? Please, try to see sense, Jenny,' Cerys begged desperately. 'Look, for all we know he was the one who shot Will.'

'Of course it wasn't him!' Jenny snapped, her eyes filling with tears.

'You don't know that,' Cerys insisted. 'Why, how do you know for certain he was ever Will's friend?'

'Because he told me so.'

'He *told* us a lot of things,' Cerys pointed out. 'We have only his word for it that he knew Will at all. He could have just said that so as to worm his way in with us.'

'Oh, he knew Will all right,' Jenny said. 'And almost certainly they were friends. How else would he have known about what had happened to our parents if Will hadn't told him? And don't look like that, Cerys. It was Hal who put me in the picture, and when I confronted Will with it he admitted it was true. I told you. All those years he had fed me a fairy story that they had been murdered by bushies, yet he had shared the truth with Hal.'

Cerys bit her lip. So she had been right, it seemed, to surmise that Jenny had known Hal before he had come to Kanunga to offer his services.

'When did you first meet Hal?' she asked.

'Oh, when I was out riding one day. He was headed this way, coming to look Will up. But he wasn't altogether sure of the reception he would get. Though he said they had been very close when they worked together on Barlinney, they had fallen out about something, it seems.'

'A bank robbery and a murder, no doubt!' Cerys interposed sharply. Jenny let it pass.

'He didn't go into details. He just said he wanted to make things up with Will because they had always been such good friends and he didn't want there to be bad blood between them. I promised to prepare the ground for him and he went into Medlock to look for a place to stay.'

'And did you tell Will his so-called friend was looking for him?' Cerys asked coldly.

Jenny shook her head. 'I never got the chance. I was preparing the ground, like I said, and then I found out the truth about our parents and I couldn't think of anything else.'

'And in the meantime you were creeping off to meet Hal,' Cerys said.

Jenny nodded. 'Yes. I let you and Will think I was going to Glenavon to see David. I'm sorry I deceived you, Cerys.'

'Yes – well, that scarcely matters now,' Cerys said. 'What does matter is that we are giving shelter to a thief and a murderer. You must see, Jenny, that I can't allow it to go on. I know you're very fond of him, but . . .'

'Fond of him!' Jenny burst out. 'I *love* him, Cerys!'

Cerys's heart sank. 'You don't. You can't. He's wound you round his little finger, that's all, and has you infatuated. You'll forget him, Jenny – meet someone else . . .'

'No!' Jenny shook her head. 'You don't understand.'

'I understand very well,' Cerys said, hardening her heart. 'He has used you, Jenny.'

'No!' Jenny's hands balled to fists. 'Don't say such things, Cerys! It isn't true! I love him – and he loves me. And I think you should know I am going to have his baby.'

Cerys felt the blood drain from her face. So that was the reason Jenny had been so unlike herself this last week – the reason she was not out working now – the reason why she was so pale and wan. It was just as she had feared. The silly girl had allowed that horrible man liberties and the worst had happened. She had fallen pregnant.

'Oh Jenny!' she groaned.

'So now you see why you can't turn Hal in!' Jenny rushed on. 'He's changed, Cerys, even if he was ever as bad as you say, which I can't believe. He's changed for me.'

'Does Hal know about the baby?' Cerys asked tersely.

'Not yet. I was waiting until I was certain before telling him. But when he does we'll be married and—'

'You are deluding yourself, Jenny,' Cerys said harshly.

It was her opinion that if Hal thought he was about to become a father, they wouldn't see his heels for dust.

'I am *not* deluding myself!' Jenny cried. 'We've talked before now about getting married!'

'When he was persuading you into his bed, no doubt,' Cerys said tersely.

A shadow of doubt flickered across Jenny's face and died.

'Not just then!' she retorted. 'How can you be so horrible, Cerys? We are going to be married and we shall live here at Kanunga. You and the children can go and live at Wells Court with Chas Wallace and leave this place free for us.'

'I think not,' Cerys said coldly. 'Somehow I cannot see Chas allowing a convict on the run to occupy his property even if I were to relent, which I will not.'

'Chas Wallace? What has he got to do with it?' Jenny demanded. There were high spots of colour now in her pale cheeks. 'It was *Will's* farm. I've every right . . .'

'Well, it's not Will's farm now,' Cerys said. 'It's mine. Or, more accurately, it is Chas's. I deeded it to him to pay my debts.'

Jenny's eyes opened wide; an expression of horror came over her face.

'You did *what*?'

'Deeded the house to Chas so that we could keep our heads above water. He promised to allow us to stay here, but I'm quite certain his generosity would not extend to a criminal,' Cerys said shortly.

'How could you *do* that?' Jenny demanded, aghast. 'How could you do such a thing and not tell me?'

'We both, it seems, have our secrets,' Cerys said coldly. 'I'm sorry to sound hard, Jenny, but I won't see you throw your life away on that man, baby or no baby.'

Jenny's face crumpled.

'Oh Cerys, please!' she begged. 'Don't turn Hal in! If you ever cared for me, please don't do it. If you and Chas won't let him stay here – well, I suppose that's your decision. Only don't turn him in, I beg you!'

'What is going on?'

Hal's voice from the doorway. Absorbed in their quarrel, neither had noticed him push it open.

'Oh – Hal!' Jenny ran to him, throwing herself into his arms. He put her aside roughly.

'What's going on, I said?'

Cerys had frozen. Oh, dear God, what now?

'Cerys is saying the most terrible things!' Jenny cried. 'She is saying that you are a bank robber and a murderer, escaped from jail, and that she is going to the authorities to turn you in. It's not true, is it? I've told her . . .'

For just a moment an expression of pure fear distorted Hal's handsome features. Then he laughed harshly.

'Of course it's not true.'

'Then tell her! Tell her we love one another and we are going to be married!'

Hal's eyes held Cerys's, cold, hard, and, she realized, very, very dangerous.

'Cerys has her own ideas on the matter, it seems.'

Cerys thought quickly. With the children in the next room this was not the time for heroics. Hal Tucker was, she felt sure, a desperate man who would stop at nothing to retain his freedom.

'I heard something in town,' she said carefully. 'It may, of course, be nothing but gossip. But I really would prefer it if you were to leave.'

'Leave?' He laughed again, harshly.

'Don't worry,' Jenny cried. 'If you go, then I shall go with you!'

He glanced at her, almost uncomprehending. 'You?'

'Yes! I love you, Hal! And I am going to have your child! If you go, I'll follow you to the ends of the earth.'

He stared at her. 'You are going to have a child?'

'Yes, Hal. *Your* child. I've waited until I was certain to tell you. But now . . .' Her face clouded with sudden uncertainty. 'You are glad, aren't you? We can be a family – you and me and the baby . . .'

'You jest!' he retorted scornfully. 'What would I want with a family?'

'But . . . you said . . . I love you, Hal! You love me!'

'I love no one! I have no place in my life for such nonsense! And if I should love, it would surely not be the sister of a man who did to me what Will Page did.'

Cerys glanced at Jenny, who was paler than ever and trembling with shock and distress, and felt her heart contract with pity. This was no more and no less than she had expected of Hal – that he would callously abandon Jenny the moment it suited him. But this was no time to worry about that. She would comfort Jenny later. And one of her questions, at least, seemed to have been answered, though from the way he spat out Will's name, it seemed clear he had been no friend to him.

'You did know Will then?' she said.

'Of course I knew him – though I've had plenty of time to

regret that,' Hal said bitterly. 'It's thanks to him I spent years locked up in a stinking cell. Oh yes,' he laughed shortly. 'Your information is good, Cerys, though I don't know where you got it. I thought New England was far enough away – and isolated enough – to hide. I was wrong, it seems, and now I must run again. So before I go you might as well know the truth, both of you. You revere Will's memory – and that disgusts me. For he was nothing but a thief, just as I was. A thief without honour or loyalty.'

He spat, and the phlegm glistening on the slab stone floor in a ray of sunlight was a manifestation of the bile and hatred that festered inside him.

'What are you talking about?' Cerys demanded. 'Will was never a thief! How dare you stand here in his home and say such a thing?'

'*His* home?' Hal laughed shortly again. 'This place is as much mine as ever it was his. More – for I've paid for it with five years of my life.' He turned to Jenny. 'You remember the first time we met? Out on the road to Medlock? I told you then I was coming to look for Will, and that was no more than the truth. But I wasn't looking for him out of friendship, as you so readily assumed. It was my intention to kill him and take back what rightfully belongs to me.'

Cerys was trembling from head to foot.

'Are you mad? Kanunga belonged to Will!'

'Ha!' Hal spat again. 'On paper, perhaps. But let me tell you, my dear Cerys, Kanunga was bought with stolen gold. The gold Will and I got when we robbed the bank at Littleton. It was supposed to be shared between us – that was what we planned when we worked together on Barlinney. Enough gold to set us both up, that was what we craved. Will had the notion to be a farmer – a damn fool idea, it seemed to me back then, but all he could think about was building a home for you, Jenny. He talked of it day and night – how he wanted to make a home for his little orphan sister. Me – well, I just wanted to be rich enough to enjoy the good things in life. Wine, women and song. That was my goal – not sitting a horse from dawn till dusk, working my fingers to the bone to make some other bastard wealthy.'

He paused, a slight, unpleasant smile twisting his mouth. Then he went on: 'We did a spot of rustling – I told you about that – but it wasn't enough for either of us. And then we heard there was bullion in the bank at Littleton, and it seemed like the answer to our prayers. We reckoned we could rob that bank and we'd be made for life. Trouble was, things went wrong.'

'Someone was shot,' Cerys said. Her voice did not seem to belong to her at all. None of this seemed real – it was like a story from a book of fairy tales. And yet, somehow, she knew all the while deep down that at last Hal was speaking the truth.

'The bank guard,' he said now. 'Thought he could be a hero – the fool. Well, I wasn't going to give up my chances of being rich for anyone – and certainly not my liberty. I shot him. What else could I do?'

'But you *did* lose your liberty,' Cerys said. 'You were caught.'

'No – we got clean away. Hid the gold and went back to Barlinney to lie low for a bit. Nobody had seen our faces, and nobody suspected two young farm hands – they put it down to bushies. Everything was going according to plan. And then Will got greedy. He turned me in.'

'But how could he do such a thing if he was in it with you?' Cerys asked through stiff lips. 'He'd have been arrested too, surely?'

'Oh, such a tale he spun them!' Hal said bitterly. 'Told them he hadn't known what I planned when we went into Littleton that day, and didn't know where I'd hidden the gold because he wanted nothing to do with it. And they believed him. Well, you know what Will was like – the picture of innocence when he wanted to be. They let him go in exchange for him testifying against me. It made a watertight case, and that was all they cared about – that someone was behind bars for the shooting of the bank guard.'

'The gold,' Cerys whispered. She was ashen now. 'Surely they cared about getting the gold back?'

'Dare say they did. Dare say they watched him for a bit if they thought he was lying about that part of it. But he was too clever to lead them to it. He went on working on Barlinney like nothing had happened, so I'm told.'

266

Cerys straightened her shoulders. 'So how do you know Kanunga was bought with it?' she demanded.

'Stands to reason,' Hal said. 'Will just bided his time. I don't know when or how he went back for it. All I do know is that when I managed to break out of jail and went looking for it myself, it was gone.'

'Someone else could have taken it!' Cerys said. 'Will worked for the money to buy Kanunga – I know he did. He wouldn't have robbed you because he wouldn't have wanted gold that was stained with the blood of the bank guard you shot.'

Hal shrugged. 'Think what you like if it makes you happy. I know what I know. Well, now you know too. The whole story. And I reckon it's time I was on my way. Didn't get what I came for, more's the pity. You weren't as well set up as I'd thought. But at least it was a place to hide out, and I've had my revenge in little ways. Setting your barn on fire – now, I enjoyed that. You spurned me that day, Cerys, do you remember? Told me to get out of your house. I couldn't let you get away with treating me like that, now could I?'

'But you were the one who discovered the fire – and you worked like a Trojan to put it out!' Cerys said.

'Well, it came to me that if too much damage was done, I'd only be cutting off my nose to spite my face. And anyway – it gave me a chance to get in your good books, didn't it? Oh yes, being here has had its amusements. Just little things, like breaking down a fence so that your cattle would stray, and all the time making out like I was on your side. And I've had my fun in other ways too.' He smirked unpleasantly. 'I'll miss you in my bed, Jenny. But there will be other girls, I dare say, just as pretty and just as willing.'

Throughout all Hal's revelations, Jenny had been standing transfixed, her white face a picture of horrified disbelief. Now her expression became one of pure agony.

'Hal . . . please! Please don't do this to me! If you don't care about me, surely you must care about your child!'

Hal laughed unpleasantly. 'Oh – and who's to say it's mine?'

'Whose else could it be?' Jenny cried.

He shrugged. 'How should I know? You're like a bitch on heat, Jenny. Anyway, I shall be long gone by the time it's born. I can't stay around here now the truth is out. And to think I thought when I got rid of old Duggan I was safe! How wrong can you be?'

'You killed Duggan, didn't you?' Cerys said.

'He didn't take a lot of killing,' Hal said scornfully. 'One little crack, that's all it was. His skull was like an eggshell. Anyway, like I said, it's time I was on my way. Now, what have you got of value, Cerys? Not a lot, I know, but I need something in lieu of wages to help me on my way.' His eyes roved round the bare functional kitchen. 'You used to have money stashed away, Cerys. But you got a little suspicious of me, didn't you, and moved the hiding place. Where is it now?'

'There's nothing,' Cerys lied.

'Oh, I think there is.' He went to the shelf, moving ornaments, looking into jugs and dashing them to the flagged floor where they smashed.

'Stop it!' Cerys yelled, grabbing at his sleeve.

His hand covered hers, then his eyes lit upon the ring which she had worn every day since Chas had returned it to her.

'Now, that's pretty!' He grasped her hand, holding it fast. 'I thought you sold that. Have you been playing games with me? Oh well, never mind that now – though I should chastise you for it. I'll have the ring, anyway.'

'You will not!' Cerys retorted spiritedly.

'Oh – and who's going to stop me? Not you, surely. Take it off.'

'You are not having my ring!' Cerys blazed.

Hal's grip tightened on her wrist. 'Take it off now, or I'll break your arm!'

Cerys knew it was no idle threat. Glaring at him she removed the ring from her finger.

'Don't think you'll get away with this!'

'But I'm going to, am I not?' He tossed her precious ring into the air scornfully and caught it again, punching the air triumphantly with his clenched fist. 'Who is to stop me?'

'Oh, I can't stop you going, it's true,' Cerys said furiously. 'But you won't get far. The troops will have the area ringed and searched, I'll see to that!'

The moment the words were out she regretted them, just as she so often had cause to regret the quickness of her tongue. Hal's face changed, his eyes narrowing, teeth baring, and with a thrill of fear Cerys realized that this time speaking without thought had placed them all in mortal danger.

And at that very moment Molly, alerted by the raised voices, appeared in the doorway.

'Mama! Mama! What's wrong . . . ?'

Cerys made to rush towards her, but Hal was quicker. Before Cerys could reach her he had grabbed the little girl by the shoulder, pulling her roughly towards him.

'You'd set the military on me, would you?' he grated. 'We'll see about that! How would you like your daughter to be caught in a shoot-out?'

'You wouldn't!' Cerys cried, aghast. 'You wouldn't take Molly!'

But even as she said it she knew that Hal was desperate enough to do anything to ensure his escape.

'You'd like to come for a ride with your Uncle Hal, wouldn't you?' he leered at Molly.

'No – no – Mama – Mama!' Frightened, Molly began to struggle, but he held fast to her small wriggling body.

'Come on now, that's no way to talk! We'll have fun, you and I. I won't hurt you so long as you're a good girl.'

Cerys rushed at him, hands flailing.

'Let her go, you beast! Let her go!'

With one blow he sent Cerys flying. She cannoned into a chair, which overturned, and she landed in an awkward and painful heap on the flagged floor.

'I'll let her go when I'm good and ready,' he sneered. 'When I'm well away from here, where we aren't known.'

He turned for the door, dragging the struggling Molly with him.

'No!' Cerys screamed, trying desperately to scramble to her feet. 'Molly! Dear God, no!'

So intent was she on trying to pick herself up and reach

her little daughter, she did not see Jenny run to the wall cabinet where the guns were kept, and Hal did not see either.

'Stop, Hal!' Jenny's voice was no longer pleading, but commanding. 'Stop – or I'll shoot you!'

Hal spun round, startled. Then, when he saw the gun levelled at him, he laughed.

'You wouldn't, Jenny! You wouldn't shoot me! The father of your child, remember?'

'Oh yes I would,' Jenny said grimly. 'Let Molly go.'

For just a moment he looked at her, the girl who had been putty in his hands, and what he saw in her face must have convinced him she meant what she said.

With a swift movement he bent, intending no doubt to pick up Molly and use her as a shield. But Jenny was too quick for him. A shot rang out, ear-splittingly loud in the confines of the kitchen, and Hal staggered backwards, clutching his shoulder where the blood spurted scarlet.

'You . . . !' He gasped. The expression on his face was one of surprise. Then it contorted with pain. 'You . . .'

Like a wounded bull he lunged forward, and Jenny shot him, again and again. He went down screaming. Cerys grabbed Molly, who was transfixed with fear, pulling the terrified child into her arms and hiding her face so that she would not see the awful sight of Hal writhing on the floor while his life's blood poured out and pooled on the flagstones.

'Oh Molly, Molly! Oh Molly, thank God!' was all she could say, and in that moment she knew without doubt that for all that she sometimes favoured Ritchie in so many ways, her love for her little daughter was equally strong and deep. When the chips were down there was no difference in the place they held in her heart, none whatever.

When she looked up again, Jenny had lowered the gun and was standing motionless, staring, stunned and disbelieving, at Hal's now still form.

'He's dead,' she said flatly. 'Oh Cerys, he's dead. I killed him!'

'You saved Molly!' Cerys cried. 'You saved us all, Jenny! You were so brave!'

'But Cerys . . .' The first tear escaped and rolled down Jenny's cheek unheeded. 'I loved him so!'

'Oh Jenny!'

Suddenly Jenny threw the gun down and ran to where Hal lay, taking his head into her lap and rocking back and forth.

'Oh Hal, Hal – I'm so sorry! I didn't want to do it, Hal, but I had to! Oh my love, my love . . . !'

Though she wanted nothing more than to hold Molly in her arms and never let her go, Cerys couldn't help but be afraid of the effect witnessing this scene would have on her. She would, pray God, forget how Hal had frightened her; what she would not forget would be the sight of Auntie Jenny, distraught and soaked with his blood as she cradled his body in her arms.

'Molly, can you be a very big grown-up girl for me?' Cerys asked, trying to sound as normal as she could manage. 'Will you go and look after Ritchie for me? Auntie Jenny and I have things to do.'

Molly nodded, her face still buried in Cerys. Cerys carried her to the bedroom where Ritchie was playing in total blissful ignorance of all that had happened.

'Mama, why did Hal fall down?' Molly asked when Cerys set her down.

'He wasn't feeling very well,' Cerys said. 'Now, just look after Ritchie for a few minutes, and then we'll go for a ride into Medlock.'

'Again?'

'Yes, again.' Cerys rumpled the silky soft hair, watched as Molly crossed to Ritchie and sat down with him, then closed the door on them.

Jenny was where Cerys had left her, still cradling Hal's body. Tears were streaming down her face to mingle with his blood, her whole body shaking with a paroxysm of grief. Cerys went to her, putting her arms around the girl.

'Jenny, darling, don't, please! He's not worth it, truly he's not.'

'But I loved him,' Jenny wept. 'Oh Cerys, I loved him so!'

'But he wasn't for you,' Cerys said, softly and urgently. 'He did terrible things, Jenny. He was a bank robber and a cold-blooded murderer.'

'So was Will!' Jenny looked up at her indignantly. 'He and Will were in it together!'

'I'm not sure I believe that. We have only Hal's word for the way it was,' Cerys said. 'But even if Will did rob the bank with him, he did it for a reason – because he was so desperate to make a home for you. Hal was different, Jenny. He was out-and-out bad – totally ruthless. Just look at how he was prepared to use Molly! And he'd have taken her, too, if you hadn't stopped him.'

'He wouldn't have hurt her!' Jenny interposed.

'Jenny – she would have been frightened to death, and then dumped amongst strangers. We might never have found her! But you know that. It's why you did what you did. And you mustn't feel guilty about it, not for a minute. Jenny – he killed Will, remember. Shot him in cold blood!'

'No!' Jenny's voice was muffled.

'He did. He as good as admitted it,' Cerys pressed on. 'He came looking for Will to get his revenge and what he considered his just deserts. And when he found him, he shot him.'

'No!' Jenny insisted. 'No, he didn't shoot Will! I know he didn't!'

Cerys shook her head in despair.

'Have it your own way, Jenny. But you can't know anything of the sort. It was Hal creeping around the night before—'

'Yes,' Jenny admitted. 'Yes, I think that might have been him.'

'—and he hid out and the next morning when he thought there was no one about, he came back,' Cerys went on. 'It's the only thing that makes sense. He came back, and he shot Will.'

'But he didn't!' Jenny raised tear-filled eyes to meet Cerys's. 'Why can't you understand, Cerys? It wasn't Hal who shot Will. It was me!'

# Twenty-One

The world rocked around her. Jenny had taken leave of her senses, Cerys thought. Shooting Hal had unhinged her.

'Jenny . . .' she whispered.

'It was me,' Jenny said again. 'I shot Will. Oh, I didn't mean to do it! It was an accident – a terrible accident! But it *was* me! I killed my own brother! And now I've killed Hal too!'

'Oh, it doesn't matter about him!' Cerys said harshly. 'But Will . . . ! How did it happen, Jenny?'

'We'd quarrelled,' Jenny said. 'I'd confronted him with the truth of what happened to Mammy and Pa – he'd admitted that Pa had beaten Mammy to death in a drunken rage and that he had overheard it all. He said he'd told me the story of the bushies to spare me the awful truth, but he was so angry, Cerys! He wanted to know how I'd found out, but, of course, I didn't tell him it was Hal. Then he walked out on me – just walked out, saying he had work to do, and I took Merlin and went for a ride, like I always do when I'm upset. When I got back there was no sign of Will, nor of his horse, and I assumed he was out on the land. And then I thought I heard someone in one of the outbuildings. Straight away I thought of the intruder who was here the night before. I had a little handgun with me. I got it out of my belt and went into the shed. And there was someone there! I couldn't see properly, going into the dark shed from the bright sunshine outside, just the shape of a man behind the bales. And he moved, as if to come towards me, and I fired! But it wasn't the intruder, Cerys! It was Will!'

'Oh dear God!' Cerys moaned.

'I still don't know what he was doing there,' Jenny went on distractedly. 'I've wondered since if perhaps he was upset too about our quarrel and being reminded of what had happened to Mammy and Pa and had gone there to be alone for a bit. But whatever . . . I thought he was an intruder, and I shot him. I shot my own brother! It was terrible – terrible! He was lying there dead and his blood was all over my clothes . . .'

'But . . .' Cerys broke off, trying to make sense of what Jenny was saying. 'Why didn't you come and tell me? How could I not know?'

'I couldn't tell you!' Jenny sobbed. 'How could I tell you something like that? I ran out again, and rode, and rode . . . and when I got back, Will had been found and you were all in a terrible state. I ran in and changed my clothes – stuffed the soiled ones in my cupboard, and left them there. I didn't know what to do . . .'

'The clothes I found hidden with your stupid sheepskins!' Cerys said. 'You told me the blood belonged to a steer. And all the time . . .'

'It was Will's blood, Cerys.' Jenny twisted her head from side to side in agony. 'Oh, I'll never forgive myself – never!'

And suddenly, for all her shock, Cerys could think of no one but Jenny, bearing this appalling guilt all alone along with her grief.

'You should have told me!' she said passionately. 'Oh Jenny, you should have told me! I wouldn't have blamed you! It was an accident, my dear – an accident!'

Jenny was doubled over, her arms clutching her stomach. At first Cerys thought it was the overwhelming grief that she was bracing herself against, then Jenny gasped, lifting her head, and Cerys saw her eyes widen in pain.

'Jenny!' she said sharply. 'Jenny – are you all right?'

'Oh Cerys!' Jenny caught her breath. 'Oh Cerys, I think . . . I think . . .'

She moved slightly and Cerys saw that there was another pool of blood on the flagged floor. Not Hal's – but Jenny's. And knew without any doubt that the day had not yet finished with them.

Jenny was losing her baby.

It was all over when they heard the sound of galloping hooves come into the yard outside. Cerys ran to the door and threw it open. To her utter amazement she saw that it was Chas. He leaped down from his horse and came running towards her.

'Cerys!'

'It's all right,' she heard herself say. 'He's dead. Jenny shot him.'

Then her legs gave way beneath her and she collapsed into his arms.

'Dear God, Cerys, what in the world possessed you to go back to Kanunga alone when you knew what Hal Tucker was?' Chas asked passionately.

They were at Wells Court. Chas had taken Cerys, Jenny and the children there, leaving three troopers who had ridden out from Medlock with Jem Routledge to deal with the situation at Kanunga. Refusing to leave Cerys, he had sent Jem to ride over and summon the carriage, then ridden home alongside it, his face dark and brooding, his watchful eyes scarcely leaving Cerys.

Once there, the children had been sent out to play with Cinders, looked after by Ned, and Jenny was put to bed in one of the spare rooms. The dose of laudanum Mary Lightfoot had given her had taken effect; when Cerys had last looked in on her she was sleeping, her hair fanned out on the pillow around her tear-ravaged face. Now Cerys and Chas were alone in the parlour, Cerys hunched on the chaise, Chas pacing the room like a caged lion.

'You should never have gone back alone!' he said again, punching the air with a clenched fist. It was utter folly!'

'All I could think of was getting Jenny away from Hal,' Cerys said. 'I wasn't to know he'd come back to the homestead and overhear what we were saying. If I'd thought for a moment the children would be in danger . . .'

She broke off, pressing a hand to her mouth. The picture of Hal holding a squirming Molly was still vivid in her mind; she thought it would be a long, long while before she could get it out of her head – if ever she could.

'The trouble is, Cerys, you often don't think!' Chas said shortly.

She bowed her head, tears filling her eyes.

'That's not fair! I know I can be a bit impetuous, but, oh, it seems I'm just facing one crisis after another! And I don't know how any more. I'm just not equal to it.'

Tenderness and remorse filled him, replacing the anger that had been born of his overwhelming concern for her and the raw fear for her safety that had raged through him when he had returned early to Medlock and been met by a worried Kitty.

'Thank God you are back, Chas!' she had greeted him, and told him as quickly as she could what had taken place.

He had been back on Lupus in an instant, issuing instructions from the saddle.

'Go to Jem Routledge and get him and as many troopers as he can muster out there without delay. Tell them I've already gone to Kanunga.'

'Shouldn't you wait for them?' Kitty had asked, anxious for the safety of her dear friend.

Chas had not even taken the time to reply. All he had been able to think of was getting to Cerys; and his anxiety had spawned raw aggression.

Now, however, he looked at her hunched there, small, shaken, defenceless, and wanted nothing but to take her in his arms.

'You've been through terrible times, Cerys,' he said. 'And you've faced them with courage and fortitude. So don't say you're not equal to it, because you have proved time and again that you are. Will would have been proud of you.'

The mention of Will's name reminded Cerys of all the accusations Hal had made against him, and the tears welled faster.

Chas experienced a sharp stab of pain. The fear and concern he had been feeling had made him almost forget the terms on which he and Cerys had parted after their last meeting – and what had prompted the crisis between them. Now it came back to him all too clearly.

'I'm sorry,' he said roughly. 'I see that just talking about him is upsetting for you.'

She looked up quickly, and her expression was almost one of surprise.

'Oh no – it's not that. It's what Hal has told me and Jenny

276

about Will – things I never knew. I thought I knew him through and through, Chas. It's all been such a terrible shock.'

His eyes narrowed. 'Do you want to talk about it?'

She shook her head from side to side distractedly. 'Oh, that he should have kept such secrets from me! I don't know what to make of any of it. But I have to tell someone, Chas.'

'Then tell me.'

And she did, her voice faltering from time to time. He listened intently, prompting her gently as she recounted the story she had heard from Hal's lips earlier in the day.

'I can hardly believe it of him,' she finished. 'I know if he did it, it was only for Jenny. But all the same . . . it's not the Will I thought I knew. Robbing a bank, betraying his partner, buying Kanunga with stolen gold . . . It's too awful to even think about!'

Chas considered.

'Perhaps he was in on the bank robbery,' he conceded. 'But only for the reasons you have said. He felt so responsible for his little sister. But if he had had any part in the murder he would never have gone to the law. From what you say, he had no need to. They'd got clean away. It's clear he couldn't live with such a thing on his conscience and realized his friend was a danger to the community.'

'But Hal said it was so that he could have all the proceeds for himself! He said that, when he was safely out of the way, Will took it all.'

'Cerys.' Chas sat down beside her and took her hand between his own. 'If Will really did help himself to all that gold, what has become of it?'

'Well – he bought Kanunga.'

'On a quarter deposit, paying the rest to the bank in instalments that crippled him. My dear girl, if Will had gold bullion salted away do you really think you would have been in such dire financial straights? You would have been living off the fat of the land.'

'But . . . Hal said it was gone . . .'

'Someone else happened upon it, I expect,' Chas said. 'Someone else is reaping the rewards. I doubt very much if it was Will.'

She caught her lip between her teeth, wanting desperately to believe him. And what he said was certainly true. Things had been tight even before Will's death. Surely he would not have been so worried about money if he had stolen a haul of bullion?

Watching the expressions chase one another across her pale face, Chas was once more overwhelmed by love for her. Dear God, he had never wanted anyone as he wanted her, never longed to cosset and protect and cherish a woman this way before. So – she didn't love him, perhaps she never would, but Chas knew deep in his heart that if he did not at least try to win her, he would have lost the most precious thing in his world. Patience was not one of his virtues, but he would force himself to cultivate it. Pride was certainly one of his failings, but even that seemed petty and unimportant now, set against his fear of losing her.

'Cerys,' he said. 'I know I cannot replace Will in your heart, and I wouldn't want to try. But I do still very much want you to be my wife.'

'Oh!' She looked up at him. 'Oh Chas, but . . .'

'I'd never force myself on you,' he went on. 'I know that at present you cannot contemplate a physical relationship, but I'm prepared to accept that. All I want is for you to be happy and comfortable. No – I want *you*, Cerys. Won't you reconsider?'

For a moment she could not speak. He could feel her hand trembling beneath his. Then she raised her tear-filled eyes to meet his.

'Oh Chas, I thought I'd lost you! And when I thought that, I knew. Of course I still love Will, and I expect I always will. But I love you, too. I love you now – and for ever. I do so much want to be your wife. And . . .' She bit her lip. 'Not only in name.'

Hope flared in him. 'You mean . . . ?'

'Yes,' she said softly. 'I wanted you when we were together before, the other day. I wanted you so much it frightened me. I felt as if I was betraying Will. But that's being silly. Will is dead. And I know that he would have understood and wanted me to be happy.'

His eyes held hers. More than anything he wanted now to take her in his arms, kiss those trembling lips, yet he held back. Her rejection on the last occasion had hurt him more deeply than he had realized; he heard what she said, was glad, and even dared to hope she might mean what she said. But he did not want to pressure her in any way – or risk rejection a second time.

'You have made me a very happy man,' he said simply.

'Well,' she said, faint surprise and disappointment in her voice. 'Aren't you going to kiss me?'

'If you're sure that's what you want.'

'I'm sure.' She turned her face up to him, wound her arms around him. 'I want you to do more than kiss me, Chas. I want . . . Oh please, won't you take me to bed and love me?'

And he did.

Afterwards she lay in his arms, as drowsy almost as if she, like Jenny, had taken a dose of laudanum, and in spite of all that had occurred today she felt safer than she could remember feeling in a very long time. She had needed his love-making as well as desiring it; it had gone some way to banishing the horrors for a little while at least. And it had been ecstasy beyond what she had ever dreamed of.

'Thank you,' she whispered drowsily.

He opened one eye, surprised.

She snuggled into him, wanting only to feel his strength and the protection it offered, the wholesomeness of him, the closeness that can be between a man and a woman. And then he spoke the words she had never expected to hear from another man, nor expected to want to, and it warmed her through, reaching the tender heart of her that not even his love-making had reached.

'Don't ever give me a fright like that again. I love you, Cerys Page.'

Coming from a man like Chas Wallace, she knew without doubt that he meant it.

It was a few days later and Cerys was in the yard, watching the children romp with Cinders.

279

The whole family were still at Wells Court, for Cerys could not face the thought of returning to Kanunga, and would not hear of Jenny going back there alone. She was still traumatized by all that had happened and Cerys knew it would be a long while before she could even begin to put it behind her and start to rebuild her life.

It would happen, of course. Jenny was young, she would love again when she was ready. Perhaps she would even come to realize what a good man she had in David Harris, who had come hightailing over, desperate with worry for her, when he had heard about the terrible events at Kanunga. But then again, he did not set Jenny on fire, Cerys knew, and basking in the delights she had discovered through being with a man who truly was the one for her, Cerys could not but hope that Jenny would settle for nothing less.

Now she came towards Cerys across the yard, pale still, but with a little more colour in her cheeks than she had had since that dreadful day, and with a little more spring in her step.

'Cerys, I've been thinking,' she said. 'About Will.'

Cerys glanced at her warily. 'What about him?'

'I've been wondering if not all Hal said might be true.'

Cerys smiled faintly. 'I'm sure it wasn't, she said. 'Hal was a bitter man, and he coloured everything they did so that it suited the way he wanted it to be. He had plenty of time to brood whilst he was in jail, and I expect he wanted to place the blame on everyone but himself. He probably even believed it.'

'No.' Jenny shook her head. 'I'm not talking about the bank robbery. I'm talking about what happened to Mammy and Pa.'

'But you said you confronted Will that last morning and he admitted it,' Cerys said, puzzled.

'He admitted that Pa was responsible for Mammy's death,' Jenny said. He never admitted being the one who killed Pa. That was why I went back looking for him. He'd cut me short before we got to that part and I wanted to hear it from his own lips. Except that I never did, because . . .' She broke off, the ready tears filling her eyes.

'Jenny, there is no point in torturing yourself,' Cerys said gently.

'No, listen!' Jenny caught at Cerys's sleeve. 'It's something I heard long ago and banished from my mind. I once overheard someone say they couldn't see how it could have been bushies who murdered Pa. Something to do with the shot that had killed Pa being 'self-inflicted'. And what I am wondering is whether perhaps when he realized what he had done to Mammy, Pa took his own life. Will wasn't much more than a child, Cerys. Do you really think he would have taken a shotgun to his own father? I'm beginning to think that Will found them both dead when he plucked up the courage to go in.' She broke off, shuddering. 'Oh, poor Will! What he must have gone through! It's no wonder he could be so dark and intense sometimes. But we have only Hal's word for it that Will had a hand in what happened – and like you said about the bank robbery, it may have been something he wanted to believe, something that diminished Will in his eyes, made him capable of anything.'

Cerys nodded thoughtfully.

'You may well be right, Jenny. But we'll never know now.'

'No. But we don't have to believe the worst, do we?'

Cerys smiled and linked her arm through Jenny's. She felt as if another weight had been lifted from her heart.

'No, Jenny. We don't,' she said.

Cerys and Chas were married at Christmas in a simple ceremony at Wells Court with an overexcited Molly as flower maiden and Ritchie toddling curiously among the few selected guests.

Kitty was there, resplendent in a new scarlet gown, and though Cerys thought she could see a shadow of regret in the older woman's eyes, her painted mouth never once ceased to smile and she offered the happy couple her sincerest wishes. Perhaps, Cerys thought, in time they could become friends. As unlikely as it had once seemed, she knew how much Chas cared for her, and trusting his judgement, she felt sure he could not be so wrong about this woman.

Jenny was there too, of course, a Jenny who was already beginning to put the terrible events in which she had played her part behind her. But she was an older, wiser Jenny who had lost much of her girlish impetuosity, a fact which managed to both sadden and relieve Cerys at the same time.

The Reverend Chalmers had come out to take the service, now he was speaking the time-honoured words of the marriage vows and Cerys and Chas were repeating them after him. And then Chas was placing the ring on her finger, his hand as steady as his voice had been, pushing it into place and holding it there for a moment.

Cerys looked up at him, then back at the ring, a simple band of gold. She had never thought to see another man's ring on her finger, now she knew just how very fortunate she had been. Two good men she had known, two good men she had loved. Two good men had loved her.

She glanced at her right hand. Will's ring was on the third finger, transferred from her wedding finger when she had promised herself for a second time to Chas. The ring had been found on the flagged floor of the kitchen at Kanunga by the troopers; they had returned it to her and Cerys had hesitated before putting it on, mindful of how she might hurt Chas's feelings. But he had smiled at her and nodded, indicating that he understood and was no longer plagued by feelings of jealousy.

He had acknowledged that Will would always be a part of her life, and he did not mind. He was sure that she was his, now and in the future.

At last the ceremony was over. Ritchie came toddling towards them. Cerys picked him up, whilst Chas lifted Molly on to his shoulders, then put his arm about his new wife.

'My family,' he said, smiling. 'I never thought to be a family man.'

'Oh Chas, we shall make quite sure that you are!' Cerys said.

And felt the shadows of the past receding in the warmth of the winter sun.